E
LE
PHANT
SHOES

Copyright © K T Fenton in 2024

Published by Pantser Press

Paperback ISBN-13: 978-1-3999-7005-1

Printed in the United Kingdom

This book is a work of fiction. Names, characters, places, and incidents either are products of the author's imagination or are used fictitiously. Any resemblance to actual persons, living or dead, events, or locales is entirely coincidental

Cover design and layout by www.spiffingcovers.com

No flies were harmed in the writing of this story

ELEPHANT SHOES

K T FENTON

To all of my senses

"None so deaf as those that will not hear.

None so blind as those that will not see."

- Matthew Henry

1

You drive past a car accident on the motorway, and you can't help but look at the wreckage; beads of broken glass and chewed up metal strewn across the tarmac as you pass by. That's what this is like. But it's different this time. Because *this* time you wonder if maybe it was *you* that caused the crash.

Where I am right now isn't the scene of some car accident. I'm not even on the road driving or being driven. I'm in a university canteen, on a lunch break between the end of the second class of the day and the beginning of the third. But as I sit here, where I can only gaze at the tragic drama taking place ahead of me, it sure looks and feels a lot like the scene of a car accident to me.

There's a girl laid out on the floor, on the other side of the canteen; eyes wide open and expressionless; the blood drawn from her now blanched face. The whole room frozen like a photograph where everyone in shot is facing the wrong way with their backs turned to the camera. Mouths gaping or covered with the palm of a hand to trap a gasp.

I can tell that the people directly around the girl are shouting her name, gently slapping her face with light but urgent taps, desperately trying to bring her to and keep her conscious.

Some are just stood about, slack-jawed. Gawking like sick sightseers at a twisted tourist attraction with a morbid curiosity. Whilst others, just a stone's throw away from the action, have their camera phones out, filming the whole spectacle and taking pictures. The rest of them, on the fringe of the unfolding theatrics, just sit there, heads turned with craned necks to get a better look.

I, too, am just sat here.

I cannot move.

Frozen in place with an icy horror at what may or may not have just happened.

And amidst all of the yelling, the frigid statues of fellow students, the video recording and picture taking – the lifeless girl laid out on the floor, on the other side of the canteen – all I keep thinking is …

… did *I* do that?

2

"How to Go Unnoticed"

I'm the type of girl who would rather catch another hour in bed than catch a sunrise.

Violently jolted awake every morning by bad dreams of some long, dark, rumbling tunnel with flickering fluorescent lights. Right after which, my eyes flutter open, and I realise it's just because my alarm clock's going off on the bedside table.

My alarm clock doesn't ring or beep, you see, it vibrates with a bright, flashing light. An alarm clock I habitually set to go off as late as possible, and always hit the snooze button of at least once. After all, it's not as if I'm missing out on anything by sleeping in.

If only I had a life a little more stirring, a little more rousing, at least then I would have all the good reason I needed to leap out of bed early. But since most days are about as mundane as they were yesterday, and as mediocre as they will be tomorrow, I'll keep right on sleeping through these equally pedestrian mornings.

That particular day was somewhat different, however. Because *that* day I was waking up in a bed I'd only slept in once, in a room I'd never woken up in before, on this, my very first day as a mature university student.

I would tell you what I was studying, but it would be irrelevant information. I'd have taken a Swahili class if it meant finally moving out of living at home with Dad. I mean, don't get me wrong, I love my dad and everything, it's just that for the past five years or so I've felt suffocated by all the cotton wool he wraps me up in, with all of his worrying and overprotecting.

As for room 448 C of Pantone Court – the shoebox I was going to need some time to become accustomed to calling 'home' – think, part Premier Inn, part teenage boy's bedroom, part hostel. A pair of garish Aztec-style patterned curtains hung in the one window I had to look out of, which didn't have all that much of a view, unless you find the drab appearance of concrete in a variety of shades of grey pleasing to your eyes. A dark red, almost burgundy, commercial-grade carpet took ownership of the floor – its only saving grace being that it was clean. But I was confident the room would look a little more 'me' once I'd hung a few posters on the uninspiring magnolia-coloured walls, and arranged some of my belongings around the room; the already quite limited space filled mostly by a cheap pinewood desk, bed and wardrobe.

Living in a student hall of residence for the first time and sharing a four-bedroom flat with three other people I hadn't even met yet, filled me with a buzz of anxiety I had some trouble ignoring, but I had to at least give this whole 'living with other people' thing a go, if I was to settle in around here.

I'm not ready for any kind of human interaction until I've first had my morning coffee and a smoke, followed by a 'bath from above' (shower to you) which I'm pretty sure was the reason my dad got me a coffee machine as a sending-off present, so I never had to leave my room in the mornings until I'd done so – although he loathes the fact that I smoke. The machine was one of those instant kinds you place a pod into and press a button. It actually made me feel sad to just *look* at the machine, let alone use it. Not because it didn't prepare real coffee, just that it caused me to think of Dad, leading me to realise that I was already missing home.

I popped a pod into the machine, and just before I hit the start button, I winced, hoping that the noise it made wasn't too loud, and that none of my flatmates were sleeping in.

I like my coffee to be lukewarm when I drink it, so I rolled myself a cigarette whilst it cooled.

Opening the one window I had, I stuck my head out as I leant on the windowsill and took a deep breath in of all that fresh morning air.

Then I lit my cigarette.

As I took a cautious sip of the coffee – which smelt and tasted more like toffee mixed with condensed milk – I pondered to myself that, back when I was just a school-aged kid and still living at home, I never thought I'd miss the sound of birdsong as much as I do now. And if there *were* any birds singing out there that morning, *I* certainly couldn't hear them.

Most days I went through my morning routine as if I were a dazed, methodical zombie. But in that tiny bathroom, foreign to my senses, where the shower, toilet and basin had all found new places to be – the mirror making up its own mind to hang on a completely different wall to the one back home – I was acutely aware of every step.

Warm shower water raining down on the back of my neck. A tingly sting of mint on my tongue with every scratchy stroke of a new toothbrush. My nostrils stung briefly by the lingering misty scent of body spray. The face I saw in the mirror being the one and only familiar fixture in that unfamiliar bathroom, after I wiped away the condensation from its cool, water-flecked surface. And I'm well aware that this may sound strange to you, but I do oh so miss the comforting drone of an extractor fan.

Like most days, I was looking to blend in, not stand out. Fortunately, I'd crammed the wardrobe full of plenty of drab items of clothing that would provide me with my desired look. Let's just say that if I'd had an invisibility cloak hanging up in there on the rail that morning, I would've worn it.

After pulling a cloudy-grey bobble hat down over my head, my fingers pull at my fringe to cover my too-big, blue eyes as best they can. A thick, lifeless-green scarf wraps itself around my scrawny neck, and a long, muddy-brown overcoat takes care of hiding the rest of me. A timid pair of dark-blue boots poking out from under it, the colour of the darkest waters.

Ignoring the great reluctance to do so, I threw a quick look at the girl I saw in the mirror, and without making contact with her big, blue eyes, I secretly wished she were a brunette with brown eyes instead of a blonde. So lost in that desperate wish, for a moment I almost forget to put a drop earring in my left ear to hide the jagged scar on my earlobe.

Brushing myself down with both hands, only then do I look that girl right in the eyes when I tell her, "You've got this, Iris."

And, for whatever reason, telling my reflection that 'she's got this' always makes her feel as if she has.

I gave myself one last look over in that mirror I already hated, let out a breath I hadn't realised I was holding in, and I was out the door. All of my hang-ups and insecurities slipping through behind me and following after …

3

"The Pebble in My Shoe"

Every morning, back home before I left the house, I'd put a smile on my face and see how long it lasted; a habit I was doing my utmost to keep alive. And so, I forced a grin and set off the stopwatch on my phone as I walked down the street, all the while muttering to myself the last words of advice my father gave to me, in a bid to calm my nerves about the rest of this uncharted day.

"Don't get a tattoo," he told me. *"Don't make friends too quickly. And for goodness sake, whatever you do, do NOT sleep with any of your flatmates."*

"So far, so good," my inner voice whispered to me as I strolled, as confidently as I was able, towards the lecture theatre I needed to arrive at in just shy of twenty minutes' time. Although, I was starting to rethink the clunky boots, as it appeared the walk to the university campus was a lot further than it looked on the map I got with my welcome pack.

The route wanted to lead me down through a dimly lit underpass; my clammy palms and racing heart sharply reminding me that I'd sooner take my chances with the traffic than go down there. Jarring flashbacks of my darkest of days sending me back to a time I'd rather forget and a shudder down my spine.

But the clouds were out the way of the sun, the fresh morning air was like two crisp apples held gently against either side of my face, and the walk was really rather delightful. The pavements lined on one side by those handsome town houses with cast iron railings. Trees, full of bright emerald leaves, too, lined the streets; sunshine spilling through them, twinkling green and yellow.

So caught up I was, in how wonderfully this morning was going, I almost didn't notice this charcoal-like smudge in the corner of my eye; a shadowy figure in a park on the opposite side of the street, where they appeared to be crouching down over something.

Nothing all that strange, at first glance, but when I took the time to stop and get a better look, the figure's hands appeared to be holding something and shaking rather vigorously.

Only then do I realise I'm not smiling anymore, remembering to stop my stopwatch.

"One minute and forty-three seconds," I said under my breath as I looked down at the elapsed time on my phone. "That's got to be some kind of record."

I looked back up in the direction of the park. *Were they OK?* And going to look again, I thought that perhaps they weren't.

Quickly looking both ways, I hurried across the road, calling out, "Hey! Are you alright there?"

The figure turned to look my way, and now that I was almost upon them, I could see that 'they' were actually a 'he'. He looked about my age, dressed all in black, and wearing sunglasses. A bird appeared to fly from his hands moments before he got up with a jolt and, losing his footing, tripped.

"Hey!" I called out again as he got back up, taking off in the opposite direction.

He didn't *run* exactly, but there was an urgency in the way he got up and left the scene.

It was only then did I think that maybe this guy was some kind of weirdo, and that I was only just now wondering what was in his hands when he shook them so vigorously, not a few moments ago.

"Hey!" I called after him, having more than just a little trouble keeping up with his pace in the clunky boots I'd chosen to wear that day. "Hey, you! What were you doing just now?"

And this guy, he was still walking away, double time, and I couldn't be sure but it looked as if he was putting something like an earbud into his left ear.

"Hey!" I called out. "Come back here! Don't you just walk away from me!"

My boot-heeled feet doing their damnedest to keep up with this guy on all that spongy grass.

"You some kind of pervert or something?" I asked him, more as an assumption than a question. "You like perving on bright, young women on their way to university, do you?"

But this guy, he kept right on walking.

"Well, you picked the wrong girl this morning, pervert!" I yelled at him.

And thinking I'd chased him off, I added a little, "Yeah, you keep walking, pervert! Not so much fun when it's the *girl* doing the chasing, now is it?"

That's when the guy stopped, dead.

And so, too, did I.

It was then, he turned back and walked right up to me; a stern finger pointed in my general direction.

"Look," he said. "Just leave me alone, OK? It's none of your damn business."

"I think it *is* my business," I told him. "Especially when I'm the one being perved on."

He went to say something, but his hanging head beat him to it.

"Right, that's it," I said, rummaging around in my bag for my phone. "I'm calling the cops."

"No!" this guy said, in a panic. "Please don't do that."

"Alright," I said, my hand held passively in my bag. "Tell me what you were doing just now, and I'll leave you be."

A drawn-out breath from this guy in black was followed by the words, "You wouldn't believe me if I did."

"Try me," I said, my arms now folded.

That's when he slowly looked back up at me.

"You really want to know?" he asked.

"Yes," I told him, "I really want to know."

Again, he appeared to sigh.

"If you really want to know," he told me, "you'll meet me here some other time."

But I didn't say anything.

Then I think he asks me something highly inappropriate for a chance meeting between two complete strangers in a park.

"*What* did you just fucking say to me?" I asked him.

"Whoa! Whoa!" he said, his hands going up in surrender. "All I did was ask if you had a phone."

"Oh," I said. "Sorry. I thought you'd just asked me if I wanted to … 'bone'."

"Well *do* you?" he asked.

"What?" I asked. "Bone?"

"No," he said. "Do you have a phone?"

"Yeah …?" I said, as if he'd just asked me if I breathed air.

"Then give me your number."

"I'm not giving you my *number*," I said, turning the side of my body my bag was on away from him. "I've only just met you."

The guy's eyebrows peeked out just over the lenses of his sunglasses, my screwed-up face reflected in them. His head lurched back, as if this approach usually worked for him when picking up girls on their way to class.

"I'm sorry," I told him. "I just don't make a habit of handing out my number to random guys, who may or may not be …"

"Perverts?" he asked.

"Actually, I was going to say … weirdos."

"Well, you'll just have to take my word for it when I say that I'm not one of those, either. But whether or not you give me your number is entirely up to you."

"What I mean is, I don't just give out my number to complete strangers."

"No, I get it."

I thanked him, by smiling awkwardly and not knowing where to look.

"You're not really all that interested," he said, turning to walk away.

And I let him.

At first.

There was something so very peculiar about this guy. Something I'd never come across in a person before. But he had gotten from me, in just a few minutes, what no person had ever gotten from me in years.

My attention.

Yes, he was a complete stranger, but there was this antsy girl within me that urged me not to let this opportunity slip away, lest I regret it. Rising up in me, this fidgety unease that I was going to miss out on something if I just let him go. What that something was I didn't know, but that just made it all the more intriguing.

I watched him walk away.

I just stood there and let him go.

That is, until I couldn't any longer.

What are you doing, Iris? the voice of my conscience whisper-shouts at me as it realises what I'm about to do.

"Wait!" I yelled after this guy, just before he was gone and out of sight.

And this guy in black, he stopped to turn and face me. But the way in which he did it, so casually, as if he always knew he would.

Pulling out a notebook and pen from my bag, I started to scribble my name and number as he made his way back to me.

"O, double seven, double zero," I muttered to myself, to make sure I didn't accidentally 'wrong number' him. "One, four, three. Six, three, seven."

Tearing the page off the ring binder, I held it out for him to take.

"Well?" I asked him.

"Well, what?" he said.

"Aren't you going to take it?"

"Take what?"

"Doofus! My number, of course!"

His whole body flinched as I grabbed his hand and stuffed the torn-off page into his palm.

I stepped back.

He just looked down at his hand with a smirk.

"Yeah ..." he said. "That's not going to work for me."

"I've just given you my name and my number," I told him. "What more do you want from me?"

"You're going to have to actually punch it into my phone," he told me, as he slipped it from out of the back pocket of his jeans.

"Fuck sake," I said. "Give it here, then."

He went on to say something else, but I just kept right on with the rant I was muttering under my breath. The phone he'd just handed me looked different to most I'd seen; the buttons, big, like those of an old lady's landline telephone. And I don't know if it was the fact that I was getting just a little exasperated by that point, but I punched in my number just like he'd told me to, without considering whether or not this was the smartest thing to do.

"My name's Iris," I told him.

"Iris with an 'I'?" he asked.

"How *else* would you spell it?"

Taking the phone back and slipping it into the back pocket of his jeans, he said, "I'll be in touch, Iris."

And just like that, he walked away.

"That's *it?*" I asked after him.

Me, just stood there feeling like a dummy, before turning to walk in the opposite direction in an attempt to feel like less of one.

"Oh, wait!" I turned and called after him. "You never told me your name!"

But this guy in black, he didn't so much as turn his head to look back at me. A few more seconds and he was gone. And there I was again, just stood there, feeling like a dummy.

But this dumb feeling was short-lived as a small smile crept up the side of my face.

Gone, as quickly as it had appeared, when I then remembered where I was, and that I was now running late for my first class of the day.

4

"No Uncertain Terms"

I was oblivious of anyone around me, on my way from the park to the university campus. They all just blurred into one another, merely colours and shapes as I walked right by them. I don't remember much of my first day. My body was in those classrooms, the canteen and studying areas, but my mind was back at the park with the curious guy I'd met there. I didn't even know his name, and yet I'd just given him my name *and* my number. But doing so felt right somehow, and it's only my number. What harm could he really do with just that? Call me until my head exploded? *Text* me to death?

I was now lying in bed, pensive, with too much on my mind to sleep. I felt a vibration buzz through me and thought it was my alarm clock going off already. But when I turned to look at the bedside table, it wasn't my alarm clock, but my phone. The time was **5:01 am**, according to the red numbers on the alarm clock's digital display, and wasn't due to go off for another couple of hours.

Grabbing my phone off the bedside table, I saw that I'd got a message from an unknown number.

Do you still want to meet? it read.

It *had* to be him.

It was stupid, because I'd been so eagerly awaiting to hear from him, and now that I had, I was unsure about it all of a sudden. I reminded myself that it wasn't too late to back out and, at the same time, I just had to know what this guy's secret was.

I took a deep breath in and, without thinking about it too much, began typing.

Yes, I texted, *I still want to meet.*

And as soon as I'd typed the words and hit 'send', I wanted to take them back, but they'd flown away somewhere, out of my reach, and I was way too late.

Putting my phone to my chest, so I couldn't look at possibly *the dumbest thing* I'd ever done, I screwed my face up, my eyes shut tight.

Feeling vibrations against my chest, I slowly brought the phone up to my face to better see the screen.

You have to promise you will keep this to yourself, the text read. *Do as I say and do not ask questions.*

OK, I texted back.

Before we meet, he continued, *you'll need to find something to bring with you.*

OK, I reply.

Something dead, the text said.

WTF??? I texted back.

An animal, he said. *Nothing too big. A rat, a bird … something like that.*

And I'm glad we were texting right then and not on a video call, so he couldn't see the face I was pulling.

But it has to be intact, he went on to say. *Dead from natural causes is preferable. Knocked out cold is just fine. But nothing messy. And absolutely NO ROADKILL.*

My face must've been a picture right then, so much so that I would have probably sent him a picture message of it, if it wasn't for the fact that I *really* didn't want him to see it.

Once you've found something to bring, he ended with, *let me know, and I'll let you know where and when to meet.*

And where exactly am I supposed to find a dead animal? I asked him.

You seem like the kind of girl that has plenty of ingenuity, he said. *So, use it!*

Thanks, I said, *but why a dead animal? At least tell me that much!*

You've already asked me three questions since you promised not to, he texted back. *You know what to do, so let me know when you've done it, and then we'll meet.*

OK, I type.

But he was *Poof!* gone before I'd even hit 'send'.

From the moment I left for my first class of the day, all I could think about was where in the hell I was going to get a dead animal from. I couldn't bring myself to *kill* one, so I would just have to come across one that was dead already. But even if I *did* find one, what was I going to do with it? Just casually slip it into my handbag? What if someone saw me? What would I tell them? That I'm studying *taxidermy?*

I even found myself scanning the streets as I walked to university, hoping I might find a dead squirrel and, at the same time, really hoping I wouldn't. After all, if I *did*, I might actually have to go through with this madness. I might actually have to put a dead animal in my handbag. I certainly wasn't going to do it on my way *to* the university campus. I could just see myself at the first seminar of the day, stinking out the entire lecture theatre from the back of the room with a decaying rodent in the bag at my feet.

Perhaps I could do some voluntary work at a dog shelter? Get a job as a cleaner at a vets, or work as a sales assistant at a pet store? Sneak out with a small dog, maybe? A chihuahua or a Pomeranian? But there was still the matter of it having to be dead. The 'dead' part was fine. 'Dead', I could handle. It was the *killing* part that didn't sit so well with me, even with how much I detested those awful handbag dogs.

I remember seeing dead animals at the side of the road all the time, back in my hometown, and how much I hated it when I came across one. Heads barely hanging on to their crushed bodies, guts strewn across the tarmac. But now that I was actually looking *out* for them, I couldn't find one, not anywhere. I tried to concentrate in class whilst making notes, but all I did was doodle dead cartoon animals in my notebook for the duration of the lecture.

On my way back to the hall of residence, giving the streets a good last look for just one, solitary, unfortunate animal that had met its untimely end at the side of the road, and finding none, I finally surrendered to the futility of my little assignment.

Throwing my bag to the floor, right after I'd shuffled sulkily through the doorway to my room, I shrugged my shoulders and collapsed onto the bed, defeated. The door still closing behind me. Staring up at the nothing of the ceiling, I figured I'd never see that mysterious guy again, and how much that sucked. He gave me one simple task, and I couldn't deliver. I was a let-down, a failure.

A lowly waster.

As I lay there, worn down to a nub and exhausted, I noticed this movement in the corner of my eye, and turned my head to see a cage, set right there on my work desk; about the size of an old, small television set, with a wheel spinning away inside. Slowly getting up, I sat on the edge of the bed and peered into this cage. I was now staring at a hamster, happily running inside an exercise wheel.

On the cage was what appeared to be a note.

Heaving myself off the bed, I went over to the work desk, snatching the note off the cage. It was from one of my flatmates. One of my three flatmates I hadn't even met yet. And it seemed they already want a favour. According to the note, after a few banal pleasantries at the beginning, they were away for the weekend and wondering if I could look after 'Harry'. Not like I had a choice in the matter, since they'd clearly taken off, leaving me with their dumb hamster and its stinky cage.

Great, I thought to myself. Just what I needed right now. *More* responsibilities!

Screwing up the note, I tossed it over my shoulder, and blew a puff of 'mildly ticked-off' air out of my 'somewhat fed-up' mouth. And then, as I sat there, getting a good look at 'Harry' and an equally bad smell of shredded newspaper mixed with hamster piss, I had what screenwriters call an *aha!* moment. This is the moment where the protagonist of the story realises something out of seemingly nowhere.

"Hello, Harry," I said to this hamster, as slowly as a snake eyeing up a tasty mouse.

Harry was now nosing the air and gnawing at the thin bars of his cage. And poking my finger between those same bars for him to nibble, I think aloud to myself that, "Maybe I *will* be meeting with that strange guy after all."

I sent a little text to the *Park Pervert* – which is what I had 'the guy' down as on my phone, since he never actually gave me his name

– all the while keeping my eyes firmly set on Harry. Who, by the clearly apparent 'nothing' going on behind those big, black eyes of his, had no idea at this point what I was secretly planning for him.

I think I may have found something, I texted.

Less than a minute went by before my phone vibrated.

Is it intact? the text read.

Yes, I texted.

Is it dead?

And I texted, *Not yet.*

5

"Killing Time"

I spent the rest of the evening completing the assignments I should have spent the *day* doing. Not so much because I felt *compelled* to, more so that it was taking my mind off what I may have to do. Looking up from my laptop at Harry the hamster from time to time. Or should I say, looking at Harry the hamster and back down at my laptop from time to time.

He looked so happy running in his wheel, with no clue as to what I was plotting for him, poor thing. Could I really do it? End the tiny life of an innocent, defenceless animal?

It's not like anyone would miss him. Well. Apart from the flatmate that dumped him on me last minute. The very same one who had entrusted me with the well-being of their beloved pet rodent. I could always tell them, Harry escaped? Had a bad reaction to some high-sugar content cereal I shouldn't have fed him?

Still, the questions remained. Could I *do* it? And if so, *how?* All I knew for sure was, I wouldn't be doing it that night. I had a few days. I'd sleep on it. But try as I might, I just couldn't drift off. Harry's shuffling and gnawing and spinning in his wheel kept me up the whole night, serving as a constant reminder of what I may or may not have to do with him when the most dreaded of tomorrows came around.

Tossing in my bed, I turned to face upwards towards the ceiling, just staring at all that black up there, and all it made me think of was death. Every now and then a car would go by outside, the headlights beaming through the curtains, wiping the walls in a hypnotic wave of yellow, the very same colour as Harry the goddamn hamster.

A glow of blurry blue and white light abruptly illuminated the ceiling space, and fumbling for my phone on the bedside table, I brought the screen up to my tired eyes.

How are you getting on? the message read.

Working on it, I typed back.

And with my phone still in my hands, I typed the words, '*How to kill a hamster*' into the search bar.

And just so you know that I'm not a total monster, I did add the word, '*Humanely*'.

There was the briefest of moments when I woke up, where everything was as it should be; I was back home in my own bed, in my own room, surrounded by all my familiar things. And then, I realised where I was, and it rose up inside me: this buzz of unease. To the point it was squeezing out all the air from my lungs.

That's when my alarm clock started vibrating. That bright light flashing away. Although, that morning, there were no bad dreams of rumbling tunnels and flickering lights, as I would've first had to have gone to sleep.

"It's time," I told myself.

Time for many things. Normal things, like getting up for my morning coffee and cigarette. Taking a shower. Getting dressed. Eating breakfast – although that's not very normal for a girl like me.

But it was no normal day.

I had no classes, and therefore nothing to keep me distracted from what I must do.

For if I *didn't* do it, I would never see this nameless guy again. That was the *only* reason I was going to do it, and no other. You've got to believe me when I say that I really didn't want to do this, and Harry would not let me forget it. All of his shuffling and gnawing and spinning in his stupid, fucking wheel.

And doing my damnedest not to look up at all that heavy guilt hanging over my head, I opened up the flap on top of Harry's cage, and reached in.

Stood at the bathroom sink with Harry in my hands, I only had the time it took for it to fill with water to decide whether or not I was about to do what I'd been torturing over in my mind for the last few hours or so. It was a simple plan: fill the sink, close my eyes, grip Harry tight in both hands, plunge them into the water up to my forearms, and slowly count to sixty. I'd feel some squirming, some wriggling; clenching my hands tighter. There'd be a few bursts of bubbles. The frantic wriggling would lessen. The bubbles, too. I'd finish counting, open my eyes, and it would all be over.

Fill, plunge, hold, count …

… over.

With the sink now full, I lifted Harry up so he was level with my eyes, looking right back into his own big, black ones, and said, "Give me one good reason why I shouldn't do it, Harry?"

Harry held still for a split second as if to consider his response.

"Just one," I add.

But of course, being a hamster, Harry said nothing. His whiskers just twitched, and it was evident to me that Harry had no fucking clue as to what was about to happen to him, let alone understand a word I was saying.

"You are very cute, I suppose," I told him, gazing into his big, black eyes, whilst stroking him under the chin.

And then something happened.

Something I wasn't at all expecting, but perhaps should have seen coming.

Harry, the innocent, defenceless, adorable little hamster …

… He bit me!

"Fuck, Harry!" I screamed, my hands springing open from their grip on him. He fell to the floor, landing on his feet, and ran under the crack at the bottom of the bathroom door.

"Goddammit, Harry!" I said as a whispered shout to my bleeding finger, right before sticking it in my mouth and sucking on it.

A few minutes later, and the bleeding appeared to have stopped. I didn't have any plasters, so I fashioned a bandage out of a square sheet of toilet paper and sticky tape. With that done, now all I had to do was find me an escapologist hamster.

Sliding down the wall of the hallway, I slumped right there on the rough, unforgiving, commercial-grade carpet. I looked everywhere for

Harry, to no avail. The communal kitchen included. Not that I was really keeping an eye on the time, but I must have been searching for the time it took to lose all hope. I realise I had almost decided on *killing* poor Harry, and although I had just a little less sympathy for him by now, I would still really rather not have had to. But this was even worse. Now I'd *lost* him. And for nothing.

What was I going to tell my flatmate when they got back from their weekend away? That I'd lost their beloved pet hamster in thirteen square feet of floor space?!

I had failed as a human being. I couldn't even look after a half-pint-sized rodent for a few days. But then, this was as much Harry's fault as it was mine. After all, he was the one that bit *me*, and not the other way around.

It was then, just when I'd convinced myself that this was all Harry's fault, all the lights go out.

Great, I thought. *Just what I need right now.*

As if this whole 'looking for a fun-size pet' thing wasn't arduous enough, now I'd have to do it in the dark! Without the aid of lights in this gloomy hallway, it would be better to just shut my eyes and fumble around in the dark with my arms outstretched. And I don't know why, but the thought came to me in the darkness that this was what it must feel like to be blind, and how much being blind must suck.

I'd underestimated the abilities of this particular domesticated rodent. It was obvious to me now that I was dealing with an expert here, one who'd clearly done this before.

"Stupid, escape-artist hamster," I mutter to the darkness. "Should have called him Houdini."

Then I realised, that was probably why my flatmate named him 'Harry'.

Realising also that I was spending way more valuable time than I should on the reasons why my flatmate named their hamster what they did, I set my mind back on the task at hand.

First of all, I needed light.

Perhaps a rat chewed through an electrical cable or something, I thought to myself.

"Holy shit!" I burst out as I got to my feet. "That's it!"

With my arms held out ahead of me, I felt along the wall until I came to the familiar smooth wood surface of the door to my room. Fumbling for the door handle, I pushed against the door with the side of my body, hastily grabbing my phone from the bedside table.

Switching on the torch on my phone, I scanned the hallway to see if there were any breaks in the cables running along the tops of the skirting boards as I made my way to the kitchen. Once there, I was straight down on all fours looking round the edges of the room. My butt sticking right up in the air, with the side of my face pressed hard against the cold, linoleum flooring, torch still in hand.

And there it was, down the side of the washing machine; what looked to be a grey, furry ball of dust in the darkness. Right next to that dustball, a cable. Gnawed almost all the way through. It was only when I reached in to pull said dustball out, did I realise what it was. Or, should I say, *who* it was.

It was Harry.

"Oh no," I said out loud, as I blew the dust off this miniature version of Mr Houdini. "I killed the little bastard."

Getting myself up off the floor, his tiny body held in my cupped hands, I let out a sigh. Remembering why I was looking for him in the first place, a wave of relief washed over me. The realisation that, if he was dead, I no longer had to kill him. And although I was happy about that, I was, too, sad that unfortunate Harry's life had come to an abrupt end like this. It did mean, however, I could now finally meet with the guy I'd been dying to see again.

"Every cloud."

With Harry's tiny, limp body cupped in my hands, I walked purposefully to my room, carefully setting him down on the bedside table and grabbing my phone.

Ready to meet, I texted.

And I waited …

… and I waited some more.

My phone vibrated.

Meet me in the park at midnight, the text said.

"Midnight?!" I blurted out, perhaps a little *too* loudly.

My eyes shot up to the ceiling as I pursed my lips.

OK, I texted back. *See you then.*

Then I typed an 'X' for a kiss.

Promptly deleting it, before hitting 'send'.

I fell back into bed, both worn out and hyped up, all at once; my phone held to my chest, with my head turned to the left.

"Now," I said to Harry, who looked as if he were just taking a little nap on the bedside table. "What to do with you?"

With the power now back on, I wasted the rest of the day killing the time of what was left of it. Just counting down the hours to my meeting that night with the Park Pervert – or 'Mystery Man', as I was now more affectionately calling him.

Harry was on the windowsill of my bedroom, sealed in his temporary freezer-bag home, with the curtains drawn partially to hide him. The window open, just a crack, to keep him cool. But it was evident, from the fiasco I'd had with Harry so far, that I would have to keep an extra close eye on this particular scaled-down, escape-artist of a hamster from here on out.

I lay on my bed looking up at the ceiling thinking, *I did it!* Well. Technically, *Harry* did it. I just took him out of his cage. *He* was the one that chewed through a cable, like an idiot, and electrocuted himself.

With my arms crossed behind my propped-up head, I quietly thanked Harry for his sacrifice – even though it wasn't exactly voluntary.

"You have no idea how much this means to me, Harry," I told him from the bed. "And I will always remember you."

How could I *forget?*

Perhaps someday I'll get a tattoo in memory of him, or at least something to commemorate the experience. There was still the small issue of what I would tell my flatmate about what happened with their treasured pet fur-ball, but I had the time to worry about that later. The dark cloud question of *What in the hell am I doing?* still loomed over my head.

I'd just started at university, and yet I'd barely thought about my studies, or making friends with classmates, or partying during fresher's week – not that I was going to anyway. As I kept reminding myself, it wasn't too late to back out of this weird little rendezvous with an equally peculiar guy. But I also had to remind myself of the ordeal Harry and I had been through, and it all being for nothing if I changed my mind at this late stage.

No.

I had to go through with it.

If I didn't, I may have never seen this guy again.

6

"Blind Date"

Stood there in the rain that was coming in sideways – for this 'sort of date' but 'not a date' – I'm thinking I really should have brought an umbrella, and that open-toe sandals were a very bad idea.

It was almost midnight, and only then was I beginning to wonder what in the hell I was doing there, as wave upon wave of bitter wind pierced right through me. Beyond the patch of yellow light coming from the lamp post I was stood under, a dense, absence of light was all I could see. And with the rain pouring down on me, showing no mercy or signs of stopping, I felt as though I'd been standing in an icy cold shower with clothes on for the past fifteen minutes.

Saturated benches collecting an infinite smattering of tiny droplets that dripped below into puddles of deep, lustrous black. Bushes blooming with flowers that know no colour that time of night, and wrought iron fences that went off, all the way into the nothing. And right in the middle of all this, there was me.

Cold, wet, stupid, me.

Oh, yeah, and there was a dead hamster in my handbag.

I checked inside said bag to make sure Harry was OK. Well. OK for a dead hamster, anyway. And yep, he was still in there. Wrapped up in an old scarf amongst all the typical contents: my purse, make-up, face wipes, accumulated dirt, and the fanny scratchings of rolling tobacco. Fumbling around in there, my fingers stroked against the familiar smooth plastic of my rape alarm attached to the keyring of a set of keys. *Better to have it and not need it than to need it and not have it,* my dad's always telling me. Double-checking I had *999* on speed dial. I'd have packed a can of pepper spray, too, if I had it.

I threw my arm out to reveal my watch from under the cuff of my coat.

23:57 pm.

I was giving it three more minutes and then I was out of here. I didn't have time for *this*. Where I should've been was back in my room. What I should've been doing were my assignments. What was I even *doing* here? I must've been crazy. I *was* crazy to have even entertained the idea in the first place. But to actually *be* there, minutes away from meeting a total stranger for the second time, in a dark and empty park. Some weirdo that could well be a serial killer, who had casually asked that I bring along a dead animal to our little hook-up in the middle of the night. That was just batshit, box of frogs, *crazy!*

As soon as the time turned to midnight, I was gone. I was practically *willing* those four, digital noughts to appear on my watch, so I could just get the hell out of there. And then I waited the longest three minutes or less I had ever stood in the rain for.

"Come on!" I told my watch through gritted teeth.

And then it happened.

The rain stopped.

00:00 am

"Finally," I said to my watch, as I turned to walk right out of this ridiculous situation.

And then, *Bam!* I walked straight into something. Something as dark and wet as the park itself. Then came the realisation that this wasn't some-*thing* I'd just walked into, but some-*one!* Totally forgotten were the rape alarm and my phone set to call 999 on speed dial. And all I could think, with my brain wildly processing this moment of abject terror, was that I could've really done with that can of pepper spray I didn't have, right about then. I went to scream, but I think it just came out as a gasp. The initial shock had already used up all the air in my, now vacuous, lungs.

But then this someone held me tight, and I caught sight of

their face in the yellow glow of a nearby lamp post. I saw Ray-Ban sunglasses and the collar of a black biker jacket.

It was him!

I let out the words, "*Oh, thank God, it's you.*"

He'd still got me tight in his arms, but I didn't feel trapped. I felt safe. He'd got me and I could tell he was saying the word *Sorry!* over and over. I could see it in his face, too. I also saw that he was laughing, like what just happened was somehow amusing to him.

Shoving him off me, I told him, "You scared the shit out of me!"

"I'm sorry," he said again, "I didn't see you. I was actually about to give up on you."

He put a hand of splayed fingers through his short, dark, wet hair and shook it of rainwater.

He was cuter than I had remembered.

But then, it was also a lot darker than the last time I saw him.

"Are you ready to see what I've got to show you?" he asked.

I nodded.

"Well?" he said.

"Yes!" I tell him.

And taking my hand in his, he led me into the deeper parts of the dank, dark, nothing of the park.

A short while later, this boy in black stopped short and dropped to his knees, telling me to kneel down beside him.

I knelt.

Touching my arm, he asked me something I couldn't have correctly lip-read.

"You've lost your *artichoke* ring?" I asked.

"No," he said. "Have you got what I asked you to bring?"

But so caught up in how I felt when I was around this guy, I almost forgot the reason we were there at all.

"Oh yes, of course," I said, rummaging around in my handbag.

Pulling out the freezer bag, and sliding across the plastic zipper, I scooped poor little Harry's body out. You could almost be forgiven for thinking he was just sleeping, if you didn't already know he was dead, with how perfectly peaceful he looked.

Still knelt next to me, this guy rubbed his hands together like he was trying to start a fire with the flat of his palms.

"You cold?" I asked him.

"Nope," he said. "Just warming up."

"Huh?"

After a few more seconds, he held out his hands, cupped together and facing upward.

"OK," he said. "Hand it over."

Carefully, I placed Harry's tiny, lifeless body in his palms.

"What is it?" he asked. "A mouse?"

"Hamster," I said.

"You killed a *hamster*?!"

"Suicide."

"Huh?"

"Long story."

"Oh," he said, "and I'm going to need your phone."

I pulled a face. "Why?"

"And any *other* recording or photographic devices you might have upon your person," he added.

The way he said it, like those public service announcements you get at the movie theatre just before the feature presentation is about to start.

"Oh, right," I said, rummaging through my bag again.

"Just slip it in my jacket pocket for now," he said.

I did as he asked.

"Now," he told me, "I need complete silence for this, so I need you to just sit there very quietly."

I just nodded.

"OK?" he asked me.

"OK!" I tell him as a whispered shout. "Sorry, I was literally doing what you told me to do just now."

"Complete silence," he told me again.

I didn't answer.

I didn't move, I didn't speak, I didn't breathe.

He breathed deeply, in through his nose and out through his mouth, whilst I did my best not to giggle. Sitting back on the heel of his boots, his eyes *could've* been closed, but they were still behind those sunglasses of his, so I couldn't tell. Me? My eyes were wide open.

Nothing happened, at first.

We were just knelt there, not a word said by either of us.

Us both, just staring at Harry's tiny body in the hands of this guy.

Initially, I figured it was simply a trick of the light, or that maybe I imagined it. But I could've sworn I saw little Harry's whiskers twitch just then. Perhaps it was just our breathing over him. Then I saw one of Harry's legs kick. Nothing again for a couple more seconds. Then his little chest appeared to swell with breath, but I was still unsure about what I was seeing. *Is this just my hopeful imagination?* I thought to myself.

Then something truly incredible happened that dispelled all my doubts.

Harry's eyes.

They blinked open.

He was alive.

My mouth, having no words to say, simply let out a gasp. It was then that this guy exhaled and seemed to come to, and when he looked down at Harry, he did it with a knowing smile.

And turning his head to face me, he said, "Still think I'm a pervert?"

7

"Now You See Me"

Getting himself to his feet, this boy in black offered me his hand to take, before throwing a name at my eyes when they weren't ready to catch it.

"Mally-*what?*" I asked.

"Ma-Lee-Us," he said again. "My name is Malleus."

"Oh," I said, clumsily taking his hand and giving it an awkward shake, before he heaved me up off the muddy ground.

"Iris," I told him. "But then, you already knew that."

"It was a pleasure for you to meet me, Iris," he told me.

"Don't you mean, it was a pleasure for you to meet *me?*" I asked.

"That's what I said."

I felt 'a moment' between us, before he brushed down the muddied knees of his jeans and told me he had to go, his hands now covered with half the mud he'd manged to rub off.

"So, I'll see you around?" I asked him, slowly walking backwards, but not wanting to leave just yet.

"You'll see *me,*" he said with a nod.

He placed an earbud into his left ear, his phone already in his other hand and tapping away at it. And as he turned to walk in the other direction, disappearing into the dark, I quietly said his name to myself.

"Malleus."

A smile finding its way up one side of my face.

He then reappeared from the darkness, and so did the butterflies in my tummy.

"I almost forgot," I read his lips saying, walking up to me as if he'd finally plucked up the courage to kiss me.

"Yes?" I said, my whole body standing to attention from my heels to my head.

"Here's your phone back," he said, handing me the phone I'd forgotten all about.

All those butterflies in my tummy dropping down dead.

He gave me another nod, disappearing into the dark again but, this time, not returning.

"Malleus," I whispered to myself again, in the hope that uttering his name would bring him back a second time.

But as earnest as that hope was, it didn't work.

Slowly, as I became aware of myself again, where I was, and what I was doing there, I tucked Harry in the inside pocket of my coat and walked, still surfacing from a daze, the opposite way, and out of the park.

It was only when I walked in the door, did I then realise how soaked through with rain I was. Peeling off my sopping wet clothes, that hung on me like dead weights, I rung them out in the shower, as best my muscles would allow. Hanging them to dry over the radiator in my room, I grabbed a towel to tend to myself.

I spent the remainder of the small hours of the morning with Harry, who was now full of life and running over my hands. Sat there, on the end of my bed, gazing down at him in my cupped hands as if he were some sort of tiny miracle.

And in a way, I guess he was.

There was a moment of sheer panic, the moment I woke up and realised I'd been asleep.

"Harry!" I said as a whispered shout.

But my worries were short-lived when I got myself up to see that he was happily running in the wheel of his cage, as if nothing had happened. I must have put him back there before I dozed off. He seemed to be getting back into the swing of the whole *being raised from the dead* thing. I, on the other hand, felt close to death from the whole ordeal. But now it was all over, and I was back inside from the freezing rain, all I felt was the warming afterglow of relief.

I lay there, basking in that comforting feeling, for what couldn't have been much longer than the time it took to sit through a TV commercial break, when there was this intermittent flashing of white light reflecting off the ceiling. It was my door light. The one that's set off whenever someone presses the doorbell-like button from the other side.

Springing myself off the bed, I made my way over to the door, opening it a crack to see who it was, where I was greeted by a face these eyes of mine had never seen to recognise. One of my three flatmates, I presumed. Talking so fast, I only got parts of what they were saying.

"Iris?" they said.

I got *that* much.

Then they said something about being "*back early*". And that they're just here to "*get Harry*".

Please *do,* I thought to myself. Before this hamster pulls any *more* stunts!

Carefully heaving Harry's cage off my work desk, I brought it over to the door and handed all that unwanted responsibility back to its rightful owner.

"*Thank you!*" I read their lips saying, and something about me being "*A life saver!*"

Not technically, I thought to myself.

They said something about "*hoping it wasn't too much trouble*".

Oh, I thought to myself. *You have no idea.* Keeping the words firmly in my mind as I shook my head, "*Not at all!*"

And I can't have read their lips right when they asked me something like if I was "*doing some drilling in here the other morning?*"

"No?" I told them, unsure if I was answering the question I thought they'd just asked.

And something about them hearing "*some buzzing coming through the wall*".

"Oh?" I said, hoping my reply fitted with the statement I thought they'd just made.

Then I thought they were thanking me again. This time, however, they did it with a sort of forced grin. The very same kind you make when someone's about to take a photo of you and asks you to smile for no goddamn reason.

"*Weird,*" they appeared to say, whilst lifting the cage so Harry met level with their eyes.

And just before they left with Harry – none the wiser to all the trouble he'd caused – and still looking at him through the bars of his cage, this newly acquainted flatmate of mine said something like, "*That's funny.*"

And something about them never seeing little Harry, here, being "*so full of life*".

8

"The Daily Grind"

Checking my reflection in the coffee shop window, it was only after I'd brushed the hair away from my eyes – that kept persisting in falling right back where it was – did I then see Malleus sat inside the café on the opposite side of the glass.

Colourful winged creatures breaking into a dance inside my stomach.

We arranged to meet at this little café he knew called The Daily Grind – the lettering written in broad strokes of white chalk against a blackboard background, right across the top of the coffee shop window-front. This was after Malleus texted me asking if I drank coffee, to which I coolly replied, "Constantly." I made it there no problem, and in good time, although I almost walked straight into a lamp post following the satnav on my phone.

Quickly bringing my hand down to my side, it seemed I'd gotten away with my last-minute adjustments to how I looked, as Malleus didn't appear to have seen me – perhaps those sunglasses of his were impairing his vision. I gave him a timid wave but he didn't wave back, and so, shrugging it off, I made my way inside. And as I walked through the door, my whole body filled with a reassuring warmth. There's just something about the aroma of freshly ground coffee beans that calms me down.

"Hey," I said to Malleus, reluctantly removing my coat.

To which he appeared to say, "Straw."

My face screwed up. "Huh?"

"Never mind," he said.

He didn't get up. He didn't even pull the stool out for me. Nor did he pay me a compliment for the way I looked – not that I'd know how to take one. And, dressed all in black, he appeared to be wearing the exact same clothes he was wearing the last two times we met.

He *did* smell good though.

There was this moment of no words being exchanged as I unwillingly unwrapped the scarf from around my neck, so I beat him to breaking the ice by offering to buy the coffees.

"No, no," he said. "I've got these. This was my idea, after all."

"Good company *and* free coffee," I said. "Lucky me."

He just smirked as he got up from his stool.

"Cortado," I told him.

"Oh, I don't speak Spanish," he said, "but you're quite welcome."

"What?"

"So, what are you having?"

"A cortado."

"Oh right," he said, slapping his forehead before heading over to the counter.

I used the time Malleus was in the queue to check my reflection in the window we were sat in. It was only when I looked back at Malleus – who appeared to have jumped the queue of about seven people – did I then see him appearing to be flirting shamelessly with one of the barista girls behind the counter. Some blue-eyed blonde who, I was pretty sure, kept shooting catty looks my way. She was making it so obvious, too. Could Malleus not *see* this?

Attempting to ignore how self-conscious I felt, with this barista bitch making evil eyes at me, I looked around the room to distract myself. Which didn't help all that much. As, when I did, I found I was completely surrounded and totally outnumbered by man buns, groomed beards and earthy tattoos of wolves, rocky mountains and pine trees. The only girls I could see in there, all *tip, tap, typing* away on their PearMac laptops. No doubt beavering away on some blog about sustainable, vegan, gluten-free living, and how best to lick rocks for their nutrients. And even though I didn't particularly rate this type of hipster crowd, I did start to feel just a little out of place.

And since when did all these people start wearing hats indoors?

But all of that I forgot about entirely when Malleus returned to save me, coffees in hand. And it was all going so smoothly until he bumped into a stool, spilling a little of what I'd ordered on my drab, dark-brown dress. Which, luckily for me, was very similar in colour to the coffee he had just spilt upon it.

Not that he noticed.

"Well," he said to me as he carefully set down the coffees. "Turns out they don't do cortados here, so I took the liberty of ordering you a … *flat white?* Kind of the same thing but bigger, apparently."

"Well," I told him. "A girl certainly never complains about bigger!"

And as soon as the words had passed my lips, I really wished they hadn't. But he humoured me by blowing a laugh out his nose, and I loved him for it.

I took a sip of my coffee, Malleus almost spitting out his own.

"What?" I asked him.

"Nothing," he said, wiping his grinning mouth with his sleeve.

Setting my cup of coffee down on the bar – which was missing a saucer and spoon, I might add – I turned to him. "Can I ask you a question, Malleus?"

"You just did," he said.

"What's with the sunglasses?"

He leant back slightly.

"That's a conversation for another time," he said.

"Oh, come on," I said. "You've *got* to tell me, now."

"Another time," he said again, but he did it with a smile, and I went quiet.

Then I think he went to put a hand on my knee, but missed. Only landing it on the second go, and my leg flinched for no reason other than it not being used to boys touching it.

"Was that some sort of trick the other night?" I asked.

"How do you mean?" he asked, bringing his cappuccino up to his lips.

"Bringing back little Harry from the dead like that."

"Little Harry?"

"The hamster."

"Oh, right," he said, cautiously placing his cup back down on the bar.

There was now a frothy moustache on his upper lip, but I didn't want to change the subject, so instead, I asked him, "It was just a neat trick, right?"

"Oh, yeah," he said. "Like I keep spare hamsters up my sleeves."

"Fair point."

"That's why I asked you to bring something dead of your own. So there would be no doubt in your mind of what you saw."

I was still staring at the milk froth on his upper lip, and it was taking everything that was within me to not tell him about it.

"Do you mind if we don't talk about this here?" he added.

"Oh no, of course," I said. "Sorry. I wasn't thinking."

"Let's change the subject."

"I think you just did."

It was then that he finally wiped away the froth from his upper lip.

"So," Malleus said. "Now you know my big secret. What's yours?"

"I don't really have one," I told him. "What you see is what you get with me. I'm pretty ordinary, really."

"Not to me, you're not. I don't know the first thing about you. Right now, you're one *big* secret."

I could feel myself blushing pink, well aware that I was probably clashing with the colour of my drab, dark dress.

"I'm really not all that extraordinary," I told him.

"So tell me about all the ordinary stuff," he said.

"OK. Well, as you know, my name is Iris, I'm twenty-one, and I'm currently studying here at the university, and looking for a part-time job, ideally related to …"

But Malleus was giving me this bored look, and my words trailed off to nothing.

"What is it?" I asked him.

"That's just stuff you're doing," he told me. "Tell me about *you*."

And I felt as though the whole cafeteria was watching me shrink upon my stool.

"How about this," he said. "If you could have any superpower, what would it be?"

"What's *that* got to do with anything?" I asked.

"You can tell a *lot* about a person from their answer to that question."

I sat there, looking up at all those exposed industrial pipes, running along and across, just above of what should've been the ceiling.

"Invisibility, maybe?" I told him without much thought. "Although, I think I already have that power."

Malleus held a look on me, as if to say … *Interesting.*

"Or maybe the power to create excitement," I added, with a laugh. "Life can be so …"

"Ordinary?" he said.

He went to place a hand on my knee, but on this attempt, he landed it first time, and my leg was more accepting in allowing it.

"I know exactly what you mean, Iris," he added.

I just looked down at his hand, realising this was only the second time I'd ever been touched by a boy, but I kind of liked it.

"Can I ask you a question, Iris?" he asked.

"You just did," I said with a wink.

Malleus appeared to blow a laugh out his nose.

"What is it that you *really* want?" he asked.

And I was back to looking up at all that invisible ceiling, whilst letting out a sigh.

"I don't know," I told him. "I guess I just want to know what the right thing to do with my life is."

Again, that same look Malleus had been giving me before. The one I couldn't quite work out.

"I feel as though I've tried so many things," I told him, "and they've all just hit dead ends."

For a moment, I lost myself in the sadness of what I'd just said out loud for the first time.

"So, come on," I told him, shaking my head free of wandering thoughts. "What's with the sunglasses? It's bugging the shit out of me now."

"Why does it matter?" he asked.

"You were wearing them the first time we met, but that was different, it was daylight. And then you were wearing them the night we met in the park."

"So?"

"It was dark. Pitch black. And now you're wearing them again, here, inside a coffee shop."

But Malleus didn't say anything.

"Oh," I said.

"Oh, what?" he asked.

"You're one of those."

"One of *those*?"

"One of those posers who wears sunglasses all the time. Even when they're indoors."

"Iris," he said, placing his hand on my leg that didn't budge an inch this time. "I think it's time you knew something about me."

Sliding off his stool and landing on his feet, he took my hand to help me down off mine.

"Oh no," I told him. "Is this the part of the movie where the guy tells the girl he wants to 'show her something'?"

And I could just tell he was shooting me this look from behind those sunglasses when he smiled and said, "Just shut up and take my arm, would you?"

9

I felt three, firm taps on my shoulder, and opened my eyes.

After we left The Daily Grind café, Malleus told me to take his arm and shut my eyes, tight. He said he wanted to take me somewhere; show me something.

"Just don't take me down through any underpasses," I told him. Telling him, "Long story," when he asked why.

It took a few rapid blinks for my eyes to become accustomed to the light, but when they did, I saw that we'd stopped at this big, knobbly log, facing out to the infinite length of a river, and that Malleus was now turned to face me.

"You're probably wondering why I got you to close your eyes," he said, touching my arm.

But instead of asking why, I just stayed quiet, granting him the silence to tell me.

"I just wanted to show you what the journey here was like for me," he said.

Screwing up my face, I told him that I didn't understand.

And with his eyebrows raised above the lenses of his sunglasses, he just threw me this look of, *Seriously?*

"Oh," I said, as soon as the penny dropped. "Oh!"

"There we go," he said with a nod. "You got there in the end."

"Why didn't you tell me sooner?"

"I just didn't want you treating me any differently, was all."

I shook my head a little, smiling serenely with understanding eyes, just before he suggested we take a pew on this knobbly log. Gestures that, I was only just realising, were completely wasted on a boy like him.

"So, like, how do you even find your way around?" I asked as I sat down next to him.

"My steps are guided," he said.

"What?" I snorted. "Like, by a higher power or something?"

Malleus's lips moved.

"You've got an *apple* on your foot?" I asked him.

"No," he said. "I've got an app on my phone."

"Oh," I say. "Right."

"Sort of like a satnav for blind people."

"So, what? You got an app on there for finding dead animals, too?"

"No. I can just sense when death is near. Whenever I'm around death, I can just, sort of, feel it."

"Ooo. Creepy."

"In fact," he added, "I can feel it, even now."

It was only then did I look from Malleus, to this place he'd brought me to.

It was only then, did I wonder, why.

Looking down from the bleak, overcast sky, I saw that the river water was a murky brown. The lonely, rusting corpses of boats, run aground and long forgotten, scattered untidily across this wasteland of shopping trolleys and traffic cones that stuck out from the mud. A dead bird, laid out on the marshy ground with greedy seagulls pecking at its eyes and innards. And what could be a jellyfish or a cluster of used condoms, washed up on the boggy shore, and flapping in the wind.

"I hear it's still a beautiful view," Malleus told me.

And all I could think in that awkward moment, was whoever had been feeding Malleus those little white lies, obviously never had it in them to tell him the truth of what'd become of this special place of his.

"My mother used to bring me here," he said, "but my memory of it has faded somewhat. Would you mind describing it to me?"

And breathing in that crisp air – the only one, good thing about this barren wasteland of a landscape – I prepared myself for the first, big lie I'd ever told him.

Looking out on all that dirty water, I described it to him as a rippling sheet of turquoise glass, stretching out, so far, it was almost impossible to tell where the water ended, and the sky, which soared into the blue beyond, began. My eyes landing on the dead bird as I told him I could see a black, silhouette triangle of birds passing overhead. Glancing at all those boat corpses, telling him that they were all moored up, bobbing happily, and wearing many coloured coats of fresh paint. Rising and falling like breathing, in the swell of that same clear water they were floating upon. And even though I knew it was better to lie sometimes, I still felt the guilt that came with doing it to a person who would never know that I had.

"Thank you, Iris," he told me, as I pushed that same guilt way down, in a place I'd never look to find it.

"I could almost see it," he said.

I held myself back from quipping in with something like, *It's probably best that you can't!* to preserve the hazy image he held of that place, in his fading memories. Lying to him, again. Assuring him that, *"It was my pleasure."* My heart, breaking under the weight of having to do so.

Sat there, just taking in the scenery, or lack thereof, there was this itch in me that I couldn't quite reach to scratch until I asked him, "So when did you first find out you had this power?"

"Power?" he asked me. "Like I'm some kind of superhero or something?"

"Well. What would *you* call it?"

"I've never really thought about it. But if I had to call it anything, I guess I'd call it … an ability?"

"So, come on," I pushed. "Tell me. First time you knew you had this ability."

And taking a deep breath in, as if the tale that followed was going to require it, Malleus appeared to ready himself to tell a story he may never have told anyone.

10

"If I Die Before I Wake"

I would always get terribly upset when it came time to return the school hamster, so when I was eight, my mother got me a pet guinea pig. He was as black as a field of tall grass at midnight, so I thought it fitting to name him 'Shadow'.

Staying up with him for most of that first night, just watching him. Fascinated by his big, black eyes and floppy ears. It must have been late, because my mother called from the hallway that it was time for me to put Shadow back in his cage and go to bed.

After dinner, I had asked my mother if I could take my dessert to my room, so I could watch Shadow run around his hutch whilst I ate it. And, for once, she said yes. But just this one time. Shadow seemed to be very interested in what was in my bowl as I lifted a generous spoonful of Devil's Delight to my mouth. And I couldn't blame him, after eating nothing but hay and kale all day.

Scooping another generous spoonful of the chocolate mousse on my spoon, I held it close enough to the bars of his hutch for him to sniff. Immediately, he began lapping at the air, his nostrils flaring.

One spoonful couldn't hurt, I thought to myself as I offered the end of the spoon to Shadow's lapping tongue.

The mousse, gone in just a few licks. Then, he was back to lapping wildly at the air through the bars of his cage again. And so, with a shrug of my shoulders, I scooped another generous helping from my dessert bowl. Shadow, near enough inhaling the air-bubbled goo on the second go. And the third. The fourth, the fifth and the sixth.

And just when I was about to scoop a seventh generous dollop from my bowl, I found it to be empty. With only the brown smears left from the last six spoonfuls. Only then realising, I'd had but a mouthful, whereas Shadow had six!

My mother called from the hallway that it was time for bed and to not forget to say my prayers.

And kneeling by Shadow's cage, my hands clasped, I rushed through my nightly prayer, saying it for the both of us.

'Goodnight, Shadow,' I whispered to my little black pet through the bars of its cage.

Shadow was still making rustling noises as I drifted off to sleep, and when I stirred, awake, he was dead still. Not wanting to disturb him from his first night's sleep in my bedroom, I slowly pushed off the covers, cautiously swung my legs out of bed and gently settled my feet on the carpeted floor. Creeping over to him, on light feet, I softly knelt by his cage to watch him sleep. He was so still, I couldn't even see him breathing.

My mother calling from the hallway that it was time to get up. To not be late for school.

'Gotta go,' I whispered to Shadow. 'See you later, buddy.'

That whole day at school, all I could think about was returning home to Shadow. First thing I did, right after swinging open the front door to my house, was dash to my bedroom and fall to my knees at Shadow's cage; expecting him to chirp with excitement, or run around his cage in an excitable frenzy. But after falling to my knees to greet him, and tell him all about my day at school, he appeared to still be sleeping in the very same spot I'd left him.

'Oh, Shadow,' I said looking down at him. 'You haven't been asleep all day, have you?'

But still, Shadow slept.

'C'mon, Shadow,' I said to him gently. 'It's time to wake up.'

But he didn't so much as twitch his whiskers.

'Shadow?' I said. 'If this is some sort of joke, it's not funny.'

Flipping open the lid to his cage, I reached in and clasped my fingers and thumb around Shadow's tiny body. He felt limp in my hand, not solid and wriggly like he usually did.

'Shadow?' I said to him, peering into the thick, jet-black hair where his big, blinking, black eyes usually were.

'Shadow?' I said again.

Although, this time I could feel my eyes beginning to well up.

'C'mon buddy,' I told him. 'Please don't be dead.'

He was held lifelessly in my hands, but I wouldn't accept it.

'Come back,' I whispered to him. 'Please come back.'

That's when my mother called from the hallway that it was time for dinner.

Then I turned my attention back to the little black ball of fur in my hands.

'Come back,' I said.

Willing him back to life with all of the life I had within me.

'Come back,' I whispered. 'Please come back.'

And I couldn't be sure at the time, but Shadow's whiskers, I thought I saw them twitch.

'Come back,' I said, my voice growing from a desperate whisper to a determined plea of the smallest of hopes.

My mother calling from the foot of the stairs, asking if I was alright.

Shadow's legs, kicking. His tiny body, swelling with breath. His eyes, blinking open.

And as I looked up from Shadow to the ceiling, as if the answer was to be found up there, I quietly asked myself . . .

'Did I do that?'

Shadow didn't eat a thing the next day. Nor did he have a drop to drink.

We, my mother and I, had taken Shadow to the vet, and they couldn't find anything wrong with him, but said to keep an eye on him, and make sure he ate and drank.

Every day, I filled his food bowl and water bottle, making a mental note of how much was in each. But after a day and a night had passed, still he hadn't drunk from his water bottle, or eaten from his food bowl. It was the same with the next day, and the day after that. A week passing, with Shadow not touching either his food or water. Days turned to weeks, and weeks to months. Shadow making it to his first birthday, having not drunk a drop or eaten the smallest of bites. All of this, I kept secret from my mother, for fear she would take him back to the vets, or worse, have him put down. Emptying Shadow's food bowl down the toilet, and pouring out the contents of his water bottle with it at the end of every *day, only to fill them both up again at the beginning of the next. Shadow's immortality, just mine and his little secret.*

Seven years passed …

By the time it came to my fifteenth birthday, Shadow's non-requirement for food and water had become a normality for us both. Although, out of the two of us, only I knew that he should have been dead by now.

And then, about a year later, my mother passed.

Soon after which, I knew it was time to let go of little Shadow, too. He no longer relied on me, and I had outgrown him. He didn't need me around to feed or water him, and I didn't need him because I was now a young man that had matured from the requirement of having a pet fitting for an eight-year-old. I was only supposed to have him for a few years, and now here I was, on the threshold of adulthood, that'd outgrown silly pets meant for little boys.

My mother, who should've still had decades of life within her, was dead. And yet, here Shadow was, living on bonus time that may never come to an end.

It wasn't right.

And whenever I looked at Shadow, with his long, black coat, that's all he reminded me of – death.

My mother was gone forever, and Shadow, from what I had gathered, was going to be around for the same amount of time.

I was going to set him free; let him live out the rest of his never-ending life in the wild. But after being domesticated for so long, I figured he wouldn't last long out there.

Instead, I donated him to a local primary school. The very same one I attended, back when I still cried about having to return the school hamster.

And when I met with the headmistress there, I had to hold myself back from saying something like, 'He'll be cheaper to keep than most,' fearing she wouldn't have understood. But then, no one ever does. Not when it comes to life never ending, and death never coming around …

11

"She's Dead, of Course"

Malleus, so lost in the story he was telling me, hadn't heard the question I'd just asked.

"Sorry," he said. "Say again?"

"So you weren't always blind?" I asked.

"From that whole story? *That's* what you got?"

"Sorry. You don't have to answer that question."

And he doesn't.

"So, if that was the first time," I said. "What did you do, next?"

Malleus appeared to exhale, as if the air that was leaving him was somehow helping to bring back the memory.

"I started small," he said.

"What?" I asked. "Like, hamsters?"

"Let's just say I brought back my fair share of flies after that."

"And *then?*"

"Spiders."

"Eww! Yuck! Why spiders?"

Just saying the word caused me to clamp my mouth shut for fear of swallowing an imaginary one.

"Because all of God's creatures deserve to live," he said.

"And then?" I asked, unsure if I really wanted to know the answer.

"Then birds. Then cats, then dogs, then …"

"Horses?" I said as a laugh.

"No," he told me. "They're way too big."

"Oh my God," I said. "Have you ever tried it out on a *person?*"

Malleus's mouth didn't appear to move.

56

"I'm sorry," I said, putting my hand on his leg. "That was insensitive of me."

"No, it's fine," he said. "It's just that every time I bring something back to life, it takes a little life *out* of me."

"Oh, I see."

"I mean, birds and cats are one thing, but bringing back something as big as a dog. That really takes it out of me."

"No, of course."

"The life always returns to me eventually, but the bigger the animal, the more life it takes. The more life it takes, the longer it takes for me to recover."

My hand was still resting on his knee.

"The last dog I brought back almost *killed* me," he said.

"Would you ever bring *me* back?" I asked.

"I hope I never have to."

Out of politeness, I let a few seconds of silence go by. After that, I could no longer hold back the one question I'd been dying to ask Malleus since we met, back at the café.

"Would you show me, again?"

"Show you, again?" he asked.

"Bringing something back."

He slouched.

"Maybe something a little bigger this time?" I added.

And I could tell, from the shape his mouth was making, that Malleus let out a sigh.

"I just want to see it," I told him. "Just one more time."

But Malleus gave me nothing, not even a look of spent patience.

"Please?" I said, with the most convincing puppy dog eyes I could muster.

Which I then remembered had no power over a guy like him.

"On one condition," he said.

I bolted straight upright, clapping my hands quickly and silently.

"It has to be no bigger than a bird," he told me. "And when I say bird, I mean, like a pigeon or something, not an albatross."

"Yes, yes," I said. "Yes, of course."

"And just like last time," he added, "*you* have to supply it."

"Deal," I said, putting my hand out for him to shake.

But Malleus's arms were still folded as I slowly took back my hand.

"You've got to meet a bear?" I asked him, after his lips moved in strange shapes.

"No," he said, slapping his legs and getting to his feet. "I've got to be somewhere."

To which I replied, "Yeah, me too."

Which was an outright lie. I didn't have anywhere to be. I could've quite happily wasted the rest of the day with him at that sad little waterfront he'd brought me to.

"Just before you go," I said.

And standing to face him, I raised my hands up to cover his ears with the flat of my palms, only removing them once he'd had his own, personal, one-minute silence.

"That's what sitting here with you was like for me," I told him.

He smiled.

"I know," he said.

I took a step back.

"How did you know?" I asked.

"I can hear it in your voice," he said.

I didn't know whether to feel relieved or disappointed.

"But how is it that you understand everything I'm saying to you?" he asked.

"You speak more slowly than most," I told him. "That, and I'm crazy good at lip-reading."

And he smiled that damn smile at me again.

"Let me know when you're ready to meet again," he said, coming in for a hug.

"I will," I said, looking into his, not quite so mysterious, sunglasses.

"Iris," he said. "I just want you to know ..."

"Yes?"

"Your eyes are the most beautiful I've never seen."

And with a quick kiss on my cheek, he pulled out his phone from the back pocket of his jeans, put an earbud in his left ear, saying, "See you around, Iris," and he was gone.

Gone.

In much the same way the enthusiasm left me, for wasting the rest of that day without him.

12

"A Lad in His Cave"

With a shrug of my shoulders, I willed myself up from the knobbly log, took one last look at that gloomy view – looking even sadder than it did, now that Malleus wasn't here to share it with me – and headed back the way we came. Not knowing, at first, which way *the way we came* was exactly, what with Malleus leading me here with my eyes shut. But it didn't take me long to get my bearings once I saw the park, and I knew exactly where I was as I passed The Daily Grind café.

Now alone with my thoughts, I thought about nothing but Malleus to keep me company as I wandered. How, when I was with him, it felt as if it were just him and me in the world. Like we'd got the whole place to ourselves. And just as I'm strolling down these more familiar streets, blissfully unaware to anything that's going on around me, my eye is caught by a flashing neon sign that reads, '**OPEN**', in red, tubed letters. And when my head turns to look, I stop to see a pawn brokers. 'A Lad In His Cave' written in rust-freckled chrome lettering across the top of the shop's varnished wood, art deco window-front.

A seed had somehow managed to sow itself in my mind, taking root there, and now I couldn't stop it from growing. But if I was going to carry out what the seed whispered for me to do, I'd have to act with some sense of urgency, as if I missed this opportunity, I may not get a second chance.

Could I *do* the thing the seed in the soil of my mind was craftily suggesting? Could I really *do* it to Malleus? Take advantage of him like that? After all his kindness?

We hadn't known each other all that long, and I know it sounds corny, but it felt more like we knew one another from long ago and had only just recently caught up. He'd shown me death in a wholly different light, and that had, in turn, brought *me* back to life in a way. The adventure of it all, and yet only ever being in one place. That sense of danger, and yet feeling totally safe. A loyal companion, in an otherwise lonely world.

Was I really willing to risk losing all of *that?*

Stood there, just looking up at that inviting neon sign. Enticed by a flashing arrow, leading the way in.

I *knew* I shouldn't do it, but I did it anyway.

I pulled open the door to that shop and stepped inside.

It was as if I'd stepped through a looking glass, and into another world entirely. Magically transported one hundred years into the past. An Aladdin's cave full of wonders, once treasured, brought here and left abandoned. Beautifully crafted instruments of music, scratches of affection adorning their glossy, lacquered surfaces. Vintage jewellery that outlived the wrists and necks that wore them. And antique furniture, bearing the scars of their historical stories.

Lost amongst all the treasures that surrounded me – both sacrificed and discarded – there was something in particular I was looking for. I wasn't even sure if I'd find it in a place like this, and it was no antique by any stretch.

Sauntering up to the counter, where an old boy with a bald head was sat behind it, feet up, and reading what looked to be a tabloid newspaper. He licked a finger to turn the page and, upon seeing me, folded the paper and set it down.

"You deaf or summing?" I read his lips asking me.

And don't fret, dear reader. I get asked this a lot. I just shrug it off whenever it happens. *You've got to pick your battles,* as my dad's always telling me. But it was a damn good thing for this particular pawnshop owner that my dad wasn't there right then to hear the way this miserable old git was speaking to me.

"So?" he said, in a tone that was probably anything but friendly.

I must have missed this old boy asking me the first time, while the newspaper was still up to his face.

"I love your shop," I said, perhaps more politely than he deserved. "It really *is* like an Aladdin's cave in here."

"Yeah, yeah," he said. "I get that a lot. Now, whaddaya want?"

I'd only been talking to this guy for less than a minute, but I could tell already that he really needed to work on his customer service skills.

"Do you happen to sell second-hand mobile phones?" I asked.

"I buy more than I sell," he said, pulling his top lip up to his nose. "But, yeah, I do as a matter of fact."

Rummaging through my bag, I pulled out my phone.

"I'm looking for one like this," I told him.

Sliding his tortoise-shell spectacles up from the edge of his nose to his eyes, he leant in close to better see the phone I was holding up. His breath, reeking of dog shit chased with a few too many shots of whiskey.

"Whaddaya need a phone for if you've already got one?" he asked. "You a drug dealer or summing?"

Stepping back so he could get a good look at me, I asked him, "Do I *look* like a drug dealer to you?"

"No," he said. "No, you don't."

And that, right there, would go down as the nicest thing he said to me on that particular visit.

"You look more like one of those low-rent street walkers," he said. "Is that what the phone's for? Your thriving business?"

He laughed out loud, and I had to wipe some of his shit-whiskey spit off my face with the cuff of my coat.

I felt like walking out, and perhaps I should have.

But if I was going to do what I was thinking of doing, this would probably be my last chance.

"Look," I told him. "I just want to buy a phone."

"Like *that* one," he said, more repeating my words than actually asking me.

"In fact ..." I added, still holding my phone up for this rude, crude, mean old bastard to see.

"... *Exactly* like this one."

13

"An Act of Betrayal"

We arranged to meet, Malleus and I, same time, same place. Midnight, the park. Except *this* time round there was a dead pigeon in my handbag – which wasn't too hard to come by, thanks to someone very recently hitting it with their car. Knocked out, cold. Dead, but still in one piece.

That was Malleus's only rule: that the animals he brought back had to be intact. He told me how he'd tried it with roadkill before. Squirrels and pheasants with their heads barely hanging on, entrails strewn across the tarmac. He told me how it didn't work most of the time, but when it *did* the results were so gruesome Malleus point-blank refused to ever do it again.

Waiting there, I felt as if I were spilling over with nerves. Not like the last time we met in the park, that was different. We were then meeting properly for the first time, and nerves were to be expected. No, *this* time I was nervous with the indecision of what I may or may not be going through with that night.

It wasn't too late. I didn't *have* to go through with it. There was still time to change my mind. I almost walked away. But before I had the chance to take a step, those four dreaded noughts on my wristwatch appeared, and so, too, did Malleus.

He greeted me with a kiss, saying, "Shall we do what we're here to do?"

But I didn't say anything in return, I just kissed him back. That kiss feeling more like a betrayal than a greeting.

He took my arm, and we walked to the very same spot he brought back Harry, the suicidal hamster. We knelt as before. I took out the dead animal as before. He rubbed his hands as before.

The only difference being when he asked me to hand over my phone.

I mean, I *handed* him a phone. It was the same size and weight as my phone. Identical, in every way, to my phone. Except that it *wasn't* my phone. It was the one I'd bought at the pawnshop. And as he slipped the phone I'd given him into the inside pocket of his jacket, I slipped out my *actual* phone from mine.

And while he set about bringing this dead pigeon back to life, I switched my phone to 'camera mode'. Clicked on 'video'. Held it up in the direction of Malleus, now knelt down with the bird in his hands …

… and hit 'Record'.

14

"A Moment of Clarity"

I know what you're thinking. *How could I do that?* How could I even *think* about doing that to Malleus? And the reason I know that's what you're thinking is because, well, I was thinking it, too.

Thing is – and here comes my defence – I hadn't really done all that much wrong at this point. Yes, I filmed Malleus bringing back that dead bird. Yes, I betrayed his trust. Yes, I had taken advantage of his disability. But no, I hadn't actually done anything with the footage.

Not yet.

I was still the only person who knew about his ability. And yet, it still plagued me: this small act of betrayal. It was as if I'd swallowed a fly, and that I may have to swallow a spider to catch it. And then what? A bird to catch the *spider?* And so it would go … a cat, a dog, and finally the horse that would finish us off. Killing the one good thing I had: mine and Malleus's friendship.

Kill it, dead.

But then I reminded myself I'd only swallowed a fly at this point. I could just stop there. Delete the footage. Never speak of it to anyone. Malleus, none the wiser.

I was thinking about all this in my usual spot for going over things when my head's just a big, rotating drum of tumbling thoughts. Lying there on the bed, and staring up at a non-specific patch on the ceiling.

With my phone still in my hands, I opened the video gallery, clicked on the video of Malleus with the dead bird, and …

… I couldn't do it.

My finger just hovered over the 'delete' icon. My mind, torn in two. On the one hand, I should've just *hurried up and deleted it already!* But, on the other, I had some pretty incredible footage here. And just *think* what Malleus and I could do with it. We could be internet sensations. We could finally be seen and heard by the world!

But I also knew Malleus didn't want all that. That he really didn't want this getting out: what he could do. That he just wanted it to be our little secret. It wasn't my power, and so it wasn't my choice to make.

But then why show me at all? Why risk it 'getting out' if that's what he was always so afraid of? To me, it was like being gifted with the most magnificent specimen of a tiger, and then just keeping it locked up in a cat carrier.

My finger was still hovering over the trash can icon as I chewed over what the right thing to do here was. I blew it all out, all this agony of indecision, as my lungs, once again, filled with troubled air. I couldn't decide what to do, and so I decided I wasn't going to do anything.

As I kept reminding myself, I still hadn't done anything wrong. And how I *really* wanted to keep it that way.

I still didn't know what I was going to do with the footage. What I *did* know, however, was that my ballooning mind was being suffocated by this ever-shrinking room.

I took a brisk walk, hoping those troubling thoughts would be left far behind me. But, it turned out, those troubling thoughts caught up with ease, as they took much longer strides than I did.

And I don't know why, but there were what felt like hands, buzzing with static, creepy-crawling up from the base of my spine and planting themselves on either one of my shoulders. The feeling of being followed. And I, not having the reassuring sense to hear footsteps keeping up with my pace behind me, kept turning my head sharply back the way I came to see no imagined stalker in sight.

Then my clawing thoughts let go their grip of my brain, as I was taken aback by where I had accidentally ended up, and the barren landscape that was now before me. I had stumbled across the one place, of all places, that might just help to still my spinning mind.

Taking a pew on the knobbly log, I closed my eyes and imagined the very same view I described to Malleus. A triangle of birds in the sky. The sky spreading out into the distance and coming back to me as a river. Boats bobbing in the swell. The sun, twinkling in a thousand golden pieces on the water's surface.

But just like when Malleus left me here that last time, it wasn't the same.

That's when it became so clear to me. That my life, much like that view, just wasn't the same without him next to me.

It was then I knew *exactly* what to do.

I would delete that stupid video, and never speak a word about it to anyone. Malleus, none the wiser. It would be like it never happened. All that guilt and shame, washed away by a sweet wave of relief, sent from my own clear thinking. And this feeling would have lasted if I'd just taken out my phone, and deleted that stupid video, sat right where I was.

But after rummaging through my bag. After shaking said bag upside down, all the contents spilling to the sodden ground. Frantically rifling through my personal effects, on my knees, with panicked, outstretched fingers.

I could have torn my hair out.

For it appeared I had, in fact …

… lost my phone.

15

"Losing It"

I tell myself to *Stay calm*, and that *Everything will be fine.* But lying and *believing* it – if you've ever tried it – is nigh impossible when you're lying to yourself.

Even so, I would at least *try* to convince myself of the half-truth that I would find my phone before anybody else did.

I'd just have to re-trace my steps.

Telling myself, *You just dropped it, is all.*

On my way back to the hall of residence, I scanned the streets like some desperate young woman looking for a dropped cigarette butt to smoke. But, ironically, all I saw were cigarette butts – and the odd dead animal by the side of the road. Where were they when I was actually *looking* for one?!

"How could you be so careless?" I muttered venomously to myself, hammering a clenched fist against my thigh, in time with the words. I must've looked like a *crazy* person, and if I didn't, I was certainly starting to *feel* like one.

Approaching me was an old man walking his dog who, upon seeing me punching my leg and berating myself with harsh words, crossed to the opposite side of the street with a look of mild concern on his face.

"What??" I hissed at him as we passed by each other.

To which he began walking all the faster, whilst still looking back at me. And then, upon realising what I had just done – which wasn't far off from socially terrorising some old timer with a dog – I stomped, double time, with my head down, the rest of the way home.

Throwing my things to the floor of my room, I fell to a crumpled heap to join them.

"What am I going to do?" I asked myself aloud, as I got myself back up off the floor and began pacing back and forth like an agitated piranha in a puny fishbowl.

Then, an *epiphany!*

I would just call up my service provider and get them to put a block on my phone.

And forgetting for just a moment, I reached into my bag.

"FUUUCK!"

And I surrender to the hopelessness of the floor again.

Only just then realising that in order to *call* the service provider, I would actually require a bloody *phone!*

And just when I think things can't possibly get any worse, I'm snapped out of my spiralling thoughts when I see a flashing of white light reflecting off the walls and ceiling. Letting me know there's someone pressing the doorbell-like button on the other side of the door.

Heaving myself up off the floor, I go to open the door, a crack, to see that it's one of my three flatmates.

"What?" I asked a little more reservedly than I did with that poor old man who was just taking his pet pooch for a walk.

From what I could read of my flatmates' lips, they were saying something about there being *"Someone here to see me"*. Jerking a thumb over their shoulder, and towards the front door to the flat behind them.

"Someone's here to see *me?"* I asked. "Really?"

But no one knows that I live here, I thought to myself. *Not even Malleus.*

"Malleus?" I said, one third to myself, one third to my flatmate, and one third to the guy who could be waiting at the door.

My flatmate then steps aside to let me by, but where I expect Malleus to be, stood there with that damn smile of his, is someone else entirely. Someone I hadn't paid much mind to in, since, well …

… forever.

Someone I had tried to forget and put behind me.

For standing in the doorway, right there in front of me, was a girl with eyes the colour of envy, and fiery red hair.

A girl I thought and *hoped* I would never, ever, again, see.

But there she was.

She was right there.

Mascara running down her face like rivers of black oil.

Fighting back tears between sharp, violent breaths.

"Amy?" I said to this beautiful, washed-up shipwreck at my door.

A girl who somehow still managed to look absolutely drop-dead gorgeous, even as a snotty, teary-eyed mess.

And after all these years, and everything that happened between us in the time before them, all this girl managed to say was, "Hello, Iris."

16

Before we go ANY further, there are some things I REALLY need you to know about this Amy girl. What I also need you to know is that just because someone never laid a finger on you, doesn't mean they never hurt you.

Amy G'dala.

'Aimz' to her close-knit circle of friends. Or better put: 'clique of followers'. People like you and I have friends, Amy had only followers. She saw people as useful tools; objects she would pick up and discard whenever she ran out of use for them.

Me?

She had no use for me, other than to keep me around to make her feel better about herself.

In all the time I had the displeasure of knowing Amy, I never knew her to have any real friends. And I would have felt sorry for her. No, honestly, I *would* have. If it hadn't been for the way she treated *me*. Someone who was once her 'best' friend.

I had no idea what I was in for with Amy when we first met at primary school. But I would gradually find out over the next ten, slow years, as the very worst times of my life painfully unfolded.

The first year began when my dad and I moved counties, relocating to the outskirts of a small town. This was quite some time before I became fully aware as to what level of malicious Amy truly was, and the lengths she would go to make my life an insufferable torment.

My parents were going through something I wouldn't have been able to understand at the time. I'd left a good many friends behind, along with the place I called home for the first eight years of my life. Not to mention, my mother, who no longer lived with us.

I dreaded that first day at a new school like I dreaded being drafted and sent to fight in some war I had no part in starting.

Would the teachers be strict? What would my classmates think of me? Would they poke fun at my accent? Would I make any friends? Would I be ostracised? Be made to walk the arid deserts of solitude, alone, and without even food, water or encouragement?

But my first day – from what I can remember of it – went surprisingly well.

This would also be the very first day I met Amy – the most popular girl in school, it turned out – who took me under her wing.

Did you hear that?

The most popular girl in the entire *school!* She actually took me under her wing.

One of the first things Amy said to me was that she just *loved* my accent. We would chit-chat, just me and her, all the time, in class, assembly and at break. We were what I had always imagined twin sisters to be like – ones that got on with each other, at least. We dressed the same, and we acted alike. We were inseparable.

Almost as if we were two minds in a shared head.

But just when I'd relaxed into the cosy reassurance of thinking that what Amy and I had would last, things took a turn. I just didn't realise at that time, it would be for the very worst.

Over time, gone unnoticed, Amy began to lose the other friends she had, who felt sidelined and left out of the little, impenetrable bubble we had formed around ourselves. That's when she began to push me away.

It was so subtle, at first.

She'd ignore me in the hallways, or pretend she hadn't seen me when I waved at her from the other side of the playground. We always sat together at lunch break, and now my seat was always taken by some other girl.

Then 'that turn' I spoke of just now, turned again.

But this time it turned nasty.

Instead of being ignored, I was being teased. It was so slight, at first, I hardly realised it was happening. Being stared at by a group of five or six of them in the playground at break time, and them giggling about me. Calling me 'Cow Eyes' on account of all that white space around my big, blue irises. One of Amy's band of beautiful bullies would give me a shove as they walked past me in the hallways.

I thought leaving primary school to begin secondary school would somehow put an end to it, but it only served in showing me what real bullying was.

Now I was being pushed into lockers. Tripped up, landing on my face in the concrete netball courts at lunch break. Those same girls, mocking me in the changing rooms after physical education about being the only girl to have started her period and having hair on their legs. All of them, ready and waiting outside the school gates, and taunting me as they followed me home. Every, godforsaken day.

Relentless.

That's the best word I have for it.

It was relentless.

I told my dad about it, pleading with him for me to move schools or get home-schooling, but he never believed it was as bad as I was making out. That it was just what happened at school. All those teenagers thrown into one big cage together, with their hormones all over the place. His vague advice was to simply "fight back". That you're only a victim if you *choose* to be.

And so, I stayed.

And I fought.

And I fought some more.

I fought back with everything I had in me to fight with. A five-year-long ritual of psyching myself up before stepping onto the canvas that was school, and returning home to my corner, purple-grey bruises with yellow halos all up the sides of my body. Slashes on my legs and my arms. Cuts across my face. A girl even tore out an earring in this one fight, leaving me with the souvenir of a rough, jagged scar to prove the story true. But what hurt the most – more than the cuts and the bruises – was knowing who was behind it all.

Amy G'dala.

The girl who once saved me, had now thrown me to a pack of wolves. She took me under her wing, and then proceeded to cut mine off just so they could all point and laugh. The cuts and bruises healing only to make room for new ones. But it's the wounds from all the low blows I took to my self-worth that are still there on the inside, yet to heal. The cuts and bruises you *can't* see because they're not on the surface.

Amy did all this without ever physically touching me, having plenty of other girls to throw the kicks and punches *for* her. She never laid a finger on me. She had given me a few small things in the beginning, but had taken so much from me over the years that there was almost nothing left to take. And, unbeknownst to me at the time, she was yet to take a whole lot more.

It was the last day of secondary school, and everyone was in high spirits; singing songs and signing each other's school shirts. I distinctly remember a copious amount of big, fat, erect penises being doodled on shirts, complete with hairy balls and projectile ejaculate.

Boys will be boys.

It was a day where we all felt like we were going to be free at last. Especially for someone like me, as it also meant there was a sound chance the bullying would stop. College wasn't at all like secondary school, from what I'd heard.

I was going to study music.

But the one thing I was most looking forward to, was getting as far away as I could from Amy and her band of beautiful bullies.

On my way home from school, for what would be the very last time, I had no idea I was walking right into their one, last send-off for me.

I remember the roads being particularly busy after school that day, so I took the underpass. And it was only when I'd walked about halfway through the tunnel that passed under the road – the sound of my footsteps resonating about the corrugated tube around me – that I saw Amy, standing at the other end as I approached her. I remember turning on my heel to walk the other way, only to see six of Amy's so-called friends waiting for me on the opposite side, and blocking my way out.

And that's the last thing I remember from that day.

Then it's just fragments. A roll of film. The frames, spliced and stuck together in no discernible order. Blurry eyed, I think I'm still laid out in that underpass. But when I look to my right, I see green waves, spiking and dipping on a black screen. I remember trying to sit up, a surge of pain laying me back down again. The soft of a mattress beneath me. Pastel-yellow walls. Dark-blue, people-shaped shadows moving behind a window of frosted glass. I call out to them, but no words make it out. I scream and I yell but, still, I make not a sound. Those same dark-blue shadows surround me. There's a sharp scratch on my left arm, the shadows all blur into one another, and as much as I try to force them to stay open, my eyes slowly close.

My eyes open as slowly as they had closed. And perhaps it was there before, and perhaps it wasn't, but this time I wake up to see there's now what appears to be a drip in my left arm. Green lines on a black screen still spiking and falling as before. The soft of a mattress. Pastel-yellow walls. Frosted glass.

And my first thought is just how quiet this room is.

A shadow rises from one corner of the room, swiftly floating over to me in a manner that causes my heart to pump icy cold blood. I gasp, but no sound makes it past my throat. Then an embrace warms my veins as I feel the shadow hold me tight in its arms, and I realise who the shadow is.

Only my father held me like that.

You're holding me too tight, Dad! I tell him. But the words fail to make it past my lips.

He then mouths words I can't quite make out. I remember telling him to *Speak up!* but, again, the words never make it out, and neither does the laugh that came with them. *I must have lost my voice,* I thought to myself. I couldn't understand why I couldn't talk. And why was my father mouthing his words to me rather than just *saying* them?

A white blur enters the room. A doctor, maybe? A bright, white light shone in both my eyes. A torch, perhaps? The rough textured, woody taste of a flat, wooden stick on my tongue. Plastic entering and settling in the canal of my ears. The familiar sensation of a remote thermometer. The white blur appears to mouth some words to me as it places a hand on my knee.

I'll never forget the way my father hung his head.

The doctor looks at me with the eyes you give a person when

you're about to give them the worst news of their entire life. He reaches into his coat pocket, pulling out a small notebook; a silver pen slipped in the binding that spirals down the side of the white, blue-lined pages.

I crane my neck to better see what he's jotting down.

Slipping the pen back in the black, spiral binding, he tears off the page, and throws my father a look with his eyebrows raised. And my father, not looking the doctor in the eyes, simply gives him a nod. The doctor slowly hands me the torn-off page, blank side up. And with the scrap of paper now in my hands, I turn it over.

My eyes, refusing to believe themselves, and the words the doctor had written, shut tight to hold in the tears that would surely bleed out of them if they didn't.

But the worst part of it all was that I couldn't even hear myself crying.

I kept that note. The one the doctor handed to me that day. I don't know why. It was silly, really. But I think I did this to let its message truly sink in. Or perhaps it's because I just couldn't bring myself to throw it away. I still have it now – slipped in one of the credit card slots of my phone case – carrying it wherever I go to serve as a reminder of how far I've come.

On the note, scrawled big in doctor's handwriting, are just three words.

YOU ARE DEAF

Words that had to be written down for me to read, as I wasn't able to hear them.

I fell asleep with that note in my hand, that first night home from the hospital. Losing count of how many times I'd read it before I finally drifted off. My dad must have checked on me in the night because, come morning, there were three more words written on the other side of that little note.

I'm so sorry

I was due to be starting college soon after my time at secondary school came to an end. As I said before, I was going to study music. And when I say, 'was', that's precisely what I mean.

This whole being deaf thing was most novel to me back then.

I had to live my daily life in a wholly different way to what I was accustomed to, and as much as I couldn't wait to get started at college, I'd *have* to. College life was just way too big of an adjustment to jump into right away at that time, with so many *other* big changes to get used to.

I tried to stay positive.

Figuring, if one of my senses had to go, I would always choose my hearing over my sight. And losing my hearing made me thankful for the other four senses I *did* have.

My psychiatrist advised I took a gap year; adjust to this new way of life, keep up with something creative as a hobby, and whatever I still *could* do without my hearing. And as much as I didn't want to hear it at the time – pun absolutely, categorically intended – I have to say, looking back with the clarity of hindsight, I now see that they were right.

So I took a gap year.

I still watched movies – except now with subtitles. I still read books – audiobooks weren't even a thing back then. And I developed a strong penchant for drum and bass music – and just about anything bass-heavy. The more vibrations, I found, the better. Much to my father's annoyance, no doubt. Although he never once asked me to turn my stereo down.

There was still so much I *could* do, that I almost forgot about all the things I *couldn't*.

I'll admit, it took a while to get used to the idea that I would never hear music again, or the sound of my own voice – or anyone *else's* for that matter. It did mean, however, I would never again have to put up with all that pop shit on the radio, the inane chatter of annoying disc jockeys, or any of those god-awful commercials slipped somewhere in-between. But, to be honest, I would happily sit through hours of all that crap just to hear a beautifully played piano, or be sat inside a car with the sound of rain pitter-pattering on the roof. All the simple stuff I so took for granted until it was taken away.

There would be things I would miss, but it also opened up a whole new way of experiencing the world. A world that most people, with all of their senses, took for granted. I developed a whole new appreciation for images. Specifically, photographic images. Deciding I would use the time – this one, whole year I had – to get out with my camera every day, and put together a portfolio of my work to apply for a photography course at college.

It's what spurred me on through that first year of silence; seldom paying mind to much else. My end goal, far off in the distance of three hundred and sixty-five days away. But with my blinkers firmly attached, it was also all that I could see ahead of me.

One year passed …

I got my portfolio together. I got into my college of choice. I got on with the rest of my life as a deaf girl.

The nerves I felt for my first day at college, were a lot like the ones I had for my first day at primary school. But it was different this time. Because *this* time I was accepted for who I was. My uniqueness: encouraged.

Liberated.

That's the best word I have to describe it.

I felt liberated.

Set free from being shoved into lockers and tripped up in the playground. The taunting, and the beatings. The name calling and being laughed at whenever my back was turned.

But most of all, I was free of Amy G'dala.

Finally, I could get on with just being me, and doing whatever was in my heart, without having to worry about what she would have done to me if I did. I was, for what seemed the first time in my life, truly and genuinely free.

Yes, I'd been held back a year, but what I had personally achieved in my first year at that college, I had not been able to do in the ten years prior, all thanks to her.

Things were good.

Really good.

And I don't know whether all good things *must* come to an end, but they certainly always seem to, eventually.

The good things, in this case, came to an end when I started the second year at that college.

It was enrolment day. I was in line to sign up for the second year of a photography course, after getting an A-plus at A-level for my submission at the end of the first year.

I looked about me; at all the other students in line for their chosen subjects. All these brilliant, like-minded people, who all wanted to be the very best they could be, but who also supported one another in being the very best *they* could be, too.

I signed the papers with my photography tutor and walked away feeling as though I was floating across the floor.

Then something arrested my attention.

Something that clutched onto my light, winged feet, and pulled them back sharply down to the ground.

This smudge of fiery red, like a crimson-coloured fly stuck in the corner of my eye.

Stopping, without looking, my gut told me to keep walking. To *not* look up. To *not* turn my head.

But I did.

I turned my head.

I looked up.

Nothing could have prepared me for who I saw in the room that day. I had put her so far out of my mind. Replaced all those dreadful memories with all the glorious pictures I had captured from behind my camera. With every roll of film I developed, and every negative I had cast light through onto glossy, light-sensitive paper, I filled my mind with so much beauty that I had almost but forgotten all of her ugliness.

She no longer existed in the world I saw now.

And this new world I had created over the last couple of years or so. This entire world. It imploded like it had been hit by a planet-killer meteorite. This heavenly sphere that I had so carefully and painstakingly crafted with my own hands, was obliterated.

I haven't been able to so much as pick up a camera since that day.

For the dark angel of Armageddon was back, and her name was Amy G'dala.

There she was.

Standing in line for level one *Music Studies.*

She was right there.

And that's where she is now.

Amy.

Stood there like a pathetic mess in the front doorway of my flat.
And after all that.
After everything I just told you.
All she had to say for herself was, "Hello, Iris."
Me.
I'm just stood here.
Looking at her in a wholly different way to the way she's looking at me.
And sighing the biggest sigh of my entire, fucking life …
… I let her in.

17

"Don't Let Her In"

I had closed the door on Amy, and now I was stepping aside to let her back through it. But what was I supposed to do? I couldn't just leave her standing there with mascara running down her face. It's not like I was prepared for a moment I thought would never happen.

"I don't know where to start," Amy said, in between her blubbering. "I'm just so sorry. For *everything*."

She actually managed to sound … well, *look*, sincere.

Sat on the edge of my bed, I held her in an awkward embrace.

"It's OK, Amy," I told her.

When, *really*, there was nothing OK *about* it.

Why was *I* the one comforting *her*? After all she'd done to me. Where was *she* when *I* needed kind words or to be held? *She* was the one that'd done the damage and just left me behind, broken, not the other way around! But there was a part of me that I didn't fully understand in that moment, that felt, kind of, *sorry* for her.

"I never forgot, you know," she said, between sharp breaths. "What I did to you."

Neither had *I*, I thought to myself. But I *had* moved past it. Replaced the bad memories with good ones. Forgiven and forgotten her. I had put her so completely out of my mind that she no longer existed in this new-fangled world I'd created for myself. But, it seemed, she *hadn't*. And in the most strangest of ways, I felt for her. That's why I invited her in. That's why the awkward hug and the kind words.

"Whatever can I do to start making it up to you?" she asked me.

Quietly, I considered the question. *I don't know,* I thought to myself. Build a time machine? Travel back to when we first met? Way back when you were still *nice* to me. Before you turned my whole, fucking, *world* upside down and shook it like an *Etch A Sketch!* And, I don't know, perhaps not have transformed into the complete and utter *Super-Twot* you became *after* that!

Obviously I didn't actually *say* all of this to her, due only to the impossibility of the suggestion. I just looked into her eyes, that appeared to be filled with a deep regret, and put a reassuring hand on her knee.

"Buy me a coffee?" I said.

Even when Amy buying me an entire, fucking, global, coffee *franchise* wasn't even going to come *close* to 'making it up to me'.

And although still sobbing pathetically, she was able to hold back her crying for just long enough to laugh, slowly look up at me, wipe the tears from her face in a black smear and say, "It's like you're in my head."

Not a word was spoken by either of us on the way to The Daily Grind café, but once there, we couldn't stop our mouths from flapping. And just to show you the extent of my mercy, dear reader, I did give Amy some face wipes; even going as far as to allow her to use some of my make-up. Although, as she did point out, she wasn't as into such "safe colours" of lipstick and eyeshadow as *I* was. Really, rather than giving her make-up, I should've probably given her some bruises of her own. Say, a broken rib, or a fractured skull. But it was abundantly clear, from just how wounded she appeared, that Amy had been beating herself up about all this *for* me, for quite some time already.

"Damn good coffee, right?" I asked her as she took her first sip.

But all she did was nod unconvincingly, place the cup down again, and appeared to make a *Mm* sound.

"So, like," I went to say, "what are you even *doing* here?"

"What?" she asked, after almost spitting out her coffee. "Like I need your permission?"

"You know what I mean."

"I'm here at university," she said. "Like, *you.*"

"Studying …?"

Bringing her cup up to her lips, she took a sip, swallowed and said, "Music."

And until that moment, I had no idea that just one, single, spoken word could set my blood boiling.

"And you?" she asked, casually.

"What?" I asked, the word 'music' still ringing in my ears.

Well.

Head.

She took another sip, looking up at me with expectant eyes, before saying, "Anyway, look at the two of us. Chatting over coffee. Here at the same university. The both of us doing degrees. I mean, what are the chances?"

Mmm, I thought. What *are* the chances? About a gazillion to one, I reckon.

Only then do I get round to asking the one question that's been pestering me since we left my room to come to this café, drink overpriced coffee, and pretend like everything's just hunky-fucking-dory.

"How did you even *find* me?" I asked her.

"How did you manage to lose your *phone?*" she replied.

To which, I scoffed.

"Very easily, as it turns out," I told her, before my whole face scrunched up. "Wait. How did you know I lost my phone?"

Amy's shoulders fell, and a small smile grew on her face. Reaching into her pink snakeskin handbag, she pulled out a mobile phone. A phone, identical in every way to the one I had lost. The only difference being, it now had a cracked screen.

"Where did you find this?" I asked her, taking it from her hands as if it were a bar of gold bullion.

"In the street," she said, her back straightening up with pride.

"Thank you," I told her. The way I said it probably sounding more like a question. Then my face screwed up. "But how did you know this was *my* phone?"

"It didn't take all that long to work out," she said. "You should have studied photography, you know. All the pictures I saw on your phone. You've got a good eye."

And suddenly the phone in my hand didn't look like a bar of gold to me anymore. More like a pile of dog shit that had been slapped in my palm.

"You should really put a lock on it or something," she told me, as she took a sip of her coffee. "You know what people are like."

Yes, I thought to myself. *You don't have to tell me.*

My eyes narrowed. "So you went through my phone?"

"Well, yeah," Amy said. "To see whose it was."

"What *else* did you see on there?" I asked her.

"How do you mean?" she asked, bringing her coffee cup up to hide her lips.

And then, realising I was about to give away more than I wanted to, I just said, "Nothing. Don't worry about it," and pretended to shrug it off.

"Anyway," I said, tucking the phone back safely in my bag as if it were encrusted with diamonds. "Thanks, again."

Feeling somewhat more relieved that my phone was now back in my possession, there was, however, this niggling unrest in me because of who'd returned it. I decided to put it out of my mind for now as Amy and I caught up. It was just like when we first met at primary school. Although, this time, it felt as if *I* were the one taking her under *my* wing.

We finished up our second cup of coffee and ended our little catch up with a much less awkward hug before going our separate ways.

It's funny how life surprises you like that. Just when you think you know the road ahead, it turns sharply round a corner. This time I was met with a girl who I thought I'd left way back down the road I came. This time, my big surprise was Amy. Yes, it had stirred up a lot of unresolved feelings from the past. Feelings of hate, and of bitterness, and of anger. But by the end of our stopping in the road to meet, there was also 'making amends', and forgiveness, and 'letting go'.

I guess sometimes you just have to accept a person for the now, and not the then.

So caught up in the whirlwind of what had just happened; this ghost from the past just showing up at my door. It was only once the whipping winds had calmed, that my mind came back down from being blown around, settling on Malleus and the video I made of him bringing that dead bird back to life.

Peering past the new cracks in the glass, I was almost disappointed as I gazed at the empty home screen of my phone to find that no one had been trying to get hold of me. Just a few emails from the university about my attendance. Or lack thereof.

But first thing's first.

I opened up my phone's picture gallery, clicked on 'video', selected the dead pigeon footage and hit 'delete'. A tidal wave of relief washed over me as I pressed the 'envelope' icon on my phone's home screen, and I began composing a text message for Malleus.

After what must have been the best part of several wasted minutes, I was about to hit 'send' when I realised I'd written a small dissertation on the subject of my adventures of the last day or so. Puffing my cheeks, I blew all the air out like a deflating balloon whilst holding down 'delete'. My eyes gliding left and darting sharply to the right like a backwards typewriter, watching the entire paragraph shrink, line by line, to nothing.

After gazing up at the ceiling, hoping to find some kind of inspiration up there, I instead just typed the word, *Hey*. No need to overwhelm the boy with a colossal mammoth of an info dump, I thought. And with another puff out from my lips, I hit 'send' and waited.

And waited.

And waited some more.

18

"Pavement Pizza"

Pacing my room like a girl who's anxiously awaiting the result of a pregnancy test, I tell myself that *A watched phone never rings.* Or in my case, flashes and vibrates.

It felt as if the best part of a day had gone by, when really it was probably no more than the worst couple of minutes, when Malleus finally texted me back with the words, *Hey, yourself.* Upon which the sound of gleeful clapping could be heard coming from the inside of my head for only me to hear.

Me: *Can we meet? I've got a lot to tell you!*

Malleus: *You hungry? I know this great little pizza place.*

Me: *I'm so hungry I could eat a pizza topped with horse meat!*

I texted that last message, complete with an emoji face licking its lips. Whether or not he would actually *know* about the emoji face licking its lips, I had no idea.

Malleus: *Meet me at Pavement Pizza ... I'll send you the deets.*

Pavement Pizza? I thought to myself. Wasn't that just vulgar slang for a patch of vomit, typically found in the street on a Sunday morning? And thinking on this, suddenly I'm not so hungry anymore.

Malleus: *See you there in thirty? Give you time to pretty yourself up!*

Me: *Like I need to?*

And tossing my phone on the bed, I go to get ready.

Malleus was already sat inside the pizzeria when I got there, and I couldn't help myself not to wave and check my reflection in the

85

shop window. First *pushing* the door, only then do I see the **'PULL'** sign on the handle. Heaving it open, the door then banged me in the arm as I stumbled through it. Now my coat sleeve's all bunched up, my handbag now hanging from the crook of my arm, and not my shoulder.

You only feel as disabled as the world around you that's not built for you.

Malleus gave me a wave as I walked over to where he was sat in a booth with what looked like faux-leather seating. The only colours in the restaurant were white, red and green, in that order. And someone had really gone to town with all the chrome in here. Harsh fluorescent lighting, brighter than the sun outside, stung my eyes as if lemon juice had just been rubbed in them.

Taking the seat opposite Malleus and scooching over, I asked him, "How do you do that?"

"Do, what?" he asked.

"How do you always know it's me?"

To which, he coolly replied, "I'd know those little footsteps of yours anywhere."

And then, in a fluster, I just go right into an info-dump about my adventures of the last day or so. How I lost my phone. How I'd done everything I could do to find it. How a ghost from the past just *Poof!* appeared at my door. When, really, all I want to tell him, but perhaps thinking better of it, is how much I've missed him.

"Sorry," I said, slapping myself on the forehead. "I'm going on a bit, aren't I?"

"No, it's cool," he said. "It's just …"

And I cringe, dreading his next words.

"It's just good to hear your voice again," he said.

And even though he can't see it, I smile in a way that says I love him for it.

That smile sagging on my face when I happened to look down at my plate.

"Errghh. Nasty," I said as I flicked a dead fly from the pizza's crust.

The fly lands on the back of Malleus's left hand, immediately springing to its feet and flying away.

"What's the matter?" Malleus asks.

And as I watch the tiny insect fly up and over the heads of hungry customers sat at the bar, and straight into the blue ring of light of an electric, bug-zapping machine behind the counter, I tell him … "Never mind."

"You're quiet," Malleus said. A red ring of tomato sauce around his mouth that I'm either too polite or too amused by to mention.

This is while I'm pensively chewing on my third slice.

I make a *Hmm?* sound. The only sound one *can* make with a mouthful of double-pepperoni pizza.

"Well," he said. "Quiet for *you*."

"Ha ha," I said. And I'm so glad he can't see me unintentionally showing him all the chewed-up pizza that's in my mouth right now.

"There's something on your mind," he said. "I can tell."

Quickly chewing up what's left in my mouth, I put the rest of my slice of pizza down on the plate with the others, and swallow.

"Well," I said. "There is something."

"I knew it," he said. "Go on."

Lowering my voice to a whisper, I said, "I just can't stop thinking about the other night."

Some heavy-set fellow sat in the next booth stops to look up from his pizza, mouth open, mid-chew.

"The other night?" Malleus asked.

"With that dead bird," I said.

A chunk of chewed pizza falls from the gaping mouth of the guy sat in the next booth.

"We can't talk about this here," Malleus said, finally wiping his sauce-spattered mouth with a napkin.

And I can't tell whether the guy in the next booth is either mildly disturbed or simply disappointed.

"We'll talk about it later," Malleus said.

No, from the way the guy in the next booth is looking down at that sorry chewed-up hunk of dough on his plate, he's definitely disappointed.

"Let's just sit here and enjoy our pizza," Malleus said.

And I must sound like a spoilt brat that's just been told that *No!*

they *can't* have a bag of Jelly Babies at the supermarket checkout, when I slump in my chair and make the most disgruntled of noises.

We finish up our pizza to the sound of the slightly uncomfortable ten-minute silence we both sit through – although I'm quite comfortable with silence by now. Only talking again when we're out of the restaurant and walking along the street, where I tell him about all the incredible things he could be doing with his ability. Working his magic in hospitals, bringing back stillborn babies. Or at veterinary practices, breathing life back into beloved pets after they've been put down. How he could change the world and its entire belief system of death!

Malleus told me that people simply wouldn't understand. The whole stigma around 'bringing things back from the dead'. How he'd more than likely be locked away for it, or poked and prodded by scientists. How the whole world would think he was a freak. That he preferred to keep it how it was: a secret. How it was just 'a little hobby' of his.

I told him he was selfish for keeping a power, as incredible as his, to himself. That bringing back dead birds and rodents was small fry. How he could do so much more if he just … took it up a notch.

"Don't you think I've already thought about all this?" Malleus hissed at me. "Why do you think I never told anyone?"

"Then why did you ever tell *me?*" I hissed back.

"I don't know," he said. "I guess I just wanted to share it with someone. Someone who I *thought* I could trust!"

I could see that I'd gone too far.

And, ironically, so could he.

"I'm only trying to open your eyes …" I said to Malleus, which probably wasn't the *best* choice of words.

Malleus just stood there, arms folded.

"… to all the great and wonderful things you could do," I told him.

His arms fell to his sides.

"I realise it's your power, your choice," I said. "But if it were mine, I'd just *have* to use it for more."

"Just stop, will you!" he snapped.

I stopped short, along with any more words I had to say.

"Sorry," he said. "This is just all too much for me to be thinking about right now."

Malleus turned to leave.

And I, having no more persuading words of my own to stop him, just let him go.

My eyes followed him as he walked away, and as much hope I had in me that he would …

… he never looked back.

19

"Of Mice & Men"

Wiping the weariness off my face with the back of one hand, I slowly got myself up from the bed, and just for a moment there wasn't anything to worry about. Not ambitious plans for bizarre powers. Not changing the world. Not even falling out with Malleus.

I must have dozed off soon after getting home, but after everything that'd been going on with me lately, it was hardly a wonder. It was then that my worries, too, awoke from their slumber. The desperate cries of a multitude of voices, all sounding just like me, echoing in my head.

Have you gone too far with Malleus this time? Do you think he hates you for it? Could this be the end of what's just beginning for the two of you?

"Oh, do shut up!" I told them all aloud.

Then I realise where I am, and hope that if my flatmates are indeed in, they'll just think I'm angrily berating my laptop because it's not hooking up to the Wi-Fi.

But my worries concerning Malleus are short-lived, as when I reach for my phone to check the time, I see that I have a text message from him. Which could either be a good thing or a really, really *bad* thing.

Shutting my eyes tight, I offer up the most sincerest and heartfelt of prayers to the gods of texting before clicking on the 'envelope' icon to read it. And, to my astonishment, not only does it appear that I haven't totally screwed things up with Malleus, it seems he's actually entertaining the grand ideas I have for his incredible ability.

I'm sorry for the way I acted, his text reads. *I've thought some more about everything you said. Say we do some good with what I can do. Where do we start?*

And it's only because this same question is all I've been able to think about since we parted ways, that I already have an answer.

And messaging Malleus back so fast it probably gives him text-whiplash, I say, *We start small.*

This accord between us didn't come without some certain ground rules from Malleus's side. Rules he set out for me in a drawn-out, but clear-cut, text message. It was agreed that we would start small, but I had to promise to absolutely, categorically, keep this between him and me. No careless talk. No leaks whatsoever. And I had to make a solemn vow to never discuss what we were planning to do, with anybody. Even with those I considered to be the most trustworthy of people in my life. It would be just him and me, with complete secrecy acting as our third and final member of our two-man team.

Mum's the word, keep schtum, zzzip!

It was my idea that we help people; be it bringing back pets or loved ones, but without their knowledge, and then we would just disappear. We'd leave no notes behind of what we had done. We'd stay only long enough to get the job done, vanishing soon after. Keeping the whole thing to ourselves. Do some good, but take no credit for it. Thus enabling Malleus to use his abilities on a grander scale whilst still retaining his privacy.

All we need do now was figure out a way of finding these people. We couldn't exactly advertise in the *Blue Pages*. Word of mouth was too risky. And we'd likely get reported, knocking door to door.

After much deliberation between Malleus and I over text message, our fried craniums had come head-to-head with a wall made up entirely of mind-blocks.

I think we've got about as far as we're going to get for one day, I texted him. *We should sleep on it. Maybe it will come to us in the night?*

Yeah, he texted back. *You're probably right. Speak tomorrow.*

And then Malleus did something that made me smile for the very first time all day.

He left a kiss.

And so, I left one for him, too.

Wondering, all the while, if he was smiling the way *I* was right now.

Once I knew for sure that Malleus was gone for the night, I pressed the 'home' button on my phone, and hit the HeadMagazine icon for a light social-media session. Just to give the cogs and wheels in my head a break from all that turning and grinding.

After scrolling for a few minutes through posts of seemingly perfect lives, and rants about ones that never seem to be, I scroll past a grainy image that immediately causes me to scroll back up again. And when I do, I see that it's actually a video. A video that looks worryingly familiar to me. The video itself is potato-quality at best, but just about clear enough to see what's happening in it.

Going against my better judgement, I hit 'play' to watch it from the beginning, which is also the moment I bolt upright. And when the video – which is less than a minute long – has ended …

… I can't help myself from playing it again.

Over and over, I play this video. Hoping that with every viewing it will make it less and less true. I pinch myself, but the waking nightmare is still sat there in my hands and staring right back up at me.

And looking up from my phone, and into the bleak light coming in through my bedroom window, I have no words.

No words, other than, "Oh," and "Fuck."

20

"Out There"

The voice inside my head, the one that sounds just like me, it tells me that this isn't happening. That I must've just fallen asleep and tumbled into some terrible place of my very worst thoughts. But as convincing as that voice sounds, I know I am very much awake and, therefore, unable to believe it.

How could this have happened? I'd only been without my phone for less than a day, and then *this!* The most disastrous thing that could've happened with it!

The video had been posted by some anonymous nobody, and was now doing the rounds on this particular social media platform. The video's title was, '*Boy holds dead bird in his hands*', with the subtitle, '*Watch to the end! You'll never believe what happens next!*' The very same video I made of Malleus bringing that dead pigeon back to life. You couldn't see our faces in the video, and I'm positive neither one of us spoke a word in that minute or less, so there was no way for anyone to know it was us, which only served to instil the very smallest sense of relief in me.

Then I read the comments, which gave me just a little more comfort. For as I read sceptical comment after sceptical comment, it was clear to me that no one was taking this video seriously, highly doubting its authenticity. I must have read at least a hundred of these comments, and not one, single person thought that the video was genuine.

That still didn't change the fact that the video was out there, but thankfully we live in a cynical world full to brimming with cynical people who don't believe much of anything anymore. Usually, this would be a bad thing, but in this case it was most fortunate. Plus the fact that Malleus didn't use social media, as far as I knew, or had much use for it without his sight. Otherwise I fear everything would have taken a sharp turn for the worst.

There was nothing I could do to stop the video from spreading like an aggressive cancer, but then maybe that was the best thing *to* do: do nothing. This video would do the rounds, nobody would believe what they saw, simply making way for some other random video, and be lost in the mix of all the internet's weird footage.

One question still remained, however.

Well, two, if you're going to get all pedantic about it.

Who put the video out there in the first place? And just how did it get from my phone to the newsfeed of a well-known, social media platfor ...?

That was the moment neurons began firing in my brain.

I daren't even say the name I was thinking for fear of me being right.

"Amy," I whispered to the walls of my room.

"Amy, fucking, G'dala."

21

"Out of My Hands"

Now that I had a pretty darn good idea as to who leaked the video, another question arose: *What in the hell was I going to do about it?* I wanted to hunt down that little, scheming bitch, and throttle her to her beautiful death. *But what good would that do?* The video would still be out there, and I'd probably have to serve a life sentence. Which, needless to say, would be a total drag.

If I *did* confront her about leaking the video, she would then know, for sure, it was me who filmed the footage. And if I knew her – which I think I bloody well *did* by now – it wouldn't take her long to figure out who the *other* person in the video was, as well.

No.

The best thing I could do here, as with the whole HeadMagazine thing, was to simply do nothing. Wait it out. Let people talk about the 'dead pigeon video' for a little while. Use up their interest for it. Something else would come along in its place, and it would all be forgotten.

As much as I wanted to scream and rant and rave about it, I knew that wasn't the clear-thinking thing to do. That *that* thing would only make things worse. That doing the exact opposite of how I actually *wanted* to react, as much as it irked me to do so, was the very best thing to do.

Don't feed it, and just let it die a slow death.

And no sooner had I let out a big sigh of relief, my phone began to flash and vibrate.

Under any normal circumstances, a text message from Malleus would've filled me with joy, but here, in this moment, all it did was fill me with dread.

So, what's next? His text read. *Any ideas?*

But so eclipsed by the whole 'dead pigeon' situation, my mind had gone dark when it came to anything else, so I just texted him back with, *Any ideas about what?*

What we talked about! he said. *My power! All the good we're going to do!*

I had hoped he'd waned off the idea, but it was evident to me, from his gross overuse of exclamation marks, that he was more stoked about it than ever.

Doing my level best not to sound too enthusiastic about the whole thing, I instead texted back the most uninspiring word I could pluck from the vacant parts of my mind to answer his initial question.

The word was, "*Dunno*".

It actually made my thumbs ache, sounding *this* dumb in a text message.

Wow, he texted back. *That's all you've got for me? "Dunno"?*

How could I get out of this without sounding like an utter jerk?

It was your idea! he added.

Come on, Iris! the voice in my head said. *You can still save this!*

What I mean to say is, I texted back. *I haven't really had any more thoughts about it.*

Whatever I was going to tell Malleus, we just couldn't do this right now. Not with the dead pigeon video doing the rounds on social media. It would get back to us, for sure. Obviously, I couldn't tell Malleus this, either, as I'm sure it would mean the end of him and me.

Now's not the best time, I texted.

Which wasn't a lie and made me feel just a little less terrible about having to keep the truth from him.

But he kept probing.

How so? he asked.

With everything that's going on right now, I told him.

Also true.

Like what? he asked.

Half-truths weren't working, so I'd just have to do what I did best and start making things up.

I've got my degree to be getting on with, I told him. *And on top of that I'm trying to find a work placement. Make friends …*

I was just laying it all on thick at this point.

We've only just met, I told him, *and I think things are moving too quickly.*

All went 'quiet' between me and Malleus for a few dreadful minutes, while I re-read the message I'd just sent him. *Oh God,* I thought. It read like the kind of text you'd send someone if you were breaking up with them, but trying to let them down gently.

Maybe I could save this.

But then perhaps I should just shut the hell up before I made it any worse.

Was it too soon to tell him that I thought I, maybe, sort of, loved him?

I just didn't want this to be it. This could be it if I didn't say something. *There's still time!* my inner voice told me. I almost had the right words. I could see them off in the distance, heading towards me at great speed, but before I could make them out, he beat me to it with the word, *Fine.*

And that was it.

No other words.

No kiss.

Just, *Fine.*

One word, and yet it told me more than an entire set of encyclopaedias *ever* could. This one, solitary word telling me that things between Malleus and I were going to be anything *but* fine for quite some time.

It was the silence I couldn't take. Even though I should be accustomed to it by now. This, though, was a different kind. One that I was not used to after all these years.

The silence of a good friend.

Too late to text him back now; say I didn't mean any of it; the whole *'taking it up a notch with his power'* thing. That I really couldn't care less about him bringing creatures back from the dead anymore. That, yes, it was amazing and everything, *incredible* even. But now I just wanted him. Just him. With or without the extraordinary gift he had.

This was my own fault, and I'd have to come up with a way to fix it, and fast. Time may be running out to backtrack here. I'd have to get on with it sooner rather than later.

So I did what most of us do when we're looking for answers. I turned to Dr Toggle, and typed, *'How to fix a broken relationship'* into the search bar.

Hunting for the answers, but not finding the ones I caught in the forums at all favourable. Answers too bleak. Too depressing to accept. Sure, I wanted answers to my questions, just not *these* answers.

Exiting the webbed world of Toggle and its insufficient ability to make me feel better about falling out with Malleus over text message, I instead hit the MyPipe icon. A whole world of hilarious video clips of cats doing daft things, hair and beauty tutorial disasters, and 'epic fails' at work compilations, all at your fingertips. But my fingertips had other ideas that night, and couldn't help themselves from punching the letters of words they were so intent on typing.

I should have just watched some stupid cat videos, but curiosity got the better of me.

And so, knowing all too well what curiosity did to that cat, I typed the words, *'Dead pigeon in boy's hands'.*

I didn't have to scroll too far down through the videos, to arrive at the one I really didn't want to find. Some anonymous nobody had uploaded it a day ago; the video currently sitting at just over four thousand views. An avalanche of comments, already a few hundred strong, written by a torrent of disbelieving, tap-happy people hidden behind keyboards and aliases, all running in the same vein of dubious comments as the ones I'd read on HeadMagazine the day, previous.

I should've just left it there.

Taken solace from the apparent fact that the people who *had* seen the dead bird footage, merely considered it to be yet another fake video doing the rounds on the internet. What I should have done was just sit back, enjoy my popcorn, and watch as people tore the show to shreds. But that pesky, inquisitive feline I'd swallowed just *had* to know. So I moved up a level, and checked TweetyPie.

And, oh fuck, what do you know.

The dead pigeon video.

It'd gone viral.

22

"Who is it?"

To the relief of the skittish sinews of my heart, most of the chatter on TweetyPie was about the origin of the video and the authenticity of the footage. Again, the posts and their direct interactions made up of dubious words, didn't seem to point to people really caring where it came from. But that didn't change the fact that the footage was still out there for all to see, and had people from all over the globe in mass debate with each other.

Sure, it was only talk for now, but I felt helpless. What *could* I do? Create a TweetyPie account? Post a comment myself? Back up the remarks of the sceptics? But then, maybe – as was the case with MyPipe and HeadMagazine – it was best to do nothing. As long as it just stayed on social media, Malleus, not using social media himself, probably wouldn't even know about its existence.

There was also the added peace of mind that whilst, yes, the footage *was* doing the rounds for all to see, it was probably nothing to worry about. Because, so far, it seemed, no one believed what they saw. But that was a big 'probably'. 'Probably' wasn't *nearly* enough for me to not worry about the dark cloud hanging over me, that could send the downpour of a shitstorm at any moment.

Then my phone screen began to flash, and when I looked, I saw that I had a text message from Malleus. My feelings on receiving something from him were divided. On the one hand, it was good to hear from him. But, on the other, what would it be about?

The text, just four words long, simply read, *We need to talk.*

Malleus told me to meet him at the park, same spot as the very first time we met here.

But why weren't we meeting at the café or the river like we usually did? And what exactly did we need to talk about, that couldn't be said by means of a few text messages?

Upon arriving at the park, Malleus was already sat there on a bench with his head in his hands, when I asked him, "So what's all this about?"

"You tell *me!*" he replied, his hands pulling away from his head as it jerked upward.

"Tell you, what?" I asked him,

"People are talking," he said.

Shiiiit, I thought. *He already knows.*

"What are people talking about?" I asked.

"Iris …" he said.

Shit. Shit. Shit.

"… I think we're being followed."

My arms fell to my sides.

"Being followed?"

"I was in the café this morning," he told me. "Where I heard a group of girls talking at the table next to me."

Fuuuuck.

"Some video they'd seen on the internet."

Fuck. Fuck. Fuck.

"Right?" I said, playing the dumbest-of-blondes card.

"A dead bird," he said. "Coming back to life in someone's hands."

"Oh?" I said.

"*Oh?*" he said. "Is that all you've got to say?"

"What do you *want* me to say?" I asked him.

"What I want you to say, Iris!" he yelled at me. "Is that you haven't seen the video yet, and for that to be the truth!"

I fell silent.

"Well?" he pushed.

"No," I told him. "No, I haven't seen it."

"Well perhaps you should get yourself on the internet," he scolded me, "because apparently it's out there for everyone *else* to see!"

He appeared to be yelling at me, so I asked him if he could

maybe keep his voice down.

"I want you to look it up," he said. "Look it up, right now, and tell me what you find."

What could I do? I couldn't exactly tell him that I didn't have my phone on me. That I left it at home. So, with a deep, reluctant sigh, I plunged my hand into the pocket of my coat and fished my phone out.

"Well?" he pushed.

"Would you just give me a minute," I told him. "I'm looking."

When, really, all I was doing was standing there with the phone in my hand, not really looking at all. Taking advantage of his disability, all over again. Buying myself more time to better think how to play this risky game.

"Well?" he pushed again.

"I can't find anything," I told him.

"Well, it's definitely on there somewhere!" he barked.

"Look," I said, slipping the phone I hadn't even turned on back into my coat pocket. "I'll look into it, OK? See what I can find."

"Let me know when you *do* find something," he said, turning and putting an earbud into his left ear.

"Nice to see you, too!" I called out after him as he walked away.

"Great," I muttered to myself. "Nice one, Iris."

Malleus didn't even know, at this point, that it was *me* who made the damn video, and he already hated me for it. I knew the footage would wear out of the temporary interest it had gained, and be forgotten in a week or so, but I wasn't so sure Malleus would let it slip from his memory quite as quickly.

With a close of the door, I was back in my room, and also back where I started. *What was I going to do?* I couldn't keep up with lying to Malleus, but I also didn't want to just dive straight in and tell him the truth about everything. So I decided, at our current stage, I would simply tell him as much truth as I needed to.

Grabbing my phone, I began to compose a text message – right after composing *myself* – telling Malleus that I'd found the video, but was still vague about the details of who was in it, where it was filmed, and who by. Malleus had already come to the conclusion that someone must have been, both, following and filming us from a distance. This assumption he had come to, all on his own, threw him off the scent and, in turn, got him off my case about me having something to do with it. It was his plan, he said, to track this person down, and that once we found the person responsible, we would make them go public on all social media platforms, admitting that the footage was merely some elaborate hoax.

I told him about the comments I'd read in regards to the video leaked on HeadMagazine. How not one, solitary person believed the footage was real. That we had nothing to worry about and, therefore, need take no action.

I thought this would be enough for Malleus to drop it, leave it behind, and move on. That we could just go back to the way things were before this footage went viral.

But it wasn't.

Malleus told me that he wouldn't be able to carry out 'his work', as he called it, knowing there was someone out there following his every move. That, until we'd found this person, it wouldn't be possible for him to simply let it go.

I hated to hear him talking like this, and resented lying to him and making it worse, but neither of us would budge from where we stood in all this. I held onto my lies, and he held onto his fears. Seeing Malleus act the way he did in the park made me loathe myself, as what all of this had done to the poor boy was entirely my fault.

With my mind spiralling – along with where I could see Malleus and I heading with the lies I kept up – I was determined, in that moment of maddening despair, to do something I felt as if I hadn't done in a long time.

I decided to tell him the truth.

23

"An Admission of Guilt"

Shifting my position on the knobbly log – that, for whatever reason, I simply could not find a comfortable fashion to sit upon today – I felt those same buzzing nerves as the ones I felt flowing through me, the very first time Malleus and I had ever met. Just that, *this* time, for an altogether different reason.

I decided to leave the yellows, greens and oranges hanging in the wardrobe that day; coming dressed all in grey to match the weather and my mood. To give myself the appearance of being honest. Honest to the girl I saw in the mirror of my room, at least.

Was I really about to tell Malleus everything? This could mean the end of us if I did. That this may be the very last time we'd ever meet. That being said, it would be better if I never saw him again, him knowing the truth, than to continue living a lie for the rest of our days together.

I looked down, checking the time on my phone, and back up, looking both ways up the river's edge to see if he was on his way to me.

He wasn't.

We'd met a good number of times by now, and almost every time we had, he was here first.

But not today.

Then my phone started buzzing in my hand; the screen flashing away. "Not now, Dad," I told my phone, just letting it ring out because I didn't have the heart to hang up on him.

There were still a few minutes to go before the time we said we'd meet came around, but not nearly enough time to get up and walk away. I had gone over in my head, multiple times, what I would say. Words circling my mind like vultures.

Looking down at the time, and back up the river, I could just about make out the shape of Malleus, a way off, but almost here.

I stretched my arm up, and gave him a keen wave, my whole face lighting up to show him that I'd seen him. And as swiftly as me realising the gesture would be lost on him, my face went dark and my waving hand fell back into my lap.

He looked the way a person does when they can't see the place they're in for what it is. The world around them so warped by their mind's twisted perception of it. It pained me to see him this way, but it was all the persuasion I needed to get the crippling guilt from off my, oh so heavy, chest.

"Hey," I called out, as I stood to bring him in for a hug.

But he said nothing in return.

He just hugged me back, half-heartedly, and I didn't want to let go of him in case this was the very last time I would ever hold him.

With us both sitting down on the knobbly log. *Our* knobbly log. Malleus looked at me; my apprehensive expression reflected in the lenses of his sunglasses, and said, "You've got something to tell me."

I nodded.

"Well?" he said.

"Oh, right," I said. "Sorry, Malleus, I forgot. Not that I had something to say. I mean, of *course* I remember I had something to say, it's just …"

I had gone through all this with myself: telling him everything. But now the moment had arrived, I'd forgotten where to come in.

"What did you want to tell me, Iris?" he asked, shaking free the cumbersome thoughts that blocked the path from my mind to my mouth.

"What did I want to tell you?" I asked myself. "Oh yes, I *do* want to tell you something, Malleus."

I was all over the place.

"But before I do," I went on to say, "I want you to know something first."

It was as if I were a girl trying to make her way home in a blizzard; not being able to see the way ahead. And just when this girl got the footing to take another step forward, she would then slip and fall on the ice again.

"OK," he said.

I had all the right words neatly lined up in my head before I got here. But now that Malleus was here, and I was sitting beside him, all the wrong words were getting tangled up in my throat.

"What I mean to say is …" I said.

Malleus hung his head.

"… I really like you!" I blurted out.

Malleus's head jerked upwards.

"Really, I do," I said. "I like you, and I never meant to hurt you."

Malleus's head went back to hanging again.

"How meeting you," I told him, "and this amazing gift of yours you shared with me, is the best, most incredible thing that has ever happened to me."

That's when Malleus's lips moved.

"How my life just hasn't been the same since you came into it."

Again, his lips moved.

"How I really don't want to lose you as a friend."

"Iris," his lips seemed to say.

"But there's something I really need to tell you."

That's when Malleus twisted his body, slapped a hand down on my leg, and appeared to look me right in the eyes when he said, "There's someone else."

"No," I said, placing my hand on his. "No, that's not it, Malleus."

"No," he said, placing his other hand on top of mine. "You don't understand, Iris. There's someone else. I've met someone else."

Cut off by his words, that came so quickly and without warning, I wasn't granted the time to properly acknowledge them. And I couldn't be sure at the time, but I think he then went on to say that he was sorry.

I wouldn't have been aware of it in that moment, but I had stopped talking. I don't recall all that much of what happened after that, but what I *do* remember is that he never so much as touched me as he got up and walked away.

And as I watched him leave, against the way he came, I may not have been able to hear myself crying, but I could feel the tears.

24

"Killer Looks"

It felt like my whole world had been screwed up and tossed in the trash as if it were a scrap of paper. My life now as meaningless as a love letter written by someone that now hates me.

And people wonder why there are walls around me that can't be knocked down.

I didn't leave my room for days after that, with nothing to keep me company but the heaviness of my broken heart. I had a good thing going with Malleus, and had only myself to blame for letting it go bad. It was over, a train wreck. And I told myself, to let the words sink in and hit home, that *a write-off just can't be fixed.*

Life without him, I didn't even want to *think* about it, let alone live it. Everything would go back to the way it was before we met: below average, under par, and so completely ordinary.

Even the sun was in hiding that day, as if the weather, too, was in mourning. Colours faded to grey, brightness dulled, and shapes blurred together, out of focus.

After wasting the past few days in bed, just staring up at a lonely looking water stain on the ceiling, I willed myself up and made an attempt to get on with this first day of the rest of my life without Malleus in it.

I'd revert back to what I *should* have been doing before he came into my life: waking up, getting ready, going to class, studying hard, heading home, sleeping, repeating. Just going through the motions, keeping myself ticking over, until the memory of him faded, the feelings weren't so raw, and the wounds had turned to scars. All the while waiting for my shattered glass heart, held together with sticky tape, to mend itself.

I wouldn't even bother trying to make new friends, and just the idea of dating anyone else in the near future left me cold in the hollow of my gut. Besides, it wouldn't be fair to the next person if I *did*. After all, how could anyone else compare with everything Malleus was, and all he could do?

I would just have to give these dreadful feelings, whirling around in the winds of misery within me, time to settle. But as sincerely as I tried to sound to convince myself, I just couldn't believe it. I'd never met anyone quite like Malleus, and I doubted I ever would.

Still, it was over, and I would simply have to begin again. Close the book on the story of Malleus and me, reluctantly pick up a new one, and open it to the first, blank page.

Many uncounted days went by, and I was closer to being settled into this new life without Malleus. I say 'closer', because that particular day I saw something that took me right back to the moment Malleus left me on the knobbly log.

Sat in the university canteen, alone, and at my usual table. I was on a lunch break between the end of the second class of the day, and the beginning of the third.

I was dressed all in black – my go-to shade of choice since I last saw Malleus – and wearing the same pair of spilt coffee and cigarette-ash-stained leggings I had been for the last week or so; a hoodie zipped all the way up with the hood pulled over my head and down to just past my eyebrows. Not that I paid much mind to attracting the stares of curious students for the new look I'd adopted, but I must have appeared to everyone else in the canteen at lunch break to simply be a girl, comfortable in her own company, that was studying a bachelor's degree in theatre and dance.

I must have glanced away from the blandwich in my hand for an idle moment, when this smudge of red caught my eye, causing me to look again.

Over in the corner, on the opposite side of the canteen, appeared to be a boy and a girl sat facing one another.

The girl had this fiery red hair, and the boy was dressed all in black.

I couldn't quite see the girl's face, on account of the boy being in my direct line of sight with his back to me. They were kissing – that much I could tell. And it was only when they stopped for a beat to breathe, did I then see who this girl was. From behind, the boy looked a lot like someone I'd tried my best to forget, and when the girl sat back from leaning into him, I saw her face.

Amy.

I could feel every muscle in my face tighten as I glared at her from across the room. Not being able to help but read the lips of someone, sat on an adjacent table, say something like, "*If looks could kill*". But I didn't even acknowledge their words with a response. I just kept glaring at the girl in my sights.

That's when Amy looked up and over at me, pulling a face that told me the boy in black was hers now. Our eyes locking as she leant into him. And with her chin rested on Malleus's left shoulder, she gave me this sly look of satisfaction.

That's when I looked deep into those pretty, green eyes of hers, and prepared my missiles of fury to be sent flying across the room.

The way they say your life flashes up before your eyes the moment you die, all those awful memories I'd forgotten about began whipping through my mind.

She had taken from me, what should have been my happy childhood. The confident, upbeat girl I should have seen in the mirror every day, and any hope I had for a bright future. Taken my hearing! And now she had taken for herself the one boy I could feel myself falling for. She'd taken so much, and so now it was time for me to take something from her. I wanted this girl to pay for what she'd stolen from me. I wanted to take her life. I wanted to end her with every fibre of my being.

I wished she was dead.

Just then, Amy's eyes glazed over, her jaw went slack, and as her eyes rolled into the back of her head, she slid off Malleus's shoulder, and fell to a heap on the canteen floor.

That car accident I told you about. The one that you just couldn't help but get a good look at as you drove by. The one you thought may be all your fault.

This was it.

25

"The Act of Going Back"

Petrified to the spot, and staring blankly at what I may or may not have done, my first and only thought was …

… did *I* do that?

When it had just happened – Amy falling to the ground the way she did – Malleus and I were the only two people in the room that knew something was very wrong. Only then, once Malleus began yelling for help, did others cotton on to the urgency of the situation. Setting off the ones closest to him, and spreading like wildfire throughout the rest of the university canteen, causing them all to stand up or crane their necks to get a better look. And although I couldn't actually hear the yelling, I could feel the fear in the room as a cold weight in my stomach.

I didn't want this.

I know I'd wanted it before, and that I'd wished it with all of my energies, but now that it had actually happened, and Amy was laid out on the floor like that, I didn't want it. I thought revenge would taste sweet, but now that I had it, it lingered there as a sour aftertaste in my mouth. My father always told me, *Be careful what you wish for. For, one day, you just might get it.* He'd said that to me so many times over the years, and I'd never really understood it.

Not until now, that is.

The question, 'Did *I* do that?', still very much on my mind as I stood in the bitter cold with the other hundred or so students, just outside the entrance to the university. Looking on, as Amy's body was loaded into the back of an ambulance in a black, zip-up bag.

Did I really kill her by just throwing her a look?

Surely it was just some freak coincidence, her dropping down dead like that. Me glaring at her, and her slyly looking back at me. Just good or bad timing on both our parts, depending on how you look at it.

One of the two policewomen called to the scene made sure I got home safely, only leaving me by myself once they were satisfied that I'd normalised. This was after they took my statement of what happened in the canteen. My account of what I'd seen. It took me answering all of the policewoman's questions to gradually return to the girl I was before the incident. After which they left with the words, "Call us if you need anything."

Under any normal circumstances, I would have quipped in with some sarcastic comment about a phone call being utterly useless to a girl like me. But this circumstance was anything *but* normal, and all I managed was a timid nod.

Now that I was alone, I attempted to get my head straight. But all I could think about was what had just happened in the canteen with Amy. Playing out in my mind like a clip from a horror movie, on a loop. And no matter how many times I watched it, I just couldn't make sense of it, and it didn't make it any less horrifying.

It cut me deep to see Amy with Malleus like that. At the time, I wanted her to die. To march over to where they both were, shove Malleus out of the way, and squeeze the life out of her pretty, little neck. But instead, I just sat there giving her the evils. And then, she was dead.

I got what I'd wished for, hadn't I? I wanted her to die, and now she had. But now that she *was* dead, all I felt was dead inside.

Had I really killed Amy just by throwing her a look?

It was then that my eyes widened. And looking up at a space only I could see, a realisation slowly drifted down from the ceiling, fell upon my head, and seeped into my mind.

Had I just gotten away with murder?

26

"Or So I Thought"

Did I really have life-taking powers behind these big, blue eyes of mine? That was ridiculous thinking, wasn't it? Killing Amy with a look. I mean, I really needed to know, but how? Oh, God. Would I have to try it again with someone *else?* Because I wasn't exactly crazy about *that* idea. Just doing it once by accident was horrible enough.

If it was, in fact, me that had done it.

Aagghh!

I felt like I was taking crazy pills!

What I needed was something to take my mind off it all. And then the thought came to me … back home, whenever I felt overwhelmed by all the things I needed to get done, I would simply write a list, and then prioritise by reorganising and numbering them from one to whatever.

Grabbing a pen from the pot, and paper from the desk drawer, I began to write a list. Just to steer my mind away from the collision course I could see it heading towards. A totally hypothetical list of people I wanted dead.

"It's just a list," I told myself. "It's not like you're actually killing anybody."

"Not at *this* point," I added.

And so, pencil in hand, the very tip of the sharpened lead hovering over the surface of the paper, I looked up and to the left, searching the filing cabinet of names in my mind for that one, first name to jot down.

But no names came to mind.

I couldn't think of anyone, because I had never wished anybody dead before.

Well.

Apart from Amy.

So I figured, instead of coming up with a specific list of people whom I thought deserved to die, I would just start by compiling a list of people who had recently ticked me off somewhat.

That's when the mean old bastard from the pawnshop sprang to mind. And then there was the barista bitch from The Daily Grind café – the one throwing me spiteful eyes from behind the counter when I was just having a cup of coffee with Malleus. But as much as the both of them had greatly displeased me, did either of these people deserve to die in the process of me trying to prove something to myself?

No.

No, they didn't.

But I really did need to know if what had happened to Amy was, in fact, my doing. And, therefore, I'd have to pick someone to test it out on. 'It' being, whatever this thing that I may or may not have, was or wasn't.

You still with me?

The pencil in my hand was still poised over the paper and ready to write a whole list of people, but that's all it did. It just hovered, not moving, as I simply could not think of just one person that deserved to lose their life for my cause.

Laying down the pencil, exhausted of names to write with it, I brought my face down and my opened hands up, admitting defeat in the darkness of my palms.

I guess the names would just have to come to me in time.

The best thing to do right now, I decided, was to get out of this uninspiring room. Go for a walk, clear my head. I was so often clearing my mind these days, but then, I'd never had so much *on* it, either.

I felt better, the very moment the light and air hit my face as I walked out the door. And with the way the hue of the colours around me appeared in the late afternoon sun, I soon forgot why I had even come out here in the first place.

Did I really need to know? Whether or not I did it? Did I care? Amy was dead. *Isn't that all that mattered?* She could no longer ruin my life, and I didn't even have to lift a finger for that to happen. *Did it really matter how she died?* It was the same outcome, either way. She was gone for good, and I was again free to get on with the rest of my life without her getting in the way. The question of *'Did I do it or not?'* was immaterial. But there was that curious cat I'd swallowed that just had to know for sure.

What I needed was somewhere quiet, where I could be left alone for long enough to think on all of this.

The knobbly log by the river would just remind me of Malleus, and I wasn't going to just double back and head home now that I'd come this far. What I needed was a peaceful corner where I'd be left to my own devices. A lonely surrounding where there would be nothing to remind me of Malleus. What I needed was a quiet place.

Then, an *aha!* moment.

The university library!

Perfect!

Nowhere was more solitary and quiet than a library.

Or so I thought.

Because upon arriving at the university campus, it was teeming with people; either crying or offering a shoulder for someone *else* to cry on. What looked like a protest taking place just outside the university building, about a hundred students strong, all with their banners held high, chanting words that I couldn't quite make out.

Seemingly out of nowhere, a girl with sombre eyes handed me a flyer with a picture of a smiling Amy upon it; the words, *'What Happened to Amy?'* written across it in pink. She then pinned a pink ribbon to the lapel of my coat, mouthed some words with her sorry mouth, and touched me on the shoulder with a reassuring hand before dissolving into the crowd around me.

Wasn't a pink ribbon supposed to symbolise breast cancer awareness?

But then, when I thought about it, I guess Amy *was* a sort of cancer.

I felt like I was having one of those lucid dreams; the kind where you're walking naked through a bustling high street. Reminding myself, self-soothingly, that I probably wasn't responsible for Amy's death. And even if I *was*, there probably wasn't anyone who had the faintest idea that was the case.

But then, that *was* a pretty big 'probably'.

Staying on course, I headed to the library, right through the horde of angry protesters and past the throng of emotional students on the ground floor of the university building. Everywhere I looked, whenever I dared look up, these goddamn posters; a picture of a smiling Amy blown up to six times her head's actual size. The words '*What happened to me?*' written in big, pink letters underneath. A '*WhatHappenedToAmy.com*' link for students to find support, to better deal with the tragic loss of someone they never really knew at all. Hashtags running along the bottom.

Were people talking about this on TweetyPie already?

And how had all this – the banners, the posters, and the flyers, this shrine to a girl nobody but me really knew – how had all this just *Poof!* happened in the space of a day and a night?

Some of the media studies students here had clearly been busy.

I could feel the watchful eyes of the posters following me down the corridors, up the stairs and across the floors as I made my way to the library. And once I'd made it to the place I was so sure I would finally find some peace, it wasn't much better there either.

More of those goddamn flyers, just like the one held tightly in my clammy hand, had been left in every study cubicle, and stuck to every computer monitor.

Amy being dead was beginning to feel far worse than when she was alive. Now she was everywhere, and practically a martyr in the eyes of everyone who studied here. The question, '*What happened to Amy?*' following me wherever I went with my shoulders hunched and my head ducked down. Much in the same way she'd been following *me* before all of this absurdity.

Resisting the urge to hurry back the way I came – through the corridors and down the stairs – I did my utmost to blend in by not making eye contact and appearing to be stricken with grief.

And maybe it was because I was overwhelmed with this whole '*What happened to Amy?*' thing ambushing me out of nowhere. Perhaps it was the guilt for what I may have done to Amy from across the university canteen the other day. Could be that it was the shame

I felt for wishing something quite so harsh for her. Or it might be that the reason I felt so … woozy, was because I just needed to eat something.

Whatever it was, I could have murdered a panini right about then.

Everywhere else in the university building was swarming with students, except for the university canteen. I guess people just weren't feeling all that hungry today. Either that or they felt that eating so soon after Amy's death was disrespectful somehow. But on the plus side, and to my delight, upon arriving at the university canteen – which was empty as a dead girl's skull – there also wasn't a queue.

Stepping up to the counter, I politely told the lady behind it that I'd have the mozzarella, sun-dried tomato and pesto panini.

She was all sad-eyed with her head bowed slightly forwards; what an apology would look like if you dressed it in white overalls and stretched a hair net over its head.

"Sorry, dear," she tells me. "But we're not doing those anymore."

"Oh," I say. "What *other* paninis have you got, then?"

"Well that's just it," she says. "We're not actually doing *any* paninis. Not since that poor, sweet girl died here the other day."

"Oh?" I say. "Can I ask, why?"

"It's what she ordered that day," she tells me. "They think it might have been the food she ate."

"Oh, you have *got* to be fucking kidding me," I muttered under my breath.

Or, at least, I *thought* I had.

"I beg your pardon?" she says.

"Sorry," I say. "In that case, I'll just take a packet of salted crisps and a can of Type 2."

"I'm afraid they've been taken off the menu, too, dear," she says.

"Are you shitting me right now?" I ask her. "Anything *else* I can't have off this poxy menu?"

"Excuse me, dear," she tells me. "This is a 'zero-tolerance of verbal-abuse' zone."

She points to a lonely looking sign hanging on the wall just above her head. A sign I would've probably seen if it hadn't been for all these *'What Happened to Amy?'* posters taking ownership of the walls.

"Do you know what, forget it," I tell her. "I guess I'll just starve to death instead."

And if this counter assistant with the sorry eyes is asking me to leave, I'm way ahead of her as I march right out of the canteen, empty-handed and with a grumbling stomach.

27

"At My Door"

I felt like I'd been holding my breath underwater, and now that I'd made it back to the safety of the place I now called home, and to the surface, I could finally breathe. But the breath was knocked out of me again when, upon opening the door, I saw yet another one of those damn flyers with Amy's smiling face lying there on the floor of my room. All that pink of the flyer's border and lettering clashing with the dark, blood colour of the burgundy carpet.

Crouching to pick the flyer up off the floor, I sat on the edge of my bed with it in my hands, and gave the words I was too jarred to look at amongst all those grieving students a read. Words about her being such a promising, aspiring singer-songwriter. How she lit up a room just by entering it. About what a brave and courageous girl she was after everything she'd been through. How much she would be missed, and how empty the university would feel, now that she was gone.

And reading these words, all I could think was …

… *What a load of complete and utter bollocks!*

That they should have got *me* to design the flyer and write the words that adorned it. Someone that actually *knew* her, and the heartless, conniving wench I knew her very well to *be!* The flyer, cheaply photocopied in black and white, with the words '*Ding, dong, the bitch is dead!*' running right across her wicked, fake-smiling face!

And, until that moment, I never knew some flyer about a dead girl could rile me up to this extent.

Now printed on an A5-sized sheet of glossy paper, frozen in time with an eternal smile, it was like she was immortal, and no one would

119

ever know the ugly truth as to who this girl really was.

According to the same flyer – that I had to unscrunch now that I'd scrunched it up in my hands – there was to be some dumb memorial service held in her memory, a month from today. Some dumb memorial service I figured I'd have to attend, God forbid I should appear aloof, or worse, suspicious.

Remembering to breathe again, I closed my eyes, and brought myself back down from the lofty heights of this violently silent, bitter rage I'd stirred myself up into. Looked down at the crinkled flyer in my hands, into those big green eyes of Amy's – the words '*What Happened To Me?*' written in bright pink letters across the top – and said aloud, "Amy. I'm still trying to figure that out."

28

"Narrow Down"

"What happened to Amy?" I scribbled at the top of a scrap of paper. Thinking, with the end of a pencil between my teeth, that perhaps *this* list would prove easier to write than the one of people I, hypothetically, wanted dead.

1) Her food was poisoned.

2) She died of sudden, natural causes.

3) She had a momentary lapse of consciousness and died hitting her head on the canteen floor.

And 4) *I* killed her, just by wishing her to death with my eyes.

Killing her, just by throwing her a look. It sounded more and more absurd with every time I thought it, wrote it or said it. But whatever the cause of Amy's death, I simply had to find out. To remove myself from the list of possible causes and put my troubled mind to rest.

There was no alternative, I could see, other than finding someone else to test it out on, but that might mean having to kill somebody in the process. I decided that it would have to be a person that deserved it or, at least, a person that *I* thought deserved it. But I just knew I wouldn't be able to let it go until I had done this one thing.

So I referred to my other list. The one that was currently sitting at just two names strong. I already had the mean ol' bastard from the pawnshop, and the barista bitch from the café, but surely there were others who far more deserved it. I figured I would just have to be patient and happen to come across them in time. Doing it now, with the whole '*What happened to Amy?*' thing still going on, was too soon. I needed to wait patiently for a more suitable time. Let it all, for want of better words, die down before I ventured out looking for answers.

This could wait.

There was plenty of time, and I didn't have to find out straight away. I justified it to myself as the least I could do to respect the sudden death of a girl – no matter how much of a bitch I still thought they were – and for wishing they were dead over a sandwich I had for lunch the other day.

Time passed, the protests fizzled out, the posters came down, and the flyers stopped being posted through doors. But the feelings people were harbouring about Amy's death were still raw. It had been almost a month by then, but my fellow students, it seemed, just couldn't let it go until they had answers that satisfied their questions.

And so, I waited longer.

29

"The Perks of Being Deaf"

That dumb memorial service I told you about. The one being held in Amy's name. The one we all had to wear something pink to. Well, the day for it finally came. A dumb memorial service I had to attend, for obvious reasons, where all sorts of delightful things were said about a girl who I was more than happy had bit the dust.

Happening to look down for a moment at the sad, little, pink ribbon still pinned to the lapel of my coat. *That's about as much pink as you're getting out of me, bitch,* I thought quietly to myself.

Every single person who went up on that stage to hold a microphone, painted an enchanting picture with their words, of a girl who had the biggest heart, and brought sweetness and light wherever she went.

A generous girl.

A kind girl.

I had to be careful not to have some violent outburst of objection to what I was 'hearing', or let even the smallest of *Pfff!* sounds leave my lips. These people who barely knew her, all talking as if they did. Could they really all be talking about the same girl I knew all too well? The service was for Amy but it felt, to me, as though it were for some other person entirely. They couldn't all be going on about the girl *I* knew, surely. I wanted to scream or, better yet, *leave*, but I couldn't do either. Instead I had to sit through all sixty minutes of it, as close 'friends' of hers said their pieces. Singing songs and playing some of her favourite music, as if just *being* here wasn't punishment enough.

Sometimes being deaf has its perks.

But worse than the gentle words that came from the mouths of her clueless followers and, what I imagined to be, the most awful 'music' I was fortunate enough to sit through in silence. Worse than all that, was that the people in this room, my fellow students, had no idea as to what this "sweet, sweet girl" had put me through. If they had, we would have chucked her flimsy body in a cheap pine box, dug a hole, thrown it into the ground with all the grace of a house brick, and yelled in unison, *'Good riddance!'*

But they didn't have a clue.

None of them did.

And so, because of this, we all had to sit here, packed in, shoulder to shoulder, like tinned sardines, in a sweaty mess of snot and tears. Miming the words to songs we'd never heard of, and sitting in silence as people made up nice things to say about some tacky tart they barely knew. All this for an attention-whore of the highest order. And I bet you, if she were here right now, Amy would be loving every, ego-inflating minute of it.

I could have stood up. I could have marched right up onto that stage. Filled them all in with everything. The bullying and the beatings. The hearing loss. The stalking me wherever I went, in a blatant attempt to completely ruin my life. And *then!* And *then!* To top it all off, slither in there like a snake in the grass and take from me the only boy I had ever felt a genuine connection with.

I could've said all those things to the people I was now sat amongst. But what would be the point? They weren't likely to believe me, the story being so completely awful, to the point of being ridiculous. No, they would have all just yelled at me to *Shut up!* and to *Sit down!* to *Have some respect!* And, on top of that, I'd be shooting myself in the foot, as then they would all have real reason to suspect me with what really happened to Amy.

So I just sat there, like the good girl who never rocked the boat. Mouthed the lyrics to the songs up on the projector screen. Read the lips of those with nice things to say and clapped when they finished. What I *didn't* have to do, however, was listen to any of that truly horrendous music.

Every cloud.

I flicked the switch in my brain to the 'off' position. I was there, in body, but my mind was elsewhere. Anywhere but stuck inside this stuffy room with all these morons. Just until this, *the worst hour I've ever had to sit through in my entire, fucking, life,* was over. All I really had to do was just sit there, as comfortably as I could, and endure the torture.

That is, until all these heads started turning in my direction.

30

"What Are You Looking At?"

I could feel the crimson colour of red flooding to my face. Every eye in the room laying on little old me as I shrank in my seat that suddenly wasn't quite so comfortable anymore. I was just glad to not be sat in front of a mirror so I couldn't see the look on my face when I clocked the head of the university, up there on the stage and looking my way, appearing to be mouthing words at me. He was saying my name, I was sure of that much, and perhaps something about me having … *Anything to say?*

Fuck.

Did I have anything to say? About what? The history the recently deceased Amy and I have?

Had.

The death missiles I was firing at her in the university canteen the other day?

I fell silent, dumbly looking about myself; anywhere but at all those faces eagerly waiting for me to speak. The head said my name again and something about Amy … *Always having good things to say about me?*

"Of course she did," the voice in my head whispers for only me to hear. *She* was the one that took away *my* hearing, not the other way around. *Typical,* I thought. Even in death, Amy knew how to put me on the spot like this.

What could I do? I couldn't leave now. I'd have to say something about Amy, and to all these people. I'd actually have to do it. I had plenty of words I *wanted* to say, it's just that none of them were nice.

The university head's hand was outstretched as he said something about me … *coming up on stage?* I could feel my soul leave my body as I reluctantly got myself up, shuffled awkwardly past the other students in my row, and made *the longest walk these feet have ever trodden* to where the head was standing on the stage. Slowly, I made my way to the front of the room, and all I could feel were the stares of a thousand eyes aimed at the back of my head.

What was I going to say? I'd have to say *something*. But I couldn't think of anything. Let alone anything *nice*. And then, suddenly, there I was, on stage. Looking out on all these intently waiting faces. I had to say something. But this was going to be hard enough, even if the words were written on paper and laid out in front of me. And then, I would actually have to *mean* the words.

Say something! I said to myself, being careful not to let the words leave my mouth, even as a whisper. *Say something, anything!*

Then it came to me.

I would just talk about all the *good* things. Spare all these people the gory details and just say everything I could think of that was favourable, without blatantly lying, in case they could tell I was being disingenuous about any of the details.

And then, before I had a chance to give my mouth permission to speak, my lips moved all by themselves, blurting out the words, "What happened to Amy?"

Oh my lord, I was talking.

"That's the question we've all been asking ourselves," I continued. "That's why we're all here today."

No lies, so far.

"I honestly don't know," I told them all. "Like all of you, I am still waiting for the answers."

And I don't know whether it's because I'm deaf, or that the faces in front of me were nothing but ears, but no one in the room appeared to make a sound.

"What I *do* know," I tell all those blank faces, "is that she will not be forgotten."

This was also true, as I certainly wouldn't forget such a vile excuse of a human being any time soon.

"When I first met Amy," I told them, "she welcomed me in as her friend, the kindest way a person could."

My audience is just blank, mute faces. And I'm quite sure, if I still had my hearing, I wouldn't hear a silence that differed all that much to the silence I was hearing now.

"Like many of you, I was drawn to her."

All those faces. Still blank. Still silent.

"She was so different to any person I've ever had the pleasure of meeting."

Those same blank faces nodding in agreement.

"She taught me how to see the world in a wholly different way."

She took my hearing.

"Because of her, I have such an appreciation for things I never had, before."

I'm deaf because of her.

"I really wish she wasn't dead."

Which is also true, as her being dead, as it turned out, felt far worse than when she was alive.

"I almost feel responsible somehow."

Careful, Iris! my inner voice told me.

"For not seeing the signs that she was unwell."

Good save! that same voice said.

"I'm really going to miss that girl. The one who taught me every lesson I needed to learn in life."

Just then, someone got up from their seat and began making their way past the people in their row. My eyes following them down the aisle and out the door of the lecture theatre. This person being the only one dressed all in black when everybody else was wearing pink.

"There are some things I really wish I'd said to that girl, but now she's gone."

And just then, I could have sworn I heard someone giggle.

"What happened to Amy?" I finished by saying. "We don't know yet, but we won't forget her, even after we have the answers."

I looked out on all those faces, each with a pair of eyes already welling up with tears.

And with a shrug of my shoulders, a tightening of my lips and a tilt of my head, I told them all, "That's all I have to say."

All I had to say that was *nice*, anyway.

My audience was stunned. Transfixed. And, for whatever reason,

I think of when mine and Amy's eyes locked in the university canteen the other day.

And although I wasn't able to hear it, I could see people beginning to clap. Some even stood up from their seats; others appeared to be cheering. And, almost immediately, everyone else followed suit by getting up from their seats also.

I was usually the girl who went about her days silent and invisible. But here, in this moment, people really noticed me and held their tongues long enough to listen to what I had to say. Having the undivided attention of so many people without interruption felt so empowering. To be the one with all the attention for once, and not Amy.

And with my whole audience out in front of me, all wiping away tears in between their enthusiastic clapping …

… I think I'd just gotten away with it.

31

"Coming Clean"

As I walked the more familiar paths that led my way back home, the calming effect of a feeling – so unfamiliar to me that my mind and body, at first, treated it as an impostor – took up its residency in my once giddy head and jittery heart. Not simply because that speech I gave in front of all of those people was over, but that Amy's memorial had let the fact that she was dead, truly sink in. Not being able to help but lose myself in all the wonderful things I'd be capable of doing, now that she was gone for good. And as a side thought, maybe I should've been doing a degree in performing arts after that little stage act of mine back there.

Now everyone thought *I* was the kind and caring girl. I'd even go as far as to say all my new admirers thought me a *heroine* after listening to what I had to say in that lecture theatre just now. But more importantly, no one was ever going to suspect me as Amy's killer after hearing all those 'heartfelt' words of mine.

That is, if I was, in fact, her killer.

Now back home and sat in front of the *click-clacking* keys of my laptop, I searched Toggle for '*how to select yes to a multitude of friend requests on HeadMagazine*'. My friends list currently sat around a measly one hundred and forty-three, going up to seven hundred and eighty in less time than it took for a day to begin and end.

Popularity was clearly time-consuming, but I didn't have all night.

Only once I'd waited until the flood of friend requests eased off – some six hundred and thirty-seven vibrations and flashes later – did

I then accept them all with a single click. Just so happening to glance over at the door, where my eyes settled on a crisp, white envelope that had been slipped under it.

Pushing myself away from the desk on the wheels of my office chair, I flipped closed my laptop, and made my way over to the door. On the front of the envelope, now at my feet, was my name. The letters shaped with clumsy intention in thick, black ink. Not even my full name. No address, and no stamp affixed to the envelope. Just, '**IRIS**', scrawled big, the way a five-year-old with a felt pen would write it.

Stooping to pick the envelope up off the floor, I stood back up with it in my hand and turned it over to better inspect it.

Opening the door and leaning out of it, I looked up and down the hall, but it appeared that whoever slipped it under my door was long gone.

Stepping back into my room, the door swung closed behind me as I took my seat at the desk again. Studying this peculiar envelope in my hands, but it giving me no further clues as to who it was from, the envelope seemed to whisper, pressingly, for me to open it. And soon after I had, I really wished that I hadn't. For as I slipped out the folded piece of paper inside and unfolded it, a jarring sensation of alarm invaded the pleasant parts of my mind. Cold, steely hands strangling the necks of my happy thoughts as I read what was written across the harsh fold of the paper.

On the note was just one word.

One, lonely, accusing word.

LIAR.

32

"Take Note"

The note *had* to be from Malleus. I mean, who *else* could it have been from? He was the only one, to the best of my knowledge, who knew that I had lied to all those people at Amy's memorial. And I'm only now wondering about all the wondrous things Amy may have told him before she croaked.

If I knew Amy – which I really, bloody well *should've* done by now – she would have, at best, shared with Malleus some choice morsels of what happened between her and I. And, at worst, lied through those perfectly straight, whitened teeth of hers about everything. Sculpting a masterpiece of a tall tale to make herself look positively marvellous, whilst painting a shoddy picture of me with every stroke of her brush-like tongue dipped in shitty, toilet water.

There was so much I wanted to tell Malleus, but would he even listen now? I still had his number. Even though he was gone from my life, I just couldn't bring myself to delete him from my phone book. Now was the time, I decided. Whether or not he'd actually *give* me the time was another matter, entirely. I figured if Malleus would just hear me out, we'd have plenty to talk about when the time came, so I kept my message brief.

Got your message, I texted him. *Now here's mine … Can we talk?*

Now it was just a waiting game. I always seemed to be waiting for something these days. A lot of waiting around and a whole shedload of disappointment. But there was still a chance something positive could come from all of this atrocity, and so I held on to that possibility's promise as I waited.

The sun was setting as I leant out of my window, smoking yet another cigarette I wasn't really craving. Dropping the butt in the sorry looking remnants of what was left of my coffee, I threw out the dregs of my fourth cup with it and looked down, with little hope, at my phone rested there on the sill next to me.

And just when I was about to call it, yet another, disheartening day, my phone hovered over the surface of the windowsill with the intermittent vibrations of it receiving a text.

We can talk, the message read, *but it is NOT in your favour.*

Now, I'll be the first here to admit that this didn't sound hugely promising, but he did text back, and so there must have been a small part of him that entertained the idea of hearing me out.

Thank you, I replied. *Speak tomorrow?*

Talk tomorrow, he texted back.

Still no kisses. Not even a lousy 'How do you do?' But it was an exchange, at least. Which, at this point, is all I asked of him.

My mind rested a little easier after that.

And so, too, did I, for that matter.

Rubbing the eyes I hadn't needed for the last eight hours or so, and stretching out the body I couldn't stop all that tension seeping into while I was awake, I reached for my phone on the bedside table to see the time. *Ten past ten.* The happiest time of the day.

Well. As long as you're reading the time off an analogue clock and not a digital one.

Then my eyes darted from the way the long and short hands shaped a smile on the circle of numbers, and down to a text I'd received a good few hours ago.

Meet me at noon, the text read. *The park.*

And in an instant, I'm frantically typing back the reply *See you there!* as if composing a sloppy message in a few, quick seconds is going to make up for Malleus having to wait well over four hours to hear back from me. I almost didn't catch myself texting a kiss out of habit but, luckily, I deleted it just in the nick of time before sending.

I had just shy of a couple of hours, so I fought against my nerves that buzzed at the idea of seeing Malleus again, and attempted to get ready at the most leisurely pace I was able. Only running into problems when it came time to dressing. I wanted to look good, granted, but not so good that it would be obvious that I was trying to. But then, not dressed so sloppily that it appeared like I wasn't trying at all.

What would Amy wear if she were meeting with Malleus?

No! I told the girl in the mirror that looks just like me. *Don't you even go there!* If this was to be the time for me to start telling Malleus the truth, I also had to stay true to myself. Amy was gone, and I was still here. That's the advantage I had over her.

I would go as myself.

Then I remembered that '*what I looked like*' would be lost on a boy like Malleus, and threw on any old thing.

Malleus wasn't at the park when I got there, bang on time. Which, as you ought to know by now, is most unusual for him. And so, sat here on this bench, I took advantage of his tardiness to collect myself. Resisting the temptation to go over in my head what I would say, I decided that *this* time I would trust that the right words would come to me.

I had already lost him once, and so, in that respect, I really didn't have anything to lose.

I must have glazed over, because the next thing I knew, Malleus just *Poof!* appeared out of nowhere. Getting up to acknowledge his arrival, Malleus made his way toward me; his walking pace telling me that he just wanted to get this little meeting of ours over and done with. And without so much as a peck on my cheek, he sat himself down; his body twisted slightly away from me; his head turned almost in my direction. And I realise he's blind and everything, but it felt as if he wasn't really looking at me. Like just having to *be* here was some massive inconvenience to him.

"So what did you want to talk about?" he said.

"Can we talk about your little note?" I asked him. "I assume it was you?"

"What's to talk about? You're a liar."

"And what did I lie about, exactly?"

"Everything you said at Amy's memorial. Makes me wonder what *else* you've lied about."

"I'm a lot of things, Malleus. But one thing I am not, is a liar."

Malleus puffed some air out of his mouth and looked away.

"Everything I said up there on that stage was the truth," I told him. "There were just a lot of things I couldn't say in front of all those people about Amy and me."

"Oh, Amy told me all about it," he said, almost cutting me off. "How you two go way back. How you bullied her at school. Beat her up so bad she had to take a gap year before college. How you've been following her around all this time and making her life a misery. How you were a total … *B-word* to her. And yet she only had nice things to say about you."

Bitch.

My eyes were welling up as he said the words. Not because I was upset about what he was saying, but because the simmering rage inside of me, for the audacious lies she had told him, was seeping out of me as tears.

"That is simply not true, Malleus," I said.

"So what *is* the truth?" he asked.

"All of that stuff she told you. The bullying, the beatings, the gap year, the stalking. It's all true."

"So you admit it then?"

"The only thing she lied about," I told him, "was, who was doing it to who."

Malleus pulled a face.

"I didn't do any of those awful things to her," I continued. "She did them to *me*."

Malleus appeared to be chewing over my words as if they tasted like sour fruit.

"I may not be able to see you, Iris," he said. "But then, I don't need eyes to see right through you."

And with that said, he got up to leave.

"Why would I lie about this?" I said, grabbing his arm.

"Oh, I think I've already figured that out, Iris," he said, as he pulled his arm away and turned to face me. "This is jealousy. Plain and simple."

Grabbing both of his arms by the elbows I told him, "No, Malleus. It's the other way round. She was jealous of *me*!"

"I don't believe you, Iris," he said, throwing my hands off him. "And I don't keep the company of liars."

Malleus, not being able to see the tears bleeding from my eyes, simply walked away.

What could I say to make him stay? What words could I use to make him listen and for him to believe them? What could I tell him so he would take me back?

If he left now, that really would be it. We would be officially over, and I would never see him again.

With my mind racing, it was then that I blurted out, *"I was the one that filmed you bringing that dead pigeon back to life!"*

That's when Malleus stopped.

"I'm not a liar, Malleus!" I yelled after him. *"There's just so much I haven't told you!"*

Only then did he turn to face me.

"Lying and withholding the truth are the same thing," he said, just standing there; somewhere between coming back to me and walking away.

"That day," I said, "when we were sat on the knobbly log by the river, the very last time we met."

Malleus seemed to stay just long enough to give me the very slimmest of chances.

"I was ready to tell you everything," I said, "but then you cut me off, and just left me there."

Malleus hung his head, his hands finding a place to rest on his hips.

"Please give me the chance to tell you now," I said.

Malleus didn't say anything. He didn't have to. He just slowly came back to me.

"I said what I said to you that day," he told me, "and left you there the way I did, because I thought you were about to break up with *me*."

"Oh, no, Malleus," I told him. "That wasn't even the *last* thing I wanted to do."

Malleus felt for the bench to sit back down on it.

"What you wanted to tell me that day," he said. "Would you tell me now?"

That's when I sat back down on that bench and told Malleus everything. Everything apart from the whole *me, maybe killing Amy* thing. I figured that could wait.

Then I gave him a brief history lesson on the subject of Amy and me. Which, as it turned out, took a wee bit longer to cover.

And no sooner had I finished, Malleus took my hand in his. No words were spoken, but this one, small gesture of his said enough for the both of us.

33

"Digging Dirt"

I never knew just how much I could miss my ordinary, mundane, humdrum life. Amy was long gone. The storms in my mind had subsided. And Malleus and I had, at long last, patched things up. But there were still some pressing questions I desperately needed answers to.

What really did happen to Amy? Was it my doing? And just how was I going to find out?

Walking in circles inside my head, I kept coming back to the same place of putting my powers – if I did in fact possess them – to the test. It was this one last thing I wanted to lay to rest. Only then would I be able to move on with the rest of my life, which I *hoped* would have Malleus in it.

Pulling open the top drawer of my desk, I pulled out a notepad, flipped through the pages, and took another glance at the list I had started writing. The list of potential test subjects for my 'potentially deathly powers' experiment. So far, inscribed on the paper in the silver of pencil lead was the old boy at the pawnshop and the coffee-shop girl. A good start, but was it enough to prove to myself that I really *did* have a fatal ability?

I mean, how many people would it take?

I didn't want to take out *too* many people in the process of finding the answers. One wasn't nearly enough, and two was *almost* enough, so I settled on three. That sat well with me. Three was the magic number, after all. Not *too* many, but enough to convince myself of the possession of the abilities I may or may not have.

I guess the only real question now, was … *Who would be this third and final person?*

Looking up and to the left, I searched every corner of my mind for this one, last test subject for my potentially deathly experiment. A name, a face. Hell, I'd settle for a vague figure from a hazy dream right now. But alas, it was all in vain. I just couldn't think of anyone I wanted dead, let alone someone who deserved it. I didn't really want *anyone* dead, but it was the only way, I could see, to know for sure that either I *did* have this rare gift or that it was simply pure chance that Amy dropped down dead whilst I was giving her the uber-evils from across a crowded room.

And then I thought … *What if it didn't necessarily have to be someone who deserved it? What if it could just be someone nobody would miss?* Someone, whose death would make the world a slightly better place just by them not being in it. But the harder I tried to shed light on my suggestive thoughts, the darker my brain's bright ideas became. This was so much harder than I figured it would be, now that I was actually having to think about who I wanted dead.

And gazing at the notepad I needn't have taken out from the drawer – my pencil spending more time between my teeth than on the paper – I guessed I would just have to come across this third person in time. For, in the meantime, I had other more pressing matters to attend to.

Before I finalised my list of potential test subjects, I would first have to do some digging. Some research into the first two people I so hastily scribbled down on that notepad. To see what they were *really* like when they assumed no one was around to watch them.

Were they really as bad as I thought them to be? Did they really deserve to, albeit potentially, die? Was I actually going to try this out on three more people?

To cleanse my mind of the muck of indecision, I would have to get my hands a little dirty. And so, my digging commenced. I figured I would begin with the barista girl at The Daily Grind café. She wouldn't be too much of a challenge to dig some dirt on, surely. After all, a girl like her was bound to be found on HeadMagazine. Thing is, I didn't even know her name, and just how was I going to find *that* out? I knew Malleus was familiar with the girl, but it's not like I could just come right out and ask him for it.

No.

This was a solo mission, and the fewer people that knew about it, the better.

A trip to the café then, I thought.

I could do with a decent cup of coffee, anyway.

Now stood in the queue, and looking past the heads of thirsty customers in front of me, I craned my neck to see if this barista bitch – as I was not *quite* so affectionately calling her – was serving behind the counter. And, what do you know. There she was, stood there with perfect posture and prettier than ever – on the outside, at least – beaming that fake smile of hers at the person at the front of the line.

So what was I going to do here, exactly? Ask for her full name? To her face?

I really hadn't thought this through.

Would I have to go to the lengths of actually applying for a job here as a trainee barista, and find out that way?

Because I really didn't have time for all that.

It was then, I realised, I wouldn't even so much as have to ask, as I noticed every member of staff here were wearing name badges. Not their full names, granted, but a first name was all I needed to get started.

The coffee bitch was serving behind the counter with this hunky barista guy. The type of guy I would secretly be wishing to get served by on any other day. But this wasn't 'any other day', and what I *really* wanted was to be served by *her*.

I would have to time this just right so that would happen – which wasn't as easy as my plotting mind had promised. Sometimes she would just get a small order, such as an espresso. Other times she would get a big order, involving cappuccinos and lattes and Americanos. Double chocolate chip muffins and cinnabons and fudge brownies – all gluten-free, of course.

This barista girl was still juggling a toaster, a blender and a coffee machine as I shuffled ever closer to the front of the queue. The person in front of me had now been served, and this hunky barista guy, wearing a name badge that read, 'BRAD', asked me what I wanted to order.

To which I told him, "Sorry, I'm still trying to decide."

Quickly getting out of that one, and secretly hoping the customer behind me was about to make a big order, I continued to appear to be studying the black slate menu board, chalked up with every combination of milk, hot water and ground coffee beans you could be pushed to think up. But the customer 'BRAD' was seeing to just ordered an espresso, whilst the barista girl was still seeing to that damn blended ice drink and cursed toasted sandwich.

Could I really say it again? That I was still undecided about which of the many coffees on offer I wanted? It would be a tad embarrassing, for sure, but I may just have to.

Just then, as luck may have it, the coffee machine 'BRAD' was operating began to steam and splutter uncontrollably, before spewing fourth a hot brown liquid on his hand, up his arm, and all over his apron.

"SHIT!!" this 'BRAD' exclaimed.

I got *that* much.

The barista girl then ran to the aid of the barista guy with what looked like ice wrapped in a damp towel. This kind gesture of hers throwing me off, as I didn't peg her as the type to care. But then, this particular barista guy was a bit of a dish, so I figured what girl wouldn't.

After wrapping 'BRAD's' hand in the towel, the barista girl hurried back to the counter, announcing to those stood behind me something about being *Sorry!* and something about us, please, giving them a minute while the barista guy saw to his now very scarlet hand. And when I happened to glance back, I could see that this was met by a unanimous groan from everyone in the queue, and I almost, *almost*, felt sorry for her.

I mean, people can be so unreasonable sometimes.

With all the drama of the malfunctioning espresso machine, for a good few minutes I totally forget that I was only *really* here to find out the name of this particular barista girl, now stood right in front of me and asking to take my order.

'JESSICA'.

I decisively order a flat white, whilst quietly thanking her name tag in my head.

So thrilled I was, on the way back home, that I'd successfully accomplished my first mission on a background check for one of my unknowing test subjects, it didn't register that there was this long, deep puddle at the side of the road, running parallel to the pavement I was walking on. And before I could even think to move to the far left to avoid being splashed, I got completely drenched, head to toe, in dirty, black, gritty water with the passing of a speeding car.

Shocked silent at first, it took me a few shallow, gasping breaths to fully realise what had just happened. Only then, after looking down at my soaked-through clothes, my arms thrown up in surprise, did I jerk my head up to see a god-awful, yellow sports car leaving me in its wake.

"Just what this world needs!" I screamed after this god-awful, yellow car. *"Another total fucking asshole!"*

A banana-yellow Ferrari, complete with a truly ridiculous spoiler, and a personalised number plate – I mentally noted as it sped off down the road – that read, **'370H55V'**.

But as I stood there looking down at myself, and all that wet grit stuck to my now-soiled clothes, I began to laugh, hysterically.

A devilish smile creeping up the side of my face, once I'd got a hold of my laughter, as I realised …

… I may have just found my third and final test subject.

34

And then there were three: the *barista bitch,* the *mean ol' bastard* at the pawnshop, and finally, *the total fucking asshole in a banana-yellow sports car.*

I had a name: Jessica.

It was time for some cyber-stalking.

Now to go about finding her on HeadMagazine and seeing what dirt I could dig up.

Clicking on the magnifying-glass icon, I typed Jessica's name into the search bar and, by the looks of things, there had to be at least fifty 'Jessicas' on here to trawl through. I knew what she looked like, but then a lot of girls looked the way Jessica did: blonde, blue-eyed, boring.

Just like me, come to think of it.

But was being boring really all that bad? Bad enough to deserve to die?

To answer that question, I would have to do some further digging. Like I said, this particular 'Jessica' was pretty unremarkable, but forty-three 'Jessicas' down the list, and I thought I may have found her.

Jessica Blowers.

My first thought being: *What an unfortunate surname.*

According to her profile, she was an aspiring dancer, slash, mobile beauty therapist, who also worked as a trainee barista on the side. Her profile bio read, *"Leave the world better than you found it"* – which I thought was kind of apt – with two red hearts either side of said tagline. A profile picture of her pouting and holding a ridiculously small dog. Small enough to fit in a handbag, but then perhaps that's the whole idea – any dog smaller than a Westie is just a pet rat, in my book.

Her cover photo was of her with, who I assumed to be, four of her friends; all on some night out; all dressed pretty much the same; all appearing to be the sort of girls who would prioritise *looking* good over having a good time.

Still, no real grounds to *kill* a person.

There were plenty of 'Jessicas' on here for me to find. Which made me think … *If she were gone, with so many of them about, would she really be missed? Would it make any kind of lasting difference to the world if she just … ceased to exist?* She had no husband, no kids. Her friends seemed to mean a lot to her, but then what were her *friends* like? What kind of people were *they?* After all, a bitch can still be loved by other bitches. I could literally go … *Eenie, Meenie, Miney, Mo,* and pick a girl out of a crowd of dumb blondes just like her.

So why *not* her?

After scrolling through her most recent posts – of which there were more than is psychologically healthy – I found they were all predominantly about one of only three things …

1) Herself.

"Hittin' the gym", "smashing *Spinning* classes", and "nailing *Body Pump* sessions".

Photos of every low-calorie, meat-free meal she had for breakfast, lunch and dinner, every, damn, day.

Whatever 'look' was the latest fad at the time of taking a selfie in a bedroom mirror, whilst holding a bright pink, cubic zirconia encrusted *iSheep* smartphone in one hand.

2) Her dog.

Hundreds and hundreds of pictures of a Pomeranian called Jezebel, dressed in many a variety of 'cute' doggy outfits, and usually featuring a make-up caked Jessica holding them up to her face whilst gazing into the camera and kissing this handbag dog in the thick of its fur.

3) The places she's been, or going to.

Machu Picchu.

Some other achingly obvious bucket-list destinations.

Ibiza a gazillion times.

So it's evident that she's pretty shallow, we've established that much. Pretty obvious. Pretty banal. In fact, from appearances, all she's got is 'pretty'. And, over a long enough timeline, gravity and age will soon take care of all that. Plus that's just what's on the outside. She wasn't a *bad* person. Not really. Not *evil*. She hadn't started any world wars or caused mass genocide, as far as I knew.

I almost felt sorry for her.

Almost.

She was clearly trying so tremendously hard to be more like everyone else than anyone else, that she'd lost herself in the mix of what everybody else looked like, and what everyone else was doing, in a bid to be affirmed by receiving more 'likes' than any of the other girls just as insecure as *she* was. She would not be missed, let's put it that way. And that's all I needed. She would be gone, the world would keep right on spinning, and forget all about her in a week or so.

I looked at Jessica's profile picture one last time, and I thanked this little photo of hers. I told it that it had given me everything I needed.

And with that, I flipped shut my laptop.

I actually felt prematurely mournful about this particular Jessica; like she was dead already, and that it was all because of me. All she had done was be totally obvious and so completely forgetful. I had to remind myself that I wasn't doing this to her because she deserved it, but because she was the ideal candidate for the experiment. Even if I let her live, that wouldn't change the way she felt about *me*, and I'd only have to go and choose someone else to be part of this little experiment of mine. So why not her? She would not be missed. The world would be no emptier a place without her.

I looked off to the side, to see what thoughts that blank space of nowhere had for me on the matter. But being something that didn't really exist, that blank space, unsurprisingly, had no opinion at all. And so, with a shrug of my shoulders and a tilt of my head, I thought to myself ... *Why not?*

And with that decision made, I began my research on candidate number two ...

35

The old boy at the pawnshop was going to prove to be a little bit more of a challenge. I didn't know his name, I'm pretty sure he didn't wear a name tag, and highly doubted he would be found on a social media platform such as HeadMagazine. What I *did* know, however, was where he worked. And so, I decided I'd just have to stalk him the good old-fashioned way.

Thing is, I'd never actually stalked someone before. The word alone made me want to tear my clothes off, leap into a shower and vigorously scrub off the way it felt against my crawling skin.

Instead, I made the decision not to call it 'stalking' but 'research'. The kind you do when studying for a big test, which, really, is what this was. But whatever I was going to call it, I'd better quit dillydallying about with making 'stalking a complete stranger' sound better to me and just bloody well get on with it.

Pretending to browse the old-school record players and vintage cameras in the pawnshop window, I stole a glance at the opening hours etched into the glass of the shop door. The times were a little all over the place, and there was no way I could store them all in the limited memory space of my head. But then, we had camera phones nowadays. We no longer had to cast anything to memory anymore, and it wouldn't be so unusual to take a photo of a shop's opening hours, now would it? I'd seen plenty of people snapping shots of timetables at bus stops or of menus in the window of a restaurant. We live in an age where people are forever taking photos. Everyone's a photographer now. We even take pictures of our morning coffees and what we had for breakfast. So this would be no stranger than that, right?

I felt so sneaky as I tiptoed away, like I was a spy working for some secret government agency, obtaining vital information for something so big, everyone around me would have no idea about its existence.

And I guess, in a way, I was.

Now I would have a good idea as to what time the old boy would leave his shop, and when he did, follow him home. Waiting outside his house the very next morning, an hour before he was due to open up the shop. Perhaps the toing and froing from his house to work would give me some clue as to what kind of person he was and, more importantly, if he was a suitable candidate for my deathly experiment.

And I do worry about myself sometimes, as this was actually starting to get me all kinds of excited.

The time was precisely **17:01**. I was waiting on the corner, just outside the old boy's shop, and doing my utmost to be as inconspicuous as possible; on my phone, head down, and wearing a drab, grey bobble hat. My clothes so dull that I simply blended in with my equally dull surroundings.

I couldn't have been waiting any longer than the time it took to properly steep a teabag, when the door to the pawnshop swung open. My eyes darted up with my head still down, pretending to have the most banal of telephone conversations. The old boy shot me a look as he fumbled for the right key to lock the shop's front door. I was still gassing away to nobody on the other end of the phone.

Just then, my phone started buzzing and flashing away in my hand.

"Not right now, Dad," I whisper-shouted to the caller ID on my phone's screen as I jabbed away at the red telephone icon to hang up.

Shooting another look at me, I saw the grumpy old bugger mumble something to himself; his top lip pulled up into a snarl as he put the key in the door and turned it locked. Realising he'd noticed me, I crossed the street to the pavement opposite the pawnshop and stood under a lamp post to continue with the rest of my phony phone call.

With a heave, the pawnshop owner pulled down the window shutters, and crouched down to lock them. Like I said, he was an old boy, and appeared to have some difficulty getting up to stand. And just like with the barista girl, there was the briefest of moments where I almost felt sorry for him when I saw that he walked with a stick. The crafty little voice inside my head whispering for me to not let my feelings get in the way of what we were trying to do here. Even so, he was a swift walker, and I had just a little trouble keeping up with him, having to pick up my pace every few steps or so.

It was quite a way back to wherever this old boy lived, as when I checked my phone and saw that we were already two thousand steps in and not yet there, he was still walking. We must have walked almost a mile by now, and still no sign of his home.

How long could I realistically keep following this guy around without him noticing he was being followed?

But my worries were short-lived when, about another six hundred steps or so later, we reached what I sincerely hoped was his home. It was a humble place; nothing fancy. Grey concrete steps leading up to the front door, with railings either side that this old boy clung onto and pulled himself up with. I hung back, some distance away, peeking over the top of a bush that walled off his garden. No flowers of any kind or colour lining the lawn; just dull, lifeless grass that had grown taller than the rusty lawnmower leant against the front facing wall of the house.

Waiting for the old boy to wipe his feet, step inside and close the door behind him, I cautiously made my way from behind the bush wall of the garden, dashed up the stairs, and scurried to the dark porch with all the cunning of a ninja-feline stalking its prey.

Looking down at the doormat, although worn with the uncountable scuffings of the soles of the old boy's shoes, I could still make out the fading words, **'NOT YOU AGAIN'**, written on it in bold, capital letters. An angry looking, chipped, stone gnome beside the front door, holding a sign that read, **'GO AWAY'**.

I tried to peek inside the house, but a blind had been pulled down, covering the wobbly glass window of the front door. So too, were the curtains drawn behind every window.

Everything about this place barking the words, **'LEAVE ME ALONE'**.

Here was a lonely old man that didn't appear to have anybody. No wife, no kids, no family, no friends. No one. Even the corroding house number, barely hanging on by a solitary nail, looked lonely. That sorry feeling beginning to pester me again. But the point wasn't whether or not he deserved to die, it was whether or not he was a suitable participant for the test I was conducting.

I tried to look at this whole thing logically rather than emotionally. He was an old man, and a rude one at that. Who appeared to have no one in his life, not even a pet. He was alone most of the time, but even if he was lonely, it didn't matter. If he didn't have anyone that knew him or anybody that even knew *of* him, then he wouldn't be missed.

And that, really, was the most important factor. He would not be missed. And, therefore, the perfect candidate.

This had been a fairly successful mission. I now knew where the old boy lived, and that he appeared to be alone most of the time, but I had to accept that I wouldn't find out much else tonight with his doors locked and the curtains drawn.

As I made my way back down the steps that led up to the old boy's house, turned the corner, round the thick, thorny bush that fenced off his home, and out on to the pavement, I walked right into something that took even my breath by surprise.

Something too soft to be a lamp post, and too firm to be a bush.

It was then, I suddenly realised that it wasn't some*thing* I'd walked into, but some*body*. As from what I could feel, with my hands out in front of me, felt a lot like a leather jacket.

"Malleus!" I gasped, after pulling him into the light of a nearby lamp post. "What are you doing here?"

"Iris?" he said, taken aback. "What are *you* doing here?"

"What am I doing here?" I said, repeating his question.

What was I going to tell him? 'Oh, just a little light stalking. Just, you know, following some random old man around in the dark, the usual.'

I had to bide my time; give myself the chance to come up with something convincing.

"If you really want to know," I told him with a wasted wink, "you'll meet me here some other time."

"Where are we even going?" Malleus asked me as I pulled him by the arm.

We'd been walking in 'silence' for the time it took Malleus's patience to wane.

"Look!" I finally said.

A poor choice of words, but I think he let it slip.

"There's a bench over there," I told him. "Let's have a sit down, and then we can talk."

And as we both made our way over, I ran around the empty hallways of my own mind, desperately trying to find any words he would believe. But even with the most wildest of my imaginations failing to come up with a believable scenario as to what in the hell I was doing before I literally bumped into him, I gave into the idea that I would just have to tell him the, albeit inconvenient, truth.

"So?" Malleus pushed.

"I was doing some research," I told him.

Thinking, 'research' sounded far better than 'stalking a pensioner'.

"Research?" he asked me. "What for?"

"I'm trying to work out ..." I said, my words trailing off into nothing.

"... if I have ..."

God, this was going to sound so dumb.

"... an ability."

"An ability?" he asked, a frown creasing the skin across his forehead.

"You know," I said. "Like what *you* can do. The whole, 'bringing dead things back to life' thing you've got going on."

"So, what?" he said. "You think you can bring dead things back to life, *too?*"

"Yeah," I told him. "Like you, but the opposite."

"The opposite?" he asked. "Like, *killing* things? You can kill living things?"

"Well," I said. "You can't exactly kill something that's already dead, now, can you?"

"I don't understand," he said.

I breathed a deep breath in, and let an even deeper breath, out.

"What happened to Amy," I told him. "I think what happened to her was because of me."

And even though I couldn't hear a damn thing, I just knew, for sure, there was this pensive silence.

"There's something I really need to tell you, Malleus."

That's when Malleus felt around to take my hand in his.

"Actually," he said. "I have something I really need to tell you, too, Iris."

I prepared for the imminent sinking of my heart; staying silent for perhaps the very worst thing Malleus could ever tell me. And turning to face me, he spoke as I watched his lips utter words I couldn't have read right.

"Elephant shoes?" I asked him, baffled.

That's when Malleus laughed.

"No, silly," he said, repeating the words more slowly. "I ... love ... you."

"You *love* me?" I asked him.

"Is that so hard to believe?" he asked me back.

And after everything that had happened. Yes. Yes, it was, actually.

"It's why I started dating Amy in the first place," he said.

I just pulled a face he couldn't see.

"I could feel myself falling for you," he told me, "and you were always blowing hot and cold. So I finished things with you before you could finish things with me. I thought seeing someone else would help me forget you, but it didn't. It could have been anyone, just as long as it wasn't you. I could see where we might be heading, and that's why I ended it."

The words had been taken from my mouth by the words that had entered my eyes.

And, for once, I had no sarcastic quip or witty comeback for what Malleus had just told me.

"Please say something, Iris," he said. "I can't see your face to tell how you're taking all this."

Had Malleus really just told me he loved me? And, if he had, did that mean he always had? That he'd loved me this whole time?

"You still there?" he asked.

"Honestly," I finally managed to say. "I'm not really sure."

"Come on, Iris," he said. "Don't leave a guy hanging."

And still unsure as to whether I was really here or just dreaming I was, all I managed to do was sit there wondering which it was.

"Well, Iris?" he pushed gently. "What do you have to say to that?"

"I don't know," I said. "Elephant shoes?"

We both sat in what I imagine were a few seconds of silence, before bursting into laughter. We laughed so hard it made my face ache. For so long that Malleus had to hold together his splitting sides.

Once we'd regained control of ourselves, I then pulled myself together and said, as seriously as I could manage, "I love you, too, Malleus." And we kissed for the very first time.

They say you can tell a lot from a first kiss.

This first kiss told me that he really *did* love me. That from this moment on we would be inseparable. That we would go on to do a great many things together, and that nothing, not even death, would separate us from the love we had for each other.

But don't take my word for it.

I've got no other first kisses to compare it with.

After a time of both our lips being softly pushed together, Malleus slowly pulled away from me. My eyes were still closed. So lost in his kiss, for however long it lasted, I completely forgot where I was.

It was only after my eyes had opened that I noticed this strange look on Malleus's face; his nose all scrunched up, with his mouth chamming at the air like he was chewing on a wasp.

"What's wrong?" I asked him.

"Nothing," he said. "It's just …"

"Just what?"

Malleus let out a breath after taking one in.

"I'm trying to think of the nicest way to say this," he said as a laugh.

"Was I no good?" I asked him.

"No, it's not that. It's just …"

Nothing existed to me in that moment but Malleus's lips and the next words to be uttered from them.

"It's just that you taste a bit like … an ashtray?"

"And that was the *nicest* way you could think to say it?" I said, rummaging around in my slouch bag for the packet of mints I didn't have. "At least I'm not the one going around licking ashtrays!"

"So, anyway," he said, shaking his head free of the last topic of conversation. "Why do you think what happened to Amy was your fault, exactly?"

Typical, I thought to myself.

This was so like Amy.

Even in death she knew just how to ruin a perfectly good moment.

36

Taking the deepest of breaths in, I readied myself for what may be the most ridiculous story I've ever told a person.

Where did I even *begin?*

"So," I began. "I think what happened to Amy was my fault because ..." but my next words were hesitant to reveal themselves from behind the safety of my lips.

And Malleus, holding onto any words of encouragement he had for me, just sat there, patiently waiting for the following words I would utter.

"Look," I put it to him another way. "I saw you laughing and kissing, over there with her in the canteen, and it just made me so ..." but my words trailed off again.

"It really pissed me off!" I blurted out.

And I could tell Malleus's attention was suddenly grabbed; his whole body flinching as I said the words with such passion.

"I saw red," I told him, "and practically burned a hole between her eyes. She was looking at me from across the room with this certain satisfaction on her face, and I was glaring right back at her."

Malleus, promptly over his shocked surprise of my sudden outburst, still seemed to be with me.

"You know how they say, *If looks could kill?*" I asked him. "Well, it was one of those looks. I wished she was dead in that moment of our eyes locking, and then, right there and then, she *was.*"

Malleus hadn't moved from the position he was sat in, while I filled him in with all of this. He didn't so much as utter a word. It was only seconds later, after I'd stopped talking, did he then shake himself free of the disbelief of what I'd just told him.

"Just so we're on the same page here," he finally said. "You think you killed Amy just by shooting her a *look?*"

"I know it sounds crazy," I said. "But, yes."

"From across the room?"

"Yes."

Feeling even more terrible about what I may have done, now that I'd said the words out loud for someone else to hear.

That's when I could feel Malleus's whole body shaking next to mine. And when I looked up, I saw that he was giggling. I had just spilled my guts to him, and *he* was finding the whole thing just a bit too amusing.

"What's so fucking, funny?" I asked him.

"I'm sorry," he said, just about managing to fit the words between fits of giggles. "It's just that you really had me worried for a minute there."

And if he could've seen the way my mouth pulled up, almost meeting with my scrunched-up nose – my arms, now firmly crossed – he would've known that his apology was *not* accepted.

"I thought maybe you'd poisoned her food or something," he said.

And even though this wasn't the case, I had certainly thought about it.

"So let me get this straight," he went on. "You're telling me that you think you caused Amy's death just by *looking* at her?"

"Why not?" I said back, somewhat ashamed, somewhat furious. "*You* have a power. Perhaps I do, too."

Malleus pulled the kind of face you do when you're dubious about the claims of a clearly deluded individual.

"Don't look at me like that," I told him, pulling the kind of face one does when someone's just made a joke about their haircut.

"But I'm *not* looking at you," he told me, setting his giggling fit off again. "Not technically."

"Why's it so unbelievable?" I asked him. "Especially for someone like you!"

"What's *that* supposed to mean?"

"You know *exactly* what I mean. You think it's normal for a person to bring creatures back from the dead the way you do? I've never met *anyone* who could do that."

"Well, neither have *I*!"

"Well, there you go, then! But if you also think you're the only person on God's green earth that has some kind of special ... ability, then you're just ..."

"Just what?"

"Ignorant!"

"Wow! I'm an idiot for thinking I'm the only one on this planet that's able to do what I do? You said it yourself, Iris. You've never met anyone that could, and neither have I!"

We both fell, for want of a better word – in my case, at least – silent. And as much as my mouth fought back to not say the words, I forced out an apology for calling him ignorant. Right after which, he apologised for laughing at me, in a manner that could almost pass for sincerity.

"Look," he said, slapping a hand down on my leg with impressive aim. "Let's say you do have this power. And I will entertain the idea for now that you might. How are we going to find out, for sure, exactly?"

"I'm already on it," I told him, my back straightening up with my words. "That's what I was doing. Before I ran into *you*, anyway."

The expression on Malleus's face: a combination of quite impressed and slightly concerned.

Malleus leant back as if to get a better look at me. "You're putting together a list of people to try it out on, aren't you?"

"Not as dumb as you look," I said, getting to my feet.

"And you're not as dumb as you sound," he told me, feeling the air for my hand to take.

Pulling him up from the bench we were sat upon, I led the way out of the park and back to my room to further discuss my plan. And although he was all very clever and everything, and had already pretty much sussed out what it was I was up to ...

... Malleus still had quite a bit of catching up to do.

37

"Reasonable Cause"

I'd never had a boy in my room before. Not even back home living with Dad. Malleus was sat awkwardly on the edge of the bed; hunched up, his hands held together and pinched between his inner thighs. And, from the looks of him, it was as if he'd never been in a girl's bedroom before. The way in which Malleus tensed up when I asked him if he wanted a cup of coffee, was like I'd just asked him if he wanted to have *sex*. His whole body recoiling in terror, the moment I slipped a pod into the coffee machine and hit the start button.

"It's OK," I told him. "It's just the coffee machine."

How loud *was* this damned electrical appliance, exactly?

"Oh, right," he said. "For a moment there I thought you were doing some DIY!"

"What?" I asked.

"You know, like drilling a *hole* in the wall or something."

"So, *that's* what my flatmate was going on about!"

"Huh?"

"Never mind."

Taking Malleus's hand, I placed the coffee cup inside his palm as he wrapped his fingers around it.

"*Wowzers!*" he exclaimed, passing the cup to his other hand and back again like a hot potato.

"It's coffee," I told him. "What did you expect?"

Grabbing my notebook, I slid the pencil out from the binder, and flicking through the pages, took a pew beside him.

"So," I began. "I already have two definite test subjects."

"*Test* subjects?" he asked.

"This mean ol' bastard that owns a pawnshop," I continued, "and …"

I had to be careful here.

"… some totally random girl you don't know that works at a café."

Malleus didn't appear to twig, so I kept right on talking.

"These first two," I told him, "were easy to find, easy to track. But this *third* test subject is proving a little more difficult, seeing as they were in a speeding car when I clocked them."

Malleus appeared to be deep in thought. Either that or his coffee still wasn't quite at drinking temperature.

"Now," I went on to say, "I did, however, recognise the make and model of the car they were driving, and made a mental note of the number plate. I can't imagine there to be *two* assholes driving around these parts, in a car as gaudy as the one I saw the other day."

That's when I turned to Malleus, who had now put an earbud in his ear and appeared to be fooling around on his phone.

"Are you even *listening* to me?" I asked him.

I was telling Malleus all of this in the hope he would have some suggestions as how to locate an asshole in a sports car, but when he told me, "Yep!" it was apparent he was already way ahead of me.

"I can get his address," Malleus told me, frantically tapping away on his phone. "But it's going to cost you."

I slouched. "How much?"

Malleus drummed his hands on his legs before announcing, "A whopping two spons and fifty doolies!"

I rubbed my hands together like a Disney villain. "It'll be worth every penny."

"Says here," Malleus went on to tell me, "that you can obtain the name and address of the registered keeper of a vehicle, if …"

I gleefully clapped my hands and, although I'm a little ashamed to admit it, I think maybe a little bit of pee came out, but I couldn't be sure.

"… *If*," he continued, "you can give reasonable cause for requiring the information."

"So all we need to do is come up with a reason?" I asked.

"That's what it says. But, whatever the reason, we need to get this form first."

"And how does one go about getting one of those?"

Malleus tapped at the screen of his phone. "Says here, you can get one from a local post office."

"Then what are we waiting for!" I said as I sprung off the bed and made a beeline for the coat rack.

"Whoa there, Nelly," he told me. "Hold on to your horses."

My left arm was already in the wrong sleeve of my coat.

"It closes in less than ten minutes," he said. "We'll never make it."

My right arm now in the left sleeve of my coat.

"Maybe not if we walk," I told him, "but we could make it if we run."

"Oh yeah," he said. "Like I ever run."

Fair point.

"It opens again at 9 am," he told me. "Can't we just wait until morning?"

My shoulders slumped as I attempted to count the hours from now until that time.

"It's sixteen hours away," he told me. "That's not even a *day*. What could possibly happen in less than a day?"

Oh, you have no idea, I felt like telling him.

Slowly, I slid my arms out of the sleeves I had mistakenly slid them into, and let my coat drop to the floor in a sorry heap.

"Aha!" Malleus exclaimed.

"What? What?" I asked, scurrying over and plonking myself down next to him, to better see what he had just found on his phone. Which didn't help at all, what with the phone screen not having any actual text displayed on it.

"Says here, you can fill in the form online," he said, as if he'd just hacked into the Pentagon.

"Good work, soldier," I said, holding up a hand for him to high-five.

And then, upon realising I would actually have to announce that I was holding *up* a hand for him to high-five, I thought better of it, and just lowered my hand back down again.

"Oh," he said.

"What is it?" I asked with crazy, wide eyes he couldn't see.

"It does say here, you can fill in the form online …"

"Yes? Yes?"

"But then, you actually have to print it, sign it, and send it by post anyway."

I slouched; a puff of air leaving my lips. "Blocked at every turn."

"It's not the end of the world, Iris," he told me. "There's always tomorrow."

"I suppose there is *one* upside to this whole thing," I told him.

"And what's that?" he asked.

"This does give us more time to come up with a good reason."

After spending the best part of a wasted hour attempting to put a list together of all the possible reasons why we needed this particular asshole's details, we came to the dead end of admitting we'd failed to come up with any good ones.

"Bake a cake?" I asked him. "How's that going to help?"

"No," Malleus said. "Maybe it's best we take a break from all this."

"Yeah," I said, "you're probably right. Let's take five, and we'll get right back to it."

That's when Malleus turned to me. "For the day, I meant."

Shutting the coffee machine off, an empty cup held in my hand, I leant on the desk in a stance that told him I disagreed.

That is, if he could have seen it.

"I know you really want to find this guy," he told me, "and I'm not trying to get in your way. I'm just saying that perhaps the reason will come to us when we're not thinking so hard about it."

This, I didn't want to 'hear'.

"Alright," I said, placing the cup under the spout of the coffee machine, and switching it back on.

And with the coffees made, I imagine the room was as silent as it was before.

Guiding his left hand to take the coffee cup from my own, I said to him, "I guess the reason will probably come to us in our sleep or something."

Whether or not I actually *meant* the words I had just said, I wasn't as convinced – my brain, running on minimum capacity after all the thinking up of ideas that weren't good enough.

Malleus shifted his position on the bed. "That's all I'm saying. Hey. I want to find this guy, too."

"You do?" I asked him.

"Well, yeah."

"And why's that?"

And although I couldn't actually hear him, I could tell he raised his voice somewhat when he said, *"Because he sounds like a total f'ing a'hole!"*

Shocked silent by his own outburst, Malleus fell quiet. We both did. That is, until we could no longer hold our poise, and burst into a fit of laughter. Malleus spilling his coffee as he doubled over, slipped off the bed to the floor, and rolled onto his back.

And quickly getting over the fact that I was probably going to lose my deposit, due to a coffee-stained carpet – no matter how hideous the colour – I, too, joined him on the floor.

It wasn't even all that funny, looking back.

And I really don't know why it tickled us so, but right then, in that moment, it just did.

Laying there on our backs, on the floor of my room, both of us gazing at the same nothing-in-particular up there on the ceiling, I felt Malleus's hand reach for mine.

And as our fingers interlinked, I turned to face him, and asked, "So what now?"

"What now?" he asked, after turning to 'look' at me. "I guess we just wait."

Somewhat baffled, I almost asked him again. Except *this* time being more clear as to what I'd meant by the question. Then I realised. Malleus thought I was referring to the whole 'asshole in the sports car' thing, when what I was *really* asking was, "What now, with *us*?"

Perfect little moments, however, are far and few between; never lasting all that long, so instead, I just held my tongue.

"Why?" Malleus asked me back. "What do *you* think?"

And looking away from him, and back up to that non-existent spot on the ceiling, I simply said, "I guess we just wait."

We lay there in a comfortable silence. Just savouring the moment of not being able to do any more. Neither of us feeling the need to come up with any kind of conversation. But even though Malleus was lying here as still and silently as I was, I could just tell he had something on his mind when he gave my hand a gentle squeeze; my eyes falling from the ceiling, and landing on his.

"You asked me once," he said, "if I'd ever used my ability on a person."

I remained silent, my mind travelling all the way back to the first time Malleus and I sat on the knobbly log by the river.

"Do you remember?" he asked.

I nodded.

"Well, *do* you?" he asked me again.

"Yes," I said. "Sorry. Yes, I do."

That's when Malleus gave me a nod, saying, "I think I'm ready to talk to you about it now."

38

"Slipped My Mind"

Once my eyes were fully open, and my body had caught up with them, the first thing I noticed was my aching back. I had been laying on the floor with Malleus – that much I *did* remember – and now that I was awake, he was no longer lying beside me.

I vaguely remember reading his lips as he told me a story.

It was this thought that lurched me up off the floor and sent my mind, still disorientated from a deep slumber, into a frantic spinning. Desperately trying to recall what it could of the sad account of Malleus's dying mother, and the great extent of his efforts to keep her alive.

I remember how the tragic tale began: Malleus was fifteen years old – which was also the year he went blind – when his mother was diagnosed with an aggressive brain tumour about the size of a small orange. But where did it go from there? And how did it end? For the life of me, I just could not pull the memory of the story back into the light, and out from the darkness of my fading recollections.

Malleus had been telling me a story. One I imagine was awfully close to his heart. A story buried deep down within him. A story he may never have shared with anybody until last night. I had fallen asleep watching his mouth, and now he was gone.

How had I managed to mess up again? And just how did I keep doing that so often?

Malleus had divulged this one thing to me, in good faith that I would 'listen' for the duration, and perhaps have had something comforting to say by the end of it. He had poured his heart out to me, and I had let it strain through my mind like a sieve. There was not all that much left in there of the story; just some leftovers, not enough of which to piece the story back together in its entirety.

And I don't know why it came over me: this uneasy feeling. But with Malleus gone, I couldn't shake off the thought of what the future held for us. And contemplating this troubling notion that clung on to me and refused to let go, made me think the worst.

A few more dreadful minutes passed before I willed myself up off the floor, against the gravity of my worries. But I didn't even have the time to think about how I would spend the rest of this lonesome day, when I noticed the door to my room being ever so slowly opened. And it was only when the door was about halfway open, did I then see who it was, unable to contain myself from bursting out with, "Malleus!"

"Jesus!" Malleus exclaimed as he stumbled through the door.

"Close," I told him with a wasted wink. "More like Mary Magdalene."

"Huh?"

"Never mind."

"I figured you'd still be asleep," he told me. "I brought coffee."

He held out a brown, corrugated cardboard cup for me to take. Which, all thanks to my outburst of his name, was now dripping with coffee running down the side of it.

"I *think* there's some left?" he said. "Either that or I'm now *wearing* it?"

"Thank you," I said, taking the cup from his hands. "And I'm sorry."

Malleus's face looked like a question mark.

"For scaring you," I told him.

That question mark tilting along with his head.

"When you came in just now," I told him, in the same tone of voice you would use to explain the laws of physics to an infant.

Malleus puffed out his chest. "You didn't scare me. Just made me jump."

Then he smiled that damn smile of his. The same one that refused to leave my mind whenever he wasn't around. And sat on the floor with our backs against the side of the bed, it was right then I knew everything was OK, and without even saying the magic words, he'd already forgiven me for last night.

But I just couldn't help myself to not make doubly sure.

"Do you hate me?" I asked him.

"*Hate* you?" he asked, pulling that question-mark face again. "Why would I hate you? I just wasn't expecting you to be awake when I got back."

"No," I gently cut him off. "I mean, because of last night."

The fact that Malleus still wasn't getting it, made me think I needn't have brought it up.

"You were telling me that story about your mum," I said, "and …"

I couldn't even finish the sentence, I still felt so bad about it.

"And you fell asleep," he said.

And even if Malleus had eyes that still worked, he wouldn't have been able to see me, I'd shrunk so small.

"It's cool," he said, tossing the words at me like they were loose change.

"You can tell me the story again now, if you like?" I said, giving him a gentle nudge with my body. "Only, this time, I promise I'll stay awake until the end."

He put a tender hand on my knee, and said, "Some other time."

"So what do you want to do today?" I sprang up as I asked the question. "Take a walk somewhere? Go for coffee? Pizza?"

And if 'unenthusiastic high-five' had a face, Malleus was now wearing it.

"Maybe go see a heavily action-based film at the cinema?" I added, throwing it in there merely to jerk his chain.

"I've got a better idea," he said, perking up. "Let's start the day by finding out where that total f'ing a'hole of yours lives."

Honestly, I'd forgotten all about the guy. But now that Malleus had suggested it, I couldn't think of anything in the world I would rather do today than doing just that.

As long as it was with him.

39

"Inconsequential Conversation"

Finally at the front of this awful queue – the one we shared with some particularly unsavoury characters who made me wish it had been my sense of *smell* I'd lost – the post office clerk must have called out, *Next please!* as Malleus gave me a gentle nudge for me to step forward, asking if I wanted him to speak *for* me. And looking up at him, with admiring eyes I wish he could see, I softly told him, *No.*

"Come on you two love birds," I read from the lips of the clerk sat behind the glass window. "There are people waiting in line who are less patient than *I* am."

We stepped up.

"I need a form?" I said unsurely, turning to Malleus for the help I had just turned down.

"Have you lost your manners along with your hearing?" the clerk asked.

"I'm sorry?" being all I managed to say.

"You forgot to say, *please*?" she informed me.

"Please?" I said, a little taken aback.

"So you need a form?" the clerk asked, not looking up at me. "Most everyone that comes in here needs a form. What kind? We've got all sorts."

I was still thinking about her previous question about losing my manners along with my hearing.

Only *then* does she look up at me and says, "Are you telling me you had all that time waiting in line, and now you don't know?"

Turning to Malleus for the help he'd offered me, not a minute ago, he spoke for me. "It's this one," he said, holding up the screen of his phone for the clerk to see.

And *she* says, "Does your boyfriend always do all the thinking and talking for you?"

I shot her a look. The very same look you give a person when they're skating recklessly on the thin ice of your patience. And although Malleus couldn't see it, he could obviously sense what was bubbling just under the fragile surface of my tolerance, when he said, "Let's not get ahead of ourselves, Iris." Before turning his attention to the clerk and telling her, "You *really* don't want to upset this one right now."

The clerk looked up at him with eyes that challenged his advice.

"Trust me," he added, a stern look on his face answering any of the following questions she could possibly ask.

It was then, an amicable expression slowly made itself apparent on the clerk's face as she looked up for long enough to recognise a familiar face.

"Malleus," she said, a smile appearing from seemingly nowhere. "I'm sorry. I didn't see you there, stood behind this one."

This one?

"No need to apologise, Nora," Malleus said back to her. "I didn't see you, either."

And just like that, it's all jovial chit-chat and friendly banter.

"And who is this lucky girl that's with you today?" she asked him.

"This is Iris," he told her, putting an arm around me. "My girlfriend."

*Girl*friend?

"Well," the clerk replied, "she seems lovely."

Which will go down as the nicest thing this Nora says about me on this particular visit.

And then she just goes and ruins it by adding, "And probably all the lovelier without the attitude."

I'd have been so pissed off right then if I wasn't so damned happy.

"Well," she says. "If there's nothing else I can help you two puppy lovers out with, here's your form."

Doing my best not to snatch the form from her hand, I secretly hoped she could see the *Fuck you* in my smile.

And in the time it takes for this Nora to glance down at the keyboard in front of her, I swipe a packet of mints off a small countertop display rack and slip them into a vacant pocket.

Malleus thanked this Nora, and with his arm still around me, guided me back, away from my furious reflection in the glass window with the speaker. Leading me to the exit of the post office and out the door. This wasn't so much chivalry as it was ensuring I didn't make eye contact with anyone in the queue and, say, accidentally, on purpose, execute them with the ferocity I was still harbouring for that downright rude office clerk.

Which was novel; him being blind and being the one guiding *me.*

"Don't you ever get sick of everyone around here knowing who you are and all your business?" I asked Malleus, as he put sufficient distance between me and the post office he'd had to personally escort me out of just now.

"Nope," he said. "Not really."

"Don't you ever want to move someplace else?" I asked him. "Have a change of scenery?"

"Now, why would I do that?" he said. "It's not like I'd be able to appreciate it. Plus, I know every square inch of Constanceville. If I moved, I'd only have to go and start all over again."

"For some people, starting all over again's a good thing," I told him.

"Not for *me,*" he said. "Besides. 'Starting all over again' just sounds like another form of avoidance."

"Anyway," I said, swiftly changing the subject to one I might actually get somewhere with. "This Nora. How well do you two know each other exactly?"

"Well enough," he replied. "Why?"

"No reason," I replied. "I was just thinking about my list, was all."

"Oh, right?" he said with a wry smile. "You thinking about maybe putting her on there, too, are you?"

"Well," I said. "There's always room for one more."

40

"Disabilities & Advantages"

Usually, handing me a form and a black ballpoint pen to fill it out with was the quickest way to send me into a self-induced coma. But as monotonously formal and boringly straight forward as this form was, I would actually go as far as to say filling *this* one in was … enjoyable. Mainly because of *why* I was filling it in. To get my own back with that asshole – the one who drenched me by the side of the road all that time ago – for an act of douchebagery he probably thought he'd long gotten away with.

After all the deliberation of last night – when Malleus and I were throwing ideas back and forth across the room, trying to come up with 'reasonable cause' to obtain the information we so fiercely needed – in the end we went with Malleus's fine suggestion of the asshole in the yellow sports car regularly parking across two spaces allocated only for disabled drivers at my hall of residence.

Isn't it gratifying when you can finally use a disability to your own advantage?

I had asked Malleus if we could fill in the form at his place - a change of scenery, more for my own benefit than for his. But he told me, "Now's not the best time." Saying, "I'm sort of living between homes at the moment." And that my room, although a little pokey, would be a far more suitable environment for the business of filling in forms such as this one.

With all the necessary details filled in, along with the supporting photographic evidence – thanks to a contact of Malleus's with insane Photoshop skills – all I needed do now was sign on the dotted line. But instead, I just chewed on the end of my pen. It was the **'It is an** *offense to unlawfully procure personal information'* part that had me gnawing on my writing implement. Plus the fact that this sure, 'no bones about it' warning was written in bold lettering at the end of the form, right before you sign and date it.

I mean, we could get in some **serious shit** for this.

Getting myself in trouble for my own interests was one thing, but to drag Malleus along with me was quite another. Did I *really* want to do this? Did I really *need* to do this? If I got in trouble for intentionally giving false information to obtain a person's details, no matter how much of an asshole I considered this person to be, there could be some severe consequences. What those severe consequences could be, I didn't know. What I *did* know, however, was that I really wasn't all that crazy about finding out for myself.

Thing is.

And this was the one thing tipping my indecision towards signing the bottom of the form. I really wanted to find this guy. Going as far as to say, I *needed* to. And that's all it took: the thought of tracking this guy down and exacting a little revenge of my own.

The pen chewing stopped. And with a muttered, "Fuck it," I took the pen and held it steadily in my hand as I scrawled my signature.

All that was left to do now was slip the form into the prepaid envelope, along with the photographic evidence and a cheque for two spons and fifty doolies, push it through the slit-like hole of a pillar box and – the very hardest part of this entire process for someone as impatient as I am …

… wait.

The last time I was both this nervous and this excited, was back when I was still living at home with Dad, the day my GCSE results were posted through the front door.

Malleus and I were now sat beside each other on the bed. Beside *ourselves*. Sharing this mutual feeling of nauseating anticipation. The envelope from the DVLA now finally in my hands. We had patiently waited for four whole weeks for this day, and now that it was here, I dare not open the envelope for fear of what may or may *not* be inside.

"I can't do it," I told Malleus, looking down at the crisp white envelope. "*You* open it."

"And just how is that going to work, exactly?" he asked me. "Unless you requested the information in Braille?"

I really did hate the fact that Malleus was blind sometimes, as it meant he got out of doing some of the more difficult stuff.

"Please," I begged him.

With an impressively well-aimed snatch, Malleus took the envelope from my hand, and with a rip and a tear and a "There you go," handed it back to me.

"Thank you," I told him, sliding the letter out from the torn paper pocket he had just made for me. "That wasn't so hard, now was it?"

"So?" Malleus asked, urging me to cut the foreplay.

"Give me a minute," I said, quietly enjoying torturing him with what he couldn't read for himself.

Reading down the letter, a smile crept up the side of my face.

That's when I turned to Malleus – looking as if he would have a seizure if I made him wait a second longer – and said, "We've got him."

41

"Mellow Yellow"

To get underway with our investigations of a man we assumed was, at best, an asshole, and, at worst, a *total* fucking asshole, we would be stalking him the good ol' fashioned way.

We had a name: Richard Heard.

What we *also* had, and perhaps more importantly, was his address.

I stood with Malleus, looking up at the towering, wrought iron gates of this monstrosity of a house. I say, 'house', it was more like a palace, and a god-awful one at that. With gold leaf practically everywhere, and what looked like Swarovski crystals embedded into pretty much everything you could see. That is, if you could bare to look for *long* enough.

Extravagantly bright; incredibly showy; utterly tasteless.

It was quite simply the gaudiest place of residence these eyes have ever had the displeasure of seeing.

Malleus was lucky he was blind.

All of this I had to describe to him, but even with my sound vocabulary, it didn't quite match up to the truly horrendous spectacle that was this asshole's, far from humble, abode. The colossal prick even had an ancient-Greek-style water fountain statue – that may or may not have been modelled on himself – mounted on an ornate plinth of carved fish and wild horses; all flapping and galloping around it. Centred right in the middle of a private roundabout in front of his disgustingly opulent dwelling.

Everything about the place declaring with boastfulness, *Me, me, me! I'm better than all of you! And kindly piss off!*

Even the house sign to this gargantuan, glittering turd of a mansion – a large golden plaque, mounted on one of the outer walls that stood either side of the gates – didn't offer any kind of courteous welcome. The words, '*Mi Casa*', etched deep into the gold's cold to the touch surface.

And looking up at all this ghastly extravagance, all I could think was …

… *What a dickhead.*

Here was proof in its physical form that, even with an obscene abundance of money, you still can't buy good taste.

But enough sightseeing of the gaudy tourist attraction that was this douche-bag's home. We were here for far more pressing matters. And although Malleus was still a little more than uncomfortable with the whole stalking thing, there was no doubt about it when it came to the fact that this guy was clearly the ideal candidate for my little experiment.

We really didn't need to do any further digging. But stalking – especially when it's to exact justifiable revenge – is just way too much fun.

The only question, really, with these high walls and locked gates that towered over us, was, *How would we get close enough to him?* And so, we kept an extra-close watch on this particular asshole over the next few days.

Fortunately for us, this asshole's life ran like clockwork. Unfortunately for us, this asshole was a very late sleeper and a very early riser. I mean, who in the hell turns in for the night at just gone midnight, only to be up at 4 frickin' am the very same day?

"Does this guy ever sleep?" I asked Malleus as I passed him the binoculars. Taking them back the very moment I realised they would probably be more useful in my *own* hands. The both of us hiding in a bush adjacent to the asshole's home at precisely **4:01 am** on a bitterly cold morning.

He was either, inside his home, walled off on every side – the gate being the only way in or out – or in one of his many high-end, luxury cars. Even if you *could* scale the walls, that stood taller than the backboard of a basketball net, or clear the front gate, there was the state-of-the-art security system that would stop you in your tracks, soon after. Not to mention the big dogs Malleus could hear barking and snarling from somewhere in the complex.

It was quite evident, from all of our extensive research so far, that the house was a no-go. That, within the confines of his home, he was, quite literally, untouchable.

Soon after he left the house for work, he would get straight into one of his many cars. And it appeared he had quite a penchant for the most detestable shades of yellow. Today's choice was a Bentley Continental with tinted windows, in the most hideous baby-shit colour. And when I say, 'left the house', he never actually left the house.

There must have been some kind of back door that led to, what I imagined to be, a ginormous garage where he kept his prized fleet of flashy cars. Which meant he never actually came *out* the front door and, similarly, never actually entered *through* the front door, either.

He was also hardly ever home, spending so much of his time in his monstrous factory, he may as well not have lived there at all. We never even bothered attempting to see if we could somehow gain access to the property under the guise of canvassers, and the sign that stated '**No visitors without appointment**' deterred us, right off the bat. And what business would two people like us, a deaf university student and some blind nobody, have to discuss with this workaholic of a man-machine to persuade him to give us a mere second of his precious time?

"No offence," I told Malleus.

To which he replied, "Some taken."

So, if we couldn't get close enough to him at home, could we get close enough to him at his place of *work*?

And so, we followed him to his whopping great factory; a building, blatantly overcompensating for smaller things. Me, wiggling my pinky-finger and whispering the words, "Little dick" in Malleus's ear, as we tailed yet another one of his positively hideous cars. But when we got there, the factory gates were even taller than those of his vulgar monstrosity of a home. No way we'd be able to infiltrate this mammoth fort with its spiked, barbed wire fences and manned security cameras, unless we worked there or owned the place.

Just how in the hell were we going to get close enough to this asshole, for me to look him dead in the eyes and wish him to death?

He was either tucked up safely in his mansion, surrounded by the metal and glass of some overpriced luxury sports car, or cocooned within the confines of his monumental eyesore of a factory. We'd been following him around for days now, and not once had we seen him outside of his home, outside one of his many tacky rides, or outside of his factory. The closest we *ever* got to him being outside was his brief commute to and from work.

The only way, I could see, for us to get close enough to him was to somehow grab his attention from the side of the road. Slow him down, one way or another. Persuade him to wind down his tinted driver's side window. If we could do *any* of these things, then maybe, just maybe, we would stand a chance.

First off, we tried me lying by the side of the road, playing dead, with Malleus screaming for help.

Next, we tried Malleus waiting to cross the road with a white cane at a pedestrian crossing, and again this asshole didn't stop.

Finally, we tried me hitchhiking at the side of the road, wearing – or should that be, *hardly* wearing – a scandalously skimpy outfit. Scantily clad with my ass showing just a little and my boobs pushed up. But he didn't pull the car over to crawl the kerb. He just honked at me – according to Malleus – as he flew by in a flash of garish yellow.

Sat on the edge of the kerb, defeated, I told Malleus that perhaps we would just have to find someone else for this experiment I was conducting. Nora, the post office clerk, being the first name that sprang to mind.

"You're not going to kill Nora," Malleus said, shooting me a knowing look.

But this guy, I told him. This asshole we'd been following around for days and days now, was untouchable. His house, his car, his factory. All completely and utterly impenetrable.

But if I could have seen past the jet-black lenses of Malleus's sunglasses, I would have also seen the sheer, unfailing determination that was still behind his eyes.

"You really want to get this guy, don't you?" I asked him.

Malleus hid his lips just inside his mouth and nodded, *Yes*.

"Why?" I asked him.

"I have my reasons," he said.

We had to keep trying, he told me. That if anyone deserved to be part of this deathly experiment of mine, it was this guy.

I told Malleus to give up. That it was pointless. Futile. But, ironically, all my words did was fall on his deaf ears.

"All we have to do is get him to stop," Malleus said, more thinking aloud than actually talking to me.

Oh my lord, I thought. *Tell me something I don't already know.*

"Get him to stop," Malleus kept repeating. "Get, him, to, stop. Get. Him. To. Stop."

And I don't know whether it was because of the early mornings or the late nights, when I exploded with, "*What are we going to do, Malleus? Stand in front of this asshole's factory gates, yelling and waving stop signs?!*"

Too exhausted to realise why, I thought it was just the shock of my outburst that had caused the look on Malleus's face. And with just enough excess energy to do so, I told him, "Sorry." I thought Malleus, like myself, was all out of ideas. But when I looked up at him from down at my worn-out feet, it appeared that an invisible lightbulb had just switched on above his head.

"What is it?" I asked him.

"Iris," he said. "You're a genius."

42

"The Lady Doth"

If you know me – and if you've been paying attention, you really, bloody well *should* do by now – I am not one to give up easily. I wanted to get this asshole perhaps more than anyone, but after Malleus and I trying what I thought was everything, I was too beat to realise that there may just be one, last thing I hadn't thought of.

"Say, again?" I asked Malleus.

"A protest," he said.

Not managing to sound even the slightest bit convinced when I replied with, "O … K?"

"Think about it," Malleus continued. "What would slow this guy down faster than, say, a hundred angry people all chanting away in unison? Every one of them, armed with banners and signs, right outside the gates of his factory."

"Go on," I told him.

"If we can somehow put that together," he said, "we've got him."

I prepared dubious words to come raining down on his parade, but he just kept right on marching with his own.

"If we can get that many people on board for a protest," he said, "he will have no choice but to come to a complete stop before his security intervenes to let him through."

"And what about all that tinted glass he'll be behind?" I asked.

A fair point that caused Malleus's tongue to cease its flapping for the first time in minutes. And even though I couldn't actually hear it, I could see that he was mumbling to himself, before he burst out with, "Eggs!"

"Did you say, '*eggs*?" I asked him.

"We'll just throw eggs at his car," he said.

"But we're here to potentially *kill* the guy," I told him, "not vandalise his car."

"Don't you get it?" he asked. "If he can't see out of his windscreen, on account of all the egg goo, he'll be forced to open his driver's side window, to better see to drive through the factory gates."

I didn't want to be a naysayer. This was a great idea of Malleus's. I just didn't see how we would pull off something that big. And even though he couldn't see my face, he could somehow tell what expression I was wearing on it, by my pensive silence.

"I know what you're thinking," he said.

"You do?" I asked.

"You're wondering where we're going to get all those people from."

I nodded.

"Iris?" he asked.

"Sorry," I said. "I mean, yes."

"You told me that you gained quite the following," he went on to say, "after that little speech you made at Amy's memorial."

And if I wasn't as blind as he was, I could have seen where Malleus was going with this.

"You were wondering what good you could do," he said, "with all that newfound popularity."

"Yeah," I said. "But what has a protest got to do with Amy?"

"I don't know," Malleus said.

Which really meant that he *did* know.

"You could tell them Amy was some big environmentalist or something," he said.

I still wasn't getting it.

"This factory," he said, "is the biggest one of its kind in the country, and to blame for most of the waste plastic that ends up in the river here."

"How do you know all this?" I asked him.

"It's no secret," he told me. "Everybody knows, and yet nothing really gets done about it."

"Well," I said. "If you're so passionate about it, why don't *you* do something?"

"Oh, believe me," he said. "I've wanted to for a very long time now. I was never able to do anything like this on my own. But together, me and you, I believe we could."

After Malleus's little speech, I decided to humour him. After all, he had humoured me about the abilities I may possess. *Perhaps this was it,* I thought. A way for Malleus to finally let go of whatever he clearly harboured for this gigantic prick and his equally enormous factory. And a method for me to test out my possible powers on an ideal candidate, who, if anything, far more deserved it than the other two test subjects I already had.

And so, with all this in mind, I set my mind to it.

Sat in the university head's office, he studied me from across his desk; eyes full of consideration as he petted his cat – a grumpy looking thing with a very distinctive ginger-and-white-striped coat. This was the very next day, when I was asking the head's permission to organise a peaceful protest in the late Amy G'dala's name.

I told him about the factory, and how it was responsible for most of the waste plastic ending up in the nearby river. That I wanted to lead a group of students in a peaceful protest outside the factory gates. How my aim was not to cause disruption, but to heighten awareness of plastic pollution, and to educate the university's students of the powerful action they could take.

I told him about how I knew Amy. *All too well.* How it was such a tragic loss for us to lose her the way we all did. *Good riddance.* What a keen environmentalist she was.

As if she cared about anything but herself. And lastly, what an incredible opportunity it would be to do something in Amy's name. *As if I gave a solitary fuck.*

Obviously, I didn't care about all this, but the head of the university stroking his stupid cat didn't know that. And I don't know if it was because he felt sorry for me being deaf, or because Amy was no longer with us, or that plastic waste was an issue close to his heart, or a combination of all three. But it must have struck a chord with him. For as he stroked his grouchy looking cat, pensively considering the idea, he took a deep breath in and gave me the green light to go ahead with the protest, on the one condition that no more than a hundred students could attend.

Things were moving speedily, and it was so refreshing not having to wait so long for something I wanted so badly, for once.

I knew I'd be making the announcement the following day. What I *didn't* know, however, was that it would be to well over a thousand students. I never would have believed that we would get the sheer volume of signatures we did. That I would have to turn away almost nine hundred people. Telling them, thank you, but that I wouldn't be requiring their services, after all.

Nothing quite like the environment, and a protest in the memory of a popular dead girl, to use as an incentive for a whole load of clueless dimwits getting on board with your own personal cause.

The protest was actually going to happen, and it was all thanks to Malleus's witty genius and my silver tongue.

Not forgetting Amy's modest contribution of being dead.

43

"Never Been Closer"

The whole crowd winced in unison as I brought the megaphone up to my face, to address the one-hundred-strong audience before me. And I couldn't be sure, but it must have been because the bullhorn I held in my trembling hand had whined with feedback. Me, looking down on them, and them, all looking back up at me. Waiting intently for my first words as I lifted the hand-held public address system to my mouth and pulled the trigger to speak. Pointing it at them like a firearm loaded with bullets forged from words.

This was about a week later, after my little meeting with the university head, where one hundred students and I – all of us wearing pink and green bibs over casual clothes – marched to the lofty gates of the colossal factory, on what was a particularly drizzly and dreary morning.

Over the heads of my fellow protesters, I could just about make out the shape of Malleus, stood, at some distance, against the darkened bark of a tree.

But this was no ordinary protest. It wasn't really a protest, at all. It was an experiment in determining whether or not I had a deathly gaze, under the guise of a peaceful demonstration outside the factory gates of the globally known fizzy drink, Type 2.

But with the pressure of so many expectant eyes laid upon me, I had all but forgotten the real reason we were all gathered here today. *Was this what it felt like to be popular?* Having everybody's complete and undivided attention, like nothing existed to them right now but me and my megaphone.

I always wanted this: to be favoured. To be needed, respected and adored. But now that I had it, I felt unclothed and on show. Less of a worshipped diva, bathed in limelight, than a tacky stripper, sliding up and down the greasy pole of some seedy strip club. I could feel this nauseating lump rising up in my throat, and yet there was no way I was going to throw up with this many people watching.

Peering past the crowd to where Malleus was still leant against the trunk of that tree, I then looked down at the very recently safety-checked, makeshift soapbox I was stood upon. Tugging nervously at the hem of this hideous pink and green bib I was wearing, all too conscious of how much attention it was calling out for with all of its screaming colour. One hundred young men and women all holding their banners and signs in eager anticipation to get on with the protest. And after a slightly more confident throat-clearing cough, I began to speak to the crowd.

"Fellow students!" I cried out. "Thank you all for coming out today!"

And there must have been another whine of feedback, because, just then, I saw one hundred faces wincing all at once.

"And what a miserable day it is, too!" I added, looking up at the ominous, purple-grey cloud above our heads. Mouths in the crowd stretching wide with tongues flapping inside them. The look of raucous laughter.

I smiled at the crowd's reaction, but inside, I was dancing the lambada to it.

"But let's remember what it is we're doing here," I continued, "and who we're doing it for."

The crowd appearing to cheer as one, as I said the words.

"We're here to make a difference," I told them, "and we're doing it in memory of our beloved friend, Amy G'dala."

Just then, I could have sworn I heard a giggle.

The very same one I heard at Amy's memorial service. Not just in my head, but with my own ears.

Shaking my ears free of what they thought they'd just heard, I continued.

"We're all here for Amy!" I said.

And there was that giggling again.

"Who *is* that??" I yelled into the crowd.

A hundred baffled faces all looked at each other, and then back up at me.

"Whoever it is," I added, "please could you kindly stop! Let's remember what it is we are doing here. Have some respect!"

Again, giggling.

In the soundproof confines of my head, a voice, sounding very much like my own, told me that I was just imagining things. Perhaps it was the added pressure of every person here counting on me, and not having Malleus by my side. It *had* to be that. No way could I actually hear the singled-out giggling of somebody in a crowd. What about all the other sounds going on around me? The rain. The shuffling of impatient feet. The inner workings of the factory we were stood right next to. Plus – and I hope you don't need reminding here – the very fact that I'm deaf as a doorknob!

If it wasn't coming from somebody in the crowd, then just where was this giggling coming from? Wherever it was coming from, I would just have to do my best to ignore it, as, from the look on Malleus's face, it was clearly evident that I was beginning to lose control of the crowd. And I just stood there like an actor on stage, about to deliver their first line but not being able to remember, for the life of them, what it was.

Then I saw something.

Something that jerked me into remembering why I was here in the first place. A garish yellow sports car, heading our way at speed. And as much disdain as I had for the man behind the wheel of said car, he had, although unintentionally, awoken me from this nightmare of a situation, and for this I quietly thanked him.

Only to then close my eyes and mutter, *Shit!* when I realised it had slipped my mind to tell everybody to bring eggs.

Looking down on the riotous mob, and back up to the yellow sports car – showing no signs of stopping – the protesters turned as one and began chanting their rehearsed mantra. Practised words of defiance directed at the yellow sports car fast approaching the factory gates.

Just then, as if the one hundred protesters and I had called his bluff, not standing down, the yellow sports car came to an abrupt halt.

"Come on," I muttered to myself. "Don't chicken out now, you bastard."

There was only one way into the factory. Malleus and I knew this. After all, we were the ones that location-scouted the shit out of this place. The asshole had two choices at this point: he could either turn back and head home the way he came with his tail between his legs, or he could stick to his guns and keep coming.

But if he *did* choose to maintain his current course, he would have to do it slowly. Yes, he could drive full speed at us; pedal to the metal, force us out of the way. But a good businessman, as he clearly was, would know that this approach would be very bad for business.

Can you imagine the lawsuit that would be set in motion soon after he ploughed through one hundred and one university students during a peaceful protest? The papers would be all over it; the factory would be shut down; and no one in this industry would ever go near him again after an event like that. He would lose everything he had built. No way was he going risk that shitstorm when he could so easily avoid it.

No.

We would stand our ground, and he would have to choose between the two actions he was going to take.

The yellow sports car rolled on its wheels towards us, as cautiously as an inquisitive rodent crawling ever closer to a baited mouse trap. The crowd showing no intention of parting to let him and his canary-coloured car through. No doubt honking away on his horn, like an amateur boxer throwing clumsy punches but not landing a single blow. Nevertheless, he continued at the pace of a snail, in an attempt to pass through the horde, but again, the horde would not budge.

It was then I noticed boxes of eggs being distributed amongst my fellow protesters, from out of the depths of unzipped backpacks. The words, **'FREE RANGE'**, stamped in big, red letters on the sides of the boxes they came in. It seemed that many of my fellow protesters had brought along eggs without my requesting for them to do so. This was the plan, after all. To temporarily blind this asshole from the inside of his car, causing him to roll down his tinted windows. Thus giving me the window of opportunity I needed to look deep into this asshole's eyes and wish him to death.

And no sooner had a dozen eggs or so been thrown, the asshole's windows, ever so slowly, began to roll down.

I readied myself, knowing this would be the one chance I'd get to act out some sort of justifiable revenge on this asshole and all he thought he could hide behind. This whole peaceful protest thing just wasn't going to work a second time.

This was it, and I was ready.

Until I saw his face.

44

"Window of Opportunity"

I had never been closer to the asshole I'd been following around with Malleus all this time than I was right now. The both of us, piecing together a monstrous face collage of what we imagined he looked like from the fragments of information we had gathered.

But right here and now, in this big moment we shared with each other, I looked this asshole dead in the eyes and saw, not some evil reprobate, spewed forth from the depths of hell, but a man. A man that looked as if he'd had the fear of God put into him by a hundred enraged faces and pumping fists; all of them wielding banners and eggs. But then, I guess being challenged and held accountable for the harmful things he had done was probably something terrifyingly novel to him.

If he were the very spawn of Satan, that *might* have lived up to my expectations. But he wasn't. He was just a man, and looked nothing like the Frankenstein's monster I had conjured up in my head over the last month or so.

And because of this, I couldn't do it.

I just could not wish this man dead.

Looking into his eyes – as blue as my own father's – and his eyes looking right back into mine, I had no resentment for him at all in that moment. I didn't have the ability to resent him because he reminded me of someone I loved, dearly. What I'm saying is that I couldn't have wished this man to death if my life *depended* on it. I didn't really want this man to die. I just wanted him to not be so much of an asshole.

And then, the strangest thing happened.

He smiled at me.

Followed by the most unexpected thing.

His car door opening.

A hundred people with confused faces surrounded him as he left the safety of his car. One by one, banners that were being held high, gradually lowered. Pumping fists, relaxed. Eggs fell to the tarmac ground. Slowly, this man waded through the horde of protesters, showing no signs of fear as he calmly made his way toward me.

With his eyes still fixed on mine, and wearing that same serene smile on his face, he looked up at me from the foot of the makeshift podium I was stood upon. And me, looking back down at him, as if a chimpanzee, dressed in a three-piece suit, had just *Poof!* suddenly appeared out of nowhere and asked me to climb aboard its spaceship.

The way he offered his hand was similar to the way you would offer your hand to a friendly dog to sniff, before petting it. I assumed it was the megaphone, now held limply by my side, that he wanted. And since he hadn't snatched it from me, like he so easily *could* have, slowly, I handed it to him as he gently took it from the loose grip of my hand.

It was then he offered his free hand for me to take, helping me down from the lofty heights of this makeshift pedestal I'd made for myself. I stepped down, and he stepped up, taking my place on the soapbox.

By now, the crowd had calmed to a gentle simmer.

And I'll never forget the look this man gave me as his eyes smiled one last time, before they looked up at the one-hundred-strong crowd before him as the megaphone was brought up to his mouth.

With the mouthpiece of the bullhorn covering his lips, he said something I couldn't quite catch. But he couldn't have spoken more than a few words as, just seconds later, he stepped down from the podium, embraced me the way a father would his daughter, and casually handed back the megaphone. Making his way back through the crowd, similarly to the path he had made for himself from the security of his vehicle to the podium.

Walking right past his car; driver's side door, still open. Keys, still in the ignition. Strolling up the road, without even the briefest of glances back, he began tearing items of clothing from his body;

first his jacket, then his tie, his shirt, his trousers, his socks, his shoes. Ripping them all off and tossing them aside. Leaving a pretty-penny trail of designer apparel and bespoke made footwear behind him as he strutted, with cheerful intention, down the street.

It all came off.

Even his underwear.

He was stark, bollock, naked.

And yet this man appeared not to give a hoot. Like he just didn't need them anymore. As if he didn't need *anything*.

I could not believe, nor make sense of it. One hundred and one pairs of eyes all looking on as the man who had everything, strolled away with nothing. Not even the shirt on his back. We all, the crowd and I, just watched him go, in utter disbelief.

Everyone, except for Malleus, of course. Who I would, after the event, have all this to explain to him.

Had this been the most successful peaceful protest in world history? Or had something else happened here, entirely? Had I done this?

If that was the case, it was yet *another* theory for me to process. And instead of determining whether or not I had the power to kill, telepathically, this one little experiment of mine, if anything, had merely provided me with the outcome of raising even more questions.

Snapping out of the dumb daze I found myself in, I swiftly told the one hundred students before me, "Good job," and that they were free to go.

And now that I'd gotten rid of all of *them*, I could finally speak to Malleus.

The very first thing Malleus asked me, once the crowd had dispersed, and the remnants of banners and eggshells had been cleared away, was, "What just happened?"

And I would have given him a straight answer. That is, if I really knew what in the hell had just happened, myself.

"What did he mean?" Malleus asked me. "What did he mean, when he said, 'You have opened my eyes'?"

"So *that's* what he said!" I exclaimed, my words exploding all over Malleus's question like eggs on a car windshield.

"Now, tell me truthfully," Malleus said. "Did you wish him to death like we planned?"

But feeling caught out by the question, like he somehow already knew the answer, I went quiet.

I could have lied. I could have told him that I tried, but, for whatever reason, it didn't work. That maybe I didn't have a power, after all. But I didn't want to lie to him anymore.

Thing is.

Would he even believe the *truth?*

I told Malleus, I wasn't able to. That I simply couldn't wish the guy dead. How, instead, I looked that man right in the eyes, and just wished he wasn't such an asshole. And how it seemed that, in an instant, he had changed. How this colossal prick got out of his car, made his way to the front of the procession, said the few words he said, and then left, butt naked, down the street.

Obviously, this made no sense to Malleus. It made no sense to *me.* But that's what happened, and I had nothing else *for* him.

"You expect me to believe that?" Malleus asked me, his face looking like that ominous cloud hanging over our heads. The one that could break and pour down on us at any moment.

"I don't expect you to believe *any* of this," I told him, "But I do expect you to believe *me.*"

"That guy knocked my *house* down to build that factory!" Malleus yelled at me. "That guy's the reason I'm homeless!"

And right then, it all becomes clear.

Why Malleus was so intent on getting this guy.

But Malleus, without another word, pulls his phone out, sticks an earbud in his left ear, and I'm just way too late in realising as he leaves me. Me, stood here in the rain, as wet as I was the other day, when that asshole soaked me with dirty water at the side of the road with one of his stupid, yellow, sports cars.

Usually, Malleus would 'look' back at me as he walked away. But not this time. And now that he was gone, I was alone. Except that *this* time, I really felt it. Alone. I was all alone.

"No, you're not," a voice said.

The words slapping the self-pity off my face.

"But you're going to wish you were," it added.

The world span around me; my wide eyes frantically darting

about to see no one in sight.

How could I hear this voice, clear as day?

"Wait?" the voice said. "You can hear me?"

"Of course I can hear you!" I told the voice.

But this didn't make any sense. Surely I wouldn't be able to hear a thing, even if that person was stood right next to me. Even if they were speaking directly into my ear with their mouth pushed right up against it.

I was deaf as a doorknob.

So how come I could hear this voice?

And without me saying a word, the voice replied, "Because I'm a voice inside your head."

45

"Tulpa"

The moment I heard the voice's last words was also the moment I started walking, hastily, and with intent. Marching, double time, before breaking into a sprint. I was headed home. No way was I about to start a conversation with a voice inside my head, in public.

As soon as I was back in my room, I closed and locked the door behind me, threw down my personal effects, hit the lights, and drew the curtains.

"Alone at last," the voice said. "So good that we're finally getting round to talking."

"Get out of my head!" I commanded the voice.

"My God," the voice said, as I happened to look down at the floor with my hands planted either side of my face. "That carpet really is 'a choice'."

"What do you want from me?" I asked the voice.

"From *you?*" the voice said. "An apology would do for starters."

"What are you doing in my head?"

"What is it that you *really* want to know?"

I was actually doing this: talking to myself in an empty room. Seriously considering the question a voice inside my head was asking me. *I've finally gone and done it,* I thought. I had, at long last, gone utterly, raving bonkers.

I figured what was happening here must have manifested itself as a voice in my head from all the craziness of the past month. This journey of mine; following complete strangers around for the purposes of some twisted experiment had ultimately landed me in destination fruit-loop.

"Ding, ding!" the voice said. "Here comes the nut bus!"

"Quiet!" I told the voice. "I'm trying to process here!"

"Well, come on. Don't keep a girl waiting. If you had just one question, what would it be?"

And I would've had to have thought about it, if I didn't already know. What troubled me was that perhaps the voice knew, too. And so, resisting the urge to ponder for too long, I simply asked the one question that burned all the others I had to ask to cinders.

"Who are you?" I asked the voice.

"I think you already know," the voice replied.

"I don't. I really don't."

"After all these years, you don't recognise my voice?"

I foraged every dimly lit, dark patch of my mind for the memories of the voices I *did* remember. Turning over every mossy stone of recollection in my desperate search for the face that belonged to this voice inside my head.

"But I haven't heard a voice in years," I told the voice.

"Oh yeah," the voice said. "The whole 'deaf thing'. Sorry. Slipped my mind."

"How did you know I was deaf?"

"Oh, there's not much I don't know about you. But I guess my voice has changed somewhat, since the last time *you* heard it, at least."

"We *know* each other?"

"More like, knew."

I would have wracked my brains at this point, that is, if they weren't already wracked.

"Can't you just tell me who you are?" I asked.

"Not a chance," said the voice. "This is just *way* too much fun. Most fun *I've* had in … God *knows* how long."

"Just how long have you been *in* my head?"

"Hard to say. After a while, I just stopped counting the days."

"So how come I'm only hearing you now?"

"I guess I finally found my voice."

"Well, I really wished you hadn't," I told the voice as I paced the length of my room. "I can't deal with this shit right now."

"Yeah, well. Tough titty."

"I don't want this," I told the voice, my hands cupped over my eyes as if that would shut the voice out.

"Do you really think this is what *I* wanted?" asked the voice. "Being stuck in *your* head?"

"This is so much worse for me. *I'm* the one that's stuck with *you*, not the other way around."

"You sure about that?"

"Look. Just leave me alone, OK?"

"And just how am I meant to do that, exactly?"

I was on my knees at this point, my hands clasped over my ears, and summoning everything that was within me. I laid, stretched out on that commercial-grade, almost burgundy, carpet with my face down and screamed, **"LEAVE ME ALONE!"**

And there was silence.

For me, there's always silence. But *this* silence was the most silent I had ever heard.

"Hello?" I called out unsurely, as I looked up from the darkness of the floor.

Oh my God, I thought. *It'd worked.*

Until it hadn't.

"You're not getting rid of me *that* easily," said the voice.

"Please leave me alone," I said, on the verge of tears. "I'm begging you."

"Oh, come on. Even a girl like *you* can beg better than that."

"You don't know what this is like for me."

"I don't know what this is like for *you?* What about what it's been like for *me?*"

"Like for *you?*"

"There I was," the voice said, "sat in the university canteen. Laughing and chatting away with our lover-boy, Malleus, when I see you giving me 'this look' from across the room. One minute, I'm just sat there, quite happily, and enjoying a gluten-free panini. And the next, there *you* are, giving me the uber-evils from the other side of the room. Our eyes lock, and for some reason I can't look away. Next thing I know, I'm looking back at myself from the opposite side of the room, except that *now* I'm lying in a heap on the canteen floor."

I fought to hold back my tongue, but it was hopeless to fight. The name was going to slip by my lips in the time it took for a few dreadful seconds of realisation to pass.

"Amy?" I asked the voice.

And just like the day she showed up at my front door in a mess of tears; mascara running down her face like rivers of black oil.

All she had to say for herself was, "Hello again, Iris."

46

"Catch Up"

Most people grow out of their imaginary-friend phase early on in life.

Those that don't, get diagnosed and medicated.

We had a lot of catching up to do, Amy and I. Although, I figured she probably knew everything, already.

"So …" I began.

"How did I come to be a voice inside your head?" Amy asked me. "You tell me. I only know as much as *you* do at this point."

Or as little, I thought to myself.

"Or as little," Amy said.

Could she hear my thoughts?

"Yes," Amy said without me saying a word. "I can hear your every thought, Iris."

Oh my God, I thought to myself, *she can hear my thoughts.*

"Oh, do get over it," Amy said. "I have."

"Well, I'm sorry," I said. "But you've had plenty of time to think about all this. I'm still catching up."

"All I know is," Amy began, "one minute I was in the university canteen with Malleus, you shot me the dirtiest look from the other side of the room, and I somehow wound up behind your eyes looking back at myself, dead on the floor."

I quietly probed every neuron in the expanse of my brain.

"There's no point doing that, Iris," Amy said. "I've already looked at everything there is to *look* at in here."

But I was too busy comb-searching my log of memories from that day, to listen.

"You really don't know, do you?" asked Amy.

"What are you having a go at *me* for?" I said. "Neither do you!"

"And I also wasn't the one who killed *you* from across a university canteen. So don't you be having a go at me, either. I was quite happy that day until you showed up with those killer eyes of yours."

"Well, so was I!"

"If you were so happy, then why did you have to go and kill me the way you did?"

"Hold on a second. Are you saying that I *did* kill you?"

"Well, duh!"

"With just a look?"

"Yeah, but you should have seen yourself, Iris. I mean, 'if looks could kill'."

"So, I *do* have a power?"

"If you could call it that."

"I knew it! I really *do* have a power!"

"Yeah, well. I've known for quite some time now, so do me a favour and move the fuck on already."

"Holy shit."

"What did I just say?"

"Sorry. This is just a lot to take in."

"A lot for *you* to take in? *I'm* the one who was murdered and wound up in your fucked-up head."

"Hey! Less of the 'fucked-up', thank you very much."

"I'm not apologising for that. And as long as I'm stuck in your head, I will say whatever I goddamn well please."

"Look," I told Amy. "I am truly sorry for what I did to you. But you have to believe me when I say that I never really meant to end your *life*. Sure, I *wanted* you to die at the time. I even shot you a look that told you that I *wished* you were dead. But how was I supposed to know that 'that look' would actually *kill* you?"

"Are you done?" Amy asked. "Because I am literally forgetting what you're saying as you're saying it. You may not have meant to kill me, but you were quite content lying through your teeth at my memorial service. Stealing all my hard-earned friends and turning them into your ass-kissing followers. Not to mention the unashamed glee you felt after you thought you had gotten away with my murder."

I choked and stuttered, saying, "That simply isn't true, Amy."

"I think it is," Amy replied. "In fact, I *know* it is."

"How do you know? How could you possibly know how *I* feel?"

"Because I'm in your head, Iris. I know everything that's going on in this crooked landscape you call your mind."

And Amy would have felt it in that moment, if she, too, could feel what I felt. That rush of cold blood, sent coursing through my veins by my heart pumping like the galloping hooves of a startled horse over hard terrain.

"That's right," Amy said. "I know what you're thinking and how you're feeling. I see what you see, feel what you feel, taste and touch everything the same way you do."

I'm never doing anything ever again, I thought to myself.

"Speaking of," Amy said. "I also know who you've been … *ahem!* 'self-servicing' to every night before bed for the last few months."

I stuck both fingers in my ears whilst making a *La, la, la, la, la, la, la, la* noise with my tongue.

"Oh, like *that's* going to make any difference!" Amy said. "Just do us both a favour and *sleep* with the damn boy already!"

"Nope!" I said. "Not listening!"

"I'm still getting used to not being able to hear anything other than your voice and mine," Amy said. "Still. Better to be deaf than dead, right?"

I think I'd rather be dead, I thought.

"And," Amy's voice continued, "I *do* have access to all your memories and deepest, darkest secrets to keep me entertained for *two* lifetimes in here."

And right now, I'm doing my very best not to recollect *any* of them.

"I can even hear your thoughts as you think them," Amy's voice told me.

"That's enough!" I yelled. "You're a voice in my head, and I'm not talking to you for another second!"

"Correction. A voice in *our* head."

"*I'm* talking! This is *my* head!"

"It was my *life*, Iris! You took my life, so I'm taking your mind. I'd call that a fair trade."

"No," I said, shaking my head in an attempt to throw Amy's

voice from out of it. "Not happening."

"All that's going to do is give us both a migraine," Amy's voice told me.

"I'm not talking to you anymore."

"Oh really? Like you get to make all the decisions in here."

"I'm going to bed," I told Amy's voice. "To sleep."

"Oh yeah?" Amy's voice said. "Good luck with that."

47

"Hey Baby"

At first, I ignored it. Then, I *tried* to ignore it. But after the longest of hours had passed, ignoring it, and *trying* to ignore it, it seemed, was no longer an effective approach.

Amy's singing began the moment my head hit the pillow. And when I say, 'singing', I mean it in the loosest possible sense of the word. Whether Amy was tone deaf or doing it intentionally, I had no means of telling. But, either way, she full well knew how much I loathed this particular song – the one she was currently murdering with her lack of vocal ability – as she had access to all my thoughts and memories.

And sitting bolt upright, my patience spent, I yelled at the top of my lungs and screamed, *"OK! OK! I'm up! I'm up!"*

"You did well to ignore me for that long," said Amy's voice, "seeing as how much I know you detest that particular song."

I was now sat up in bed, my face smothered in the darkness of the palms of my hands.

"I always found it quite catchy," said Amy's voice, "but seeing as you don't, and now that you're up and I have your attention, let's talk."

"I'm so tired," I told Amy's voice. "Can't we talk later?"

"Nah."

"Just give me one hour. Please."

"An hour?! I've been stuck in here for God knows how long now, I've only just found my voice, and now I can finally talk, you don't *want* to?"

"I just need some time to get my head straight."

"There isn't anything to *get* straight. Everything's all bent out of shape for good because of you."

"I know, and I'm sorr-"

"Yeah, yeah. We've already covered this. And all the apologies in the world aren't going to help you change the fact that, if it wasn't for you, I'd still be alive right now and not trapped in the mind of a complete psychopath!"

"But if you've already waited this long, surely another hour won't hurt?"

"Maybe not for you, but then you weren't the one who had to do all the waiting around inside somebody else's head."

"I can appreciate that, bu-"

"Never knowing when it was going to end. It's been pure, unadulterated hell."

"It sounds awful. Truly, it does."

"And just for the record, I *hate* coffee."

"You do? But we both had coffee that day you just showed up out of the blue."

"We're getting off topic. And maybe no talking out loud from now on. Someone hears you, and realises you're having full-blown conversations with yourself, you're going to get yourself locked up in a nuthouse, and I'm pretty sure that would suck vast amounts of donkey dick for the both of us."

"But how can I speak to you if I don't use my mouth?"

"*I* don't have a mouth. Just think the words. I'll hear them."

This was going to take some getting used to. Like learning to speak the King's English all over again. Just without the use of my lips, teeth and tongue.

"But speak up," Amy told me, "because there's a lot of noise in here. I can pretty much shut most of it out, but you've got one crazy loud brain."

"This is so messed up," I said out loud for the last time.

"You don't need to tell me."

"Perhaps I could just keep my voice down for now. Just until I've got this whole 'talking inside of my head' thing down."

And even though Amy didn't actually *say* the words, I could just tell, somehow, that she agreed.

"Maybe we should come up with some ground rules," I said. "That is, if you're not going anywhere, anytime soon."

"All thanks to you," Amy's voice chimed in.

"Let me finish. We're going to have to learn how to co-exist."

An endorphin-like sensation in my mind, telling me I'd piqued Amy's interest.

"You're in my mind," I continued, "and you experience all my limb movements and senses."

"Kind of stating the obvious," Amy said, "but, check."

"Except that you cannot control them, whereas I can."

Amy managed to stay silent for just long enough for me to continue.

"So," I told Amy, "I'll be the one in charge, as I'm in command of the body."

"That's not fair," Amy said. "Just because I'm a mind without a body, doesn't make me any less in charge. And let's not forget who it was that put me here in the first place."

"But I didn't *mean* to," I told Amy, "it was an accident. How was I supposed to know you were going to drop down dead and wind up in my head, just because I threw you a look?"

"You may not have *meant* to," Amy said, "but you *wanted* to. You *revelled* in it. You took *advantage* of the situation. You literally got away with my murder!"

"Alright," I told her. "I'll admit I did enjoy it just a tinsy winsy little bit. I wanted you to die, and then, you did. But after everything you did to me, don't you think you maybe deserved it? I mean, what if we were both to go back in time and switch roles, and I did all those horrible things to you? Wouldn't you have secretly wished me dead, too?"

Amy didn't say a word, but her silence could have filled the pages of an entire journal.

"As for you occupying the free space in my head," I told her. "Do you really think I wanted that?"

"You may not have wanted it," Amy said, "but perhaps you deserve it. I mean, this way you haven't really gotten away with my murder at all. Now I can spend the rest of your sorry life, in your head, making you pay for what you did to me."

"But, I thought we were going to talk about how we could make this work for the both of us?"

"After this little exchange we've just had, I think you've just fucking convinced me otherwise. I think, instead, I'm just going to come up with ways to make your miserable little life a living hell."

After that, it was as if the mute button on the remote control of Amy's voice was jabbed on by her own spiteful finger.

Amy was living rent-free in my head, and now I wasn't sure how to evict her.

And as I sat there on the bed, my face back in the darkness of the palms of my hands, I thought about all of the terrible things that had ever happened to me, and how *this* thing had to be amongst the very worst.

48

"Stare Down"

Imagine being stuck in a lift for eternity with your very worst enemy. Now think of the elevator version of your most hated song playing on repeat through a tinny, crackling speaker.

My life, true to Amy's word, had become a living hell.

Hounded by her wherever I went, everything I attempted to do became an impossibility. I couldn't sleep. My appetite was lost. Every time I took a sip of coffee or a drag on a cigarette, she would sing that wretched song all the louder. The mundane day-to-day things I had so taken for granted all this time, affected to the point of being unbearable. And if I never again heard the song Amy was singing to me on a vicious circular loop, it would be too soon. She had taken over my entire life, and I could see that if I didn't make some kind of deal with Amy, the voice inside my head, it was just going to go on like this …

… forever.

I told myself, I wouldn't give up. That I would just simply ignore this voice. Hanging on to the hope, in the hell that had become my life, that the voice would eventually fade into the background. I made a solemn vow to myself, if I could just withstand this torture for as long as it took to get my mind back, I would eventually come out the other side with my life as well.

But Amy wasn't giving up that easily either.

It had become some intense staring contest, with both participants standing to win or lose everything. I could feel my stinging eyes, struggling to stay open, welling up and about to blink. And after many, many, uncountable, torturous hours of this battle of straining peepers, I finally retreated to the quiet place that was my room, surrendering to the superior force that was Amy.

"Alright, Amy," I said to her, in a tone filled to the brim with all the desperation it had collected in this single day. "You win."

"One day, four hours, and three, whole minutes," Amy's voice announced. "I'm impressed."

"What is it that you want, Amy?"

"Finally! The right questions."

And suddenly, without Amy's atrocious singing voice bouncing off the walls of my mind, I realised just how quiet it was to my ears that usually heard not a sound.

"What I want," she told me, "is for you to do whatever I tell you to do. And in return, I promise not to slowly drive you insane."

So completely beat I was at this point, all I managed to say in return was the word, "Fine."

"I'll give you what's left of today to rest," Amy said, "but make the most of it, because, come tomorrow, I will return and my demands will begin."

And with a worn out "OK" from me, she was gone.

But even with her not around to punish me, and the sheer bliss of the silence I ordinarily took for granted, I wasn't able to savour the rest of the day for the not knowing of what would follow when the night made way for the morning. Granted, I knew she would be back, but what exactly was she going to make me do that would satisfy her wants? And was it co-existing that she was interested in, or was it more that she wanted, to exact revenge on me for what I had unintentionally done to her?

One thing I knew for sure, however.

And that was that I certainly wasn't looking forward to finding out.

49

I never even bothered to set an alarm to wake me up that morning, for I was more than certain I'd be getting all the help I needed with that.

"BRRRRRRRRRRRRRRR!" Amy's voice rang in my ears. *"This is your early morning wake-up call!"*

And it's a good thing I wasn't sleeping on the bottom bunk of a bunk bed when I lurched forwards, awake, otherwise I would have woken up tomorrow with a sizable bruise on my forehead.

"Get yourself up and dressed!" she barked. "We've got a loooong day ahead of us!"

And right then and there, not a moment after that rude awakening, I just had this inkling that this was going to be the first of many woeful days ahead of supreme and absolute purgatory.

Once I was up and dressed, I checked my reflection in the full-length mirror, like I always would, before leaving the safety of my opinion-less room.

"Seriously?" Amy said. "*This* is what we're going out looking like?"

"What's wrong with what I'm wearing?" I asked her.

"It would be quicker to tell you what's *right* with it."

"Want me to change?"

"Don't bother. If this is a fitting example of the sort of clothes we've got to work with, we'll be here all week."

"This is how I dress, so you're just going to have to deal with it."

"Careful."

As we headed out the door, I asked Amy what she was going to make me do first.

"How about some clothes shopping?" Amy replied, a hint of sarcasm telling in her voice.

"C'mon, Amy," I said. "I'm being serious."

"First, a coffee. After all, I know how you can't start the day without one. Better make it a ristretto. This is going to be quite a day."

She almost managed to sound as if she actually cared.

At least I'll be getting my caffeine fix, I thought. *That is, before the hellish first day of the rest of my miserable life commences.*

Once at The Daily Grind café, we (Amy's voice and I) craned our shared neck to see if the barista bitch was working that morning.

"All in good time, Iris," Amy's voice assured me.

"I don't know what you're talking about," I said under my breath, looking down at the ground.

It's only then that I realise just how dirty the floor is.

"I know the plans you have for this one," Amy told me. "This barista bitch of yours. We'll get round to her when the time's right."

And even though Amy was just a voice in my head, I could tell, somehow, that she winked after she had said it.

"How's about first we use your powers to get that hunky barista guy to sleep with us?" she said.

"Hunky barista guy?" I asked.

"You know," she said. "What's his face? Bryan? Brandon? Brady?"

"Who, Brad?"

"Brad! That's the one!"

"Can we please just get a coffee first? I haven't even woken up yet."

That's when Amy clicked her tongue.

"Oh, for goodness sake, Iris," she said. "You're such a muffin muzzle."

Now at the front of the queue, I thought about my order.

"You're going to order a chai tea latte," Amy said, abruptly.

But I don't want a fucking chai tea latte, I thought to myself.

"This isn't about what *you* want, Iris," she said, interrupting my thoughts. "Not anymore, it's not."

They say, the only two things you have control over in life are your thoughts and your actions. And now it felt as if I'd lost all control of even *them*.

I couldn't believe what was about to transpire. This would go down as the very worst thing that had ever happened to me in a coffee shop. And a very decent one at that. Behind the counter was an industry-standard grinder of freshly roasted coffee beans, a state-of-the-art espresso machine – complete with a milk frother and thermometer. An expertly trained maestro barista, fully competent in carefully crafting a beverage of perfect temperature, consistency and aroma, just for me.

Here I stood, in an independent café, with all of its wondrous ways of consuming freshly prepared coffee, and actually about to order myself a weak, watered-down beverage with the overpowering taste of appalling spices.

The hench barista guy, 'BRAD' – from his name tag – said something to me from behind the counter. I figured he was probably asking me for my order, but I hesitated just long enough for Amy to start singing that damn song she'd been punishing me with all of yesterday.

"Alright!!" I screamed.

But not in my head.

Out loud.

The barista guy's mouth looked as if it used God's only son's name in vain as he bolted upright from the counter.

"Sorry," I said, composing myself. "A chai tea latte."

"Decaf!" Amy added.

"Are you fucking kidding me?" I muttered under my breath.

"Oh, and you forgot to say 'please'," I heard Amy say from within my head.

"Decaf," I tell the barista guy. "Please."

The look on the barista guy's face when I said it: "A chai tea latte." Like I'd just ordered a flower vase of liquidised squirrel with a dusting of powdered gherkins.

"I'm trying new things," I told his troubled eyes.

To which, he merely looked at me a little less strangely.

"See?" Amy quipped out of nowhere. "That wasn't so hard now, was it?"

I pulled a grimace.

"I thought we were here to get coffee?" I muttered through gritted teeth.

"If I had told you we were off out to grab a chai tea latte," she coolly replied, "would you have still come down here?"

"Fuck no," I told her.

"Well, there you go then," she said.

She was already inside my head, and now she was getting right under my skin, too.

Grabbing mine and Amy's takeaway cup of freshly prepared disgustingness, I thanked the barista guy, if not perhaps rather unconvincingly. Looking down at the cardboard cup in my hand with a look of pure revulsion masking my usually socially acceptable face, as Amy and I both headed out the door of the café. The door having not yet shut behind me as I took a cautious sip from the ribbed cardboard cup, spitting out what I had just sipped immediately afterwards.

"Uurgh!" I said in a spew of shitty-coloured liquid. "Gross!"

Resulting in me getting some very odd looks from some of the customers sat outside.

"*What?!*" I squawked at them all as I took another sip and spat it out in much the same way I did the first time.

You should have seen the looks I got for *that*.

"Oh, for goodness sake," Amy said. "Take a proper sip and swallow this time."

And there's me, battling the mighty sensation of intermittent retching. Forcing myself to swallow the truly vile beverage down a throat that just would not accept it.

"Ahhh," Amy said, after I finally managed to keep this revolting drink down. "That's better."

I used the sleeve of my coat to wipe my mouth, but that awful taste still lingered, sat on my tongue and lining my throat.

"I don't normally drink this shit," she added, "but I figured I'd give it a go. Horrible, agreed. But your reaction was so totally worth it."

"Fuck you, Amy," I said under my breath.

Tossing the rest of … whatever the hell that drink was, in a roadside drain, I threw the cup in a nearby bin before rummaging around in my bag and pulling out a pack of cigarettes. Even burning tobacco had to taste better than that drink I'd just been subjected to.

Flipping the packet lid open, I slipped out a cigarette from the pack and lit up.

"Jesus, fuck!" Amy said, coughing hard.

"What?" I asked as best I could with a lit cigarette still between my lips.

"Sucking on that cancer stick the way you are!" she said. "Are you trying to kill us *both?!*"

"You don't smoke?" I asked her, fast losing my enthusiasm for how this morning was going.

"No, I don't!" she said. "I mean, I *used* to. But I quit, like, well … some time ago."

"Oh right," I said. "Why *did* you quit?"

"I don't know," she said. "I guess so I wouldn't die so young."

We both fell silent for a moment.

Before the both of us burst out into an uncontrollable laughter that made our shared jaw ache.

We were still just a stone's throw away from the café; people in the outdoor smoking area all looking over at us with screwed-up faces. Muttering amongst themselves in a plume of vape smoke, wisping up from their e-cigarettes.

I imagine this scene wouldn't have looked quite so crazy if Amy had actually been there in person and laughing with me. We would have just looked like a couple of fun-loving gals, buzzing on caffeine and having a good time. But she *wasn't* really here. She was in my head.

And I must've looked like a lunatic.

Especially when I glared over at a group of hipsters congregated outside the front of the café and screamed, *"Oh, you're just jealous because the voices are talking to me!"*

50

Seeing as the both of us occupied the same mind, I figured Amy and I really needed to be on the same page as well. And so, too weary to care how she would react – after the whole café fiasco – I decided to confront Amy, the voice in my head, with some ground rules of my own.

"We need to make this fair," I told her, taking a pew on a nearby bench.

"Fair for me, or fair for you?" she asked.

"Fair for the *both* of us."

"Go on."

"You like chai tea lattes, and I like flat whites," I began. "You don't smoke, and I do."

"I never said that I actually *liked* chai tea lattes," Amy quipped in with.

"The point is," I told her, "we both share the same space in my head. I think it's only fair that we make some compromises with the things the other person likes and dislikes."

"Fair?" Amy said. "Let's talk about fair. I was alive and happy. You killed me. I got stuck in your head. That's on you. And now you want to talk about *fair?*"

"Do you really think I actually *wanted* this?" I asked her.

"But you did want me dead, right?" she said.

"I did, but-"

"You got a certain, sick satisfaction from it, did you not?"

"Sort of," I said, looking down at the ground littered with dog-ends.

"You'll get to fill your lungs with tar once we're done talking," she told me.

The promise of my next nicotine fix being all I needed to snap myself out of the longing for it.

"If there was some way I could go back," I told her, "I would never have looked at you the way I did that day. I would never have wished you dead."

"Only because now you have to put up with me as a voice in your head," she snapped.

"I was jealous," I told her, "and that's the only reason the thought ever popped into my mind to begin with."

"Jealous?" Amy asked. "Because of *Malleus?*"

"Seeing the two of you together like that," I told her, "I just couldn't hold back the thought of wanting you to die."

It was as if Amy shifted to get comfortable within the cramped confines of my mind before she asked, "Want to know the very last thing that went through my mind before I died?"

I didn't ask her. I just let her tell me.

"I wished that I was you," she said.

"But, why?" I asked. "Why ever would you want to be *me?*"

"Because," she said, "Malleus was never going to love me the way he loved you."

So taken aback by her words, my words had been taken from me.

"You can have that cigarette now," Amy told me.

But I didn't light up. Not right away. It was as if the blaze of the grudge I'd been holding onto for Amy all this time had been extinguished by her words.

"I could really do with a proper coffee, too," she added. "If you don't mind?"

And upon hearing those words, I have never stomped to a coffee shop so hastily.

To say we got a few strange looks, as we walked back through the door of the café, would be a massive understatement.

"Don't mind them," Amy said to me from within our shared head. "I never did."

I couldn't believe that I was even thinking it, but I was actually starting to appreciate the company of Amy's voice. It made me feel more self-assured somehow. More assertive.

"Why, thank you, Iris," Amy told me.

It kept slipping my mind that she could hear my every thought.

And by the time I'd realised it, I had jumped right to the front of the queue; the hench barista guy giving me that look again from behind the counter. All those waiting patiently behind me, no doubt muttering away between themselves about the brazen girl that had so rudely pushed her way to the front of the line just now. But why should I care what these people had to say about me? It's not like I could hear them. Plus the fact that I was here with the most popular girl in town.

Technically.

"A flat white, please," I said to the barista guy with a beaming smile upon my face.

"What's that?" I asked Amy.

To which, I added, "Fuck it. Make that, two."

Granted, I *was* acting like a bit of a twat this morning, but the people around me, they were complete and utter twats on a full-time bases, and really had nothing to say on the matter.

Grabbing the freshly prepared coffees from the hunky barista guy, I looked down at the sorry looking beverages in my hands and wondered why my usual love-heart hadn't been drawn atop of the velvety milk. And with looks of utter contempt from some of the other customers, I threw them all back a look of my own.

"Oh, go fuck yourselves," I told them all.

To which I quickly added, "No, don't!" as I suddenly realised what might happen if I didn't, before exiting through the door of the café with my head down and making a beeline for the nearby park.

"Before we go any further," Amy began, as we sipped on a coffee that, for whatever reason, didn't taste quite as lovingly made as usual. "I just have a few ground rules of my own."

Setting our coffees down on the bench we were sat upon, I promptly stubbed out the best cigarette these lips have ever sucked on.

"Then," she added, "we can get on with the sordid business of living together."

Amy's brief silence allowing me the time to sit as comfortably as I was able before she began.

"Firstly," she announced, "no doctors or therapists, and absolutely no medication to suppress me."

"Gottit," I said simply, observing the all-seriousness in the tone of her voice.

"Secondly," she continued, "no recreational drugs or alcohol to drown me out with."

"But I don't *do* dru-"

"And most importantly," she told me, "you are not to talk to anybody about my existence as a voice inside your head."

Not even Malleus? I thought to myself.

"Especially not Malleus," she told me.

"I've got to keep this all to myself?" I asked her.

"All to *our*-self," she said, correcting me.

I fell silent as I thought about what Amy was asking of me. I shared *everything* with Malleus, and him, with me. How was I going to keep something this big, to myself?

But then I was reminded by Amy that she held all the cards, and all *I* had was a crappy hand. So, really, what choice did I have? And so, mindful of all this, I reluctantly accepted her terms.

"So what now?" I asked her.

"Let's take a walk," she said.

"Where to?" I asked.

"Let *me* worry about the 'where'," she said, "you just worry about the walking."

"And don't fret," she added. "I won't make you take the underpass."

51

"Checking In"

We hadn't been walking for the time it took to order and prepare a decent cup of coffee – with Amy tagging along for the ride in my head – when we came across a place Malleus and I knew all too well. Just this time with its gates swung wide open, and ground-workers swarming the area the way ants do a dropped ice-cream cone on the pavement. Scaffolding covering everything you could see, and everywhere there were contractors, all beavering away with impressive synchronisation.

With so much activity and so much now missing, the place was almost unrecognisable. For where we were now standing, Amy and me, was the entrance to the once gaudy mansion of the asshole who once lived there.

Even the brass house sign that once read 'Mi Casa' had been removed and all of the god-awful yellow cars, along with the ghastly water fountain statue, were gone from the driveway.

Clearly a lot had changed since the last time this big CEO and I had locked eyes. And me wishing him to be a better version of himself had to have had at least *something* to do with it. But as to what was taking place with the bustling spectacle before us, I had no idea.

"Can we stop here for a minute?" I asked Amy.

"Keep it moving, Iris," she told me. "We've got shit to do."

"Just give me five minutes."

"First you ask for one, now it's *five?*"

"Five and no more."

Amy went silent as if to consider the request, but before she got the chance to reply, I saw Richard Heard – the big CEO, formally known as '*the total fucking asshole in the banana-yellow sports car*' – emerge from what was now just a square-shaped hole where the front door used to be.

I could tell, from her silence, that Amy was still mulling my gentle demand over, but I figured a heartfelt *Please!* couldn't hurt in tipping her decision in my favour.

"You've got five minutes," she finally replied. "And I'm timing it."

In a grateful whisper, I thanked her, rushing over to where the big CEO was, calling out his name as I did.

"Mr Heard!" I called out. *"Mr Heard!"*

But so lost amongst the mix of the organised chaos, I simply wasn't getting his attention.

"Richard!" I yelled. *"Richard!"*

Still, not even a head turn from him.

"Oi!" I hollered, in one last ditch effort. *"Dick!"*

The look on the big CEO's face as he turned to look in the direction my voice was coming from; braced, mouth open and eyebrows raised.

This initial expression of startled concern, instantly relaxed into a gentle smile, his eyebrows settling, upon seeing who the voice belonged to.

Handing a clipboard to a man wearing a hard-hat with a suit, he began making his way toward me, arms outstretched, the way I imagine the father of the prodigal son's would have been, as he saw his boy, off in the distance and returning home.

After gently pushing me away to get a better look at a face he wouldn't anytime soon forget, and grasping my shoulders to award me with the most earnest of embraces, only then did he speak.

"My darling girl," he declared, in much the same manner an old friend would. "So good to see you."

I sensed something in this man had truly changed for the better, and for the first time, it filled me to overflowing with positivity about the powers I possessed.

Once he'd released his keen hold on me, I asked him plainly what it was that he was doing here, and he told me. But thinking I may have misread his lips, I had to ask him again.

"A shelter for the homeless," he said, his voice full of the good kind of pride.

I asked him about the factory, too, and he assured me nobody would be losing their jobs. That the factory was to be revamped into a plastic-waste recycling plant; terminating, as of immediate effect, the production of the fizzy soft drink, Type 2. The plastic manufactured for the bottles of said drink, including waste plastic from other sources, would be recycled into clothing for the homeless; who would then be given free residency in the brand-new, state-of-the-art facility that was previously this CEO's home.

Telling me, he never needed all that space, anyway. That he was living far larger than he should have. It was "high time", as he put it, he did something truly worthwhile with all the wealth and power he possessed.

And for whatever reason, I thought about the powers *I* possessed.

"Just enough," he said, "is the right amount."

Politely, he told me that it had been truly wonderful to see me, but that he had much to do and very little time.

"Yeah," Amy said from within my head, "I know the feeling."

Richard told me that he and I would speak again, no doubt. But just before he left me to return to all the coordinated chaos going on behind him, he told me that he knew my friend, Malleus, from way back. That he recognised Malleus when he saw him stood under a tree during the protest. The very same tree this big CEO walked right by, butt naked, and back down the road to his stately residence just days ago.

Malleus, he said, was the last person he saw that day as he made his way back to the mansion, and it was only once he had reached home, did he then have the realisation of who the boy under the tree was. Malleus would've just been a scared little fifteen-year-old blind kid, the last time he saw him, all those years ago.

This man, this big CEO, who now had a name and wasn't just some faceless monster, never forgot about Malleus, try as he might. But it wasn't until the day of the protest did he then have his eyes opened to what he had done to the lives of so many people, Malleus included. And now that his eyes were fully open, for perhaps the first time in his life, he planned to make amends for the trail of devastation he had left in his wake.

Starting with the boy who used to be that fifteen-year-old, blind kid.

Richard slipped both hands into his trouser pockets, his left hand pulling out what looked like a business card. A business card that had little to no purpose, now that the soft drink Type 2 was no longer being mass-produced at that colossus of a factory.

Taking a gold pen from his jacket pocket, he clicked the little, diamond button at the end of it and scribbled something on the back of the card.

"Here," he said, handing it to me.

Taking the card from his hand, I couldn't help but be quietly impressed by its thickness and its smooth, matte finish as I looked it over. On the front read the words, *"Richard Heard, CEO of Type 2"*. It was only when I flipped the business card over, did I then see that he had scrawled, in a hastily enthusiastic manner, his private phone number on the back.

"Be sure to tell Malleus to give me a call," he said.

And offering the gold pen for me to take, he told me to keep it.

"You opened my eyes, Iris," he said, his hands clamped to either side of my shoulders.

Was this powerful business tycoon about to cry in front of me? Stood just outside the gates of his own sculpted empire?

"Thank you," he said. "You have changed my life and the lives of many others."

And with that, he was gone. Back into the hustle and bustle of busy ground workers, and disappearing into the bowels of the house. A building, slowly transforming into something that would benefit so many more people than the one man who barely lived there before them.

I just stood there, awestruck. Looking down at the hefty gold pen in my hand and back up to the astonishing spectacle before me. Taking it all in with a quiet, yet hopeful, disbelief.

"Whoa," Amy's voice came from within the confines of our head. "What exactly *is* this power of yours?"

Still lost in wonderment, I'd almost but forgotten about her.

"I'll let you know when *I* know," I said.

And Amy, pedantic as ever, and always having to have the last word, quipped in with, "I'll know when *you* know, anyhow."

52

"Unfinished Business"

Stood on two aching heels and ten sore toes, Amy and I were finally on the opposite side of the street to the place she wanted to bring me to. I say, 'bring me', it was more like 'bring *her*', as I was the one doing all the walking for the last ten thousand steps or more.

"What are we doing here, Amy?" I asked her. "My feet are killing me."

"What do you *think* we're doing here?" she said. "We've got some unfinished business to attend to, of course."

Looking back at us was a pawnshop. The very same one I visited a while back when I bought that duplicate smart phone. A phone I so foolishly used to make a recording of Malleus bringing a dead pigeon back to life.

God, I miss that guy.

Malleus, I mean.

Not the pigeon.

I knew as soon as Amy had answered my question, what she meant by 'unfinished business'. Back when I was in the process of putting a list of three people together to become unknowing participants in an experiment to test, what I thought at the time, were simply my potentially deathly powers.

So much had happened since the time I'd first chosen this particular test subject, that I had entirely forgotten about their part in these twisted little trials of mine.

Just being here, again, gave me a taste for a retribution I had lost somewhere along the way. But now, as I looked across the road from the opposite side of the street, my eyes being led by the stripes of a zebra crossing, up to a sign in the door that read, **'OPEN'**, in red, neon letters. And me, just about able to see past the warped glass of the shop window; squinting my eyes to peer inside and see that mean ol' bastard behind its distorted surface. His feet up on the counter and reading a newspaper. Those very same tortoise-shell spectacles rested on the end of his nose.

Yeah.

That kind of brought it all back in floods.

53

"Trampling On Eggshells"

Pushing open the door to the pawnshop and stepping inside, I turned the sign on the door over from *Open* to *Closed* as it shut behind me; twisting the brass knob to the left, locked.

Pretending to take great interest in all the gadgets and gizmos aplenty that surrounded us, we thought to ourselves, Amy and I, about what it was exactly that we wanted to wish for this particular miserable old bastard of a shop keeper.

"Let's just kill him and get it over with," Amy piped up from inside my head.

"Hush now!" I hissed under my breath. "Let's really think about this. I mean, we still don't even know if this is going to work."

"Seriously?" Amy hissed back. "You've already killed *me*, and caused a big CEO to do a complete one-eighty-degree turn. Of *course* this is going to work!"

The miserable old git, still behind his counter, folded his newspaper in half to throw us a look. Tutting, his top lip pulled up in a snarl, he shook his paper and disappeared behind it again.

Sure, he was a miserable old codger. He appeared to be a lot of unsavoury things from what I'd gathered of him as a person on my last visit, but did I really want to end his *life* over it? Sudden death for him was a step further than I desired to tread with this guy. And now that I'd recently found out that I did indeed possess a power, and that it was so much more than a mere deathly gaze, I had discovered that it was more of a commanding influence than a deadly weapon to kill with.

I had to remind myself that it was *me* who came into *his* life, and not the other way around. He never waltzed into *my* room, it was *I* who had walked into *his* shop. All I need do for this man to not exist in my world was to never again set foot in this place.

It was just that, back then, when I was still working out whether or not I had an ability, and in need of participants to play crucial roles in an experiment to test my possible powers out on, he was close enough – in my eyes at that time – to being an ideal candidate, in that he would not be missed. That being the primary reason this grumpy old git had made it to the shortlist. But now that I'd had the revelation that my powers were so much more than I initially thought they were, I could now do some good with them.

This crabby, over-the-hill geezer – no doubt reading all about how the whole world was going to hell in a hand-basket, from behind that counter – probably wasn't always like this. But a hard life, with all the things it so generously gives and then cruelly snatches away, had more than likely shaped him into the disagreeable old miser I could see, sat behind his desk. Held up in his shop like a socially inept hermit, and shutting the world out. Barely existing, let alone living.

I mean, sure, I *could* kill him, with all that in mind.

But I could also do something even better.

I could make him *live* again.

I made a guess in my own mind that this old boy was pushing seventy, which meant he still had time to live out the rest of his life to its fullest. So that's what I decided to wish for him. I walked right up to where he was; hiding behind his big, barrier-like desk – which I'm willing to bet he found safety from being behind – with all of its solid wood, thick glass and dense steel coming between him and anyone who entered his domain.

"You again," the mean old bastard said, more to himself than to me. "What do you want *this* time?"

I just looked at him. I looked him dead in the eyes. And he looked right back into mine.

A look of utter contempt adorning his down-turned face as he removed his feet from being rested upon the desk he was sat behind. Standing up to full stature – and yet still shorter than I was by a head's height – he removed his tortoise-shell spectacles and set them down, leaning forward in my direction, his hands planted arrogantly on the counter. And that, right there, was the moment his expression faded from one of annoyance, to one of sheer wonderment.

I had him.

"Now that I have your complete attention," I said to this lonely old man, who didn't look quite so cocky now, "let me tell you what it is that I want."

Maintaining my arresting stare on him, I continued.

"I want many things," I told him, in a quietly confident tone. "But for starters, I want you to be nice to me."

He just gazed back at me, bug-eyed.

"In fact," I continued, "I want you to be nice to *all* the customers who come into this little shop of yours."

His mouth looking as if it were stuck in an eternal, silent scream; shock and awe adorning his face as I said the words.

"And whenever someone comes into the shop and says, '*It's like an Aladdin's cave in here*'," I tell him, "you're going to laugh like it's the first time you've ever heard it."

The old boy was on his way down to being on his knees at this point, as Amy whispered from inside my head.

"What?" I asked Amy. "How do you know that? Huh? How come you can read minds all of a sudden? Whatever."

The old boy blinked, looking as if he were coming around again, before I fixed my stare back on him and said, "You have a wife."

Amy whispering some more to me, the way a close friend would whisper a secret in your ear.

"She's in the hospital," I said.

Amy's whispers continued.

"You're having an affair with another woman," I hissed.

I could tell this old boy wanted to look away from me, but, for whatever reason, he couldn't.

"You hate yourself for it," I told him.

Amy whispered to me some more.

"But not enough to not do it again," I growled.

That's when this old boy started talking to God.

"You are to break off this affair," I told him, "and you are to never tell your wife or anybody else about it as long as you live."

Amy whispered some more to me.

"You are to call your sons as soon as you return home," I said down to the mess of a man by my feet. "You are to play a bigger role in their lives from now on."

Try as he might, this old boy couldn't look away.

"You've got all the time in the world," I told him, "so spend it on the things that truly matter, and not on all this toot."

Whisper, whisper.

"Get in touch with your old friends," I told him. "Some of them may even still be alive."

Whisper, whisper.

"Oh, yes," I said, "and sort out that mess of a garden of yours, would you? Have some gratitude for the things in your life."

Coming to a halt with my words, I asked Amy, "Is that everything?"

We had literally reduced this old boy to a shell of the man he once was. It was as if he were a brittle, hollowed-out egg with everything that was inside of him all sucked out.

"Yeah," Amy casually replied. "I think we're done here."

Looking back at him from the door to the shop, the old boy was still just knelt there, bawling like a big baby by his desk. All that guilt and shame, that self-pity and self-loathing, just blubbing it all out.

The old boy looked as if he could do with a few minutes to himself, so I left the *Closed* sign as it was when I went to grab the brass doorknob. But just before Amy and I made our grand exit, something came to mind, last moment, and we locked the door again.

Rifling through my pockets, I pulled out a gold pen. The very same one Richard Heard, that big CEO, gave me earlier today.

"Oh," I said, as I made my way back over to the sorry heap on the floor that was this old boy.

"There is one, more thing," I said, standing over his trembling, curled-up body.

Slowly, he looks up at me. The same way a puppy would, after being caught ripping a brand-new bean bag to smithereens.

And holding up the heavy gold pen for this shell of a man to better see, I politely asked him, "How much will you give me for this?"

54

"Eating for Two"

Amy and I made our grand exit from the pawnshop, my handbag now stuffed with every last note, and rattling with every last coin from the drawer of the shop's cash register.

"That's everything I have," the pawnshop owner had snivelled as I handed over the heavy gold pen for him to take.

But the shared elation Amy and I felt, as we waltzed out the door to the shop, soon wore off now that we were back out on the drab grey of the street. I mean, how exactly does one follow what we'd just done? It's not like we'd grabbed a cup of coffee just now.

"Let's go get that barista bitch," Amy suggested a little *too* enthusiastically.

I forgot she could hear my thoughts. Probably my fault for thinking about coffee.

"Haven't we done enough for one day?" I said to her, more as a plea than a question.

To which she replied, "Fair enough." A hint of disappointment telling in her voice.

It can't have been easy for Amy being stuck up there, the way she was. I would have found it near enough unbearable, so she was doing pretty well in my mind.

Get it? 'In my mind.'

"How's about I treat you to lunch?" I asked her. "But only as long as you don't get me to eat anything gross."

"Now why would I do a thing like that?" she asked me. "After all, I'd have to eat it, too."

"I just want to be clear. I am not going to be letting you put any quinoa or tofu anywhere near my mouth. Shared or not."

"Don't worry your pretty little head. What the fuck is 'quinoa', anyway?"

"So what'll it be?"

"Well. Seeing as how I can't get fat anymore, I guess I can pretty much eat whatever I want."

"Hey. Anything you want."

"*Anything* I want?"

"Anything at all. We can have *lobster* for all I care."

Amy hummed, as if to consider the question.

"Take me to Old McFarmer's," she said. "What I want is a grande patty."

Have you ever taken a bite of a burger to the sound of screaming orgasms coming from inside your head?

No.

Neither have I.

Amy's moans of ecstasy reverberating off the walls of my mind as I chewed and swallowed.

"Oh my God!" she moaned. "That's *soooo* good!"

"Could you keep it down?" I asked her through gritted teeth. "You're embarrassing me."

"Don't stop! Faster! Faster!"

"If I eat this burger any quicker, we're both going to choke to death on the damn thing. Now could you *please* stop showing me up in public."

"Oh, would you relax. It's not like anyone here can actually hear me."

"Yes, but *I* can hear you. And right now you're acting as if you've never had a grande patty before."

"Just shut up and take another bite, would you? And chew harder!"

"Wait a minute. You mean to say you've never *had* a grande patty?"

"Oh, I've had plenty."

"Then why is it you're acting like such a meat-whore right now?" I asked her. My mouth so full of chewed-up burger and bread, only the muffled vowels of my words were making it out.

"Because I've never actually tasted one, alright!" she snapped.

I stopped chewing. My face all screwed up. "But you said you've had plenty before?"

"And I *have*," she told me.

"So why is it," I asked her, "every time I take a bite, you're having mouth-gasms up there?"

"Because! This is the first one I've ever tasted!"

"I don't follow."

Amy went quiet.

Quickly chewing and swallowing, I wiped my mouth with a napkin, and set the burger down.

"Well?" I pushed.

Amy threw a mumbled something at me that I didn't quite catch.

"Say, again?" I asked her.

"Anosmia!" she exclaimed. The word coming out, quick as a sneeze.

"Anosmia?" I asked her.

"Anosmia," she said, slow and sad. "I have anosmia."

I took a moment to ponder this word cloaked in vague familiarity. Knowing I'd heard or read it somewhere – more likely, read it – but not remembering to know what it meant.

"It means I can't taste anything," she said, the shame telling in her voice. "Well," she added, "not until I wound up in your head with a tongue that works, at least."

That's when another word came to the forefront of my mind, from all the way back there in the dark place of rarely used and forgotten words.

"You're confused," I told her. "I think you mean, 'ageusia'."

"Ageusia?" she asked me. "What the hell is ageusia?"

"The inability to taste."

"So then what the fuck is *anosmia*?"

"It means you can't smell."

"You're shitting me, right? So all this time I've been sounding like a total frickin' *idiot*?!"

"Oh, I wouldn't worry too much," I reassured her. "I always thought you were an idiot, and this is the first time you've ever told me."

Amy went quiet.

I'd meant it as a dig, but I could sense she was wounded by the humiliation that had just smacked her in the face, so instead of adding insult to injury, I kept things going by asking her, "Why did you never tell me?"

"I don't know," she said. "I guess so you wouldn't treat me any differently."

"Oh, Amy. I really wish you'd told me sooner."

"Yeah, well."

"Could've saved you from years and years of embarrassment."

"Oh, go do one, would you."

But even without actually having facial features, I could tell she said it with squinted eyes, a little shake of her head, and a wry smile.

And right then, between the last bite and the next, there was this beautifully rare moment between us; sat quietly in that busy fast-food restaurant, while the colours and shapes of people in a rush buzzed around us. A moment where we finally found that we had something real in common: a missing sense.

"Can we *pleeeease* finish the rest of this burger, now?" Amy asked me eagerly.

"Course we can," I told her, grabbing the burger with both hands and bringing it up to our mouth for another big bite.

"And do you think maybe once we've finished this one," Amy added, "we could maybe get another?"

55

"On Our Mind"

Sat, defeated, outside some deli called Graze, after demolishing most of a gargantuan platter of grande nachos set before us not fifteen minutes ago – that could have fed a small village, I might add – Amy and I pushed the plate of tortilla crumbs and leftover jalapeños away from ourselves; our shared stomach working overtime with the abuse of force feeding it had just taken.

"You miss him, don't you?" Amy asked me.

"Who, Malleus?" I asked.

"I know that's who you were thinking of just now."

"Don't *you*?"

"I miss the *sex*," Amy said, wistfully.

"Yeah," I said, lost in a daydream.

Before the words, "Wait. *What*?!" exploded from my mouth.

"Ooops!" she said. "Did I say that out loud?"

"You two had *sex*?" I hissed at her, not even believing the *question*.

"A few times," she said. "He was so desperate to lose his virginity, and I was more than happy to help."

And if Amy had a physical face for me to slap, I would have done so right about then.

"I've gotta say, that boy wasn't bad," she went on. "I mean, for a blind virgin. He *did* need a little help with finding the right hole to slip it in, but then, what guy doesn't?"

"Oh, Amy!" I exclaimed in disgust.

"Funny," she said. "That's exactly what *he* said just before he, well … finished."

230

"Ughh!" I said. "I now can't wipe that off my imagination."

And right then, as I held the horrible image of Amy and Malleus getting intimate with each other in my mind, I realised I'd never had my heart so cruelly crushed at the same time as almost having the contents of my stomach violently evacuated.

"*You* were the one to get that first kiss though," Amy said. "Could've done with a little more tongue, but what a kiss!"

"Oh my God," I said as I plunged my face into the palms of my hands. "You were there for that too, weren't you?"

"You should call him," Amy suggested. "Drop him a text or something."

And still processing that same horrible image, I told her, "Yeah. I don't know about that."

What I *did* know, however, was that the last time Malleus and I had spoken was after the protest, and *that*, as well you know, did *not* end well. But what was I going to do about it? I couldn't simply look him in the eyes and *wish* him to like me again. If my powers were wasted on him, I guess I would just have to do it the way everybody else did, and wait patiently for him to be ready to talk. Waiting back home seemed like the best place to do it. And the *only* place that I – or anyone else for that matter – was safe from the abilities I was still getting to grips with.

Not that she didn't know already, but I started the conversation with Amy, once we were back home and laid there on my bed, about some of the things on my mind.

"So, how come you were able to read that old boy's mind?" I asked her. "I know I asked you before, but we were kind of ... preoccupied."

"What?" she said. "The mean old bastard back at the pawnshop? Seriously? It's taken you *this* long to ask me again?"

"Well," I told her, "not that you didn't already know, but it *was* on my mind to talk to you about it."

"I don't know," she said. "I used to *think* I could do it. Mind read, I mean. Before I wound up in here. I would always have an idea as to what someone was thinking before they said it. All this is as new to *me* as it is to *you*. How the hell did you kill me with just a look?

How come I'm now confined to your head? I have no idea, Iris. I'm just going with the flow with all this."

I lay there quietly, slowly digesting Amy's words, along with the bad mix of food in our churning stomach.

"How long have you been able to do this whole *messing with people's minds'* thing?" she asked me.

Good question, I thought to myself.

"It's why I asked," she told me.

"I wouldn't call it 'messing with people's minds'," I said.

"Oh, no? What *would* you call it, then?"

"I don't know. Turning bad people into good people, I guess."

"And how is it that *you* get to decide who's bad and what's good for them? You're no saint *yourself.*"

"Neither are *you!*"

"Yeah, but I'm not the one with the mind-altering powers here."

"Do you think I *wanted* these powers? I didn't *choose* to have them."

"But you *have* been using them, haven't you?"

And if I suddenly had my hearing back, I imagine I would have just heard the deathly silence of the room; silent as the inner workings of my useless ears.

"How many people have you used them on, so far?" she asked, already knowing the answer. "So there's the old boy you reduced to a quivering wreck on the floor of his own shop. That big CEO that's now completely lost his mind. And then there's me, who you, with all intention or not, murdered."

And while I was doing my very best not to think it, she was, however, making some very convincing points.

"So, no, Iris," she continued. "You didn't *choose* to have this power, but you do get to choose how you *use* it, and whether or not you should use it, at all."

I thought carefully about my next words.

"Look," I told her. "I'm sorry for killing you, Amy. Truly, I am. And I'm doing my very best to make up for that by using my powers for good."

"Won't bring me back though, will it?" she seethed. "You could alter the minds of everyone in the *world,* and I would still be just as dead."

"But in a way, you kind of *have* lived on."

"Being stuck inside your head is no kind of living."

All I could think about was how sorry I was.

"Yeah, yeah, yeah," she said. "You're sorry. I get it. The word's just noise to me now."

She's right, I thought to myself.

"I *know* I'm right," she said. "I don't need *you* to think it, too!"

Clearly, the word 'sorry' had become a worn-out smudge. Like what I had done to Amy was the very thing I had so angrily written in pencil, and so desperately tried to rub out with the eraser of good deeds. And so, on the paper of my mind, I made a mental note to myself with the permanent marker of my memories to make no more apologies.

I just took her life.

But, *Amy*.

She had lost *everything*.

"I know I've asked before," I told her, "but is there *anything* I can do to make it up to you?"

"Make it *up* to me?" she asked. "You could spend the rest of your pitiful, little life trying to do just that, and you wouldn't even come *close* to making it up to me."

I went to say something more, but she, too, had something more to say.

"To do that," she went on, "you would have to somehow put *my* mind back in my *own* head, attached to my *own* body and, by some means, bring me back to life!"

Her words causing me to ponder the notion that there may just be a way to give Amy precisely what she wanted. For us to be even. Both of us free of this truly bizarre situation we had not long found ourselves in.

But first we needed somebody, and the incredible gift they possessed.

And that wasn't going to be so easy.

56

"Worth a Shot"

Here's the thing. Even if I *could* get hold of Malleus, let alone get him to *speak* to me, there was no way, in *my* mind, I would be able to get him on board with the plan I was formulating for Amy to get her own head and body back.

But there was still a hope in hell's chance it could work, and I felt we had to give it a shot, at the very least. I owed Amy *that* much. She owed me a lot, too. I was just too polite to point that out to her with everything else she was dealing with right now.

Firstly, we would have to locate Amy's dead body. Once we had done that, we would then get Malleus to bring her lifeless corpse back to life. I would look into her glazed-over eyes, that I imagined would look as if there were nothing behind them, being no mind inside.

No different to when she was alive, then, I thought to myself.

To which Amy blurted out, *"Fuck you, Iris!"*

Anyhow, I would look into her dead eyes and wish Amy's mind back into her own, job done.

"Nice plan," Amy said, "but just how are we even going to attempt to do all of that?"

And as simple sounding as 'the plan' was, she did have a point. I mean, at this point, we didn't even know where her deceased body *was*.

There were three places Amy's corpse was more than likely to be right now: the morgue, the medical examiner's facility, or the cemetery. It could still be laid out on a cadaver dissection table; sewn up in a Y shape with waxed string after an autopsy to determine the cause of death – which, I imagine, was still a mystery to everyone but

Amy and I – or it could just be buried in the ground someplace. But wherever her body was, we would still need the assistance of Malleus and his life-breathing powers.

The only problem was, and I did mention this to Amy – not that I needed to, seeing as she knew my thoughts the moment I thought them up – even if we *could* get Malleus talking, let alone get him to meet with me, it would mean I'd then have to tell him everything. That I *did* kill Amy with just a look, and that I know this, only because her mind somehow transferred into mine. That she had told me, in person, from the confines of my cerebral matter, that this was the case, and that I was now able to have full-on conversations with her in my head. And it was *this* thing that would remove any doubt left in Malleus's mind that I was crazier than a box of frogs.

That is, if that's what I *told* him.

I could just tell him *so* much. The truth, just not the *whole* truth, and a few other things thrown in *with* the truth. How bad I felt about Amy's death, and how I still entertained the idea that it was my fault, and that it was eating away at me from the inside. That if there was any way we could bring her back, that would alleviate the burden of the guilt I felt. The culpability that I was so sure would never leave me until the day I had put right my wrongdoings and brought her back to the land of the living.

We only needed Malleus for the *'bringing back to life'* part of the plan, the rest we could do ourselves. We would find Amy's body – and who better to find the body of a dead girl than the mind of said dead girl? Amy would help me find her own body, Malleus would work his magic, and I'd finish up by transferring Amy's mind back into her own head. Her mind gets returned to its rightful owner, and I, at long last, get rid of her as a voice in my head.

"Charming!" Amy piped up with. "I'm ever so sorry that I'm such an inconvenience to you. *I* being the one whose life was taken so prematurely. My mind now wedged inside your skull, and existing merely as a voice!"

She was sounding more and more like a broken record by now. A vinyl copy of the very worst song ever written. The one you were so sure you had broken in half over your knee weeks ago, and yet, here it had somehow magically put itself back together, grown legs, and found its way back onto the turntable to play for the umpteenth time.

It was time, I thought, *to take a sledgehammer to this particular record player.*

"You're not the only one that's suffered here!" I yelled out loud. "I've suffered too!"

Going on to refresh her memory of all the bullying I endured. The beatings and the backstabbing. The violent toing and froing of our toxic, bipolar relationship. The drastic loss in confidence I had for myself. The hearing loss! All the things that I had been subjected to, and how all those things were done to me or taken away from me intentionally. By her! Not to mention stealing Malleus away by feeding him lies about me. That what I had done to Amy had been an accident, and all I wanted was for everything to go back to the way it was before all of this insanity!

Amy, alive.

Malleus and I, on good terms.

And me, happy. *Truly* happy. For once in my entire, miserable life.

I never would have thought it, but for the first time since before Amy showed up out of nowhere as a voice in my head, I actually missed being deaf. Because all I heard from her after that was a sweet, sweet silence.

My sledgehammer, it seemed, had done the trick.

57

"Epitaph"

Perhaps it was because everything had already been said, or maybe this was just Amy's version of an apology, but quite some time went by with nothing said by either of us.

Finally giving in to the quiet that was incapable of producing any result, it was Amy that broke the silence by suggesting we go for another walk. And so, persuaded by her words for lack of having any bright ideas of my own, I left the hushed confines of my room with her. Where we were walking to, I didn't know. And as frustrating as it was that she knew my every thought, and I didn't know just one of hers, I'd still rather be the one in charge of the body and not stuck inside someone else's head.

At long last we arrived at the place Amy was leading us both to. A place I hadn't been before and wouldn't normally choose to go. Not until I was dead, at least.

"What are we even doing here?" I asked her.

"If you have to ask," Amy said, "then you deserve to be here, permanently."

Oh right, I thought to myself, whilst face-palming myself in my mind when the penny dropped.

"But, what about Malleus?" I asked her.

"Would you keep your voice down?" Amy told me. "There could be other people here."

"But, what about Malleus?" I asked her again as a whisper.

"We'll get to that," she told me, as we walked down a shingle path through the crooked landscape of headstones. "There's just something I want to check out first."

These places usually creep me out – even during the day – and so does death in general, but I *did* have the company of a ghost this time.

Sort of.

Amy asked me to keep turning my head, steadily, to the left and to the right. Scanning the graves either side of us as we walked at a snail's pace through the headstones. Some proud and upright, others leaning over and sunk into the ground. And in doing so, I couldn't help but be mindful of the fact that I must've looked like a right weirdo.

Amy told me to stop where I was and to head over to a modest, white, marble headstone she'd spotted. It couldn't have been there long, this particular headstone, as it was still so immaculate. A headstone, easy to pick out amongst the others that had darkened with decades of rain and moss and dirt.

Amy said for me to walk very slowly over to it, and to stay quiet. It was only when we were stood right in front of this particular headstone, could I then read what was written upon it. Amy asked if I could take a closer look, keeping my head still as she read the words etched into the stone.

"*Amy G'dala*," she read aloud. "*Two thousand and two, to two thousand and twenty-three. Beloved daughter, and cherished friend to all who were blessed in knowing her. She saw the rainbow through the rain.*"

A bouquet of flowers had been left against the stone's face, and, by the looks of them, very recently. White lilies. Coincidentally the very same colour as the pale, flowy maxi-dress Amy had picked out for me to wear on this little outing of hers. I counted twenty-one flowers, exactly. My eyes beginning to well up the moment I realised every flower left there likely symbolised each year Amy had lived.

"It's OK, Iris," Amy said to me gently. "You can cry."

Amy and I shared the same emotion at the same time, as our tears ran down my face.

"I know we agreed no more apologies," I said through the tears, "but I'm sorry, Amy. I am so, so sorry."

"I'm not crying because I'm dead, you dummy!" Amy said. "I'm crying because they got the colour of my headstone wrong!"

Quick as a reflex action, I looked back up at the white, marble headstone.

"Anyone who knew me," she said, "would have known my favourite colour was pink!"

I knew that, I thought to myself.

"'*She saw the rainbow through the rain*'," Amy scoffed. "What a load of soppy, sappy, horse-shit!"

I actually quite liked it, but I did my best to keep that thought to myself.

"And I *hate* white lilies!" Amy exploded with. "They smell like cat's piss!"

I looked back down from the gravestone to the lilies. And if Amy had knees right now, I reckon she'd be down on them and tearing those perfect flowers to confetti.

"Did nobody ever *listen* to me?!" she screamed from inside our head.

"*I* listen to you," I said, doing my best to sound encouraging.

"That's different!" she snapped. "You don't have a choice!"

Fair point, I thought.

"There's another reason I'm crying right now," she continued. "Just look at the ground."

"I don't see anything," I told her.

"Precisely."

"I don't get it. What am I missing?"

"The ground. It hasn't been touched."

"So?"

"If the ground hasn't been touched, it means they never dug a hole."

And me, the big numbskull that I am, I'm still not getting it.

"Meaning," she said, "I wasn't buried. I was cremated!"

This is when Amy began to laugh; just a nervous giggle at first, which then broke into a full-on guffaw.

"What could be so funny right now?" I asked her.

"*I* was the one who always wanted to be cremated!" she erupted with. "I went on and on about it all the time. I was so hell-bent on being cremated because I was so afraid of being buried alive!"

I didn't know what to say, and I didn't dare laugh.

"It's OK, Iris," she told me. "You can laugh."

But instead of laughing, I just giggled.

The way you do when you're in a place – a church or a library – where you have to sit in silence and behave yourself, which just makes the *not* giggling all the more impossible. It's contagious, too. Especially when you're sat next to the person that's *having* the giggling fit. And that's exactly what Amy was having right now: a giggling fit. Which I eventually succumbed to.

Like they say: *Sometimes all you can do is laugh, to keep yourself from crying.*

58

"Ways of Making You Speak"

And so, with no body to dig up and resurrect, the plan was rendered redundant. But what I was really disappointed about – and perhaps a little selfishly so – was that, with no dead body to bring back to life, there was also no need for Malleus. I did feel equally bad for Amy, as I had really got her hopes up about getting her own head and body back.

But say we *had* managed to pull this off – bringing Amy back – those classic good looks she'd been so reliant on would be long gone by now, having been an all-you-can-eat maggot buffet for the last several months. And even the most potent of designer perfumes wasn't going to mask that signature stench of rotting meat. Plus, how were we even going to *begin* to explain Amy's sudden resurrection to all those grieving students after her being dead for so long? I could just see the contorted expressions on all their faces, recoiling in horror as she staggered back into the university canteen; the zombie version of her former self, with her decomposed flesh and hollowed out eyes, and being all like, "Surprise!"

Obviously, it goes without saying that Amy knew all of this without me actually having to tell her.

As we left the cemetery, our hysterics now under our control, there was someone on our shared mind.

"We should just call him," Amy suggested. "I mean, what's the worst that could happen?"

But, in the short time I'd got to know him, I knew Malleus better than that. He got like this sometimes. He also clearly didn't like being lied to, and especially not by me.

But here's the thing.

I hadn't.

Just then, because I was thinking back to the day of the protest, and all that had happened with Richard Heard, that big CEO, I remembered the business card he gave me. It was still in the pocket of my coat when I put my hand in there to feel for it.

Maybe *that* was the answer.

If he, the big CEO himself, could tell Malleus exactly what happened that day, as ridiculous as it sounded, maybe *then* he would believe me. The saying *easier said than done* sprung to mind, but now all we need do was come up with a way to give Malleus the inclination to talk to me.

And even though they kind of were already, Amy and I put our heads together.

Oblivious to the passing of time – back in my room, where ideas were being thrown back and forth between Amy and I – we were so engrossed in coming up with a way for Malleus to start talking to us again, we had completely missed a text message come through from him, a good while ago, that simply read, *We need to talk.*

Sometimes, when you do nothing more but sit there and think, the answer presents itself. Admittedly, the text message was short and not at all sweet, but frankly, I was just happy to hear from him.

I replied to his text by agreeing that we really *did* need to talk, and arranged to meet with him at The Daily Grind café in the time it took to look presentable in public and arrive there on foot.

Amy made the suggestion that I make an effort; apply some smoky eyeshadow to make my eyes "pop". Perhaps a little "rouge" to make my lips appear fuller. Maybe wear something skimpy that accentuated my tits and ass. A recommendation I quickly shot down, gently reminding her that she was forgetting something of significance about Malleus.

I could literally show up wearing a bin liner, pink fluffy bunny-rabbit slippers for shoes, and peanut butter smeared all over my face, and he would *still* be none the wiser.

Even if Malleus *could* see, I knew he wouldn't be fooled by all that tacky slap and tarty clothing, anyway. Malleus liked me for me, regardless of what I looked like or how well turned out I was. He wasn't at all like so many other boys I'd heard about. And that's because he *saw* me. Not just what I looked like, but for who I was underneath all that false advertising of make-up and clothes. All the parts that most people, with their sight, missed completely. He wasn't with me just for my looks, he was with me for everything else. He wouldn't let me get away with bad behaviour or a nasty character trait just because I was beautiful. He saw the beauty within me, and loved me all the more for it.

He really saw me.

"Alright, alright, we get it!" Amy snapped. "Now quit fannying about and let's get out of here, already!"

Of course, Amy was right.

I just didn't admit it out loud.

My agreement with her was throwing on any old thing and heading out the door.

We spotted Malleus from some distance as we approached the café. He was sat outside – even though he didn't smoke, and there was a bit of a chill in the air – and it appeared he'd beaten us to ordering a coffee.

Once he was in earshot of us, I called out, "Hey!" But getting nothing back as a jovial greeting, I just made my way over to his table and plonked myself on the chair opposite.

"Wow, these chairs are cold," I said to him, looking for a suitable place to put my handbag and finding none. "You wanted to talk?"

"I'll go first," he said.

"Alright if I quickly grab a coffee?"

"This won't take long."

"Mind if I smoke?"

"I don't care if you burst into flames."

"So," I began, full well knowing the answer to my following question. "What is it that you want to talk about?"

"Why did you feel like you had to lie to me?" he asked.

"*Lie* to you? Why did you never tell me you were *homeless*?"

"Just answer the question, Iris."

"Lie to you about what?" I asked him playfully. "That doesn't exactly narrow it down for me."

"You know exactly what. That ridiculous story you told me, the day of the protest."

"But that's just it. I *didn't* lie to you."

"You really expect me to believe what you told me that day?"

"I know, more than anyone, how absurd it sounded. But it *was* the truth."

"Take me through it again. Tell me the whole farcical tale a second time, would you?"

"My story hasn't changed. So what's the point?"

"After everything we had to do, to get close enough to that guy. And you bottle it, right at that last crucial moment."

"I know what it looks like."

"Bad choice of words," Amy sneakily whispered to me from within my head.

"Quiet!" I snapped at Amy.

Malleus flinched, almost spitting out his last sip of coffee.

"I get that you're angry," I tell him, "and I'm truly grateful for everything you did to help me. Everything you just said is right. It'
s what happened *after* that, that you've got all wrong."

"Then, please," Malleus said, "enlighten me."

I took a deep breath, in secret. One only Amy and I would've known about.

"You're right, like I said," I told him. "I *did* have the chance to kill that guy. He was so close I could see the colour of his eyes. Blue, just like my dad's. And it was in that one little moment. That one, tiny, window of opportunity that I ..."

Malleus quietly judged me from across the table as my words trailed off into nothing.

"I just couldn't do it," I told him.

"So, you admit it then?" Malleus said. "You folded right when it mattered."

"Yes. But it was what happened *after* that was so strange."

Malleus put an earbud in his one ear as he got up from the table, saying, "I've heard all I needed to hear."

"Would you cut the amateur dramatics, and sit the fuck down," I told him, grabbing the sleeve of his black leather jacket in a tight fist.

And if Malleus could've seen the look in my eyes, he would've dropped down dead, right there and then.

"I couldn't look that asshole in the eyes and wish him dead," I continued. "*Not* because I 'chickened-out', but because death wasn't really what I wanted for him in that moment."

Malleus must have been literally glued to his seat. Otherwise, I fear he would have probably just got up and left.

"I just wanted that guy to be not so much of an asshole," I told him. "So that's what I wished for him."

And I just have this feeling that once I'm done with this little monologue of mine, Malleus is going to up and leave the very same way he did when he left me on the knobbly log.

"And then the strangest thing happened," I told him. "This big CEO. He gets out of his car, his eyes fixed on mine as he makes his way towards me through the crowd. He told me, just the other day, that I had 'opened his eyes'. I know you heard *that* much."

The only parts of Malleus that move are his shoulders when they shrug.

"And then," I continued, "after the few words he said up on that soapbox, he leaves. Through the crowd and down the street. He left his car just sitting there, keys still in the ignition."

There's this glint of light in Malleus's sunglasses as I'm talking. That same glint you see in someone's eyes when they're humouring some outlandish claim of yours.

"And I know you still don't believe it," I told him, "but he walked butt naked down the road, leaving a trail of clothes and shoes behind him."

I took a breather to centre myself.

"Now," I told him. "You can choose to believe me or choose *not* to, but that's what happened. I'm many things, Malleus. Deaf, and maybe even a little bit dumb sometimes."

From the way his mouth moved just then, I could tell he sniggered.

"But one thing I am not," I told him. "As of right now, at least. Is a liar."

I had no more words to persuade him with, but what I *did* have was the big CEO's business card with his personal number scrawled on the back of it.

"Give me your phone," I said to Malleus.

The way he looked at me. Like I'd just asked him for both kidneys.

"If you want the truth," I told him, "but you don't believe me. Then perhaps you'll believe it from someone else."

"And who might that be?" Malleus asked.

"The horse's mouth."

Snatching Malleus's phone off him as he reluctantly handed it over, I punched in the big CEO's number and hit 'save to phonebook'.

"There you go," I said to Malleus, near enough chucking his phone back at him. "Now someone that you might actually *believe* can tell you the exact same story *I* just told you."

Malleus held onto his phone as if I'd just snatched a newborn baby from his arms just now.

"I saved the number under '**N**'," I told him as I rose from the table. "'**N**' for '*Not* such a total fucking asshole'."

Malleus just sat there, aghast, as I pushed the most uncomfortable chair I've ever sat upon back under the table. Leaving him there; that dumbfounded look still on his face, as if the wind had just changed.

If Malleus didn't want to believe me, then fine. I had done and said all I could. And if this one last thing I did for him still wasn't enough, then at least I had someone who *did* believe me. Someone who saw the whole darn thing with my own two eyes, just as I had.

Even if they *were* just a voice in my head.

59

"Theory and Practice"

I should've felt bad about leaving Malleus at the café, the way I did, but it actually felt kind of good. Liberating, even. This must have been how all those empowered independent women felt on a daily basis.

"Alright, queen bee," Amy chimed in with. "Let's not get ahead of ourselves here."

"Huh?" I asked her. So lost in my thoughts of my own independence of men that I'd only just found the words Amy said.

"We need to talk, too," Amy said. "I think I may be onto something."

"Oh, yeah?" I asked her. "And what might that be?"

"The reason I wound up as a voice in your head."

"Not this again. If I had any idea as to why that was, you'd already know."

"Maybe you're like this collector of souls or something," she told me, a twisted sort of excitement telling in her voice. "Like, when you take a life, you absorb it or whatever?"

"OK. I think someone needs to take a lie down."

"Or. And get this. Maybe it was *me* that made the jump from my head to yours?"

"Jump? What do you mean by 'jump'?"

"I'm just saying. Maybe I have a power, too."

"Come on, Amy. That's pathetic. Even for a girl like you. Don't be such a copycat, it looks desperate."

"Why's that pathetic? *You* of all people have a power."

"That's different."

"Different, how? Malleus has a power, and you didn't believe *him* at first. Then he didn't believe you when you thought *you* might have a power. And now that I'm saying *I* may have a power, you don't believe *me!*"

What I had to say next, took a whole deep breath in before I could speak it.

"I think that you're simply just a voice in my head," I said. "A manifestation of everything shitty that's happened in my life."

"Oh, don't you quote your bullshit, psychology textbook, psychobabble at me," she said.

"I'm serious. I think the whole protest thing getting out of hand was the one thing that finally pushed me over the edge, and now I'm stuck with you as a voice in my head."

"*You're* stuck?! *I'm* the one who's stuck! And I'm not just some 'manifestation'. I'm real!"

"There's no point us arguing like this. Going back and forth the way we are isn't going to bring us any answers."

But silence was all I got from Amy as a reply.

"Let's entertain the notion that you may have a power," I told her. "I think it's quite clear by now that *I* do, even though I've only tried it out on two people so far."

"*Three* people," Amy chimed in with. "I never *did* thank you for that."

"Two, three, whatever. The fact is, I may have killed you with just a look. The question is, how did your mind end up taking occupancy in my head."

"Oh, 'occupancy'!"

"Oh, I'm sorry. Is that word not in your limited vocabulary?"

I took her silence as a 'yes' before carrying on.

"Either you, or me, or someone else has done this to us," I told her. "*I* certainly didn't wish you into my own head, and I'm pretty sure you didn't, either."

"Damn *right* I didn't!" Amy exploded with.

"So. There's still the possibility that somebody *else* did."

"But, who? Who would wish this on us?"

We were both reduced to a hush. A rarity for girls like Amy and me.

"Do you have any enemies, Amy?" I asked her.

"Is that really a question you need to ask?" she replied. "I mean, *everyone* has enemies."

"What about mutual enemies? Know anyone that hates us *both?*"

"Not that I *know* of."

"So, if no one hates the two of us, it's got to be that either you or *I* did this."

"But why would we do this to ourselves? *I* didn't want this, and you … you sure as *shit* didn't want this."

"Is it then possible that we did this by accident? Much in the same way I accidentally killed you?"

"Yeah … but really, you *did* want me dead."

"I don't know. Maybe the moment your body died, your mind, like you said, somehow jumped from your head to mine?"

"Actually. Now that I've heard *you* say it, it does sound pretty ridiculous."

"But hasn't *everything* that's happened of late sounded pretty ridiculous? I mean, to 'normal' people?"

"Speak for yourself."

"I'm speaking for the *both* of us. We are not ordinary people, Amy. And, like it or lump it, we have to accept this in all of its glorified lunacy."

And right then – after I'd said my piece – I could tell that Amy agreed with me. Not because I could read her mind all of a sudden, but because she didn't say a word in response.

She never interrupted me once.

Time passed as Amy and I talked, and as it did, it gave Malleus the time *he* needed to finally come round and forgive me for all the things I hadn't actually done wrong in the *first* place.

"You've got a pot of *tea* to make?" I asked him as we stood a stone's throw away from The Daily Grind café. "I'm pretty sure they can make one here *for* you?"

"No," Malleus said. "I have an *apology* to make."

"An apology? From *you?* I'm privileged!"

"OK, OK, get over it."

I didn't say anything. I just stood there, expectantly, with my arms crossed and my head on a tilt.

"This is me waiting," I told him.

"Waiting for what?" he asked.

"My apology."

"But I just did, didn't I?"

"No, you didn't. All you said was that you had an apology to make. You never actually apologised."

"Do I really need to?"

"Well, of course you do. That's how apologies work."

And with a face that didn't exactly convince me that he meant it, Malleus exhaled the smallest of sorries.

"I'm sorry?" I said. "I didn't quite catch that. I mean, I realise I'm deaf as a doorknob and everything, but even *I* had trouble reading your lips just now."

Those same lips of his, not moving.

"Oh, c'mon," I told him. "I've apologised to you *plenty* of times. All I want is just one, tiny expression of regret from *you*, for once."

"I'm sorry," he said. Spitting it out, quick, as if the words tasted like anchovies on his tongue.

"See? That wasn't so hard, now was it?"

I could tell Malleus was beginning to get a little riled up by now. He *had* just apologised to me. And here we were, talking again. So I swiftly changed tack before the both of us had the chance to run aground.

"Let's go get coffee," I said, as I offered my arm for him to take. "Shall we?"

But, of course, Malleus didn't take my arm.

"I'm holding out my arm," I told him.

To which he merely responded with a baffled expression.

"For you to take," I added.

Being spontaneously romantic with Malleus was close to impossible sometimes, but, on the plus side, I'd never once caught him eyeing up other girls whenever we were out together.

Every cloud.

And taking his arm in mine, I, for once, did the leading.

Amy promised to stay quiet while Malleus and I waited in line at the café. Usually, I hated standing in queues, especially for something as meagre as a cup of coffee, but it did give Malleus and I time to catch up. As I told him about the last few days, I was mindful not to slip up about Amy being a voice in my head, and to leave any talk of her out of the details. Waiting in line also gave me ample time to decide what it was exactly that I wanted for the barista bitch that worked there.

To be perfectly honest, I had only just been reminded about this certain member of staff, now that I was back in line at this cafeteria. Amy, however, hadn't so easily forgotten and was giving me plenty of suggestions from within our shared head. Most of which were pretty brutal, even for my taste. This particular barista girl, it turned out, seemed to have had a problem with Amy, too.

When she was alive, at least.

And from the suggestions Amy was making, it was abundantly clear that she had far less capacity than I did for tolerating "super-twots" like this "jumped-up, thunder-cunt" of a "coffee bitch".

Her words.

"I thought you were going to leave Malleus and me *to* it?" I muttered to Amy under my breath.

"You say something?" Malleus asked.

"Oh, nothing," I replied.

And once Amy was quite finished with vocalising her designs for this particular barista girl, Malleus and I talked some more.

"So," Malleus began. "As you've probably already guessed by now, I spoke with Richard."

"Richard?" I asked him, a little slow on the uptake.

"You know. Richard Heard, the big CEO."

"Oh, right. Yeah, I was sort of able to put that together for myself. What did you guys talk about?"

"Let's just say, he's made me a very generous offer."

I didn't ask Malleus what the offer was, I just told him, "That's good to hear."

"Which reminds me," he said. "Why I didn't tell you about the whole … 'homeless thing'."

I remained silent, just looking up at him whilst waiting on his words.

"I just didn't want you thinking any less of me, was all," he said.

"Malleus," I told him gently. "There is nothing you could tell me to make me *ever* do that."

Malleus smiled, as if he could see the sincerity in my eyes.

"But where are you even living right now?" I asked him.

"Well," he said. "People around here don't call me 'The Sofa Surfer' for nothing, let's put it *that* way."

My mouth cracked into a sad smile; a few moments of no words said passing before Malleus asked, "Sure you didn't pay that guy off?"

"Who? Richard?"

"Get him to tell me that crazy story?"

"Oh, sure," I said. "I bribed a billionaire to tell you the tallest tale you've ever heard, just so we could still be friends."

Malleus looked down at all the scrapes and scuffs he couldn't see on the cafeteria floor.

"I'm sorry, Iris," he said. "Really, I am."

I just wish that Malleus could've seen my face right then, so that he could have known, for himself, that he needn't have apologised.

"You told me the truth," he added, "and I called you a liar."

I held his arm in a sort of hug, resting the side of my head on his surprisingly comfortable shoulder.

"I think most people would have thought I was just making it up," I told him. "It's just that you're not 'most people', Malleus."

I could feel the vibrations of Malleus's words as he tilted his head to rest on mine.

We were almost at the front of the queue, by now.

"There *is* something else we need to talk about," Malleus said, after I lifted my head to look at his face. "As it seems that you really do have a ..."

Malleus's words lowered to a whisper.

"... You can 'do things'," he finished with.

"It certainly appears so," I said, unbothered that we were surrounded by all these people with their eyes and ears that still worked. They wouldn't believe the words '*I have a power!*' if I stood atop a table and yelled down on them all at the top of my lungs.

"Thing is," he continued, "I haven't properly seen it for myself, yet."

And trying to think of the nicest way I could say this, I told him, "And you never *will*."

"You know what I mean," he said.

"You still don't believe me?" I asked him. "Do you?"

"It's not that. It's just …"

His words getting lost in the air like steam rising up from an espresso machine.

"Remember the first time I showed you what I can do?" he said. "The night I brought back Harry for you."

"Harry?" I asked him.

"You know, Harry. Harry the hamster."

"Oh, *that* Harry. I forgot about that little guy. What's this got to do with him?"

"Well," he said. "I brought Harry back that one time, and you needed to see me do it again with that pigeon, remember?"

"How could I forget," I said, more to myself than to Malleus.

I didn't need the gift of sight to see where *this* was going.

"You want me to demonstrate my powers to you, again?" I asked him. "Don't you?"

"Well," he said. "Yeah."

"Then you, my friend, are in luck."

That's when Malleus gave me this look of both intrigue and concern, all at the same time.

And placing a reassuring hand on his chest, I told him, "Because I was just about to show you."

60

"Second Opinion"

If it was no longer sudden death that I wished for this particular barista girl, then what exactly was it that I *did* wish for her? It's only fair to say, she was usually serving people in the early hours of the morning; those *don't talk to me until I've had my coffee* customers, with all of their less than polite demands and nigh impossible to meet expectations. Seeing to person after person, all at their very worst, very first thing of the day.

Still, all things considered, she didn't have to be such a colossal *bitch* to me.

She was lucky I found out before today, all the other things I could do with my newly acquired powers, asides from the ability to kill. Otherwise, just minutes from now, the coffee she was about to prepare for me would have been the very last thing she would have ever done.

This girl was as rude as she was bitchy, and the only thing she seemed to be any good at – in the limited time I had been graced with in getting to know her – was being the very two things I mentioned previously. She couldn't even make a decent cup of coffee for crying out loud! Or perhaps it was that she *could*, but chose *not* to. I swear she made my coffees with decaffeinated coffee beans, not just once, but *every damn time*, and it was so completely past the point of evident that our hatred for each other was more than mutual.

There was *plenty* I wanted to change about the girl, when I took the time to think about it.

I wanted to feel welcome whenever I came here for a cup of coffee. I wanted to be smiled at when it was my turn. To be asked how I was doing that morning. But more than all that, I just wanted her gone.

Not dead.

Just … gone.

Malleus and I were now at the front of the queue, and as luck might have it – but maybe not so lucky for her – Jessica would be the one serving us.

"Good morning, Jessica," I said to her through my best shit-eating grin, my face more than likely appearing to her as if it were lit up by artificial light.

And Jessica, for whatever reason, looked as if she were about to burst into tears at any moment.

"I always thought it unfair," I told her. "Me knowing *your* name but you not knowing mine."

Jessica looked at me as if she had understood not one word of that last sentence.

"If I had it my way," I went on to say, "we'd *all* be wearing name badges."

After receiving next to no reaction whatsoever to that last comment, and perhaps just a *little* too impatiently for my liking, she asked, "What do you want?"

It seemed I was being asked that question with regular frequency these days: '*What do you want?*' Not, '*What can I get you?*' or '*What'll it be?*' She may as well have been actively tapping her foot with her arms crossed when she said it. But then, after pondering her question for a moment, it was probably the most fitting question she could have asked me.

"What do I want?" I said, repeating the question back at her, whilst pretending to look up at the chalked blackboard menu for inspiration.

And moving my gaze down from the board above and behind her, I fixed a stare on this 'Jessica' and said, "Look into my eyes, and I'll tell you."

"What just happened?" Malleus asked me, with what I imagine would have been a sense of urgency in his voice.

We had just walked out the door of the café, coffees to go in our hands, leaving behind the spectacle that was still taking place inside. I could only look back and watch, whereas Malleus could actually hear the whole darn thing, and, strangely, he had a better sense of what was going on in said café than *I* did.

I could see that Jessica was now stood atop a big round table inside the coffee shop, but Malleus could hear what she was yelling so passionately at everybody, just beyond the thin glass of the coffee shop window. According to Malleus, she was now shouting down to all of the customers indoors. Regular patrons, who were, just moments ago, quietly sipping on soya-milk cappuccinos and gluten-free skinny lattes.

Apparently, and only because I had Malleus and his ears that actually worked, she was raining down on them all with some Old Testament Bible material, like some sort of manic street preacher. Calling them all *Hypocrites!* and a *Brood of snakes! Posers!* and *Narcissists!* and various other choice phrases. And although I couldn't hear all this going on, what I could see were the petrified faces looking back up at her, as if she were the second coming in female form. The masks they usually wore on a daily basis, slipping and falling to reveal skin, pale with bewilderment. All of them, seized in terrified wonderment as to what in the hell had happened in the past five minutes for this usually quite pleasant and reserved barista girl to be behaving in the outrageous manner she now was.

Did you know that the word 'barista' isn't anything special? That it simply means, 'bar person'? Just thought you should know before I forgot to tell you.

Anyway, I was looking back at the café from the safe distance both Malleus and I were at, and laughing my ass off. But when I happened to glance at Malleus, in between howls of laughter, I could see that he was not as amused as I was.

"This isn't funny, Iris!" Malleus scolded me, his hands clamped to either side of my shoulders with impressive aim.

"Oh, come on," I told him. "Where's the devil in you? What's wrong with a girl just wanting to have a little fun?"

"What did you do?" Malleus asked me.

From the only two things I could decipher, those being Malleus's facial expression and body language, it was clear to me that he genuinely wasn't fooling around. And so, seeing as he wasn't exactly revelling in all this comical absurdity the way *I* was, I took Malleus back in time with me by five minutes, to bring him up to speed with what just happened.

"So?" that barista bitch asked me, her pretty sapphire eyes clearly less than bothered about my answer than even *she* was. This was roughly five minutes before Malleus and I left the café with our coffees to go. Me, I'm still pretending to have a good old look at the menu board, making it appear as if I'm carefully considering which coffee, from the plethora of varieties available to have.

"What do I want?" I asked myself a second time. And if my ears weren't completely useless, I would have heard this lovely, charming girl blow air out of her bitchy little mouth just now. "I think what I really want right now is …" I say, this barista bitch back to giving me those eyes of hers again.

"… a change in your attitude," I tell her out of nowhere.

The look on this girl's face. Like I'd just told her I knew her deepest darkest secret, the precise time and date she was going to die, and what she was going to have to eat on her lunch break that day. The looks I would have seen on the faces around me, if I hadn't been so preoccupied with the optical tug of war I'd got going on with the barista girl right in front of me.

"From now on," I continued as I held eye contact, "you are to treat other people in the way you, yourself, would expect to be treated."

For once, not a word from this barista bitch.

"Myself included," I added. My eyebrows raised above eyes a few shades bluer than hers. And this barista girl, not being able to look away, just gazed back into my eyes with that same abject terror I saw in the eyes of that old boy at his pawnshop.

I had her now.

"You're to start becoming more yourself," I went on. "Stop being influenced by those vacuous morons on social media and the latest fleeting trends. You were born to stand out, Jessica, not to blend in."

A blank face in front of me taking all of this in.

"As of right now," I tell her, "you are to become your true self, Jessica."

Amy, being able to read this barista girl's mind, was feeding me with lots of juicy info about her.

"You're to dump that useless, cheating, self-important 'boyfriend' of yours," I told her. "You're to lose all those fake 'friends', too. Quit this shitty job while you're at it. You wanted to be a dancer, Jessica. There's still time. Get rid of all the dead weight. This isn't just some lame HeadMagazine cull. The 'friends', the 'boyfriend', the job. It all has to go so you can finally start focusing on yourself."

Still, all I'm met with is a pretty, blank face.

"But don't worry," I tell her, "you won't be alone. You'll have me. And with all of your interfering acquaintances, along with that controlling prick of a boyfriend, out of the picture, I think we really have a shot of becoming friends. *Best* friends, even. Best friends *forever.*"

"Hey!" Amy cried out from within my head.

"OK," I told Amy, "maybe not *best* friends. Those would be big Jimmy Choo's to fill. But *good* friends, sure."

I paused to consider if there was anything else.

"Is that everything?" Jessica just about managed to say. Her eyes as wide as a rabbit's caught in the glaring headlights of a speeding sports car.

"Not quite," I replied.

I was enjoying this.

It was usually the other way around; Jessica being the confident one as I sheepishly ordered a cortado, quietly wondering if I had pronounced it correctly. And here she was, looking like a girl whose soul was about to be sucked out and devoured as an entrée by a demonic entity.

"There's just one last thing I want from you, Jessica," I said, leaning in. My eyes fixed, dead, on hers.

"A cortado," I said confidently, turning to Malleus and slapping a hand down on his shoulder.

"A cappuccino?" he said.

"To have in, or take away?" Jessica asked me, a gormless look on her face.

"Take away," I replied. "And, screw it. I think we'll have those for free."

"No charge," she said, the way I imagine a beautiful fleshy robot would.

I was still getting accustomed to the fact that I had a power, but this was awesome. No one had *ever* listened to me before. Apart from maybe, Malleus, but that's different. Now people were listening. *Really* listening. And I was getting free coffee with it, too.

Thinking about it.

I wouldn't have to pay for coffee, ever again.

But back to Jessica, poor thing.

This would all be over soon. She would snap out of it, and *3 … 2 … 1*, she'd be back in the room. And then, she would finally be free to live her life the way she always wished to.

Or should that be … live her life the way *I* had just wished her to?

Whatever.

Our coffees came quickly, and beautifully prepared as ordered. So she *was* able to do it!

She had even gone to the trouble of drawing a sweet little love heart in the velvety milk of mine.

"Aww," I told her as she handed me the cup. "You shouldn't have."

Now I could be with Malleus *and* have Jessica as a friend. *I could really do with a friend*, I thought to myself. *I know I have Amy but, and no offence to her, she's just a voice in my head.*

"Some taken!" Amy said from within my head.

What I had always wanted, what I'd *longed* for, was to have a real girlfriend. Not a 'girlfriend', but a friend that's a girl.

You know what I mean.

Someone to watch *Filthy Frolicking* with for the gazillionth time, or paint my nails French Ombre for me, or go clothes shopping at Primarni. And it's not like I could do any of that girly stuff with Malleus. Plus, 'that lift' in *Filthy Frolicking* would be totally lost on him, let alone being able to apply nail polish to nails he can't even see.

I know all of this probably sounds pretty shallow to someone like you whose been there and done that, but I've never had it. What Amy and I had was close, but it never went the distance. It was incomplete. Broken. Damaged almost beyond repair. And this one thing: having a girlfriend to do all of this with, would surely fix it for me.

I'm snapped back into the room when Jessica, ever so politely, asked me, "Is there anything else?"

I had almost walked away there, when one last thing sprang to mind. Leaning in close, I whispered to her, "See that table over there?" Using my thumb to point behind me at a big round table in the middle of the café.

"Get up on that table," I whispered, "and tell all these people here what you *really* think of them."

61

"For Nothing"

They say it's amazing what can happen in a day, but with my newfound powers a whole lot could happen in the time it took to prepare a very decent cup of coffee. What was also apparent, however, was that Malleus certainly wasn't impressed. He'd asked me to fill him in with the details of what happened in the café just now, and I had taken him through it, moment by moment, so what was his problem with the whole thing?

"I got us free coffee," I told him. "The least you could do is show me some gratitude."

Malleus threw his coffee cup down; exploding in a splash of brown and frothy white as it hit the pavement.

"I don't give a *damn* about the free coffee!" he yelled at me. "What I'm more concerned about, as of right now, is you!"

"Look," I said. "I may have got a little carried away with that barista girl in there just now, but you've got to admit it was fun, right? I mean, I totally got away with it!"

"This isn't fun, Iris! This is messing with people's minds!"

"See?" Amy piped up from within my head. "Told you!"

"You, stay out of this!" I told her.

"Stay *out* of it?" Malleus asked. "I was stood right next to you when it happened!"

"That wasn't meant for you," I told him.

"What?" he asked.

"Anyway," I told him. "I'm not 'messing with people's minds', I'm changing the minds of people for the better. This is a *good* thing I'm doing here. Surely you of all people can see that?"

'See'?

Why were my words always so poorly chosen?

"But it's *not* a good thing, Iris," he snapped. "And it's not up to you to decide what's good for people, either!"

"Hey!" I snapped back. "I didn't *choose* to have these powers!"

"No, you didn't," he said, appearing to lower his voice. "But you *do* get to choose how you use them, or whether you should use them at all."

And there's this déjà vu feeling that I've had this conversation before.

"Have you ever taken the time to think?" he asked me. "What you can do. That maybe it's more of a curse than a blessing?"

"Oh, you *would* say that," I said.

"And what do you mean by that, exactly?" he asked.

I was holding onto the words so tight, but even with all the powers I possessed, I couldn't hold them back, slipping from the tongue I was biting down on and tumbling out of my mouth.

"You're just jealous," I told him.

The words promised they'd be so delicious to say when they were in my head, but no sooner had the words left my lips, they left a bad aftertaste in my mouth.

"Jealous?" he asked me. "Is *that* what you think of me?"

There are things you simply can't take back. You can't take back a rock once it's been thrown. You can't put toothpaste back in the tube once it's been squeezed out. You can't take back words once they've been said.

"Why would you ever think I was jealous?" he asked me.

The way he was 'looking' at me: burning a hole through each one of my eyes.

So I hit back just as hard as the stare he was firing at me when I said, "Because!"

I tried to hold myself back. To not finish the sentence. But my powers of commanding influence were useless to me, here.

"Go on," he told me.

But I didn't even have to say the words, they just spilled out all on their own.

"Because I can completely turn people's lives around for the better," I told him. "And you …"

"Go ahead," he told me. "Say it."

"All *you* can do is bring dead pigeons back to life."

"Wow," he said, slipping his phone out from the back pocket of his jeans. "Just, wow."

I went to make an apology, but his next words broke it in two.

"And just for future reference," he said, untangling the cord of his headphones. "It's not what you can get away with, but what you can live with after you've done it."

And as he put an earbud in his left ear, turned and walked away, the only words I so desperately wanted to say were the right ones to make Malleus stop and come back to me.

But the words that usually came so easily …

… never did.

62

"Two Cents"

"Honestly," Amy piped up from within our shared head. "You two. If yours and Malleus's relationship were a book, I would have taken it back to the bookstore for a refund by now."

"OK," I told Amy. "Thank you so much for your unsolicited opinion."

"Actually," Amy continued. "Scratch that. If yours and Malleus's relationship were a book, I would have ripped the pages from the spine, torn them to shreds, thrown them in a trash can, doused them in gasoline, and tossed a lit match in along *with* them."

And as much as I didn't want to hear this, I tended to agree with her – which also meant, she already knew. We really had to stop doing this, Malleus and me, but then this was *my* fault, not his. It was *me* that had to stop messing things up the way I always did. What made it all the worse was the fact that we'd just started talking, and then I went and did it again. Maybe I *was* getting out of control and becoming a little reckless with this nearly newfound power of mine.

I had done what I considered to be good things with it. Altering the selfish ways of a big CEO. Transforming a grumpy old git into a more compassionate man. And then there was the barista girl, who … I mean, c'mon. Was a bit of a bitch. That's what I had done. *I* did that. And I was proud of myself for it. I mean, how *else* would you use the abilities I possessed?

It was as if my conscience was being pulled apart by the opinions of two very different horses. One horse that sincerely believed I was using my powers for their intended purpose, and a second horse, deeply troubled by how I was wielding this newly found capacity of mine.

I didn't *really* believe that Malleus could be jealous of me, as he didn't strike me as the jealous type. Plus, he could bring things back from the *dead* for crying out loud! And even with all the things I now found myself able to do, I still couldn't do *that*. I was just upset that he wasn't behind all I was doing, the way *I* was.

After amicably discussing it, Amy and I agreed that going back to my room wasn't even on the *list* of the very last places in the world we wanted to go right now – the lonely emptiness we were both filled with. And I realise it may not make all that much sense to you, but we wanted to be outside, just hidden. Around strangers and, yet, alone.

We let our minds come together as we walked. Now that we knew my powers were so much more than I had at first thought – that I could do almost *anything* with them – the possibilities were infinite. Their potential only limited by how creative we could be in how we used them.

You want someone to love you at first sight? *Bam!* You've got it. Got someone in your life you want rid of? *Pow!* Gone. Is there something you want to be? *Boom!* Go be it. We could literally do anything here. Shoot for the moon, because even the sky wasn't in our way to limit us.

I say, 'we' and 'us', as I figured Amy and I were kind of one and the same now.

Both of us, so consumed with the thoughts running around in our shared head about all that we could do, we almost walked right past the pawnshop. The very same one where we used said powers on an aged miser. We figured we should probably check in with the old boy like we did the big CEO; see what had changed in him. But the shop was closed. The opening times on the door said that the shop *should* have been open today, but, for whatever reason, it wasn't.

An instant rush of cold circulated my body in a flow of icy fluid.

Was he dead?

"Could be," Amy said.

Had we killed him?

"We?" Amy asked.

Had he killed him*self?*

"Only one way to find out," she told me.

And no sooner had Amy said it, I knew precisely where she meant for us to go. And so, I began walking; double-time. Before breaking into a light jog. Before breaking into a full-on sprint. The kind of run you'd break into along the platform of a train station as you waved goodbye to a loved one on board a carriage and bound for a place you'll never go.

My legs were worn-out pistons by the time we reached the old boy's house. My lungs, full of fire. Almost falling to my aching knees, to thank a god I wasn't even sure existed, when I saw that the old boy's garden was now tended to. Grass, cut. Hedges, trimmed. Flowers planted in the rich, ground-coffee-like soil that surrounded them. Borders made up of smooth white pebbles, glinting the way settled snow does when the sun's hanging low in a wintry sky. And stood at the foot of the steps, swept clean of moss and dirt, I could see that the curtains, once drawn, were now wide open and letting in all the light of the outside.

Making my way up the steps and to the porch, the doormat that used to read, 'NOT YOU AGAIN', along with the hard, stone gnome holding a sign that read, 'GO AWAY', were gone and replaced with a 'WELCOME' mat. A friendly, fluffy white cat greeted me in the doorway by brushing against my leg, seeming to wait expectantly for the next time someone happened to open the front door to let it back in.

Crouching down to the level of my bent knees, I shimmied along the bottom edge of the front room window. Then, ever so slowly, craned my neck, and peeked into the window to see inside. What I saw filled my heart with the same warmth a shot glass of sweet liquor would, your throat.

For there, inside, I saw a laid table.

A large roasted turkey in the middle, amidst all the trimmings of roast potatoes, Yorkshire puddings, honey roast parsnips and a steaming gravy boat. Sat around the set table were the serene faces of three generations, all holding hands with their heads slightly bowed, and giving thanks for the meal they were about to receive. And at the head of the table, there he was. That very same old man that, not two sunrises ago, was asking me, in a wholly testy manner, what it was that I wanted.

And if that grumpy, old git had asked me that very same question, right now, in this ever so touching of moments, I would have simply told him, 'This'.

I felt such contentment as I trotted back down those steps, thoughtfully swept for the arrival of whom, I imagine, were this old boy's family; people he probably hadn't seen or spoken to in years. But once I was strolling down that long road, against the grain of the direction I'd come, this joyous feeling abandoned me and a certain sorrow crept in, unannounced. I knew I felt it: this downheartedness that gradually caught up with me, I just didn't really know why. Especially after witnessing such a heart-warming scene, and being so relieved that the old boy wasn't, for want of better words, 'brown bread'.

Was it that my work here was done? Was it because of yet another fallout between me and Malleus? Or was it that I now felt myself at a loss as to what to do next?

With this little 'experiment' of mine now over, concluding that I *did* in fact have a power, and that it was so much more than a deathly gaze. The result being that I had affected the lives of three people for the better. One for the very worst, if you include Amy in all of this.

"It's not so bad," Amy reassured me. "I'm getting quite settled in by now."

I thanked Amy, but not in my head. I felt like actually saying the words, out loud, like I really meant them.

So what now? I thought to myself. Or should that be, *who* now? Sure, it felt wonderful that I'd finally done some good with my powers, but I couldn't help but think, after all I had done for other people, what about me? What did *I* want? If there was only something I could do for myself with this ability of commanding influence within me.

But there *was* one thing. And that was that I could really do with a friend right now.

"You'll always have *me*," Amy said. "Seeing as I'm stuck in here for the foreseeable future and everything."

Knowing she could hear my thoughts, I thanked her without the use of my lips, but Amy could sense there was something else I was holding on to.

"What is it?" she asked me, already knowing the answer.

"It's just that …" but my words fell into the abyss of reluctant sentences.

"Just what?" she asked me, pushing me for the answer she already knew.

"You're not …" I said, attempting to finish this tricky sentence a second time.

"What?" she asked me. "Real?"

I didn't actually say, 'yes', for being too ashamed to. I just closed my eyes and nodded.

"And whose fault is that?" she asked me, knowing full well the return.

And I, out of both sugar-coated words and convincing excuses, fell silent.

"I may not be here in body, Iris," she told me. "But I *am* here in some form."

Amy's voice vanished into a deafening silence after that, and the deafness I had so been missing all this time, returned to me, right when I wasn't ready for it. And as much as I grappled with the right words to say – begging her on imagined knees to come back and talk to me, to let me explain myself – Amy had already disappeared off somewhere.

Somewhere, even *I* couldn't find her.

63

And so, with Malleus giving me the silent treatment, and Amy playing hide and seek within my head, I had no one but myself to talk to. And that wasn't exactly going to be riveting conversation, now was it?

Was I getting carried away with my powers? *Had* I become too proud? Out of control? Or was what I was doing, and *had* been doing, all coming from a good place and with the best of intentions?

I couldn't rely on myself for the answers to these questions, with the current state of my mind rendering me an unreliable source. What I needed was someone who knew me, *really* knew me. Somebody who'd seen all my hidden, dark places, but still saw all the virtuous purity, lit up from inside of me.

But who did I have if I didn't have Amy or Malleus?

This wasn't something I could talk about with just anyone, as they would never understand. My version of the events of the last few months probably sounding, to them, like the outlandish stories of a madwoman. They would just look at me with those bug eyes, swelling up with concern, and I'd be off to the loony bin in no time.

This wasn't some 'delusion'. I wasn't 'imagining' all of this. I was *not,* as I've been so called, 'crazy'.

That didn't mean, however, that there wasn't someone out there who could, at least, hold me back from going over and over it all in my rowdy, chaotic, cluttered library of a head. Perhaps a 'timeout' from all the craziness of the last week or so was just what I needed. Something simpler and tidier to occupy my complicated and messy mind with whilst waiting for either Amy or Malleus to come around.

And since they were the only two people I could really talk to about this whole 'power thing', I was left with the only thing I *could* do, which was to simply wait it out.

And I knew *just* the person to help me do that.

I'd just have to find them first.

64

"Drink-Slap"

The last thing I remember doing was sending Jessica Blowers (the barista bitch) a friend request on HeadMagazine, and Toggling *'Cats that look like Hitler'* whilst I waited for her to accept it.

Then I just woke up here on my bed, with no recollection of what happened in between. I had no memory of the walk back to the hall of residence, and I couldn't recollect returning home to my room. Nor could I recall ever going to bed.

I put the memory lapse simply down to exhaustion, and nothing more. Perhaps I'd underestimated just how much all that had happened recently had affected me. And as much as it did concern me some, it was probably nothing to worry about, as it had never happened before.

It was still light outside, so I grabbed my phone off the bedside table to see what the time was.

9:01 am.

And in doing so, saw that I had a good few text messages from a number that wasn't saved to my phonebook.

Gr8 2 hv a catch up last nite! the first text read.

FanC hookin up again sumtime? said another.

And, *RU alive? LOL.*

These texts were harder to read than some people's *lips* could be.

Who *was* this person that I had no recollection of ever talking to?

Who is this? I texted.

It didn't *sound* like Malleus, and it wasn't his number, so who in the hell was it that I was supposedly speaking with last night? But I wasn't wracking my brains for long, as, almost immediately, I got a reply along with the answer to my question. It was Jessica. You know, the girl I used to affectionately call the 'barista bitch'. The very same 'Jessica' that worked, or should I say, *used* to work, at The Daily Grind café.

But just *how* did she have my number?

Did we go out drinking last night?

I didn't *feel* hungover.

Cupping my hand over my nose and mouth, I breathed out to smell my breath for that stale aroma of too many chain-smoked cigarettes. And, if I *had* been drinking, my breath would have reeked of gin, which it didn't. But if we *had* been out, this Jessica and I, just how was it that I couldn't bring to mind the events of the night before, and how she got my all-important digits?

Wer U out drinkin last nite?? another text came through, with a *LOL*.

Nope, I replied. *Just completed my 'post-drinking' checks. That is a negative.*

LOL, she texted back. *UR funny.*

I do try, I told her.

To which she just replied, *LOL* for a *third* time.

It always seemed so disingenuous to me: 'LOL'. I hated text-speak, full stop. I mean, we have proper keyboards on our phones now for Pete's sake, and not solitary buttons assigned to three or four letters of the alphabet.

I texted back the abbreviation, *SALTS*, which was totally lost on Jessica. Asking me what I meant with, not one, but *three* question marks.

S.A.L.T.S., I told her. *It stands for 'Smiled A Little, Then Stopped'. I find it's more accurate.*

She was clearly still not getting it, as she then just went on to change the subject with … *So. Do U fanC doin sumthin again?*

Thing is, and like I pointed out before, I don't remember what it was that we did the *last* time. Obviously, we caught up, but how exactly? And, just a little more worryingly, what was *said?*

Let's meet up! I told her.

I would have suggested for us to meet at The Daily Grind café, although, in light of what had transpired the last time we were both there, that was probably a little further than a bad idea. But before I even had the chance to think up a more appropriate rendezvous, Jessica beat me to it when she texted, *I NO dis gr8 place.*

People always seem to know these 'great places' nowadays.

Do U know that deli place, 'Grey's'? she asked me,

Wow. She actually knew where to put the comma and apostrophe. Mind, blown.

I don't, I said.

And then I stupidly asked if it was any good, like she might take me somewhere truly terrible.

YAAASSS!!! she texted back, with maybe two more exclamation marks, *As* and *Ss* than was necessary.

Only then realising she probably meant, *'Graze'*, and not, *'Grey's'*. And that, upon this realisation, I *did* know the place. But I chose not to correct her, and just let her give me the directions I wouldn't need anyway.

Giving in to the irrefutable matter that I was beyond famished, I ordered a pretzel bagel with pastrami, gherkin mustard and Monterey Jack cheese, with a side of chunky coleslaw and skin-on fries. Which, in contrast, made me feel like a bit of a glutton, as Jessica just graciously asked the waitress for a salad and a glass of water.

I was expecting Amy to pop up out of nowhere and exclaim, *Boring!* but she never did.

Strangely, when I took a moment to ponder it, I couldn't actually cast my mind back to the journey *to* the deli. Probably my misty daydreams of Malleus clouding my memory of the mundane or something. And just where had this green, long-sleeved shirt jumpsuit I was now wearing appeared from? I mean, I quite liked it – now that I'd taken a few dreamy seconds to admire the way it flowed effortlessly over my body – it just wasn't the sort of item I would usually pick out when clothes shopping, or ever even dare to wear. More so the sort of thing Amy would throw on in a rush on her more, shall we say … 'casual' days.

And, for whatever reason, when mine and Jessica's food finally arrived at the table, I was reminded of my eighteenth birthday, where my dad brought a cake into the darkened room for me to blow the candles out.

Where *was* Amy? Surely she could see what I was up to: making a new girlfriend, and not including her in the experience.

Then my left eye began twitching erratically, like it was furiously attempting to communicate with me via Morse code, prompting Jessica to ask if I had something stuck in it.

"Just some dumb fly," I told her as she leaned in close to better see.

"There," I said, pretending to scoop the fictitious insect from my tear duct with the tip of a finger, and flicking it away. "Got it."

"So," Jessica said to me.

She always seemed to start any new subject with a 'So' before she began talking. Which wasn't all that annoying. At first. But after a while, once I realised she did it often, only *then* did it become a little tedious. I wasn't, however, going to let something as trivial as repetitiveness become a bother to me, as I was just happy to make a new friend. Even if I had *told* this particular new acquaintance to start liking me with the powers I had used on them just the other day.

Still.

A friend is a friend, no matter how you obtain them.

We talked about all sorts. Granted, not the sort of things I was actually interested in, but it felt good to be talking the way I imagined popular girls would. Mostly talk of gossip and boys and sex stories – of which I had no genuine ones of my own. But I was happy to fabricate some filthy tales from the material of stories I'd gathered from other, more sexually adventurous, people in the past.

I also couldn't help but notice that, aside from her using the word 'so' to begin every, goddamn, new topic, Jessica also said other words with all too regular frequency. Words such as, 'like', and 'sort of like', and 'kinda like'. Luckily for me, I could only *see* the words being spoken by her lips, and couldn't actually *hear* them. Otherwise, I'm afraid to say, I may have had to 'end her' over that bowl of soggy leaves she was munching her way through.

"So," Jessica said. "I don't know if you noticed, but I almost burst into tears that morning you came into the coffee shop."

"You did?" I asked her, pretending not to have had a clue.

"I was five hours into an eight-hour shift," she continued, "and you were the first person to be nice to me all day."

I took a sip of my smoothie to get me out of having to say something.

"Also," Jessica said, looking down at the sad little plastic straw she was stirring in her glass of water. "I just wanted to say thanks again for being such a good listener last night."

A weird thing to say to a deaf girl ('being a good listener') but I chose not to correct her on that petty technicality.

"Oh," I said. "You're … welcome?"

"You're the only person I've told," she went on to say, looking as if she were about to burst into tears like she did back at the café that day.

And just when I was about to ask Jessica to refresh my memory with what was spoken about, my hand jerked in a spasm as I lifted my drink to my lips, and before I had the time to realise what I was doing, I tossed the entire contents of my glass of strawberry and banana smoothie right in Jessica's salad-munching face.

"Oh my God!" I exclaimed as Jessica just sat there with her hands held up. Frozen, in a moment of brisk shock. Covered in a thick splash of pinkish-red and little black strawberry seeds, now dripping from her hair and face in a yogurt-like goo.

"I am so sorry," I told her, desperately scrambling to my feet. Coming to her aid with anything close to hand and absorbent to clean her up with.

"Can we get a towel, please!" I yelled at a waitress who was clearing a nearby table.

"I am so, so sorry," I told Jessica, as I tended to her with a pathetic napkin that was severely inadequate for a job this messy.

I'd lost count of how many times I had apologised to Jessica, as I couldn't say sorry enough, but instead of being mad about it, she actually began to laugh. Like I had merely thrown a lightly soiled serviette at her just now.

"It's fine," she said, wiping the pinkish sludge from her face in big handfuls of goop. "I wasn't really enjoying this salad, anyway."

I really thought that might be it: this little mishap of mine. The deal-breaker that brought mine and Jessica's brief, budding friendship to an abrupt end. Either that, or I may have just had to use my powers of commanding influence, again. Look her in the eyes, tell her to forget what had just happened, and move on with the rest of our happy lives of being best friends forever. But neither happened. She didn't care, nor did I have to *make* her not care. She just casually towelled herself down like nothing had happened and said, "So."

"Fancy doing something later?" she asked me, like I hadn't just thrown an entire strawberry-based-smoothie at her just now.

"Sure," I told her.

"How's about a girly night in?" she asked. "Chick flicks, snacks, a little nail-painting?"

"It's like you're in my head," I told her.

My lord, I thought to myself. *Imagine that!*

And as alien as Jessica's idea sounded to me, it sounded most favourable in comparison to all the reoccurring craziness, as of late. At last, I was going to watch *Filthy Frolicking,* eat *way* more cheese puffs than I ought to, and have my nails painted … with another girl! It was what I'd been dreaming of since I was a schoolgirl. I had only *heard* about these girly nights in, but I had never actually experienced one. And now that it was being offered to me on a silver platter, all I could say, in the most casual of ways, like this wasn't a big deal at all, was … "Cool."

It was finally going to happen. I would, at long last, get to see, first-hand, what one of these girly nights actually entailed. I had waited almost ten years for this, but having to wait a few more hours was almost unbearable, to the point of me bursting like an over eager piñata.

I thought that just this girly meeting alone would be more than enough to cause Amy to seethe from inside of me and break her silence, but it wasn't.

She never made a peep.

And as much as I liked having my head back all to myself – and I know this may sound downright batty to you – I was actually starting to miss her a little bit.

After settling the bill, which Jessica insisted she take care of, we said our *See you laters.* A slightly awkward affair, where I went in for a peck on the cheek, whereas *she* came in for a full-on hug that lasted maybe a little longer than was comfortable for me. Some of the tacky to the touch, smoothie goop on her clothes transferring onto my own. And, for whatever reason, the memory of the last time I saw my dad popped up in my mind, when he held me in his arms before sending me off to university.

As Jessica and I parted ways, I walked home, hoping that this little meeting of ours would jog some kind of memory as to what Jessica and I got up to the other night. And I don't know if it was the way the sun was reflecting off the water of the quay that ran parallel to the pavement, but I was reminded of the warm sand of that foreign beach I strolled along barefoot whilst on a college trip abroad.

As for what happened immediately after I sent Jessica that friend request yesterday, I guess it would just come to me like it always did.

When I wasn't being so hard on my brain for not remembering.

65

"In a Corner"

I had to keep telling myself that this was actually happening. Mostly because I had no one else to tell me until either Malleus or Amy started talking to me again.

We were in my room, Jessica and I, painting each other's nails whilst we scoffed cheese puffs and watched *Filthy Frolicking*. Although, Jessica wasn't drinking a drop of the two bottles of wine I'd bought for us, which, much like the whole 'salad thing' at the deli, made me feel like a bit of an alcoholic by comparison. It was what I'd always imagined it to be: two girls chatting and snacking, only half watching the film that was playing in the background.

But try as I may, I just couldn't shake off this troubling feeling. We were having fun, sure, but how did we get here? How, exactly, did we *get* to this point?

And how come I was dressed in this pink, zip-up onesie all of a sudden?

The walk home from Graze deli was the very last thing I *do* remember. I ordered a bagel and Jessica had a salad. I remember a horrifying incident where I chucked an entire smoothie over her. I vaguely recall what we talked about, but that was normal, right? What I *don't* remember was returning home, and how we landed here so suddenly. Gassing away and stuffing our faces with cheese-flavoured maize snacks, one eye on the movie, and the other on the French Ombre Jessica was painting on my nails.

It felt good, all this, but in the same breath I was admittedly freaking out a little.

This was the third time I had experienced a memory lapse in the last couple of days.

I tried to push it all to the back of my mind for now, not wanting to ruin this precious moment Jessica and I were sharing. I had finally made a friend to have a girl's night in with. Or should I say, *made* a girl befriend me, by force, so she *had* to spend a girly evening in with me.

But what was the difference, really? *Having* a girlfriend to do this with, or *making* a girl do this with you? It was the same outcome, either way. I had wanted this for a mighty long time, and how I got it really didn't matter to me. What *bothered* me was the fact that I could not remember how we got here.

I even thought about asking Jessica to help me fill in the big gaping holes of lost time in my mind, but that might just serve in 'weirding her out' and cause her to *un*friend me – if that's even a word – as fast as she had *be*friended me.

But then I realised something. She was as helpless as a puppet on a string; her every move controlled by a wiggle of my fingers and a flick of the wrist. Whatever I did or said, and however she reacted to it, I could just look her in the eyes and give her a new command, or simply make her forget.

She was mine, whether I decided she liked it or not.

What I *didn't* seem to have any authority over. What was *really* bugging me, and not allowing me to savour the lovely time I was having with Jessica, were these memory lapses that were out of my control. It plagued me to the extent I couldn't take pleasure from the nail polish Jessica was carefully applying to my lovingly manicured hand. The stench of chemicals, burning my nostrils. The cheese puffs, like bland dirt in my mouth. The movie, just a blur of colours and shapes in motion. Jessica's squirming red lips and flashing white teeth. An orange-crumbed tongue flapping in her darkened hole of a mouth. Gabbing away too fast for me to catch the words that came from it.

I needed a moment, but I couldn't exactly have it in front of Jessica.

But as luck may have it, I had to pee.

Excusing myself for a toilet break, I got up from where I was sat, cross-legged, on the bed with Jessica, and dashed to the bathroom, shut the door, locked, behind me, and turned the extractor fan on to mask the sound of my voice with its dull droning.

Amy and I had some catching up to do of our own.

Running my hands under the tap's cold stream of the bathroom sink, I cupped both hands together to collect enough water to splash onto my face. And looking at mine and Amy's shared face in the mirror, I called her name.

"Amy?" I said, as quietly as I was able, really hoping Jessica couldn't hear me talking to anybody but myself in here.

But met with nothing, I tried again.

"Amy?" I said a little louder.

"You can do better than that," a familiar voice said, from out of the nowhere of my head.

"Amy!" I exclaimed, perhaps a little too loudly.

"Oh, come on," she said. "Say it like you mean it. Show me how much you want me back."

"Amy," I said, but only a little louder than the first time.

"Is that really the best you can do?" she asked me.

"But, Jessica," I told Amy as a hushed shout. "What if she hears?"

"You really think I care about that stupid girl in there?" she asked me. "The one you prefer to me? The girl that's more real to you than *I* am?"

But my awareness of the girl on the other side of the bathroom door, caused me to fall silent.

"Call out my name!" Amy barked. "Shout it like you're shouting it from the rooftops! Or I'm out of here. And *this* time, I will not be back."

Taking a breath in, deeper than any breath my lungs had ever taken, I prepared everything that was within me to cry out Amy's name.

But just before I did, she stopped me.

"It's OK, Iris," Amy told me. "I just wanted to see how serious you were. I'm not going to ruin this little 'friendship' of yours by making Jessica think that you're a nut-job, so don't worry your pretty little head about it."

"Where have you been?" I whispered to her.

"Where *haven't* I been, more like," she said. "Take a pew on the toilet, and I'll tell you whilst you pretend to take a piss."

I took a seat on the cold porcelain and pretended to pee.

"I just want to start by saying," I began, "I'm sorry about where our last conversation led us to."

"About me not being 'real' enough for you?" she asked.

I nodded.

"It's ancient artefacts," she told me. "So, totally over it."

"I'm sorry you've been stuck up there with no one to talk to," I told her.

"What? You think I just found myself a dark little corner to crawl into and sulk in?"

"What *were* you doing up there?"

"You mean, whilst you were wasting time larking about with this dumb 'girlfriend' of yours? Let's just say I've been busy."

"Busy doing what?"

"Watch this."

That's when my left arm began rising up, all on its own.

"What are you doing?" I shrieked, as my arm rose past the height of my chest and above my head.

"What am *I* doing?" Amy asked, the hand of my left arm falling from where it was held high to meet with the side of my face. "What are *you* doing?"

"This isn't funny!" I pleaded with her.

"No, it's not," Amy said. "But *this* is!"

The palm of my left hand then began repeatedly slapping the side of my face, hard.

Tssch! Tssch! Tssch!

"What are you doing, Iris?" Amy chortled, gleefully. "Why are you hitting yourself, Iris?"

"Please!" I begged her. "Stop hitting me!"

Again and again and again, my hand struck the side of my face with violent wallops.

Tssch! Tssch! Tssch!

"But I'm *not* hitting you, Iris," Amy said. "*You* are."

Tssch! Tssch! Tssch!

I wrestled with my left hand to pull it away from smacking the side of my face, and as suddenly as the slapping began, it stopped. A burning sensation on my left cheek and a ringing in my ears, coming to the forefront of all that sharp smacking that was ahead of them.

"What was *that* for?" I snapped at her, smoothing away the sting with the very same hand that'd caused it.

"That," she said. "Was to show you who's now in charge."

"Since when have you been in control of my body?" I asked her, as I checked the side of my face in the mirror; four glowing-red fingers and a palm now slapped across it.

"Oh, only a day or two," she said. "I've been using the time you're asleep to practise. And you're confused. I think you mean, 'our body'."

And with the sting on the side of my face, along with the ringing in my ears, beginning to fade, a realisation slowly came to the surface.

"Wait a minute," I said. "At Graze deli. That was you, wasn't it?"

"What?" she asked me. "The 'smoothie incident'? Yep! That was an act of 'me' alright."

"And the eye twitches. They were your doing, too, weren't they?"

"Oh, they're just me getting started."

"What *else* have you been doing up there?"

"Oh, I've had plenty of places to go," she told me, "and much to do whilst I've been stuck in here and left to my own devices. With all the time I needed to conduct a few experiments of my own."

A flush of icy-cold blood coursed through my veins.

My heart, now beating in my head, and trying to punch its way out.

"Experiments?" I asked her.

"You know," she said. "Like the ones you were conducting when you were going through that whole *do I have a power?* phase."

"Like, what *kind* of experiments?" I asked her.

"Oh," she said. "You'll see."

66

"Forget You Ever Knew Me"

I'd been in the bathroom, conversing with a voice inside my head, for way longer than is reasonable to simply urinate and wash your hands.

"Can we please talk about all this properly when we're alone," I asked Amy, more in a way that was desperately pleading than asking.

"We *are* alone," Amy said.

"I mean, *alone*, alone."

"Yes, of course. Get back to your 'girly night in'. I know this is your first one, which is great and everything, if not a little pathetic."

"Thank you," I told her, flushing nothing but water down the toilet, and pretending to wash my hands under a running tap.

I prepared myself to have to explain to Jessica, the moment after I'd walked out the bathroom door, why it was that I'd spent quite so much time on the toilet talking to myself. And maybe it was because the movie was dragging on a bit, or that she'd eaten far too many maize-based snacks, or that she was high off nail-polish fumes.

But, Jessica.

She was asleep.

At least, I *hoped* she was.

I stood over Jessica, just watching her. I could see from the gentle rise and fall of her small but perfectly formed C-cup chest – that I'm not too proud to admit I was a little envious of – that she was still breathing, and breathed a sigh of relief of my own. Her left hand still plunged inside the bag of cheese puffs as she slept.

Taking the empty foil bag from her orange-dusted hand, I screwed it up as quietly as I could, and tossed it in the office bin under my desk. Clearing away all the other items from the bed –

mostly used make-up sponges, nail files, and nail-polish bottles in a variety of garish colours – I gently wedged a pillow behind Jessica's head, and attentively wrapped her up in the bed covers. Then, same as before, I stood up straight, and took a step back to look down at her. She looked so serene and at peace, it was hard to believe this was the very same girl that had been so animated just minutes before. Gesticulating wildly with her hands as she dished out all that juicy hearsay with such passionate enthusiasm.

Jessica appeared so peacefully lifeless that I completely lost myself in the stillness of the scene before me. Causing me to almost leap out of my own skin, when Amy, the voice inside my head, spoke, declaring, "Alone at last!"

"Goddammit, Amy!" I snapped at her in a whispered shout.

"She does look dead though, right?" Amy went on to say. "Which reminds me. What I wanted to talk to you about."

"I thought we were going to talk later?" I hissed. "When we're alone?"

"We *are* alone," she said. "Technically. And it *is* later. By one minute and forty-three seconds."

Taking a seat at my desk, but still keeping an eye on a sleeping 'Jessica', I reluctantly agreed to hear Amy out.

"OK," I told Amy. "But only until she wakes up."

"Of course," she replied, in a snake-like voice.

"What do you want, Amy?" I asked her, plainly.

"Wow," Amy said in sarcastic surprise. "You're even starting to *sound* like her."

"Like who?" I asked.

"Schmuck!" Amy spat at me. "The idiot that's asleep on your bed right now!"

"She is *not* an idiot!" I spat back at her.

And even though I couldn't physically see her, I could just tell that Amy was giving me this cocky look with her arms folded.

"Alright," I said. "She is a *bit* of an idiot, but don't bring *her* into all this, it's not *her* fault."

"Anyway," Amy said. "Let's forget for a minute about the dumb blonde that's asleep on your bed right now. There's something I've been dying to talk to you about."

"Go on," I said, really rather reluctant to know.

"I worked it out," Amy told me. "What really happened that fateful day in the university canteen."

"But I thought we already spoke about this. That I *do* have a power. That I killed you with it."

"I played the memory of that day over and over. Studying it, slowed down and sped up, forwards and in reverse."

"I killed you, Amy. It's as simple as that."

"The very last thought that went through my mind. Right when we locked eyes from across the room. How I just wished that I was you."

"And *I* wanted you dead. That's why you died."

"That was the moment my mind jumped from my head and into yours. That's how I came to be a voice inside your head. I 'mind hopped'. If you had've *killed* me, that would never have happened."

"So I *didn't* kill you?"

"No. I mean, you probably *would* have, but I beat you to it."

"So what are you saying? What are you *really* saying?"

"What I'm saying is that I want to have a body. And my mind back in a head of my own."

"But haven't we tried this already? That day at the cemetery?"

"I didn't say, '*my* body', Iris. I said, '*a* body'."

It took a few teetering seconds for the penny to drop, but when it did, it dropped as hard as a money bag.

"No," I said. "I am not going to let you hijack the body of an innocent girl, just so's *you* can have one."

"Oh, no?" asked Amy. "You were prepared to *kill* this girl, and that was just for the sake of some silly experiment you were conducting. You were more than happy to do it *then*. And like you said, she won't be missed. Plus, this isn't just for me, Iris. Wouldn't you like me out of your head, too?"

And without knowing my answer to Amy's question, I fell silent for just long enough for her to take the opportunity to continue.

"When I disappeared," Amy said, "I disappeared, deep. I hid in parts of your mind, you forgot were ever there. And in those places, I found memories. I began experimenting with them. And not only did I find that I could bring memories to the forefront of your mind,

I also found I could erase them. So, I started small. Starting with your short-term memory. What you did in the last five minutes. The last half hour. The last hour. The last day, and so on. I did this for two reasons. One, to mess with your head, and get your attention. And two, as a bargaining chip, if I ever needed it."

And even if I *could* hear, I wouldn't have heard my gaping mouth make a sound.

"If you don't do this for me," she continued, "give me Jessica's body. I will begin erasing *more* memories. Starting with the ones from long ago, right up to the here and now.

"Souvenirs in your mind of the first time you set foot on a foreign beach, slipping away, like hot white sand sifting through your fingers.

"The happy recollections of your eighteenth birthday, blown out, like the flames that once danced on the candles.

"The memory of the last time your father held you in his arms, leaving you, in much the same way you left *him* to get on with the rest of your life.

"I'll keep doing this until I have caught up to the present. Right up to the minute. Right up to the second. That's when you'll forget what it was you were doing five minutes ago, or what you were going to do five minutes from then. You'll forget your name, until you finally forget who you are. When you look in the mirror, you won't even recognise your own face. I'll keep going until there's nothing left of you, and all that's left is me. I will assume my place in your head and in your body. Imagine it, a prisoner in your own head, with me at the helm. You will move to the back, and I will move to the front. You'll be finished, whereas I'll just be getting started. I will become you, and you will become nothing.

"I think I might even begin with the memories of Malleus," she told me. "Perhaps, after that, he and I can finally be reacquainted. Or maybe I'll leave the memories where they are; crush him with cruel words instead. And in that silent moment, right when his heart breaks, all *you'll* be able to do is watch.

"Plus, I'll have your powers," Amy finished with. "And God only *knows* what I'm going to do with *those*."

A short, sharp gasp entered my mouth; my eyes, stretched wide as a chill was sent up the length of my spine.

"So what's it to be, Iris?"

But I didn't answer Amy's question with words. My answer was shaking Jessica awake. Waiting right up until the moment I could see into her eyes, and that her eyes were fixed on mine. She awoke almost immediately, with a moan I imagined but never heard.

Rubbing her eyes, she asked me what the time was.

"You really don't want to know," I told her. "I'm so sorry, Jessica. Forget you ever knew me."

And with Jessica's eyes, now open, I looked deep into them. And as our eyes locked, that's when I told Amy to make the jump from my head and into Jessica's. I stared deep into those tight, black pinholes, circled by a sapphire ring, with all of that ivory-white around them.

Right up until the moment Jessica's face relaxed, her eyes blinked, and I could no longer hear Amy as a voice inside my head.

67

I was still locking eyes with Jessica as I wished one, last thing for her. One, last act of kindness. And in a wholly different way to how I did with Amy that fateful day in the university canteen, and with a heavy heart laden with guilt, I began to wish Jessica to death.

You have to believe that I really didn't want Jessica to die, but with all the aggressive designs Amy had on her and I – taking ownership of our minds and assuming her place within either mine or Jessica's body – it was the fairest thing I could see, in that flash of a horrid moment, to do.

And I had to act quickly, before Amy had the chance to realise what I was *really* doing. Not giving her what she wanted, but getting her out of my head, and saving Jessica from the hell of what Amy was planning on doing with her.

That being the *only* reason for what I had just done.

My mind was still playing catch-up with what had just happened as I stood over Jessica; wishing there had been something else I could have done with all the powers I possessed. A more preferable outcome, where Amy was gone, and Jessica was still here.

So involved with my strategy of making, what I considered the best of a terrible situation, I hadn't thought past to the other side of it, and landed myself in another hopeless place where I had no idea as to what to do afterwards.

Amy was no longer in my head – of that I was quite sure – and Jessica was just lying there, lifeless on the bed as if she were still asleep, just not breathing. And if her eyes weren't wide open, frozen in abject terror like they were now, that's all you would have thought.

I was still knelt by the bed with my hand rested on one of Jessica's knees.

"I'm sorry I ever laid eyes on you," I told her as I stroked her eyes closed with the thumb and fingers of one hand. Only then did the gravity of the situation rise up within me, pulling tears from my eyes, and dragging them down my face.

I'd never seen a dead body before. At least, not *this* close up. Amy's lifeless corpse was all the way over on the other side of a university canteen when I thought I'd 'accidentally/on purpose' killed her that day.

What was I going to do now? I hadn't thought far enough ahead of what I'd just done to know.

The only people I could call for help, I could count on one hand with a finger and thumb to spare: Malleus, my dad, and that big CEO, Richard Heard.

If I called Malleus, this would be *the* thing after *everything*, that pushed our already teetering relationship over the edge and into oblivion.

And what would I tell my dad, exactly? He didn't even *know* about my powers, and if he *did*, he would have thought me delusional.

As for Richard, the big CEO, I'm sure he would have *wanted* to help. That is, if he could. But all the money in his multiple bank accounts, combined, wasn't going to bring this poor girl back from the dead, *or* exorcise Amy's mind from Jessica's hijacked head.

Malleus, my dad, and Richard Heard, the big CEO.

These were the only three people I could call.

And so, instead, I just called an ambulance.

This was the first time I'd ever called emergency services in my entire life. And it was just as well – what with me being deaf – that my phone was already registered to enable me to do this. After making their way through a list of questions with me, the operator said that the ambulance was approximately fifteen minutes away. Giving me just enough time to pull myself together, think logically about the whole situation, and make use of the one quarter of an hour to get my story straight before the paramedics showed up.

I figured I'd keep it simple.

Me and Jessica were having a girly night in. I took a bathroom break. And then, somewhere between Patrick Swayze saying, *"Nobody puts Baby in a corner,"* and 'that lift', I came out of the bathroom to find Jessica slumped on my bed. *'The Time of My Life'* – a song I haven't heard since I left secondary school – still playing in the background.

Probably.

I called an ambulance, not because there may have been a chance of saving Jessica; she was gone, and there was no way for anyone to bring her back – apart from maybe, Malleus. But he wasn't here, and even if he *was* here to do it, there was still Amy to contend with.

I called the ambulance, not to save *her*, but to save *myself*.

If I hadn't, we would've *both* lost our lives, just in different ways. Her slumped on a bed, and me rotting in some dingy prison cell. But before I could think any more on this, blue flashing lights began bouncing off the walls of my room.

The paramedics arrived, carried out their checks, noted the time of death, and took Jessica's body away in a black, rubber, zip-up bag. It was all so quick, that I wasn't graced with the time to fully process what had just happened. And I couldn't help the thought crossing my mind that I'd just got away with murder again. The only difference being that *this* time I didn't feel in the least bit good about it.

Obviously, they had their questions – the paramedics – which I gave my answers to in a frank but heartfelt manner.

It was the deserved guilt that followed, however, that made all this feel very different somehow. When Amy dropped to the floor, right after I shot her 'that look' in the university canteen, I still wasn't sure, back then, whether it was because of me.

Even when I found out later that it may well have been, some time had passed and, by then, I just didn't feel all that bad about it. But *this* time I knew precisely what I was doing, and I had done it to a girl who hadn't really done me much wrong to deserve it. Jessica was merely a red mark, made in the centre of a white rope, whilst Amy and I played tug of war with each other.

Amy was gone – and perhaps deservedly so – but then, so was

Jessica. This was never about her. She just had the dumb luck of catching the attention of the eyes Amy and I shared. Getting caught up in the violent crossfire Amy and I had going between us. She just didn't know it. And, because of this, she never stood a chance.

This time, it felt all kinds of wrong.

And I just knew, deep down in my pained gut, that I would, somehow, pay dearly for this.

I just didn't yet know how, or when.

After all the theatrics of blue flashing lights and paramedics geared up with a defibrillator and an oxygen mask, I was now alone, and I really felt it this time.

Alone.

Even the word itself sounded lonely.

And being alone with my thoughts, at a time like this, was not a good thing. What I needed was someone, other than myself, for company.

Which is funny.

Not funny, ha ha.

Just, funny.

Only because I had ended the life of a girl who was providing me with what I so desperately needed less than an hour later.

The time was precisely, **11:34 pm.**

Which, from where I was lying on the floor, looking up at the bright-red, upside-down numbers of my alarm clock on the bedside table, read like the word, '**HELL**'.

I tried not to read too much into that.

Was it too late to call somebody? Even if it wasn't, who did I really *have* to call? And I already knew the answer to this next question, but, whose fault was that?

What I decided I *wouldn't* do, was go round and round in the hopeless circles of whether it was right or wrong, what I did to Jessica. Chewing it over, like a fatty chunk of steak that would never break down enough for me to swallow.

I didn't need to talk about what happened with Jessica; the blue strobing lights, the paramedics, the body bag. I just needed someone who knew nothing about what had taken place tonight, and to talk about something else – *anything* else – as long as it wasn't about that particular sore point of a subject.

What I needed was a distraction.

And so, with my phone in hand, and scrolling down through the contacts in my rather sad and empty looking phonebook, the tip of my finger wasn't swiping up the phone screen for long, when it got as far as 'D'.

'D' for 'Dad'.

But when I hit 'call', and it started ringing, that's all it did. It just rang. He never picked up. He would *always* pick up. Eventually, the ringing gave in before I did. And disappointedly setting my phone down on the desk, I waited, in the hope he would call back. But as hopeful as I was that he would, and as much as I needed him right now …

… he never did.

68

It was the slow rise of sunlight, glowing just behind the curtains, that gently woke me. A warm glow filling my room with a haze of orange and yellow. And just for a moment, everything was as it should be.

Once my sleepy eyes were fully open, however, and my dreamy mind had caught up with them, it was then I noticed the scrunched-up packet of cheese puffs in the bin under my desk. Bottles of nail varnish still scattered on the floor. The buzzing static on the TV screen. A lingering powdery processed cheese smell, and an overpowering scent of chemicals, sharply reminding me of all that took place in this very room just last night.

With my head now securely back in my possession, I went over everything that had happened before I fell asleep. I had done the right thing in calling the ambulance; that much I was sure of. Jessica's death still plagued my mind, but what choice did I really have with everything Amy was threatening us both with? I still maintained the belief that I had made, what I thought to be, the best of what was a truly terrible situation.

Anyway, it was done.

And there was no going back to make a different choice.

My thoughts now, more or less, settled in my mind, I laid my head back down on the pillow, and rested a little easier. For whatever reason, reminded of the first time I woke up in this bed after my first night's sleep in this once strange room.

Getting myself up off the bed I was accustomed to by now, I went through the familiar motions of my usual morning routine.

Looking in the mirror one last time, as I always did, just checking everything was in place before leaving out the door.

A reassuring feeling took its rightful place within me as I walked down the street. Soothing my whole being with the fuzzy warmth of an invisible, cashmere hoodie. I didn't have a place in mind as to where I was going. Neither did I consciously make the decision to simply let the morning guide me. It just took me without me even thinking about it.

I was only quite sure this wasn't some lucid dream, but if it was, I was certain it was one I'd never wake from. And I never did, because it wasn't. I had nothing pressing to do, and nowhere urgent to be, with all the time in the world not to do it in, or ever get there.

Still, I felt incomplete somehow, because there was someone I dearly missed. Someone I looked forward to actually seeing again, and not just as some sentimental memory in my mind. It had been, how many days I don't know, which made me wonder how much they were missing me, if at all. Was it over between us, and I was just left so far behind that I didn't *know* it? I certainly wasn't going to *push* for an answer, as that would no doubt just push them further away. But just because touching base with this certain 'someone' by phone may not have been the thing to do, there were other, more old-fashioned ways to do it. I could always just happen to run into them by chance.

So I took a casual stroll, and as I did, passed all of our familiar places.

Being a Sunday, the café was closed this time in the morning.

The park, too, was empty.

So I headed for the river; rays of sunshine flickering on the rippled water and onto my face like a thousand golden kisses as I sat on our knobbly log.

With no one else around, I felt as if I were the only girl left in the world; one of two lone survivors of an apocalypse, on the search for the last surviving boy.

Next was the pizza place, which was also, and unsurprisingly so, closed.

Then there was the pawnshop, which although I knew not

to be open today, caused a smile to creep up either side of my face, reminding me of the good I had done with my powers.

That smile only lasting as long as it took me to realise that this pawnshop was also one of the last places I could hope to run into this 'someone'.

And although it was most doubtful they would be there, I walked a little further to the very last place in the world I thought they'd be.

Pressing the button on the intercom, I waited.

Not that I had much use for one, mind, but I had to at least give this a shot.

After all the work this place had undergone, you could only tell it was the same home as before because of where it was situated in relation to everything else that remained unchanged around it, and those same gates that still stood so tall. Gone was the gold leaf and gemstoned everything. The house sign on the wall, just off to the side of the lofty gates now read, 'Mi Casa Es Su Casa', but instead of a gold plaque, the words were etched into smooth, white stone.

It was then, a red light began to flash on the intercom panel.

"Hello?" I said into the microphone grille. "I don't know if you can hear me?"

And if there *was* somebody talking to me on the other end, I certainly couldn't hear them, but I could feel the vibrations of what could be a voice speaking back to me.

"My name is Iris," I told the grille. "I'm here to see Richard?"

As soon as the light stopped flashing, I stopped talking and just waited, hopefully. A few more seconds of silence, and the gates began to move inward on their runners. Shimmying through, sideways, the moment they opened wide enough for me to do so. That's when the front door to the house opened outward to present an especially proud looking Richard. Who, upon seeing me stood on what used to be the driveway of his once gaudy mansion, made his way down the steps that led from the door, and towards me. And with arms held out at either side of him, like an overly friendly scarecrow, he asked me, something along the lines of, "What do you think?"

What I really wanted to say here was, *Probably way more than I should!*

But instead, I simply said, "Wow."

"It's so good to see you, Iris," Richard went on to say. "I suppose you're here to see Malleus?"

"He's here?"

"Has been for the last few days now. Would you like me to send for him?"

"Oh, no. You don't need to do that."

"It really is no problem."

"No. That's probably not a good idea."

"Can I ask why it is you're here, then?"

You just did! I thought to myself. But it was a good question. What *was* I doing here?

"Is there something you need?" he asked.

Another good question. *So* good, I didn't even have an answer for it.

"Shall I let him know you called, at least?" he asked.

"Can you tell him to meet me somewhere?" I said.

"Yes, of course. Where and when?"

"First place we ever met. Tell Malleus I'll be there at noon."

Richard nodded, looking down at what would have once been his two thousand spondoolie shoes.

"But only if he actually wants to," I added.

Richard nodded his head, *yes,* but this time he put a reassuring hand on my shoulder, telling me, "He really does love you, you know."

"I know," I told my shoes.

Richard then lifted my chin with a gentle hand, saying, "I don't think that you do."

I know, I thought to myself. At least, I *thought* I knew.

"Doesn't take someone with eyes to see it," he told me.

Richard gently gripped my shoulder one last time with a friendly hand, only letting go to slowly walk back to the front door of the house, hands in pockets. Leaving me stood at the gates, wistfully thoughtful of his last words to me.

And walking out through the gates, now slowly closing and gently ushering me out, I smiled when I looked back up at that big old house. Not because of what I had done here, but because somewhere, in one of the many rooms of that house, was a boy that loved me.

69

"The Absence of Dark"

As I sat there, on one of the many vacant benches of the park – the back-lit leaves like a canopy of green above me – forgotten nerves, undisturbed since that first time I met with Malleus in amongst these same trees, reminded me of their presence.

Checking my wristwatch from time to time, I thought about everything Malleus and I had shared with each other. The places we had been – both physically, and in our minds – and all that we'd been through together. It'd been quite the journey. And this. This felt like the destination. But I still had this feeling way down in my gut that this wasn't quite the end of our story.

One, slow hour passed with me just sat there waiting on that bench. Feeling like the forgotten lemon of a big and empty fruit bowl; the yellow of my maxi-dress matching the colour of the way I felt. And I sighed, because that's all I could do. It took a lot for me to give up on Malleus, and so it required everything in me just to will myself up from the bench I was sat upon. Feeling more lonesome than ever as I made my way out of the park, back the way I came. If I just had Malleus here with me, I wouldn't have needed the company of another soul in the world right now.

Just then, no sooner had I made the wish in my mind, my wish was granted. It was the strangest thing. Because as I happened to look back at the bench I'd left behind, I saw the sketchy shadow of a figure making their way toward it. The awkward shuffles of a boy making his way through a world, so dark, he literally had to feel his way through it. Navigating the environment around him with best guesses as where to land the next step. And even though my voice had been stolen from me in that moment of quiet disbelief, I could still just about manage to summon up enough sound to call out his name.

It was only when I finally held Malleus in my arms did I truly believe it was him, for I thought perhaps my eyes were deceiving me. His first words to me being how much he'd missed my voice, and mine, how much I'd looked forward to seeing his face. But how good it felt to hold each other again: that was something we *both* shared.

"You're late," I told him, biting down on a smile.

"No, I'm not," he replied. "I'm right on time."

"Yes, you are. I said, twelve, noon."

"It *is* noon."

"Not by *my* watch. I've been waiting here for over an hour."

I could see that he was doing his utmost not to laugh, and so I asked him, "What's so funny?"

"I think I see what's happened here," he said, nodding his head in time with the words.

I just threw him a look that he couldn't see, to catch.

"You haven't got the right time," he said.

"I think I know how to tell the time," I told him.

"Did you also know that the clocks went back an hour last night?"

"Oh, right," I muttered under my breath. "That would explain it."

Malleus then rummaged inside his jacket and pulled out a small, black, rectangular box, no bigger than a TV remote.

"Here," he says, as he hands the box to me. "I got you something."

"For *me?*" I asked, gently taking the box from his hands.

And thinking it's a fancy watch or a shiny, new bracelet, I tell him, "Aww, you shouldn't have."

To make the moment last, I slowly pull the box apart to reveal what, at first glance, appears to be a black, rubber wristband.

Turning to Malleus, I ask him, "What *is* this?"

"A peace offering," he tells me.

"No, like, *really*. What *is* this?"

Malleus's lips moved in ways I couldn't quite decipher.

"A street crap?" I asked him.

"No," Malleus said, laughing. "A *SleepStrap*."

"Oh," I say. "Thanks."

"Here," he says. "Let me help you put it on. Hold out your arm."

With the rubber wristband thingamy held in his one hand, he holds the wrist of my right arm in the other, and with impressive technique, fastens it, not too loose, not too tight.

I hold my arm out, quickly twisting it all the way to the left, and all the way to the right, to better see the face and fastening of this strange wristband, asking him, "So, what does it do? Help you sleep?"

Malleus just laughs.

"Actually," he tells me, "I think it's supposed to wake you up."

"Oh, right," I say. "How?"

"You set a time, and it vibrates to wake you."

"Oh."

"To be honest, I wasn't really sure what to get you."

"No," I say, without first engaging my brain.

"I kept the receipt," he tells me. "So I can always take it back if you don't like it."

"No," I say again.

And I don't know if I'm just saying it out of politeness, or that it's just taking me some time to catch up with the fact that the gift wasn't some fancy wristwatch or a shiny new bracelet, but I tell him, "I love it."

"You hate it," Malleus says, grabbing for my arm and feeling for the fastening on the band to undo it.

"No," I tell him, pulling my arm away. "I think it's really sweet."

And I'm back to admiring this strange new wristband thingy, again.

"Were there other colours?" I ask him.

"Why?" he asks me. "Did you want a pink one?"

"God, no! It's just that it's so …"

"What? Black?"

"Well. Yeah."

"What can I say? I've got a thing for black. Not that you hadn't noticed, already."

"Why *do* you like black so much? I mean, it's all you ever wear."

"Because I still know what black *looks* like," he says. "It's all I can ever see anymore."

"But this is for *me* to wear," I tell him. "*I* can still see colours, so why did you get me a black one?"

"I just figured," he says, "this way, whenever you look at it, it'll always remind you of me."

Tripping up on each other's excitable words, I told Malleus that perhaps he should go first. And whilst he talked, I held my tongue, like a wave I was trying to sweep back out to sea with a broom. Malleus told me that he was sorry for the way he'd acted last time we met at The Daily Grind café. After all that drama with Jessica, the barista girl, standing on tables and raining down hell fire on the regular, hipster clientele.

My whole body shuddered as a chill went up my spine, quickly shaking my head in a bid to throw off the distressing memory flashes of last night.

Malleus goes on to tell me how he'd been thinking about the powers he possessed, and how perhaps I was doing the right thing in using mine. That maybe he was wrong for merely treating his powers like a private hobby. "Selfish", as I'd once put it. How upset he was that, even with the dead pigeon video footage as proof, people, with their doubtful hearts and narrow minds, just couldn't believe in something so wonderful, because the world was so full of things that claimed to be real, and so often turned out not to be.

"If there was only some way I could put my powers on display," Malleus told me. "For all to see with their very own eyes. Maybe *then* they would believe, with it all happening right there in front of them.

"If we could somehow get enough people together," he went on to say, "and show them all what I can do, with no distractions, maybe *then* they wouldn't be able to deny it. Maybe *then* they would understand."

But now that I had powers myself, our roles had somewhat reversed. Now *I* was the hesitant one, when it came to the idea of going 'all out' with Malleus's whole 'bringing back the dead' thing. After everything Malleus and I had talked about, in regards to our powers, I thought we were going to wear one another's secret like a heavy necklace we vowed never to take off from around our necks. But if this was really what Malleus wanted, then I had an obligation to support him, because that's just what friends do.

But as great an idea Malleus thought this was, and as much as I wanted to agree with him, to feel what he felt, I didn't. To me, it felt more like we were both gradually sliding into the jaws of a sinister something, trapping us behind its teeth and swallowing us whole. And as much as I tried to warn him off the idea, he didn't take heed of my warnings that simply fell on his deaf ears.

I gave Malleus the task of coming up with a way for him to demonstrate his power to the masses. I did this, not to palm off all of the responsibility on him, or to shy away from my own personal involvement – I was here for him, in whatever capacity. I did this, to give me more time to come up with a reason for him *not* to do this. To save him from himself and what I was so sure would happen.

One thing I was always good at, in the time I'd known Malleus, was coming up with problems to his every solution. Malleus would also need my assistance with whatever ideas he came up with. That whatever plans Malleus had, he wouldn't be able to see them through without me.

As much as I needed him, he needed me.

At least, I hoped he did.

70

"Special Abilities"

"A mallet hose?" I asked Malleus.

This was when Malleus and I were back in my room, throwing ideas back and forth. When I say, 'throwing ideas back and forth', what I *really* mean is that Malleus was throwing ideas at *me*, and I was just throwing them right back at *him*.

"No," Malleus said through a laugh. "A talent show!"

"You want to put on a talent show?" I asked again, just to make sure we were both on the same page of certifiable insanity.

"With your help, of course," he added.

So, he *did* need me. I was glad that he'd said it because *that* meant I could start dumping stumbling blocks along the road to the fruition of his batshit-crazy idea.

And everything was going so well. So well, that I should've seen this coming.

"You're probably wondering why a talent show," he said, almost as if it were a question.

And although he couldn't see the look of utter bewilderment in my eyes, he could, no doubt, hear the silence of my pensive mouth.

"You want to get a whole lot of people together," he went on to say, "you invite them to a place where everybody gets to be involved. Gathering them in a setting where they all have the opportunity to show off what they can do."

To be fair to Malleus, it *had* been working for well-known TV talent shows for years: *Britain's Got Skills, Pop Hero, The Z Factor.* I had to admit this was a good idea, but I didn't want Malleus knowing that, for obvious reasons. And so, I continued in the vein of my dumb-blonde responses, as, so far, it seemed to be working. Playing dumb wasn't going to be enough, however. It was time to start hurling 'problem-grenades' at his every assault of good ideas.

"And just where are we going to get all these people from?" I asked.

"That's where *you* come in," he said.

I'm almost embarrassed to confess that I really wasn't expecting him to say that, but now that he had, I knew exactly where he was going with it.

"All the popularity you gained after Amy died," he went on to say. "All those followers of yours. You can get them all on board."

"But that was ages ago," I told him.

"The *protest* wasn't all that long ago. You got a hundred people together for that. You could easily round up a few hundred people for *this*."

Not only was Malleus full of bright ideas, he was also worryingly enthusiastic about them, so I attempted to throw him off with some more snags to entangle his trailblazing thoughts with.

"So how's it going to work exactly?" I asked him. "How are you going to …?"

My words trailed off as I tried to think of a fitting verb to use. 'Perform', 'exhibit' and 'demonstrate', all springing to mind.

"How am I going to show everyone my power?" he asked.

Malleus always had the simplest way of putting things. Something that I usually loved about him, but here it was keeping him in control of where this conversation was going.

"Much in the same way I showed *you*," he said.

"Yeah," I said with a hidden satisfaction. "Bit of a problem there. There's no way they'd actually allow you to bring a dead animal into the university building."

Even with him wearing sunglasses, the disappointment on Malleus's face was evident from the way his mouth tightened and his nose scrunched up.

"It's OK, Malleus," I said, putting an arm round him. "We'll think of something."

"You don't want me to do this, do you?" he asked me, shrugging my arm off his shoulders.

With every stride we took with our words, I could see we were headed ever closer to yet another fallout, so I treaded carefully.

"It's not that," I told him. "I'm just trying to work out the best way for you to do this."

"Well, ears are all I've got, Iris!" he barked, "So, tell me!"

The both of us falling silent, as I quietly considered the right words to use as a reply. If this really was what Malleus wanted, then all I need do was be in his corner. So, really, there was only one question I need ask.

"You really want to do this?" I asked him.

"Yes!" he told me. "I've given it a lot of thought, and this is really what I want to do!"

"OK," I said softly. "I'll see what I can do."

"Thank you," he said.

The way he said it. Sounding more like a 'finally' than a 'thank you', but I took it as one, all the same. I still had the strongest of senses that this was a very bad idea. A sense I would have to do my best to lose.

For, in the meantime, it looked like I had a talent show to organise.

71

"Must the Show Go On?"

So preoccupied I was, with making posters and flyers, I had almost but forgotten what I was doing it all for. Busy auditioning applicants for the talent show, and meeting with the university head – who had now sadly lost his grumpy looking ginger-and-white-striped cat. This missing cat of his being pretty much all he went on about in the one long meeting I had with him. Even going as far as to asking me if I wouldn't be too put out handing out 'LOST CAT' flyers, and hanging up posters around the university, in a bid to find this precious, pet feline of his.

With all of these other things whirling around in my busy head, I had to make a conscious effort to remind myself that all this was for Malleus. A public demonstration of his life-breathing powers, under the guise of a talent show for all. Setting the date for a month from now, giving me just enough time to put it all together. And apart from the minor issue of health and safety to consider when bringing dead animals into the university building, we were on our way to being set for one hell of a show.

In the line-up so far, we had the more customary acts of singers, dancers and magicians, along with the more unwonted applicants; including that of contortionists, performance artists and freestyle rappers – most of which I had to tactfully turn away for not being quite … how should I put it? 'Appropriate' for the show. I even thought about signing *myself* up for the show. But then, after giving it a little more consideration, decided against it.

These people weren't yet ready for what *I* could do.

For most of that month, all I did was live, breathe, eat and sleep the preparations for this little talent show of ours. Giving myself thirty days, and getting it done in just twenty-three. Allowing Malleus and I one, whole, uninterrupted week together to do whatever we pleased in the lead-up to the big day of the show. Time to spare for all the things we *should* have done by now, if it weren't for … well, you know …

… everything.

All the things 'normal' people would have done on first dates, such as meeting for coffee. The only difference being that *this* time round, we sat talking about more regular things as we sipped from our cups. Everyday, run-of-the-mill stuff, and nothing about all-powerful abilities getting out of control, or some crazy plan we were concocting. Just the regular kind of 'getting to know you' chit-chat. Everything we missed the first time round, without all the weirdness blocking the flow of us actually finding out about the reassuring ordinariness in one another.

The simple things in life, I've come to find, are often the most meaningful.

Malleus even taught me how to read Braille. And I wish I could have returned the favour by teaching him how to sign, but, as it turned out, this is way easier to learn if you can actually see.

For what was probably the first time, things between Malleus and I finally felt … ordinary. Not in a boring way. More so, in a pleasantly familiar way. We ate out at a fancy restaurant and flirted with the waiting staff.

We went clothes shopping for outfits for the talent show. Well, *I* did. Malleus just tagged along. *He* wanted to stay 'true to himself' and wear what he usually wore, whereas I wanted something a little more special.

Ever since I turned eight – around the time my dad finally began letting me choose my own clothes and dress myself – I had always dreamed of owning a red dress. Just like the one my mother was wearing in the only photo I have left of her; the one I secretly saved from the ruthlessness of my father's angry hands as the others met their fate, torn up in the bottom of a waste-paper recycling bin.

My mum, sat proudly upon the bonnet of my dad's then brand-new E-type Jaguar. Way back when my parents were crazy, stupid happy and hopelessly in love. Long before I came into their world and ruined everything, along with the once taut skin of my mother's stomach.

And whenever I see that colour, be it a beautiful sunset, a London bus, or even something as ugly as a bleeding nose, I think of her in that red dress.

Red: a colour I never had the nerve to wear until now.

And what better occasion than a talent show I was personally presenting. And as I stood there, admiring my reflection dressed shoulder to ankle in red, in the fitting-room mirror of some fancy department store, I just wished both my mum and Malleus could have seen how fabulous I looked – although, he did say how lovely my body felt as he ran his hands over the dress's silken fabric.

And I don't know why I suggested it, as I was pretty useless at it, but we went bowling, too. Me, stood beside Malleus, running up to just before the foul-line with him, guiding his arm down and back up again to release the ball. It also doubled up as a trust-exercise, as he quite heavily relied on me not to lie about our scores. He did win a few games – which was impressive, if not a little embarrassing – and although he didn't see it, I'm pretty sure he heard the *Thud!* of my butt hitting the deck of the polished pine flooring when I slipped over, on one of my turns to bowl. A *Thump!* that promised to show up again as a sizable bruise the next day. But the whole thing was such a hoot that it didn't matter how many strikes in a row Malleus scored, or how many times my ball ended up in the gutter.

Of course, some things were out of the question, like, say, go-karting or a rock concert, but we weren't at all short of things we *could* do with each other. We went to the pictures to see a movie that wasn't too reliant on action or its sound effects – although I do like the deep, booming sensation of low bass notes as they tremble through my body. We'd pick a suitable film; I'd watch as I read the subtitles, whilst Malleus just sat there beside me, listening intently to the dialogue. And even though one of us couldn't see the actors' faces, while the other didn't catch the tone of their voices, we could still be entertained. We could still have a good time. We could still snack on overpriced popcorn, and gulp down a gallon of flat, watered-down Coca Soda until our bladders were fit to bursting.

Leaving the darkness of the movie-theatre, we took a stroll – my eyes stunned for a moment by the contrasting light of the outside, and tonguing popcorn kernels still stuck between my teeth. Malleus knew I loved walking by water, so he brought me back to 'our river'. Taking a pew on our knobbly log about halfway, where I didn't have to lie to him about the view, since it was a fine, dry day, and the river had now been miraculously cleared of the expected clutter of traffic cones and shopping trolleys.

Nor were there any dead birds.

Which reminds me: I got a tattoo. *Sorry, Dad.* One of a dead cartoon hamster with two *Xs* for eyes. I designed it myself, based on some of the doodles I made during lectures, and wear it proudly halfway up my forearm – even though it's hiding under a layer of petroleum jelly and a bandage for now. And I realise I may have thrown myself into being friends with Malleus a little hastily in the beginning, but hey, of all my father's words of warning, breaking two out of the three pieces of advice he gave isn't bad going for a girl like me. And in my defence, I never did sleep with any of my flatmates. I tried to persuade Malleus to have 'ink done', too. Telling him he should get a dead cartoon-pigeon, maybe, and how totally bad-ass that would make him look. But what would be the point, he argued. All that needless pain for something he would never see, to appreciate.

It was actually kind of fun: coming up with ways round the day-to-day things people with their sight and hearing took for granted. Almost going as far as to say we actually felt *sorry* for people who had all of their senses, because, to them, they were just a given and not always truly appreciated.

Sure, I would never hear the latest song to come out on the radio, and Malleus would never know what celebrities looked like on TV. But I could still see the way pinkish-white blossom blew off a tree in the wind of a blue-skyed day, and Malleus could still hear the hiss and burst of waves at a beach as they came rolling in on tumbling spindrifts.

What's more, we had each other. I truly appreciated my sight, and Malleus, his hearing. I could still describe to him, what I saw, much in the same way *he* could, what he heard. Where one of us lacked, the other made up for it. We filled in the blanks for one another. Fitting together, like the lost pieces of two different jigsaw puzzles. Everything felt worthwhile when I was with him. And in a world that so baffled us both, we made complete sense.

"I am your ears," he had told me.

To which I replied, "And I am your eyes."

We had quite the time in those seven days, and probably found out more about each other than most people discover in a lifetime. I think it's because, when I was with him, I would just let my guard down. Malleus telling me that when he was with me, his walls just crumbled. We could just be ourselves with each other and open up in ways most people would never dare. Still, the days leading up to the talent show crept up on me before I had the chance to glance back and realise. As if it came as some huge surprise to me that what Malleus and I had those last seven days, couldn't last forever.

With only another day to go, and the fact that the day of the talent show was almost upon us, this crest of the good times we had been riding was inevitably going to come crashing down. Our seven days together were almost up, and I had this sinking feeling that we would never have days like those again. I should've been enjoying what time Malleus and I had right now, but I dreaded tomorrow like I dreaded death after a life not lived. One eye on my time with Malleus, and the other on the ever-shifting sand of an hourglass.

I just wanted to get this talent show done and out of the way, or better yet, not do it at all.

What was it that I was so afraid of happening? Or was it worse to know? To be told what that bad thing was before it happened. Like knowing the exact time and date of your death, and the way in which you would die.

Thing is.

If I *had* known before time, I would never have even entertained the idea of a talent show. And I certainly never would have let Malleus be a part of it. But I *didn't* know. Not at *this* point.

And despite my own reluctance tugging at me to cancel the show, "The show," Malleus told me, "must go on!"

72

"Pop Goes the Cherry"

It wasn't often, if ever, that I saw Malleus nervous.

We were lying on my bed together, as if we were two spoons resting in each other's curve. We had been kissing, but I think this time it was headed somewhere, which made *me* a little nervous, too. You see, something I never felt the need to tell you until now was that, if this was to lead to …

… well. You know.

This would be my first time.

But Malleus wasn't to know, and I intended to keep it that way. At least for now. He didn't *need* to know, and I figured the whole, 'making love for the first time' thing, didn't require any more added pressure than it already came with, and so I kept that one, little detail to myself.

I believed Malleus cared about me, *loved* me, even. He didn't strike me as the type of boy to take advantage of a girl by getting her drunk, or tricking that same girl into bed by making out he'd misplaced his house keys, and could he, possibly, maybe, spend the night at her flat. Offer her a sensual back-massage with her bra and top off or something.

If I were to choose when I lost my virginity, it would be tonight.

And if I were to choose who I would lose it *to*, it would be Malleus.

The way he so gently caressed me; exploring every inch of my body with his tender hands, as if I were made of the most fragile of glass. I have no idea how long he was doing this for – my skin, yearning for his touch, just under the delicate fabric of my clothing –

as I was too blissfully unaware to pay any mind to the time.

But it was Malleus that made the first move by shifting his position and propping himself up on one arm. The way he did it being more like a question than a proposition, as if he were asking for my permission with his body. My whole body breathlessly whispering, *yes*. My lips speaking for me, telling him to kiss them again.

This was right after I'd sneakily popped a mint in my mouth.

He was on top of me now, but I didn't feel trapped, I felt safe. He pulled his T-shirt off, and I unbuttoned my blouse. Kicking off his shoes, I shook off my own. Slowly, we helped each other undress. Malleus did struggle with the fastening on my bra, and I had just a little trouble unpeeling him from his skinny jeans, but since when did doing anything for the first time ever go smoothly? It's not like we were being closely scrutinised by a panel of judges, ready to give us their scores the very moment we finished.

This was for us, and for us, alone.

Doing my best to block out any thoughts of my own father – only because he was the man that ever so thoughtfully supplied me with them – I roll onto my side and reach into the drawer of the bedside table to retrieve a sealed box of condoms.

Suddenly Malleus's whole body froze up.

"What's wrong?" I asked him. "Are you not OK with this?"

"No, I am," he told me. "It's just that I think your phone's going off."

I quickly glanced at my phone flashing away on the bedside table, telling him, "Whoever it is, they can wait."

Then, without thinking, I asked Malleus if he wanted the lights on or off, to which he just pulled a face, telling me that it really made no difference to him.

I was always forgetting.

Asking Malleus, "You *will* let me know if I'm too loud, won't you?"

To which he just smirked and nodded.

A subtle answer of no words that never worked the other way around.

He started slow, all the while asking me if I was OK. And even though I kept telling him, *yes,* he kept on asking. So I told him to just shut up and kiss me some more.

I shouldn't have to tell you what my first time was like. In fact, why am I telling you any of this at all? I think I've told you plenty enough, already. I lost my virginity to Malleus tonight. That's really all you need to know. Now leave us be, and skip right to the next chapter.

There's nothing more for you to see *or* hear, here.

73

"Tonight's the Night"

Today was the big day.

Not only because Malleus and I had woken up in the same bed together, but that the talent show was roughly nine hours away, and there was still much to be done before that time. Tickets were sold out, so all there was to do now was go through a dress rehearsal and get the booked lecture theatre ready for a little over three hundred people. Twenty-four acts – twenty-five if you included Malleus – and three hundred spectators.

I always regarded myself as a spectator, and someone like Malleus as an avid participant in this vast show called 'life'. And tonight he'd be up on that stage, putting on a grand display of what he could do, to the most people he'd ever shown, as I cheered him on from the sidelines.

I went through my usual routine of getting ready for the day, except that this time, Malleus was here and going through it with me. Which was sort of romantic, even though he was kind of holding me up with how long he took in the shower. And although the ominous feelings about the show were still there – haunting me like spirits with unfinished business – once we were out of my room and walking hand in hand down the street together, I was able to get past my demons with every step of intention we took, until they were far behind us.

So distracted I was with my thoughts of the upcoming show and the way in which the side of Malleus's face caught the morning light, before I even had the chance to realise, we had already walked halfway through an underpass. Malleus coming to an abrupt halt, asking me if I wanted us to double back, to which I just squeezed his hand and said, "No. Let's keep going."

"I have a confession to make," Malleus told me as we walked. "About last night."

"It's OK," I said, pulling him in tight by his arm. "I already know."

That's when Malleus stopped walking. "How could you know?"

"Amy told me everything," I said, now facing him, my hand still in his.

"Amy told you I was a virgin?" he asked.

My hand loosened its grip. "*Virgin?!* What? No!"

"Then what are you going on about?" His hands retreating to hide inside his jacket pockets.

"So, you *didn't* have sex with Amy?"

"No! My first time was with you, last night."

"Ahhh. That *would* explain it."

"Screw you," he said, quickly nodding with his head on a tilt.

"You already did," I told him, yanking his hands from his jacket pockets, and pulling him close.

Whispering in his ear, "Four times."

Malleus and I would now have to part ways. He had things he needed to prepare for his act, and I had a show to put on.

He was always my favourite hello and hardest goodbye.

After saying the longest of farewells, I held onto him tight, not letting go until he did. I could have held on to him until death parted us, but Malleus was stronger than I was when he gently told me that he really needed to get going.

Putting an earbud in his ear – as he always did before leaving me – I watched him turn and walk away. The dark outline of him, that I knew so well by now, getting ever smaller with each awkward little step he took. I realise that he couldn't actually *see* me whenever he walked away, but he would usually turn his head as he did, almost as if he were looking back at me.

But not this time.

Secretly, I hoped this was because, if he had, he wouldn't have been able to carry on walking and, not being able to help himself, would have just come running back to me.

That is, if he ever *ran*.

And I don't know why it came over me: this blue feeling that covered me like the denim on denim I was wearing that morning, but it felt as if this was going to be the very last time we ever saw or heard each other.

And in a way, it was.

74

"Hidden in Plain Sight"

From behind the safety of the stage curtain, I watched. My watchful eyes, keenly aware of the empty seats rapidly beginning to fill up as people shuffled in single file through the double doors at the back of the room. As ushers took tickets from the hands of excitable folks, ripping off the stubs and handing them back. As showgoers took to their designated rows and seats. As smiling faces, beaming with anticipation, whispered amongst themselves.

All of this, I watched.

I, like all of them, being a spectator, too.

Everyone was here: the audience and the acts; the stage manager and the runners. Three media studies students operating cameras, ready to record from their positions amongst the crowd. All present and accounted for.

All except one.

Someone, whom all of this was for.

I checked my watch again – a watch I was certain I'd turned back an hour, about a month or so ago – and here we were, just minutes away from showtime.

"Goddammit, Malleus," I muttered under my breath.

At least, I *hoped* I did.

I realise he'd had to spend most of the day getting his act together for tonight, but he had nine whole *hours* to do that, so he *must* have been done by now, surely. *I* was the one that had to organise an entire, bloody talent show. All *he* had to do was find a few stupid dead animals. How hard could *that* be?

In less than three minutes, he was going to be officially late. But then maybe this was a good thing. Perhaps Malleus was never meant to go public with what he could do. I was so sure people wouldn't understand; that he would be heckled and booed off stage. This is what I'd wanted, after all, for him to change his mind about the whole thing. Sure, I'd put a lot of woman-hours and elbow-grease into all this, but the show could still go on without him, and no one would be any the wiser.

Just one minute to go, and it's showtime, whether he's here or not. Fifty-five more seconds, I'll walk up those stairs, the curtains will part, and I'll announce the start of the show everybody's been waiting for.

The stage manager gives me the ten second countdown before I'm due to go on, and that's when it happens. Suddenly, with Malleus not here beside me, I don't feel as though I can do it. I physically can't go on. If he were just here to tell me, '*You've got this, Iris,*' then I'd be fine.

But he's not here, and so, neither am I fine.

I watch the hypnotist-like fingers of the stage manager going ... *3 ... 2 ... 1 ...* and then something kicks in, like I'm on autopilot. As if someone is doing all this for me. My legs carry me up those stairs, and as the curtain opens wide, I stand before the crowd in my silky, red dress, like the queen of hearts surveying her kingdom. And then – much like my ability to get up on that stage, and in front of all those people – the words, stolen from my mouth just moments ago, are returned to their rightful place upon my tongue.

"It's so good to see you all here tonight!" I told all those faces I couldn't see. "And since I can't actually *hear* you, that's really all I *can* say!"

But with these stage lights, so bright, I can't tell if that joke was well received, or just fell flat on its laughable face.

"It's going to be quite a show, I can tell you," I continued. "And I'm sure you'll all have a blast."

Then it was time to tone it down a bit.

"But let's remember the real reason we're all here tonight."

And I don't know if it's nerves, or the searing heat of the lights, but I'm just glad to be reading from an autocue right now, as I've completely forgotten myself.

"We're all here for Amy," I read off the scrolling screen of white letters on a black background.

Pausing for a beat to listen out for any giggling.

"Amy," I say again. "Who we lost some time ago."

Still, no giggling.

"What happened to her, we still don't know."

That much was true.

"But this show, which we're holding in her memory, is a fundraiser for a brand-new charity called *'What happened to …?'* *'W.H.2.',* for short. A charity for girls, just like her, who have been taken away from us too soon, and with no explanation as to why."

Sort of true.

"And, if you knew Amy …"

Which they all really, bloody *didn't*.

"… you would have known just how talented she was …"

Or *wasn't!*

"Which is why we thought it apt to hold this show in her memory."

Forgotten but *not* forgiven.

"This show will be being recorded tonight, and all profits from the *DVD* copies sold will be donated to the aforementioned charity, 'W.H.2'."

Or Malleus and I could just pocket the money and *run?*

"As I said before, it's so good to see you all here, and supporting what we all think is a great cause."

Me? I'm still thinking about what I could do with all the money from the *DVD* sales.

"With that being said, please sit back and enjoy the show!"

And even though I couldn't actually *hear* the applause, I sure as hell could *feel* it.

"So without further ado, please give it up for our first act. The dance trio, *'Three's for the Crowd'!*"

And, from what I *could* see, the crowd went wild.

I have to admit, it was a fantastic opener – even if I, being the one who decided the order of the acts, do say so myself. The crowd erupting into a round of applause the moment the dancers pulled their last move and struck a pose for the finale of their routine. They got such an incredible response from the people in the audience that I second-guessed myself as to wonder if I had maybe 'blown my wad' in having them open the show.

Thing is, if they thought that a bit of street-dance-bopping was impressive, just wait until they saw what *Malleus* could do. I had initially put Malleus right in the middle of all the acts, in a bid to hide him amongst the magicians and the illusionists, hoping that the people here would think that's all his act *was*: a trick. But eleven acts in, and Malleus was still a no-show.

We were almost halfway through now, with an interval, before the rest of the acts took to the stage for the second half of the show – which was going well, at least. It's not as if the whole thing relied on Malleus actually *being* here, or that it rested solely on his shoulders. Which is funny, as the whole point of the show was for Malleus to demonstrate his unique talent to an audience. But with things running like the inner-workings of a Swiss-made wristwatch, it had gone clean out of my mind what the whole point of it all was.

By the time it came to the interval, I had succumbed to the fact that Malleus just wasn't going to show up, and yet, strangely, I was unsure how I felt about it. On the one hand, I was relieved that perhaps he was having second thoughts about going on stage in front of an audience to exhibit his abilities. And on the other hand, I felt a heart-sinking sadness I didn't fully understand, as I really thought he was ready, and that this was what he'd always wanted to do.

Malleus, if he *had* shown up, would have performed his act by now. Lost in the mix of magicians and illusionists, where the audience would have thought his talents were nothing more than the impressive skills of an experienced conjurer. And as relaxed in the warmth of relief I was, there was still this certain sorrow that came with the disappointment I felt. Putting it down to all the days spent and running around, headless, that had gone into this little occasion of mine, and how many precious hours it had swiped from Malleus and I simply spending quality time together.

But now that it was actually happening, along with how well the show was being received by the audience, and so thoroughly enjoyed by the participants, I was also filled with a fuzzy buzz that came with the quiet pride I felt. I had finally done something – without the help of my powers – really quite spectacular. Gathering together the powers of talent of the people around me. A personal reminder to myself, the ones performing on stage, and a whole crowd of people, that we all had something amazing inside of us, and that it didn't require supernatural powers for anyone to be …

… extraordinary.

But what Malleus and I possessed, what separated us from most people, was that we were gifted in ways that made us phenomenally special. Words fell far short of describing what *we* could do. One of us: a bringer of life to the dead. And the other: a girl who could wish anything for a person, and have it come true for them. We were quite the unlikely heroes, Malleus and I, and could only do *so* much on our own. But together.

Together we could make some real changes around here.

As I stood at the sidelines, looking on, as budding singers and musicians took to the stage, I had accepted, albeit reluctantly so, that the talent show everybody thought this was, was merely that, and not some incredible opportunity for an equally incredible boy I'd met in a park one morning. A boy, dressed all in black, who'd finally decided to step into the light and show this dark world what he was capable of. A wondrous boy I'd fallen so completely in love with. And that, if he didn't show up tonight, with all these people applauding him, and me right behind him, then he probably never would.

It was now time for the last act, and we were about to go out with a bang in the form of a vocalist, who, I had to believe when I was assured, was very talented. Watching her on the stage, I could only imagine she sang beautifully, and I also believe, if I could hear, I would have heard the silence of captivated spectators as she projected her voice toward them all; performing vocal acrobatics and hitting all the high notes.

She was all lit up in pink – which, being Amy's favourite colour, was no accident. Apparently, the song the girl was singing was also the very same one Amy had once chosen for her funeral, that I imagine had come a lot sooner than she'd expected. So taken in by the hypnotic lights and the stillness of the room, I completely lost myself for a few dreamy minutes. Never realising to acknowledge the arrival of the very last person in the world I thought would ever show up.

"Malleus!" I exclaimed, somewhere between falling over backwards and coming in for a hug.

"Iris?" Malleus said, feeling the air with one hand outstretched. "Is that you?"

"You're late," I gently scolded him as we held each other briefly. "And I know my watch is right this time."

And with the pink light illuminating his face, I saw his mouth form the words, "Any idea how hard it was to find a dead *dog?*"

"*Some* idea," I told him.

"Anyway," he said. "I'm here now. Better late than never, right?"

But it wasn't better. It would have been better if he'd never shown up at all.

"You were supposed to be here *hours* ago," I told him.

"How far are we into the show?" he asked.

"The last contestant's already halfway through their act."

"Then there's still time. I'll just go on, after."

I told him, that wasn't going to work. That he was simply too late. That he'd missed his chance. What I *didn't* tell him was that the whole point of placing him right in the middle of all the acts, was to protect him. To hide him amongst the magicians and illusionists, so that what he did would just be seen as a neat trick by everyone here.

But Malleus was as stubborn as he was determined. He had got it so firmly in his mind that tonight was the night, and there was nothing I could do – even with all the powers I possessed – to stop him. I couldn't simply look him in the eyes and make him *not* do what it was that I really didn't *want* him to do, in front of all these people.

I could tell, from the standing ovation of the audience, that the singer, our very last act, had reached the crescendo of the song, and was now acknowledging the appreciation of the crowd with a curtsy. And because of this, I was swiftly running out of the time I needed to convince Malleus that he was just too late. That this was a *seriously* bad idea.

All this, I told him, but his dogged ears wouldn't hear it. He had already pushed passed me, and was feeling his way to the steps that led up to the now empty stage. The audience still on their feet; three hundred pairs of hands applauding the girl who had just closed the show with her most beautiful rendition of dead Amy's favourite song.

To most everyone here, the show was over, but maybe there was a way I could buy myself some more time to convince Malleus *not* to do this. It wasn't too late for an encore. Get the fat girl to sing another song. I was sure there were other equally terrible ballads doing the rounds in the current top-forty chart. But I could see now that she was in floods of tears, blubbing away, and being consoled and tended to by some of the backstage staff. And, from the state of the poor girl, probably didn't have another song left *in* her.

And as much as I really didn't want Malleus to do what he so had in his head *to* do, I couldn't just leave him to do it alone. He needed me right now, maybe now more than ever. I'd fast run out of fingers and toes, counting the times he'd been there for me, and so I just *had* to do this one thing.

And so, muttering obscenities for only Malleus to hear, I dashed over to where he was – now clumsily grabbing at the handrail that led up from the foot of the stairs – and hooking his left arm in my right, I guided his steps, up, and onto the empty stage.

75

"Out of the Bag"

Stood there before the crowd with Malleus – I, dressed shoulder to ankle in red, and he, all in black – I was acutely aware of nerves I'd not been conscious enough to feel before this moment. The glaring lights, so bright, I couldn't pick out just one face in a sea of people I knew was there. Exposed to a room full of people shrouded in darkness. But mostly, the nerves I felt, I was feeling on Malleus's behalf.

Malleus had brought on stage with him a large, black duffel bag. Containing what I imagined were the dead creatures he'd been scavenging for all day. What those creatures were, I didn't know, but I would soon find out, along with the tentative audience, all dead still as the creatures in his bag.

Two backstage runners swiftly brought out a prepared folding table from one of the wings, flipping down the legs, locked, and setting it down at the centre-front of the stage. This, Malleus placed his duffel bag upon, with my assistance, and taking a careful step back, signalled for me to make the introduction with a subtle nod.

"Ladies and gentleman!" I announced to the blackness out ahead of me. "Fellow students and friends! This is my good friend Malleus. The very last act of tonight's talent show."

There was a wave of random flashing as the stage lights bounced off the bright white paper of confused spectators flipping through the glossy pages of their show programmes.

"I would tell you what Malleus's talent is," I said as the white flashing settled to a still black, "but as actions speak so much louder than words, I will, instead, simply allow him to show you. And as he does, I ask you to keep an open mind, and that you suspend your doubt and disbelief as he demonstrates the powers he possesses. I, myself, didn't believe the very first time he showed me what he was capable of. But now that I do, I, too, hope *you* can believe."

All I could see was black, whilst all I imagine Malleus to have heard was silence.

"This is the Marvellous Malleus," I told the darkness, "with whom I am well pleased to share with all of you."

Giving either side of Malleus's shoulders a supportive squeeze with my trembling hands, I slowly backed away. The very same way a parent would, letting go of a child learning to ride a bike without stabilisers for the first time. Hiding, off stage, in the shadows of the curtain, allowing Malleus to have his big moment.

I was proud of him for being so brave but, in the same breath, fearful the people in the audience wouldn't understand the wonderful spectacle they were about to witness. I had to put these thoughts behind me now, for I'd done as much as I could in warning him, supporting him, and preparing the way for him. This was it. I would just have to take a back seat now, and leave it in the capable, life-giving hands of Malleus. This was, after all, what he'd wanted.

All I had to do now was have his back.

From behind the shadow of the stage curtain, I could just about make out the faces in the crowd. Mouths, hushed. Three hundred pairs of eager eyes gazing up at the stage with undivided attention as Malleus, lit by a solitary spotlight, began unzipping the black duffel bag. Me, quietly imagining the sound of the zipper, scoring through the muted air, in a room full of deathly silent people.

Reaching inside the now unzipped duffel bag, Malleus pulled out a small glass jar with a metal screw lid, no bigger than one of those single-serving jam jars. Containing something so small, even *I*, the very closest person to him, couldn't make out what it was from the short distance away I was stood. Malleus, then, setting the jar down on the table for all of us to better see.

Holding down the 'talk' button on the walkie-talkie in my hand, I instructed the cameramen, set up amongst the crowd, to zoom in on the little glass jar. This way we could all better see what was held inside from looking up at the huge projector-screen, hanging over

Malleus's head at the back of the stage. From what we could see of the enlarged image on the screen, there appeared to be a dead fly inside the jar; on its back, its legs, stiff in the air.

Picking up the glass jar, Malleus unscrewed the lid and tipped out the tiny insect into the palm of one hand, holding it steady for a moment so we could all get a good look. He then cupped the other hand beside and just underneath the hand that held the teeny, inanimate insect. And Malleus, I imagined remaining as silent as those watching, began to focus his energies into the insect, bereft of life, in his tentative, bowl-shaped hands.

And then, it happened.

The insect's wings began to twitch erratically. The legs, too. Both twitching with ever increasing frequency as the insect appeared to come to life. Just then, the insect sprung to its legs, walking in circles and along the creases of Malleus's palms, before flying off into the blinding lights over the heads of the audience.

Still, there appeared to be a deathly silence as Malleus, once again, reached into his big, black duffel bag.

Peering passed the spotlight fixed on Malleus, I could only make out vague shapes moving out there in the darkness. And even though I couldn't actually hear an applause, I clapped quietly for him, all the same.

Next, Malleus pulled out a similar glass jar to the one before, again, with a screw lid, just slightly larger in size. Inside was a spider, on its back and legs curled up like a fist with spindly fingers, as dead as the tiny fly before it.

I took a step back as soon as I saw it, covering my mouth with one hand, and pressing against my chest with the palm of the other. Doing my best not to make a sound as he unscrewed the glass jar and tipped the spider out into the other, free hand.

Setting the glass jar down, and in much the same way as he did the fly, he cupped the spider in the palms of both hands. The whole room hushed with people watching intently as Malleus willed it to live. Eight legs, twitching in turn as the not so tiny insect came to life and ran over Malleus's hands, before carefully placing the spider back in the glass jar and tightly screwing the lid closed.

Taking my hand away from my mouth, only then did I swallow.

Stooping to better see the crowd's reaction, I was so sure I could see people clapping this time. At least, I *hoped* that's what I was seeing. If they *were* applauding, Malleus could at least hear the encouraging sounds of palms smacking together, including my own.

Malleus then carefully lifted out a shoebox from the duffel bag. Slowly taking off the lid to reveal a dead bird, nestled in what looked to be newspaper shredding. Tilting the box towards the crowd, the bird was presented to the audience to inspect it for themselves on the big screen behind him. Ever so gently, he removed the lifeless body of the bird from the shredded paper, and putting the now empty shoe box aside, held the dead feathered creature in both hands.

As Malleus willed it to life, you could see it took considerably more force to do so than it did with the two tiny insects before, because, this time, his hands shook from the effort. What was also apparent was that it appeared to take far longer to bring the dead bird back to life than it did the fly and the spider. But just when the audience and I had almost given up on the drifting hope that anything was going to happen …

… the wings fluttered.

Legs, twitching. Eyes, blinking open. The wings, beginning to flap. Until they flapped so wildly, Malleus lost his grip on the bird. The bird, flying out of his hands and over the audience's heads.

This, I could tell, got a huge reaction from the crowd. Faint shapes I could just about make out in the mass of people as they applauded. A sea of paired hands, pulling away and crashing together. All this motion of shadows around a darkened room, with Malleus being the only one, fixed in place, and bathed in light.

I couldn't believe it.

They were actually taking this for what it was: a boy demonstrating his extraordinary powers in the most simplest of ways. That, or they were just applauding in wonder at a very talented and entertaining trickster. But, either way, it didn't matter. What mattered was that he was being well received.

That is, until he pulled out the *fourth* lifeless creature from his duffel bag.

An animal, appearing much larger than a bird, and wrapped in a shiny, black, plastic bin bag. The protruding lumps of the creature's body and limbs being the only clues the bag gave as to what was held tightly inside.

The whole crowd were still applauding for the bird Malleus had just brought back to life as he loosened the drawstrings of the black bin bag he had just pulled out. Fingers in mouths, whistling. Mouths stretched wide open, cheering. Hands, smacking as Malleus reached inside the bag and got a hold of something much larger than a bird.

It was only when Malleus got a good firm grip of the animal inside, and carefully removed it from out of the drawstring bag, that the whole audience suddenly froze, all at once. Three hundred pairs of hands, shooting up to cover gasping mouths. Hands frozen between coming apart and smacking together. Horrified eyes, impossible to avert, because of what Malleus was now holding up by the neck.

And even though I couldn't actually hear it, I just knew the room had, once again, filled with a deathly silence.

For in Malleus's tight-gripped hand, and being held aloft for all to see, was a dead cat.

A dead cat with very distinctive orange and white markings.

76

"Stage Fright"

Like everyone else in the room, I recognised this cat from its very distinctive markings. An orange-and-white striped cat we'd all seen somewhere before. But this wasn't just *any* cat. It was the university head's cat. The very same one that had been missing for a good few weeks now.

I was confident Malleus hadn't first killed the cat just to bring it back to life, and that he must have simply come across it some place: a park or by the side of the road like he usually did. But everyone *else* in the room didn't know that, including the head of the university, who was now making his way from the back of the room, and up the centre aisle of row upon row of seats. His face, at first, pale as the white stripes on his limp pet feline's coat, turning scarlet as swiftly as he was now approaching the foot of the stage.

Any doubts I had about the audience's horror at what they were witnessing were gone as soon as the lecture theatre lights clicked on, and I saw the horrified looks on all their faces. And it was only when the head began yelling up at Malleus from the foot of the stage, that Malleus stopped short of what he was about to do with the dead cat in his hands. Malleus just stood there, stunned, in much the same way *I* was, a little way back from the front edge of the stage. Frozen to the spot like a frigid statue, not knowing what on earth was going on, nor the reason as to why there was suddenly an uproar of appalled and angry voices, just moments after he lifted a dead cat from the black, drawstring bag.

I looked down at the head yelling up at Malleus, and out towards the tempestuous sea of outraged people. Some stood up on their chairs, shouting with venomous mouths and pointing vicious fingers toward the boy on stage holding the dead cat. The rest of them glued stuck to their seats; silenced by a paralysing awe, unable to do much more than look on in abject horror.

I was just so very thankful, in this sudden moment of shock and distress, that there was one person in the room that couldn't see what I could.

It was only once I'd taken in the terrible scene playing out in front of me, and processed it, did I then realise that I must act with a critical sense of urgency. Calling out Malleus's name, I dashed over to him, where he was still stood holding the lifeless feline at his side, by the neck. In a state of shock, not too dissimilar to most of those in the crowd before him.

Carefully taking the cat from his hands and cradling it in my arms, I took it over to the front of the stage. And I don't know why, but I stroked its lifeless body and kissed it in the thick of its fur, before handing it to the university head; his arms outstretched, desperately, to receive it. And in that camera flash of a moment the head and I shared as he took the dead cat from my hands, what he said, I'll never forget. But so disabled by his question, I had no able answer for him.

All we were trying to do here was show all of these people something truly wonderful. All Malleus wanted was to breathe life back into that cat. A cat that, if the university head had kept a better eye on it, wouldn't have been dead in the first place.

His eyes like daggers as he bellowed at me, "What is *wrong* with you two?"

He then made his way back through the centre aisle, cradling the dead cat in his arms as if it were still alive – and it *would* have been if he had just left Malleus to work his magic. But it was too late now. The head had already left out one of the doors at the back of the room and was gone.

Then, realising Malleus was still just stood there, not knowing what in the hell was going on, I made my way back to him and took his hand in mine; his whole body, a tremor.

"Iris?" he asked. "Is that you?"

"Yes, Malleus," I told him. "It's me."

"What just happened, Iris? What did I do?"

"It's not what you did, Malleus. It's who you were doing it *for*."

With the dazzling glare of the lights in the room illuminating the crowd, I could now see all of their enraged faces. They appeared to be chanting something over and over, but from this distance, and with my eyes still becoming accustomed to the blinding lights, I couldn't, for the life of me, make out what.

"What are they saying?" I asked Malleus as we held hands on that lonely stage.

But Malleus just stood there; head down, his lips not moving. Looking as if he were the light that had entered the darkness, but, alas, the darkness had not understood it.

Giving his hand a gentle squeeze, I asked him again.

That's when Malleus sombrely raised his chin, and slowly turned his head to face me.

77

There are some questions you simply shouldn't know the answers to.

We should have left the stage; gone home. Just kept ourselves to ourselves for a little while, and waited for this whole thing to blow over. But we didn't. Malleus just stood there, and I asked the most foolish of questions. And, looking back, I do so really wish I hadn't.

I asked Malleus what they were chanting: the people in the crowd. All those people that took their sense of sight and hearing for granted. And, no sooner had Malleus told me, something terrible began to grow inside of me. It started in the pit of my stomach. Simmering there before boiling and coursing up behind my chest. Rising like searing acid in my throat and taking its place in my head and behind my eyes. This frightful thing that I couldn't stop from building up inside of me, I would not be able to hold back once I'd let it out.

My big, blue eyes, enlarged to over a hundred times their actual size on the projector screen above and behind my head. Those colossal, sapphire peepers looking out on a startled crowd, like a tidal wave about to come crashing down upon every eye looking back up at mine on the enormous screen above and behind me.

And with three hundred pairs of eyes fixed firmly on my own, I couldn't hold myself back from wishing something mightily unpleasant for each and every one of them.

78

"Exit Stage Left"

Grabbing Malleus by the arm, I led him off the stage, down the stage steps, and out one of the fire exits at the back of the lecture theatre. The beady eyes of all those '**LOST CAT**' posters hung on the bare concrete walls, following us as we bolted out of the door and across the foyer of the university building. And I couldn't be sure in the rush of that frantic moment, but I think Malleus was trying to ask me something, because whenever I happened to glance at him, in between looks ahead to wherever we were headed, his mouth was moving. Something about what in the hell was going on, no doubt.

And as we ran off the university campus, I quickly turned to him and said, "You really don't want to know."

So afraid for us both, I was, it went entirely out of my mind what all this was like for Malleus. Ever tried to walk around your own home with your eyes closed, let alone *run* with them closed, *outside?* I mean, sure, Malleus knew this town better than anybody knows the back of their own hand, but not at *this* pace.

I had not a clue as to where we were going, or what we'd do when we got there. I just wanted to put as much distance as we could between *us* and that lecture theatre we'd left behind. But with every desperate stride we took, I just knew that no matter how fast or far we ran, there would be no hiding from this. That this wasn't something we could simply outrun.

There was a place, however, that would at least give us some time – if time was all we were afforded. Two lefts, a right, and another right, and there it was: the park. Which was fitting, being the very first place Malleus and I had met. The only difference being that *this* time we weren't here for him to give me a private show of the secret he'd kept to himself for so long. *This* time we were two people, running and hiding, pursuing the ample time needed to prepare for something I'd set into motion by what I'd just done.

Looking back now, it would have been better if we'd simply stayed put where we were in that lecture theatre. Just remained there on that empty stage, with all those panic-stricken people clambering all over each other in a frenzied throng. But hindsight has twenty-twenty vision, and back there, on that stage, looking down on all those terrified faces with eyes full of vengeance, I had lost what it was to see clearly, the best thing to do.

"What are we running from?" Malleus asked me as we hurried through the park. "The screams, Iris! What did you *do?*"

"You'll just have to believe me, Malleus," I said. "The less you know, the better."

Then a troubling thought came rushing in to bother my worries, but way too late.

Shittle-sticks! The cameras!

The ones that had recorded the whole talent show from start to finish.

Fucketty-fuck!

With my brain racing, I asked Malleus to tell me about the first time we met, to slow my galloping mind.

"What did you think of me?" I asked him. "First time we met?"

The look of absolute perplexity on Malleus's face as he asked me, "What?"

"Just answer the question!"

"Why?"

"Because I'm trying to think about anything but what's going on right now!"

But Malleus's face hadn't changed in the light of my phone's torch.

"Well!?" I screamed at him.

And he just comes right out with it, when he says, "I don't know! Nosey?"

"Nosey?!" I asked, perhaps a little too loudly for two people hiding from what was inevitably coming after them. "I think 'inquisitive' would be a better way to put it."

"Iris," Malleus said. "Tell me what you did."

"Anyway," I told him. "That's not what I meant when I asked you what you first thought of me."

"Iris!" Malleus said. "What did you do?"

"Don't change the subject," I told him. "What did you *think* of me?"

"I don't know," he said. "I thought you were a very curious girl."

"And?"

"And … and I just knew, somehow, you were searching for something. Something that you believed existed but were so sure you'd never find."

"And what was that?"

"I don't know. Something real, I guess. Something that was …"

"What it appeared to be."

"Yeah."

"How did you know that? About me, I mean."

"Because I was searching, too."

"You were?"

"I was lost, and you found me."

And resting my head on his surprisingly comfortable shoulder, I told him, "We found each other."

We sat there as quietly as we could, for as long as we could, hidden in that dark, damp spot; my once lovely, new, red dress, now tattered and torn. And I don't know who realised first; whether it was me seeing the blue flashing lights, or Malleus hearing the sirens, but the people I just knew would be after us, were closing in. I thought we would have more time, but when you've done something as terrible as I just had, they come looking for you pretty damn quick.

Gripping Malleus's leather jacket – soaked through with the rain dripping from the tree leaning over our heads – I told him to deny any involvement he had with me to them. Deny that he ever knew me. That was the only way, I could see, that he would be safe after what I'd done. The police were close now, and although I couldn't see them through the thick of tree trunks and bramble bushes, Malleus told me that he could hear them getting ever closer.

"I have to go, Malleus," I told him.

"No," he said. "Don't you dare leave me."

"I shouldn't have brought you here. I should've left you behind."

"Whatever you did, Iris. I'm part of it, too."

I begged him to let go his hold of me. To let me run. Out of the park and somewhere else. Just so he wouldn't get caught up in everything I'd made happen back at the talent show.

But even if he *had* let me go, it was way too late by now. Malleus told me he could hear boots crunching leaves underfoot. Me, telling *him* I could see the sweeping beams of flashlights. The park around us shrinking smaller with every step they took, slowly closing in on our hiding place amongst the refuge of the trees.

I could only imagine the shrill wail of the sirens Malleus told me about. And when I told him of the blue lights I could see, flashing through branches and bouncing off rain-dropped leaves, Malleus then turned to me and said the strangest of things. Something I wasn't at all expecting, but probably needed to hear moments before they moved in to separate us and take us away.

"Whatever they offer you to drink, drink," Malleus said. "And whatever they give you to eat, eat. Don't tell them *anything*. And if you have to tell them *something*, make it, *'no comment'*.

"Just remember," he added. "I'm your ears."

"I'm your eyes," I told him.

And although I didn't know it yet, and just as well at the time, that would be one of the very last things Malleus ever said to me.

And if we'd had the time to hold each other …

… I would've never let go.

79

"Across a Table"

The closest I'd ever been to being in a room this small was the ensuite bathroom, back at the hall of residence.

There were no windows in the shoebox of a room I now found myself in. No colour anywhere or pictures hanging up. Just four, ribbed, soundproofed walls, all the same drab shade of grey. A large mirror on the wall beside me, like that of a window frame, being the only difference to the other three walls that boxed me in.

Alone I sat in one of the four corners of this room; a chair with a hard back, fixed, bolted to the ground, being my only comfort.

Without a clock to watch, I had no idea as to how long the detective was gone for, but it felt as if a simple trip to a nearby vending machine was taking far more time than it reasonably should, and that perhaps I should have just said *No* to his question about me being hungry.

Counting the ribs on the soundproofing tiles being all I had to keep my mind stimulated, all the while wondering who was on the other side of that one-way glass. And even though I was fully clothed, albeit in the shabby overalls the police officers had provided for me – my own clothes being soaked through with rain – the idea that someone could be looking in on me made me feel as if I weren't wearing anything at all.

Stripped of all my personal effects, with nothing upon my person – not a watch or a phone – to know exactly how long it had been since I was left here in this bare and soulless room. Daring not to move, nor even mutter comforting mumblings to myself, as I knew the ones looking in would more than likely be listening, too.

The only thoughts holding my sanity together in a room like this one were my thoughts of Malleus, and where he was right now. That if Malleus was still here somewhere in this building, I was so sure everything would turn out just fine.

Across a cold, steel table, and in the opposite corner of the room was an office chair on wheels with a supportive back; the only other object to keep me company as I waited, patiently as I was able, for whoever was next to come through that door. But not a moment before I had acknowledged my own impatience with a puff of air from my lips, the door was pulled open, and in walked the very same man who left me here. This time armed with two paper cups, a couple of chocolate bars, and what looked like a folder tucked under his arm.

"I hope you like coffee," he said, carefully handing me one of the cups.

And tossing a chocolate bar my way, he added, "It's either that or tap water."

Rolling the office chair on wheels to take his seat in front of me – close enough for me to tell that his last drink was a cup of instant coffee and that he was a smoker – he slapped the folder, thick with papers, down on the table.

Looking down at the sad little paper cup in my hand, filled with a watery brown liquid, I told him, "Thanks." Only wishing he'd warned me about how hot the paper cup was before he handed it to me.

I took a cautious sip as this detective appeared to read me my rights. And swallowing, the hot liquid stung my throat for one short, sharp, second as a bitter aftertaste of watery cocoa and cardboard flowed over my tongue.

The detective read off the sheet of paper in his hands, fast, and far too hastily for me to accurately read his lips. I'd only gotten as far as unwrapping the snack he'd brought me. So, just so as not to look guilty, I took another forced sip from the cup and an obligated bite of the bar of chocolate.

Guilty people are never hungry, I remember my dad once telling me. *A little thirsty, maybe, but never hungry.*

"I don't suppose I could have my cigarettes back?" I asked the detective, hopefully.

To which he simply replied, "You suppose correctly."

The detective told me something about this interview being recorded, and was I OK with that. I nodded. Only after which did I then realise just how long I'd been sat in this drab, grey, shoebox of a room when I read the lips of the detective stating the time, right after he hit the little red button on the tape recorder.

And fidgeting in my static chair, I braced myself for the onslaught of questions this detective would be firing my way.

And I don't know why it had taken me this long to realise – all those drawn-out hours spent waiting in this dull and uninspired room – but just then, it came to me that I wouldn't actually have to answer *any* of this detective's questions, for I had the powers of commanding influence on my side.

If it could work for a powerful CEO, a mean ol' bastard that ran a pawnshop, and a bitchy barista girl, then it could work for this weak-minded fool of a detective.

And looking him right in the eyes, I ordered him with complete confidence to, "Stop the interview!"

But the detective, he just looked right back at me, and said, "Say again?"

"You are to stop this interview," I told him. "Get up from your chair, open the door to this room, and let me go."

But this detective, his jaw didn't go slack, his eyes didn't go wide. He just told me that he would do no such thing. Telling me, "I will keep you here for as long as I need to."

"What?" I said in utter disbelief.

"This interview will end when I say it ends," he told me.

"No," I told him. "You will do as I tell you. You will …"

And then it dawns on me.

For whatever reason, I think about the powers Malleus has. How he told me how each time he brought something back from the dead, it took a little life out of him. How each time that he did it – brought something back – the life would always return to him, but how it would also take time to come back. The bigger the animal, he said, the more life it took. The more life it took, the longer it would take for the life to come back to him.

Then I thought about my powers, and how perhaps they were similar in that each time I used them they took a little something out of me, too. After all, I had just very recently used them on three hundred people. Perhaps I had used up my reservoir of power for the time being. Maybe my powers were depleted and, like Malleus's, would take time to come back to me. Maybe *that's* why they weren't working. Maybe I just needed to be patient; wait it out; give them time to return.

Thing is, I could've really used them right about *then*.

That's when the detective threw me a look through squinted eyes, swiped his thumb across the tip of his tongue, and turned to a section of the file marked with a red tag.

"Now," the detective began. "There's been some very unusual activity in the area, the last several months, and plenty more before that."

I could feel my face beginning to flush red with being caught out.

"And something you really need to know about me," he added, "and the upstanding citizens of this fine town we call Constanceville is … we do *not* like change."

And even though I'd been an *unofficial* citizen for barely a year.

Yeah.

I *had* noticed.

"So, let's see," he said. "There was the closing down of the Type-2 factory, and the homeless shelter that was built on the very same plot of land the mansion of the CEO of said factory sat. This happened soon after a peaceful protest you led just outside the factory gates."

And no sooner do I think I'm about to blush, I can literally feel the blood draining from my face.

"We then conducted an interview with the owner of a pawnshop," the detective said, "to see if he could provide us with any information about the unusual goings-on in the local area."

I'm trying my best here to not make my stiffened facial features appear as if they have the foggiest idea as to what this detective is going on about.

"We've dealt with him before," he said. "This old boy. And, for once, he was very informative. Which, from our many previous dealings with him in the past, was very unlike him. He was actually very friendly and accommodating. Maybe a little *too* friendly. Causing me to suspect that he was trying to cover something up."

My eyes haven't left the detective's. My head, fixed in place. The muscles in my face haven't moved.

"Do you know the pawn brokers?" he asked me, looking up from the file on the table.

"*A Lad in His Cave,* it's called."

I just shook my head and made a face; dampening the sound of the ringing bells in my mind.

"That's funny," the detective said, "because the old boy said you'd visited his shop on two separate occasions. The first time being when you purchased a mobile phone from him, and a second time where you sold *him* a solid-gold pen worth over one hundred thousand spons."

"*That pen was worth one hundred thousand spons?!*" I blurted out.

"So you *do* know the place I'm talking about?"

"Erm … yes? Yes, it's all coming back to me now. Now that you've mentioned the pen."

That's when the detective throws me this look that I can't quite decipher.

"About a week later," he continued, "we were called to the scene of a café, local to the area, where one of its staff members was acting out of sorts and behaving rather aggressively to the customers."

I can tell this detective's studying me for any signs of recognition on my face.

"Which," he added, "according to the other staff and regulars there, was very unlike them."

And I'm forcing my eyes to stay on the detective's, and not allowing them to wander around the room.

"How well did you know Miss Amy G'dala?" the detective asked.

And if Amy were still occupying space in my head right now, I just know she would have piped up and quipped in with something like, "*Gotcha!*"

"*Quite* well," I said.

Only having to repeat myself, after the detective asked me to speak up.

Flipping open the hefty looking folder between us, the detective licked a finger and turned to a page marked with a red tag.

"Says here," the detective said, "that both you and Miss G'dala attended the same school. Primary *and* secondary. Is that right?"

I just made a *Mm-hm* sound in agreement.

"Were you two friends?" asked the detective.

"Of sorts," I said.

"Of sorts?"

"We were friends, but on and off."

"Would you say Amy G'dala was a bully?"

"Not so much a bully, just … inconsistent."

"Did she ever bully *you*?"

I didn't answer the question immediately. I just sat there, all the while wondering whether it was better to tell the truth or just say *no*. But it was my silence that spoke for me and, really, was all the detective needed to hear.

"What do *you* think happened to Amy G'dala in the university canteen that day?" asked the detective.

She got what she deserved, I thought to myself.

"I honestly have no idea," I told him.

"So," the detective went on to say. "There was the sudden death of Miss Amy G'dala. The one-hundred-and-eighty-degree turn that big CEO made, from running a fizzy drink factory, to sheltering the homeless. The dramatic transformation in personality of the old boy at the pawnshop. And then there was the highly unorthodox behaviour of a usually pleasant and polite coffee-shop girl, who then dies as suddenly as your good friend Amy G'dala did, all that time ago."

And now that this detective had mentioned it, and now that I looked back …

… I'd been busy.

"Five rather unusual occurrences," he said, "seemingly unrelated, apart from one constant."

My body is still. My head is fixed. My mouth is mute.

"You," the detective said. "You were present, in some way, for each and every one. Which tells me, you know something."

I just sat there, using my right to remain silent.

"You know something," the detective said, "don't you, Iris? You know what it was that happened here to these four, seemingly unrelated, people."

All too well, I thought to myself. Keeping that thought to myself as best I could.

"Well, Iris?" the detective pushed.

"You've got to believe me," I told the detective, "when I say I really have no idea."

"After a search we conducted of your room," the detective went on to say, "we found a scrap of paper in the office bin under your desk. A list, three people strong, written on it in pencil. *The mean ol' bastard, the barista bitch, and the* ... ahem! *Total F'ing A'hole in a banana-yellow sports car.* Does this mean anything to you?"

On the outside I simply shrugged my shoulders, but on the inside I tensed up, taut as a bowstring.

"Nope," I told him. "Doesn't sound like the sort of list I would write."

"Funny," the detective said, "because that's where we found it. In that bin, in your room. What's also strange is that the three people on that list sound very much like given nicknames for the three people I aforementioned: the old boy at the pawnshop, the coffee-shop girl, and that big CEO. Is there something you're not telling me, Iris?"

"I honestly don't know anything about that list," I told him.

"We also checked out the recent search history on your mobile phone," he told me. "You know, you really should put a lock on it or something. You know what people are like these days."

"I would," I told him, "but then I really have nothing to hide."

"Then why was it that you fled the scene after that little talent show of yours?" the detective asked.

My throat so choked up that no words made it out of my mouth as a reply.

"So, like I said," he went on, "we checked out your recent search history. Want to know what we found?"

I didn't say anything; too busy trying to bring to mind all the things I had recently searched for on the internet.

"*Bird comes to life in boy's hands. Cats that look like Hitler.* And a little more alarmingly, *How to humanely kill a hamster.*"

"That one I can explain," I told him.

"We also found a whole lot of photos on your phone," the detective said. "You really should have studied photography. You've got a good eye."

"Thank you," I said, more as a question than a reply.

"But the one that caught our interest," said the detective, "was the one of the opening times for the A Lad in His Cave pawnshop."

"Is that a crime?" I asked the detective.

"We also saw how you'd sent a friend request to Miss Jessica Blowers," the detective said. "Not two days before she died, I might add."

"That was just bad timing," I said.

"Numerous missed calls from your father," the detective said, "over a span of months, which were never returned. And an outgoing call made to him just minutes after Jessica was pronounced dead in your room and taken away by paramedics."

"Also, bad timing," I told him.

"So," said the detective, "I think you can appreciate how mightily suspicious all of this looks."

And I had to admit, this didn't exactly paint me in a good light.

"And," said the detective, "we haven't even *begun* to talk about the events of that little talent show of yours, earlier tonight."

80

"Don't Look Back"

"I have reviewed the video footage of the talent show," the detective said, "and I must say, it makes for some pretty disturbing viewing."

A statement he needn't have made to me, despite the fact that I hadn't yet seen it for myself.

"Upon reviewing what was recorded on those cameras," the detective went on to say, "I really am stumped as to what to make of it."

Promising start, I thought quietly to myself.

"Shall we take a look at the footage?" he asked.

And I, having no real choice in the matter, just nodded.

The detective signalled to the mirror on the wall beside us. His right hand, raised, with only his index-finger extended. Twirling it like he was stirring an invisible, upside-down cup of coffee. Pushing himself backwards, the detective scooted on the wheels of his chair towards the door to push it open. And in much less time than it took this detective to fetch two cups of crappy coffee and a couple of lousy bars of chocolate, a camera was brought into the room. A camera that I instantly recognised as being one of the three cameras set up amongst the crowd at the talent show. Along with that, a TV monitor wheeled in on a trolley and positioned against one of the drab grey walls and plugged into a socket.

Thanking the officer who brought it in, the detective switched on the TV monitor, and after a few seconds the screen filled with static that grew in brightness as the monitor warmed up. Wiring the camera up to the monitor, the detective pressed a button on the camera, lifted his right hand up to cover his mouth, his left hand rested on his hip, and sat back on his chair.

The first two hours of the video were filled with act after act, which the detective fast-forwarded through. Skipping right past all the dancers and singers, the magicians and illusionists, all performing their specific talent at two-point-five times the speed they were at the actual time of recording. It was only when we reached the part where a folding table was brought onto the stage, and Malleus had set his black, duffel bag upon it, that the detective finally pressed the play button.

"Close enough," said the detective.

We watched a little of Malleus's performance – the part where he breathed life into a bird that then flew into the stage lights and over the audience's heads.

The detective leant back on his reclining chair, and turning his head to look at me with a wink, he said, "Neat trick."

But I knew it wasn't Malleus's spellbinding talents of resurrection that this detective was interested in viewing with me. Rather, it was what happened immediately after Malleus pulled a dead cat from a drawstring bag.

And when that moment came, that's when the cameraman zoomed out to show about a third of the audience in frame; hands waving wildly, angry fists in the air, and condemning fingers pointing towards the alarmed boy, dressed all in black, on stage. The camera then zoomed back in for a tight shot of Malleus as I joined him on stage; the crowd wild with rage by this point.

Of all the dead cats Malleus could have found, it had to be the one the university head lost.

The detective asked me if I knew what the crowd was chanting. I told him that I had no idea, but the look on my face from the camera footage said otherwise. And with the camera lens closing in on my furious expression, so that the audience could see the piercing blue of my despising eyes on the big projector screen behind me, that was the moment I wished something mightily unpleasant for each and every one of them.

At this pre-climactic point of the footage, the detective hit the pause button; my hate-filled eyes filling the frame; asking me, what it was that I was feeling in that moment.

"I mean," the detective followed up with, "if looks could kill, right?"

Oh, if you only knew, I thought to myself.

I had to give him *some* kind of answer, so I just told him that, "I felt upset."

"You don't need to tell *me*," the detective told me with wide eyes. "You look positively *seething!*"

I just sat there, hushed and so completely serene. Appearing, to the detective, the total opposite to how I looked paused on the screen of that monitor.

"Thing is," the detective continued. "You're deaf, right?"

"Right," I replied, my eyes squinted, like he had just asked me if I was female.

"So how is it that you knew what the crowd was chanting?"

I straightened up in my chair. "Because Malleus told me."

The detective leaned in close – his breath, stale with vending machine coffee and too many smoked cigarettes. "What if Malleus was lying to you?"

"Malleus would never-"

"What? *Lie* to you?"

The detective folded his arms as he sat back. "That boy's not as clean-cut as he's been making out for you to believe. The file we have on *him* makes the one we have on you look like a pamphlet."

"But Malleus has always-"

"You've trusted *everything* that boy has told you?" asked the detective. "Who do you think it was that tipped us off about the incident at the coffee shop with the usually pleasant and polite barista girl?"

"He was probably only trying to-"

"Malleus was in a room just down the hall," the detective continued, "telling us *everything* he knew about you. We were satisfied with his answers and we let him go. That was *hours* ago, and yet, here *you* are, still in this room and *defending* him!"

Malleus wouldn't do that to me, I thought quietly to myself. *And even if he had, I couldn't be too mad about it because none of this was his fault.*

I was the one that did that terrible thing to all those people at the finale of the talent show. And looking back with calmer eyes, I knew I shouldn't have done it. It's just that the hurtful words the crowd were chanting in unison upset me to the point where I retaliated with a thoughtless reaction. I couldn't hear, with my own useless ears, what they were saying, but I could read Malleus's lips when he slowly turned to face me.

I imagine it all started with the calling out of just one, ignorant person; igniting the rest of the mob like a blazing forest fire started with a single match. And just like that, they were all yelling those hurtful words. Inflaming me with such a compelling rage, I could no longer hold it back from striking down on every pair of eyes and ears in that swarming multitude before me.

Did they not know the struggles of being deaf, like me, or blind, like Malleus was? But from the mocking faces I could see in the crowd – all chanting those wicked words as one – it wasn't a question I need ask, as they clearly had not the empathy to imagine.

So that's what I wished for them all.

To know, for just one day, what it was like not being able to see or hear.

Smiling at the dumbfounded look on all their faces as their eyes widened and their mouths fell slack.

I didn't make the conscious decision to look up and out into the crowd; my angry eyes did that for me. So enraged I was, I could only glare at them all with a scorn that hell didn't have the fury to match. And that is how, at the finale of the show, there was a room full of panicked and disorientated people. All blindly clambering over one another, screaming out but not being able to make a sound.

Of course, it wasn't forever, and just a day, but I was sure that if they never learned anything else from attending university, they would learn dearly from the lesson I had just taught them.

"Can we please get back to what it was we were talking about?" asked the detective as he snapped his muted fingers in my face.

But so lost in the flashes of memories from earlier tonight, all I could say was, "Sorry, *what* were we talking about?"

"About Malleus's part in all this."

"But that's just it," I told the detective. "All he did was demonstrate his talent to a room full of people."

The detective fell back in his chair, the look in his eyes slowly fading from engaged interest to bored disappointment. A puff of agitated air pushed from his lips as he sat forwards, flipping the file in front of him, closed.

"Let's talk about the day your friend died," he said.

Which *one?* I thought to myself.

"Jessica," he said, saving me from asking. "Miss Jessica Blowers."

Oh, *that* one.

"We have the medical report," the detective said, "and it states that Jessica died suddenly."

And as I watched the detective's lips, I just wanted to die right there and then.

"In fact," he continued, "the way in which Jessica Blowers died was not too dissimilar to the way your old friend Amy G'dala did."

And with the detective mentioning Amy and Jessica in the same sentence, a thought popped into my head.

"Do you mind if I ask whether she was buried or cremated?" I asked the detective.

"Who, Jessica?" asked the detective. "Why do you ask? Did you not go to the funeral?"

"No," I told him. "Unfortunately, I couldn't make it. I just wanted to know."

"She was buried," he said, plainly.

The detective was still talking as my mind drifted elsewhere; passing through the door to this room, floating down the corridors, and passing through the many double doors that led the way out of the police station. Soaring over the landscape of paths and greens; of roads and of buildings. Before settling on the final resting place of Jessica Blowers, where her body lay peacefully resting in the six-feet-deep soil of a cemetery. Amy's mind still trapped inside the skull of said dead girl. Her very worst fears of being buried alive, now realised, for however long it took for Jessica's brain to decompose.

"Earth to Iris?" I saw the detective's lips say.

"Sorry," I said. "You were saying?"

"Take me through everything that happened in that last day you spent with Jessica."

As you well know, my memory was a little broken up that day

– what with Amy messing around up there in my skull – so I told the detective what I *could* remember. That Jessica and I had brunch at Graze deli. I had a bagel, she had a salad. I left out the whole *me tossing an entire smoothie over Jessica* thing, as I didn't want this particular detective thinking me any crazier than he probably already thought I was.

"And what about the time between leaving Graze deli," the detective said, "and the evening she spent at your place of residence?"

But here's the thing: I couldn't. I had no memory whatsoever, of that window of time. I was point-one-per-cent off from being pretty damn sure that nothing of much significance happened, so I would just have to make something up. What that vague something would be didn't really matter, as the only thing I could see of being any real interest to this detective was Jessica's mysterious and impromptu death in my room.

"Take me through that evening," the detective told me. "Everything that led up to you finding Jessica dead in your room."

You know what happened as well as I do, but this detective wasn't to know that. So I stick to the mundane facts: we were having a girl's night in – snacks, painting each other's nails, a chick flick, the usual. I excuse myself for a bathroom break, and when I return, I find Jessica slumped on the bed. Thinking she was just sleeping, I try to wake her. But after failing to bring her round myself, I immediately call an ambulance. The paramedics arrive, pronounce her dead at the scene, and take her body away.

"That's all I know," I tell him.

"Did you know she was pregnant?" the detective asked me.

And thinking I'd misread his lips, all I could say was, "… What?"

"Jessica," the detective said. "Did you know she was pregnant?"

81

"Epiphany"

I'm not entirely sure of what happened just after the detective uttered those six, dreadful words, but the next thing I know, my eyes flutter open and I'm laid out on the floor; my mind taking me back to that underpass on the last day of secondary school. Turning my head to the left, I see an empty office chair on wheels, and the ribs of soundproofed walls. I'm still in the police interview room. It's then I recall the very last thing the detective said to me.

Jessica.

Pregnant.

It was this short, sharp, surge of memory that lurched me up off the floor.

And with the detective's last words still ringing in my head, my only thought was that I just wanted to die, right then and there.

Desperately pacing the room, I tell myself lies to ease the ache in my gut. *This isn't happening. The detective is mistaken. I must have misread his lips.* My head is in my hands as I look down at the floor, not wanting to face the truth ahead of me. But it's no good; I'll have to look up at some point. And when I do, I'm looking right back at myself in the reflection of the one-way glass mirror hung on the wall. I look like a half-smoked cigarette; my face blotchy with red, the tracks of tears running from my eyes and to my ears. The face of the girl that turns all she touches to shit.

My mind races with all the moments I so foolishly used this cursed power of mine. So fiercely wanting to go back to that day with Amy in the university canteen and not have looked at her the way I did. To never have known that I ever had this damned ability in the first place.

To have taken the underpass that first morning. To have not crossed the road. To have never met Malleus.

But I can't go back.

As much as I want to, I have no powers to turn back time, or to undo all the damage I've caused.

I glare at the girl I see in the mirror for all of the irreparable havoc she has wreaked. The stupid girl that just could not move past her own curiosity. The one that just couldn't let it go, and had to mess with the minds of three more people after she thought she may have killed a girl in a university canteen just by shooting her a look. The dumb, blue-eyed blonde that so selfishly took an innocent life and the tiny life inside it to save her own.

And as I look into the eyes of this girl I have grown to despise, it comes to me. That just because I have no control over the major screw-ups of my past, doesn't mean I can't make a decision in this present moment for the benefit of everyone around me in the future.

I'd never tried this before, but if it worked on Amy, that big CEO, the old boy at the pawnshop, a barista girl, and three hundred people unfortunate enough to get on the wrong side of me, then, maybe, just maybe, it could work on me.

And maybe it was better this way. How perhaps Malleus was right, in that my abilities *were* more of a curse than a blessing, when I thought back on all the harm I had caused with them. Messing with people's minds. My own recklessness with my abilities pushing Malleus to abandoning me. So preoccupied with all I could do with my powers, it had stolen from me all those precious opportunities to speak with my father. Blinding and deafening all those people at the end of the talent show. Burying Amy alive.

Killing Jessica and her unborn baby.

How it would be best for everyone if I were just gone, so I couldn't cause any more havoc.

Plus, I don't think I could even trust myself. My powers may have left me for now, but they would no doubt be back, and the carnage would continue, never ending …

… forever.

And with everyone having given up on me, or gone, or dead, or buried alive, would I even be missed? I mean, if there were really no one left around to miss me? Or would the world be a slightly better place just by me not being in it? Maybe I deserved to die. Perhaps in death I could finally do some good. Maybe this was where I was always headed with everything I wanted in life and all I wanted to be.

Little old me: the girl who once swallowed a fly, and all the other things she swallowed to catch it.

It would never end …

… unless I did this one thing.

For the longest time, what I thought I *really* wanted was a more exciting life, and to know the purpose of it. But now that I looked back after all that'd happened, I think all I truly *needed* was a friend. It's only now do I realise that I was blessed with just that, that first day I met Malleus in the park. That what I should've done was be content with that. And that, if I *had* been, could've saved myself, along with all those in my path, and all those in my wake, a whole lot of bother. But I was all out of time now, and had squandered my best chances. I was down to just two equally unappealing options: either continue living like this, and accept the great cost of doing so, or put a stop to myself, and die to my own selfish ambition.

Staring at my own reflection, staring back at me, I straightened myself up, and adjusted these hand-me-down clothes I was now wearing. I checked myself over, and I was ready. It was time to leave. I breathed in my last deep breath, and on that last deep breath's way out, I told the girl in the mirror, "You've got this, Iris."

My very last thought, right before I was about to wish something for myself for the first time, was that I just wanted to see Malleus's face, one, last time. That if he were here right now to hold my hand, and tell me that everything was going to work out just fine, I wouldn't be afraid of having to do this alone.

But Malleus *wasn't* here.

He'd left me.

Left me for good.

I really *was* alone.

And looking deep into those big, blue eyes of mine reflected in the one-way glass of that mirror, I focused all of my energies into them, wished harder than I ever had done; summoning all the dark ferocity of the powers within me, *and …*

82

"Dead Room"

You wake from a nightmare, and you don't realise you were just dreaming even after you awaken. Your eyes are open but your body is still catching up. You can look around the room but you cannot move. That's what this is like. But it's different this time. Because *this* time you're so sure that the bad dream was *you* and all the terrible choices you made.

All I can see is black, until a buzzing around the wrist of my right hand jolts my eyes open, and all I can see is white.

My spine feels as if it's chiselled from a block of ice, and I can tell, only from the sensation, that I'm lying on my back. I can see, but I'm unable to lift even a finger. And all that's ahead of me, is this dazzling, white light.

The wrist of my right hand continues to buzz.

Bzzz, bzzz, bzzz.

Where *am* I?

A lingering stench of chemicals clinging to the hairs of my nostrils, leading me to the assumption that I'm in a hospital.

Now that I've noticed, it feels as if there are no arms wedded to my shoulders, no legs wedded to my hips, and no head wedded to my neck. Just a limbless body laying here, looking up with fixed eyes at what could be a ceiling as I attempt to recollect my most recent memories.

Still, my wrist continues to buzz.

Bzzz, bzzz, bzzz.

I remember Malleus and I running away after the finale of the talent show. The trip to the police station after they found us hiding in the park. The interrogation room and the detective. My eyes and the mirror. But after that, it just ends, like the missing reel of a movie.

Bzzz, bzzz, bzzz.

It's as if I had been reading a novel. Slipped a bookmark between the pages and set it down for a while. Only to find, when I pick the book up again a little later, that several pages have been torn out. Like the story has just ended abruptly, and skipped a good few chapters. As if I have been trying to follow the story so closely that I've lost the plot entirely.

In the time it takes me to think up anything else that has happened between here: wherever 'here' is. And there: the police interview room; I can now wiggle my toes.

I try rolling onto my side, but my head is fixed in place from whatever is wedged underneath it. To the left of me – once the feeling in my neck has returned – is a steel table and a white tiled wall. Turning my head as far as it will go to the right, I see the same thing: a steel table. The only difference being a clock that hangs on the white tiled wall behind it.

To give me at least some kind of bearing on how long I've been here – whatever this place is – my eyes strain to see the time. But with my vision so blurry, I just can't make it out. It could be ten-to-two, or it could be ten-past-ten, or neither. The hands on the clock appearing like thick, black, doubled-up lines, making it impossible to tell. Its circular frame floating away from wherever I try to fix my eyes upon it.

Bzzz, bzzz, bzzz.

Something on the back of my left hand makes itself known by means of a sticky sensation. And when I can finally lift my arm enough to bring my hand up to my face, it appears that a yellow square of paper has been stuck to it, with what looks like fuzzy words written upon it. Moving my hand closer to my face, the two words come into focus, scribed on the note with what looks like the scrawling of a five-year-old with a black marker-pen.

GET UP.

And when I lift the other arm to check my right hand, it, too, has a Post-it note stuck to it. Again, with the same two words.

GET UP.

And what looks like a black band wrapped around my wrist, the very same place that incessant buzzing is coming from.

Bringing my arm closer to my bleary eyes, I then see what it is. It's the SleepStrap. My mind slowly conjuring up the memory of Malleus gifting it to me whilst we were sat on a park bench.

Clumsily pressing at the strap's face, I must've hit the right spot, as the buzzing, then, stops. The note stuck to the back of my hand, reminding me, with some urgency, to **GET UP**.

And if it wasn't for these shooting pains in my chest and lower abdomen – that sear through my insides like tiny knives – I *would* have done by now. Those tiny knives turning to stabbing blades with jagged edges in my stomach as I try to sit up for the first time. Lying right back down again the very moment I give in to the agonising pain.

In the briefest of moments I have to notice, however, I think I saw someone in the room with me. Perhaps it was just a trick of the light or a shadow, but I could have sworn I saw someone lying there on the ground beside the steel table I'm on. I just didn't get the ample time to properly see. Falling back down as quickly as I had attempted sitting up.

I know this is going to feel like leaning my entire body weight onto a long and rusty sword, but I just have to get up somehow. And so, summoning everything that's in my mind over the matter of what my body is about to feel, I prepare myself for the imminent pain, and pull myself up with every muscle fibre of my being – in what is going to be the most excruciatingly painful abdominal crunch I have ever attempted. My guts torn to ribbons by a rotating steel dagger that churns my organs as I will myself up to a sitting position.

On any regular day, if I had woken up in my own bed with this level of pain, I would have laid right back down again and called an ambulance. But this is no regular day and, clearly, I have not woken up in my own bed. This place, whatever it is and wherever it is, I just simply have to find out, no matter the level of pain it causes me. To know where I am and what in the hell I've missed, since I gazed into that interview room mirror, is worth the pain.

Sat all the way up, I'm now able to better see around the room, except now it feels like there are fire ants crawling up from my belly to my chest and across from one breast to the other. I go to scratch at the erratic itchiness they cause, but when I do, I feel ridges of thick wire running along where it feels like the tiny insects are crawling and biting.

Looking down, I gasp, as across my chest and down the middle of my lower torso are these thick, black stitches. Ice cold blood sent pumping around my body as I realise that, if I've been stitched up, I would've first had to have been cut open.

From where I am, now sat up on the unforgiving cold of the steel table, I'm granted my first proper look around the room. Ahead of me, a wall of oven-like doors, numbered '1' to '21' and what looks like a price tag tied to my right toe with string.

A question, like a chill to my bones, filling my mind with a frigid notion.

Am I ...

... in a *morgue?*

Looking all around me from the cold steel table I'm sat upon. Two polished-steel tables either side of me. And everywhere else; the floors, the walls, the ceiling. There is this white ... everything.

"I'm in a morgue," I tell myself.

And not a moment after these utterances are made to myself – in the hope that saying the words out loud will somehow make any of this any less horrifying – it's then I realise something even more terrifying ...

... I'm stark, bollock, naked!

Like a shot, my right hand, along with the arm it belongs to, do their utmost to cover my hardened nipples. My chilly 'lady bits' hidden by the clasped fingers and palm of my left hand. This is also the point I realise I have missed everything that occurred between me wishing myself to death in the mirror of an interview room, and waking up on a metal slate, in a room kitted out for the deceased. Like it has all just flown right by me whilst I was in the deepest of slumbers.

Now that I think of it, I'm only *quite* sure that I'm not dead. Unless, of course, this is the afterlife. But this isn't what I imagine the tranquillity of heaven to look like, nor does it appear the nightmarish place I have in my mind hell to be. Could this then be somewhere in the middle? Somewhere in limbo? I don't consider myself to be a 'bad' person. But then, after giving it further consideration, I'm not all that 'good', either.

No, I tell myself.

This sort of thinking is silly.

I'm sure this is just a morgue.

But the question's still there, lingering in my mind that's racing to catch up with where I now find myself. That if this is a morgue and I *have*, in fact, been dead and am now alive, what has transpired in this opaque window of lost time for that to occur?

Scanning this blank canvas of a room, and it giving me no clues as to how I've wound up here, my eyes fall on the dark patch on the ground. Hungry to feed the curiosity inside of me with more than just white walls and whatever the blurry clock says the time is.

I move slowly, so as not to disturb the sleeping black blur on the ground next to me. Warily sliding myself off this cold steel table, my feet meet with the biting chill of the unforgiving tiled flooring. My body aches with a thousand icy claws that grip my muscles as I crouch to better see the vague shape I'm standing over. It's only when I touch the black, blurry figure of someone asleep, with a cautious hand, that any doubts in my mind it's a person, are gone. They're lying on their side in a most uncomfortable looking position, almost as if they have just fallen there and collapsed in a heap.

Giving the body a sharp poke with the index-finger of my right hand, I prod the body, once.

Then three times, quickly.

No response.

"Hey," I whisper.

Giving the body a good shove, saying, "Hey. Wake up."

Nothing.

The body just continues to lie there.

Getting a good firm grip with both my hands clasped on their right shoulder, I take a breath of readiness in, and with one big heave, roll them over onto their back. Even from this short distance, their face is just a smudge of fleshy colours – my eyes still unaccustomed to the glaring fluorescent lights – so, craning my neck, I lean in closer until I am almost nose to nose with them as their face comes into razor-sharp focus. A face that causes a smile to creep onto my own. A face I know so very well by now.

"Malleus," I call to the familiar face as a whisper.

"Hey, Malleus," I say again, lightly tapping the side of his face with a delicate hand. "Hey. C'mon. Wake up."

"Malleus?" I say to his blank face. "Malleus, if this is some kind of sick joke, it really isn't funny."

That's when my premature joy slowly turns to the closing in of dread, as a realisation makes itself known in my mind.

That if I was dead, and am now alive, then …

"No," I whisper to the empty air between us.

"No!" I yell at him, searching his body with desperate hands for any kind of sign of life, and finding none.

"Oh, Malleus!" I beg him. "What did you *do?*"

If I could just look into his eyes.

If I could just wish him back to life.

If I could just …

But I can't.

Even with all the powers I possess. Powers to alter minds and behaviours. Powers to change everything a person is. Powers to *kill!* But no powers within me to breathe life back into someone who has given up their own life for mine. No matter how much I love them and don't want to ever lose them. Even if I was willing to offer my *own* life in exchange for theirs.

And for the first time since I realised I even *had* these powers …

… I feel completely and utterly powerless.

83

I know that I'd wanted to see Malleus's face just one last time before I died.

This, however, is not at all what I had meant.

The unwatched clock continues to tick unnoticed as the whirlwind inside of me subsides. A turbulent cyclone that has just ripped the roof off everything I hold dear. And with the second hand *tick, tick, ticking* on that unperturbed circular face – oblivious to what I'll have to confront once this swirling tornado has calmed – it takes those further uncounted minutes to ready myself in accepting that the boy I love is gone.

There's still the smallest of chances that this isn't actually happening. A chance I am most willing to take if that's all I'm afforded. Even the very worst of situations I could conjure up in my own mind are more favourable than this purgatory I've been left abandoned in. Waking up naked in a morgue with stitches up and across my body. Malleus lying dead on the floor next to the steel table I woke upon.

Clinging onto what little hope remains in me, that this is just some harrowing nightmare I'll wake up from, the moment I take a second look at Malleus and that face of his. That's how dreams usually work for me. Some terrible scene will be playing out like a projector screen in the cave of my mind; perhaps running for my life or flying up and out of danger's way. And in trying to escape, I might fall over a cliff edge or tumble from the roof of a building. And as I plummet from that lofty height, I'll be jolted awake the moment I hit the ground below. Only to wake abruptly and breathe a deep sigh of relief that can come only from the realisation of what I was just experiencing – as tangible as it felt in that unconscious moment – wasn't real.

But as my unblinking eyes make their way up from the black Chelsea boots, to the torn black jeans, to the black leather jacket, and to the head of this seemingly dormant body, I doubt greatly that this is simply some awful dream I'll wake from, and that the expected wave of relief is not going to flow over me this time.

Just before my eyes make it to the face of this lifeless body, I shut them, tight. Putting off looking upon that face for the time it takes the second hand on that lonely clock to travel a complete circle. Malleus isn't dead right now – not in my own mind, at least – and I just know, the very moment I open my eyes to look, I won't be able to deny that he is.

If I just keep my eyes shut. If I just don't look upon his face, he won't be dead right now. But I *do* open them. It *is* Malleus. He *is* dead. And upon seeing his face – that remains expressionless – I weep.

And with every drop that comes from my eyes, I feel like I lose a little more of him with each tear that runs down my face and onto his.

By the time the last tear is cried out of my eyes, I can see clearly where the hands on the clock are – still hanging on that lonely white wall. But it's too late, as, with Malleus gone, it no longer matters what the time is.

If I know Malleus – which I believe I do – he wouldn't have done what he has for no reason. He will have left me with something. Some kind of explanation or a clue, at the very least. A letter or a note. He always seemed to have secret things hidden within pockets or some sort of trick up his sleeve.

Rummaging through the pockets of Malleus's jacket, my hands cut short their search when they feel the familiar texture of paper concealed within an inside pocket. I'm still lying here with him, on my side, as I pull out what looks to be a padded envelope from his jacket pocket; the number '1' written on it in the thick, black ink of a felt pen. And as I do, two more envelopes reveal themselves from behind the first; the numbers '**2**' and '**3**' written upon those, also.

Breaking the seal of the first envelope, I tear it open, and there inside is a piece of paper; folded twice, once from top to bottom, and then, again, from left to right.

Unfolding the piece of paper to reveal what appears to be a word-processed letter.

Hello, Iris, it reads.

Or should I say, 'Medulla', as that's the name you're going to have to get used to being called from now on.

If you're reading this, then it worked. It also means that I didn't make it. But that was the price of your life. A price I paid gladly.

I brought you back because your death was my fault. The talent show was my idea. You tried to stop me but I persisted. You thought it was a bad idea, and yet organised the whole thing for me anyway. But that's what friends do. They do things for each other, even when they don't want to.

You've probably worked out by now that you're in a morgue. And please do your best to not freak out, but you've been dead for a good couple of days now. They say you died suddenly during the interview at the police station but, unlike them, I think I know how. It was the mirror in the interrogation room I was in that gave itself away.

I don't know what the police detectives told you exactly, but they said that you had put the whole thing on me and that they had let you go hours before I was released. Needless to say, I didn't believe them. I would never believe that you could do something like that. I just wished you had trusted me. We could have both made it out of this whole thing alive and still been together.

They performed an autopsy – hence the stitches I'm sure you're aware of – and they still have no idea how you died exactly. I have contacts here at the morgue, so they gave me a little time alone with you. Time enough to bring you back. No one knows what either of us can do, and I intend to keep it that way for your sake. I know it can't be easy seeing me dead like this, because it wasn't easy for me, either. Having to prepare myself to touch your cold skin, or place my hand on your chest and not feel it rising and falling. And when I stand next to your lifeless body, I'll just be glad that I can't see it.

My sight, I can live without, but I can't live without you.

I will explain more later but, for now, you really need to do as I say. Iris is a dead girl now, and you're going to have to start living, from today, the first day of the rest of your new life, as an entirely different person. You'll still be you underneath it all, of course, just with a new appearance and identity. You won't be recognised by anyone who knew you before and, in time, you will be forgotten by the people you're leaving behind.

There's a black duffel bag on the floor next to me — the same one the police returned to me after the talent show. And don't worry, I did have it dry-cleaned. The bag contains everything you'll need to get far away from here and disappear; including some plain black clothes and shoes, a wig, brown contact lenses and an ID card. Hope you like your new 'Goth' look. You're a brunette now, and your head's already been shaved, so that'll save you some time.

And as I read the words, my left hand automatically shoots up to feel my head.

And it feels really, really strange.

You probably won't like the photo on your new ID card … the letter goes on to say … but then, again, who does?

There's plenty of cash in the purse I've left for you, and if you do happen to spend it all at once, don't worry. More will be transferred, once a week, into an account I've already set up for you. Don't worry about where it's coming from, just accept it. Keep your head down, and lay low for a while. And if you do manage to do that, you must never come back. Especially not for my funeral. And I mean that, because I know, all too well, what you're like.

Now get dressed, grab your stuff, check yourself one last time in whatever reflective surface you can find, and get going. Because, I don't know about you, but places like this really creep me out.

I'll tell you more once you're well on your way.

Malleus x

PS The sunglasses are yours. I figure you'll have more use for them than I ever will. And, in a way, you always did.

Reading through the letter, again – just to let all of Malleus's words truly sink in – I do exactly as he tells me. And even though the words are hard to read through the tears that keep coming, and how much it pains me to push back the emotions that overwhelm me, I fight with myself to do it. Dressing myself with the plain clothes he's packed for me. Adjusting the dark wig atop my head. Placing the brown contact lenses over the corneas of my eyes. Sliding my feet into a pair of black plimsolls.

And grabbing the clutch bag, a purse tightly loaded with fifty-spon notes and my new ID, I look around the room for the closest thing I have to a mirror. The best I have, being the glass viewing-window into this death-filled room.

It doesn't really matter what I look like; not this time. Just as long as I look nothing at all like myself. And with a straightening of my midnight-coloured top, and a shallow breath in and out, I go to head out the door. Only getting as far as touching the cold, metal panel on the door as I hesitate between exiting this bleak, empty room, and taking just one last look back at Malleus. And as much as I need to just let him go and leave, I can't.

Not just yet, anyway.

Steadily, I walk back over to where I left him lying there, as if I have all the time I don't. Kneeling down so I'm almost level with him on the floor. Leaning over, I kiss him one last time on his cold, blue lips. Whispering something in his ear. Something I will never tell another soul for as long as I live.

Something just for him.

And when I come back up to look upon his face one last time, that's when I catch my own anguish reflected in the lenses of his Ray-Ban sunglasses; reminding me of the one physical thing he's leaving with me. The one thing that will always remind me of him.

I had always imagined the colour of Malleus's eyes to be brown. Like staring into a deep, dark, bordering on black, shot of espresso.

But when the black lenses leave his eyes as I carefully remove his sunglasses, they are no colour at all. Just a cloudy, whitish-blue. Like a splash of milk poured and stirred into a glass of water. It's only now that I wish I'd never seen them, so I never knew the difference between what I'd imagined they'd look like and what they actually did. His eyes, so much more beautiful in my mind's eye than they actually were. I had never seen his eyes until now, but then, he'd never seen mine. And perhaps my eyes were so much more beautiful in *his* mind than they actually were.

Slipping the arms of the sunglasses to sit securely on my ears, the tinted lenses in front of my eyes turning the room a darker shade of cream, I will myself up and hurry over to the exit door with purposeful steps that fake like they don't care. Knowing all too well that if I look back a second time, my feet will never let me leave him. And as much as I want to, and how it takes everything in me *not* to

…

… I never look back.

84

"Read by Touch"

A glorious amber sun is rising up from behind sloping hills that steadily rise and fall, like breathing, off in the distance. An out of focus blending of lemon and cherry bricks; triangles and squares with soft edges; blurring together as houses rush past in the opposite direction. And with trees whipping by my window in a fuzzy strobe of coffee browns and bottle greens, I feel the peace that comes with knowing I am well on the way with my journey.

In the second letter, simply marked with a '2' – the one I read perched on a bench on the platform – Malleus had told me to catch a train. Watching the ever-changing view fly by through the dense glass window of my cabin, I feel both a reassuring sorrow and a wistful sort of hope, all mixed together in the same nostalgic receptacle that stirs up everything that's happened between Malleus and me, since that first morning with the bird that flew from his hands in the park.

Outside my window, the grassy greens and the sky's red tinge; the black shadows of hills off in the distance, reminding me of both Malleus and Amy. The angel on my left shoulder and the devil on my right; I don't think they changed me, I think they just brought out of me what was already there.

And then, the soothing landscape is swiped from my eyes as the train speeds through the blackout of a tunnel. But dark as it is, I can just about make out the pinhole of light that will come soon after, if I just press the side of my face firmly against the glass. And sure enough, after a few more moments of crossed fingers, the light arrives as it always tends to do.

Malleus gently instructed me, once I was well on the way with my journey, to read the third and last letter, simply marked with a '**3**'. Unfastening the buckle of the clutch bag, held securely at my side, I flip the flap open and pull out the envelope. To have Malleus speak to me again, especially if it's to be for the very last time, causes my hands to tremble as I tear across the top of the envelope with an eager finger.

Slipping out the folded paper tucked inside, I take a deep breath in before unfolding the letter, and begin reading from the top, savouring every word.

Dearest Medulla,

If you're reading this third letter, and you managed to hold yourself from reading it back at the morgue, on your way to the train station, or sat on the platform, then you are well on the way with your journey. A journey that will take you to as many places as you wish to go. A journey that will go on for as long as you want it to. But you must keep moving. You are never to return to the place you're running from. You are a ghost to the place you have left behind, but you will be a heroine in the places you go from here.

And don't worry, nobody's going to come looking for a dead girl.

There is one thing, however, that I ask of you. And that is that you use your powers, only for good.

I'm gone, but that doesn't mean you have to forget about me. I was with you for as long as I could be, but you will have to leave me behind now, as I can't come with you any further.

There is only one more thing I want to say to you, and this I want you to remember, always. There's something I left for you in the left breast pocket of your jacket. Something to keep. To take out and look at whenever you feel like I'm far away.

It's something I want you to know … always.

Malleus x

Carefully folding the letter and slipping it safely back into the torn envelope, I raise my right hand up to the left breast pocket of the jacket I'm wearing. Pressing against it with my fingers, flat and together, I can feel something. A piece of card, perhaps, just behind the smooth texture of the fabric. Only *just* smaller in size to the pocket that so tightly holds it.

With my right hand still held there, I unbutton the breast pocket with my left hand, and reach in with my right to pull out a small piece of plastic-coated paper, about the same size and thickness of a business card. Studying the card I hold in front of me with the thumb and finger tips of both hands, at first glance there doesn't appear to be anything written on it. And flipping it over, it's apparent that there's nothing written on the other side, either.

It's just a blank, white card.

Unclear as to why Malleus has left me this sparse, meagre scrap of plastic-coated paper, I allow my crestfallen arms to drop into my lap. What does it mean? Is this some sort of *joke?* If it *is*, it's a bad one. What is Malleus trying to tell me by leaving me with a blank card? Is he leaving me with *nothing?* Is *that* it?

I can feel my eyes stinging from the tears that threaten to come with both the annoyance and dispirit I feel. And after everything I've been through. After everything *we've* been through! *This? This* is his parting gift? The very last thing he will ever leave me with?

My arms are still flopped in my lap where I've left them. Staring blankly at all the whirls of scratches on the surface of the cabin's window as I fight hard to hold back a monsoon of tears. A solitary drop, bleeding out as I close my eyes, hidden behind Malleus's Ray-Ban sunglasses. And all I can think about, in this most hopeless of moments, is Malleus, and how he's never felt so far away.

Then the most curious thing happens.

As my thumbs – all by themselves, and without intentional thought – rub at the surface of the card I hold in my hands. Tiny bumps, like raised spots, dotted at random across the card's surface. And no sooner have I felt them, I raise the card back up to my eyes to better see, tilting the seemingly blank card back and forth, in the tangerine light.

This isn't some joke in poor taste. This is the one last thing Malleus is telling me before I embark on the rest of my journey without him. His way of waving me goodbye from the train station platform as I leave on a train to journey to a place he will never be able to follow me to. A journey that will go on for as long as I desire it to.

It's Braille; I can see it now.

Promptly running a finger along the raised dots, it appears to be only a couple of words long. Two words that don't quite make sense to me, at first. And so, I run my finger over them again. The tiny bumps whispering the same two words over and over, but still not making any kind of coherent sense.

It's then that I figure it out.

The two words are something I'd mistakenly thought Malleus to have said to me before. I forget when and where, exactly, but I think it was just before we shared our first kiss. And even *then* I didn't quite understand his words at first, and had him repeat himself. Just two words, but they're the only two words I really need to hear right now and always. It's perfect, actually. They are the best parting words anyone could ever say to me. A little private joke between the two of us, but words that fill me with the warmth of coming home.

And slowly stroking a finger over the small relief of dots, a smile creeps up my face. A smile that will go on to last for the rest of the day, and *every* day I run my fingers across these tiny, little bumps.

Acknowledgements

I would first like to thank **Mary Jones**. Without her support, the book you're holding in your hands may have never seen a printing press, and she has only some idea of how much that means to me. Thank you for believing in me and my story. All my love to you.

My beta readers (**Angie Foreman**, **Jenny Dunlop**, **Lizzie Brien**, & **Russell Stott**) for all of their invaluable feedback, for helping me in telling my story better, and for spurring me on to finish.

Stefan Proudfoot for the incredible book cover he designed.

Liz Bourne for the stellar job she did of the editing & proofreading.

And to everyone at **Spiffing Publishing** for putting up with me being an insufferable nightmare since … well. That's debateable.

About the Author

K T Fenton is a drop-out of both the universities of Lincoln & Suffolk. Their debut novel, Elephant Shoes, is their first self-published book – since going down the traditional publishing route looks like a total drag. They live alone with their dog, Rascal, on a council estate in Essex, UK.